THE BROTHER-HOOD OF THE ROSE

THE BROTHER-HOOD OF THE ROSE

DAVID MORRELL

A Novel

St. Martin's/Marek
New York

Design by Manuela Paul

Library of Congress Cataloging in Publication Data

Morrell, David.
    The brotherhood of the rose.

    I. Title.
PR9199.3.M65B7   1984   813'.54   83-21324
ISBN 0-312-10608-4

First Edition
10 9 8 7 6 5 4 3 2 1

for Donna
The years go faster, my love grows stronger.

Teach them politics and war so their sons
may study medicine and mathematics in order
to give their children a right to study
painting, poetry, music, and architecture.

—John Adams

THE ABELARD SANCTION

REFUGE

Paris. September 1118.

Peter Abelard, handsome canon of the church of Notre Dame, seduced his attractive student, Heloise. Fulbert, her uncle, enraged by her pregnancy, craved revenge. In the early hours of a Sunday morning, three assassins hired by Fulbert attacked Abelard on his way to mass, castrated him, and left him to die from his wounds. He lived but, fearing further reprisals, sought protection. First, he ran to the monastery of Saint Denis near Paris. There, while recovering from his injuries, he learned that political elements desperate for Fulbert's approval were conspiring once more against him. For a second time, he took flight—to Quincey, near Nogent, where he founded a safe house that he named "The Paraclete," the Comforter, in honor of the Holy Ghost.

And finally found sanctuary.

SAFE HOUSES/
GROUND RULES

Paris. September 1938.

On Sunday, the twenty-eighth, Édouard Daladier, minister of defense for France, broadcast the following radio announcement to the French people:

> Early this afternoon I received an invitation from the German government to meet with Chancellor Hitler, Mr. Mussolini, and Mr. Neville Chamberlain in Munich. I have accepted the invitation.

The next afternoon, while the Munich meeting was taking place, a pharmacist in the service of the Gestapo recorded in his logbook that the last of the five black 1938 Mercedes had passed the checkpoint at his corner drugstore and had arrived before the innocuous-looking stone facade of 36 Bergener Strasse in Berlin. In each case, a powerfully built plain-clothed driver stepped out of the car, surveyed the pedestrians on the busy street without seeming to do so, and opened a passenger door from which the only occupant, a well-dressed elderly man, emerged. As soon as the driver had escorted his passenger safely through the thick wooden door of the three-story residence, he proceeded to a warehouse three blocks away to wait for further instructions.

The last gentleman to arrive left his hat and overcoat with a sentry behind an enclosed metal desk in an alcove to the right of the door. For reasons of tact, he wasn't searched, but he was asked to surrender his briefcase. He wouldn't need it, after all. No notes would be permitted.

The sentry examined the man's credentials, then pushed a button beside the Luger beneath his desk. At once, a second Gestapo agent appeared from an office behind the visitor to escort him to a room at

4

the end of the hall. The visitor entered. Remaining behind, the agent shut the door.

The visitor's name was John "Tex" Auton. He was fifty-five, tall, ruggedly handsome, with a salt-and-pepper mustache. Prepared for the business at hand, he sat in the one remaining empty captain's chair and nodded to the four men who'd arrived before him. He did not need to be introduced; he knew them already. Their names were Wilhelm Smeltzer, Anton Girard, Percival Landish, and Vladimir Lazensokov. They were the directors of espionage for Germany, France, England, and the Soviet Union. Auton himself represented America's State Department.

Except for the captain's chairs and the ashtray beneath each of them, the room was totally barren. No other furniture, no paintings, no bookshelves, no drapes, no rug, no chandelier. The starkness of the room had been arranged by Smeltzer to assure these men that no microphones had been hidden.

"Gentlemen," Smeltzer said, "the adjacent rooms are empty."

"Munich," Landish said.

Smeltzer laughed. "For an Englishman, you come to the point abruptly."

"Why do you laugh?" Girard asked Smeltzer. "We all know that at this moment Hitler is demanding that my country and England no longer guarantee the protection of Czechoslovakia, Poland, and Austria." He spoke English for the benefit of the American.

Avoiding the question, Smeltzer lit a cigarette.

"Does Hitler intend to invade Czechoslovakia?" Lazensokov asked.

Smeltzer shrugged, exhaling smoke. "I've asked you here so that, as members of the same professional community, we can prepare for any contingency."

Tex Auton frowned.

Smeltzer continued. "We don't respect each other's ideologies, but in one way we're all alike. We enjoy the complexities of our profession."

They nodded.

"You have a new complication to propose?" the Russian asked.

"Why don't you boys say what the hell you're thinkin'?" Tex Auton drawled.

The others chuckled.

"Directness would ruin half the enjoyment," Girard told Auton. He turned to Smeltzer, waiting.

5

"No matter what the outcome of the impending war," Smeltzer said, "we must guarantee to each other that our representatives will have the opportunity for protection."

"Impossible," the Russian said.

"What kind of protection?" the Frenchman asked.

"Do you mean money?" the Texan added.

"Unstable. It has to be gold or diamonds," the Englishman said.

The German nodded. "And more precisely, secure places in which to keep them. The proven banks in Geneva, Lisbon, and Mexico City, for example."

"Gold." The Russian sneered. "And what do you propose we do with this capitalist commodity?"

"Establish a system of safe houses," Smeltzer replied.

"But what's so new about that? We already have 'em," Tex Auton said.

The others ignored him.

"And rest homes as well, I presume?" Girard told Smeltzer.

"I take that for granted," the German said. "For the benefit of my American friend, let me explain. Each of our networks already has its own safe houses, that is true. Secure locations where its operatives can go for protection, say, or debriefing or to interrogate an informer. But while each network tries to keep these locations a secret, eventually the other networks find out where they are, so the places aren't truly safe. Though armed men guard them, a larger opposing force could seize any house and kill whoever had sought protection there."

Tex Auton shrugged. "The risk is unavoidable."

"I wonder," the German continued. "What I propose is something new—an extension of the concept, a refinement of it. Under extreme circumstances, any operative from any of our networks would be given a chance for asylum in carefully chosen cities around the world. I suggest Buenos Aires, Potsdam, Lisbon, and Oslo. We all have business there."

"Alexandria," the Englishman suggested.

"That's acceptable."

"Montreal," the Frenchman said. "If the war doesn't turn out to my benefit, I might be living there."

"Now wait a minute," Tex Auton said. "Do you expect me to believe that, if a war is goin' on, one of *your* boys won't kill one of *my* boys in these places?"

"As long as the opposing operatives remain inside," the German

6

said. "In our profession, we all know the dangers and the pressures. I'll admit that even Germans sometimes need to rest."

"And calm the nerves and heal the wounds," the Frenchman said.

"We owe it to ourselves," the Englishman said. "And if an operative wants to retire from his network completely, he'd have the chance to go from a safe house to a rest home and enjoy the same immunity for the rest of his life. With a portion of the gold or the diamonds as a retirement fund."

"As a reward for faithful service," the German said. "And an enticement to new recruits."

"If events proceed as I foresee," the Frenchman said, "we may all need enticements."

"And if events proceed as I expect," the German said, "I'll have all the enticements I need. Nonetheless I'm a prudent man. Are we all agreed?"

"What guarantees do we have that our men won't be killed in these safe houses?" the Englishman said.

"The word of fellow professionals."

"And the penalties?"

"Absolute."

"Agreed," the Englishman said.

The American and the Russian were silent.

"Do I sense reluctance from our newer nations?" the German said.

"I agree in principle, and I'll attempt to appropriate funds," the Russian said, "but I can't promise Stalin's cooperation. He'd never submit to shielding foreign operatives on Soviet soil."

"But you promise never to harm an enemy operative as long as he's in a designated safe house."

Reluctantly the Russian nodded.

"And Mr. Auton?"

"Well, I'll go along. I'll kick in some money, but I don't want any of these places on American territory."

"Then with these compromises, we agree?"

The others nodded.

"We'll need a code word for this arrangement," Landish said.

"I recommend *hospice,*" Smeltzer said.

"Unthinkable," the Englishman replied. "Half of our hospitals are called hospices."

"Then I recommend this alternative," the Frenchman said. "We

7

are all learned men. I'm sure you recall the story of my countryman from the Dark Ages: Peter Abelard."

"*Who?*" Tex Auton said.

Girard explained.

"So he went to a church and was given protection?" Auton said.

"Sanctuary."

"We'll call it a sanction," Smeltzer said. "The Abelard sanction."

Two days later, Wednesday, October 1, Daladier, France's minister of defense, flew back from the meeting with Hitler in Munich to his home in Paris.

His plane landed at Le Bourget Airport. As he stepped outside, he was greeted by surging crowds who shouted, "Long live France! Long live England! Long live peace!"

Waving flags and flowers, the crowds broke through the sturdy police barricades. Reporters rushed up the aluminum gangplank to greet the returning minister of defense.

Daladier stood dumfounded.

Turning to Foucault of the Reuters News Service, he muttered, "Long live peace? Don't they understand what Hitler plans to do? The stupid bastards."

Paris. 5 P.M., Sunday, September 3, 1939.

An announcer had just come on the radio, interrupting the Michelin Theater to say, "France is officially at war with Germany."

The radio went silent.

In Buenos Aires, Potsdam, Lisbon, Oslo, Alexandria, and Montreal, the international safe houses of the world's great espionage networks were established. By 1941, these networks would include Japan, and by 1953, mainland China.

And sanctuary was formed.

BOOK ONE
SANCTUARY

A MAN OF HABIT

1

Vail, Colorado.

The snow fell harder, blinding Saul. He skied through deepening powder, veering sharply back and forth down the slope. Everything—the sky, the air, and the ground—turned white. His vision shortened till he saw no more than a swirl before his face. He swooped through chaos.

He might hit an unseen tree or plummet off a hidden cliff. He didn't care. He felt exhilarated. As wind raged at his cheeks, he grinned. He christied left, then right. Sensing the slope ease off, he streaked across a straightaway.

The next slope would be steeper. In the white-out, he pushed at his poles to gain more speed. His stomach burned. He loved it. Vacuum. Nothing to his back or front. Past and future had no meaning. Only now—and it was wonderful.

A dark shape loomed before him.

Jerking sideways, Saul dug in the edge of his skis to stop himself. His pulse roared in his head. The shape zoomed past from right to left in front of him, vanishing in the snow.

Saul gaped through his goggles, hearing a scream despite the wind. He snowplowed frowning toward it.

Shadows gathered in the storm. A line of trees.

A moan.

He found the skier sprawled against a tree trunk. There were bloodstains in the snow. Beneath his mask, Saul bit his lip. He crouched and saw the crimson seeping from the skier's forehead, and the grotesque angle of one leg.

A man. Thick beard. Large chest.

Saul couldn't go for help—in the chaos of the storm, he might not be able to find this place again. Worse, even if he did manage to bring back help, the man might freeze to death by then.

One chance. He didn't bother attending to the head wound or the broken leg. No use, no time. He took off his skis, removed the skis from the injured man, rushed toward a pine tree, and snapped off a thickly needled bough.

Spreading the bough beside the man, he eased him onto it, careful to let the good leg cushion the broken one. He gripped the end of the bough and stooped, walking backward, pulling. The snow stung harder, cold gnawing through his ski gloves. He kept tugging, inching down.

The man groaned as Saul shifted him over a bump, the snow enshrouding them. The man writhed, almost slipping off the bough.

Saul hurried to reposition him, tensing when he suddenly felt a hand behind him clutch his shoulder.

Whirling, he stared at a looming figure, "Ski Patrol" stenciled in black across a yellow parka.

"Down the slope! A hundred yards! A shed!" the man yelled, helping Saul.

They eased the skier down the hill. Saul bumped against the shed before he saw it, feeling corrugated metal behind him. He yanked the unlocked door open and stumbled in. The wind's shriek diminished. He felt stillness.

Turning from the empty shed, he helped the man from the Ski Patrol drag in the bleeding skier.

"You okay?" the man asked Saul, who nodded. "Stay with him while I get help," the man continued. "I'll come back with snowmobiles in fifteen minutes."

Saul nodded again.

"What you did," the man told Saul. "You're something else. Hang on. We'll get you warm."

The man stepped out and closed the door. Saul slumped against the wall and sank to the ground. He stared at the groaning skier, whose eyelids flickered. Saul breathed deeply. "Keep your leg still."

The man winced, nodding. "Thanks."

Saul shrugged.

Scrunching his eyes in pain, the man said, "Massive foul-up."

"It can happen."

"No. A simple job."

Saul didn't understand. The man was babbling.

"Didn't figure on the storm." The man scowled, his temples pulsing. "Dumb."

Saul listened to the storm, soon hearing the far-off roar of snowmobiles. "They're coming."

"Did you ever ski in Argentina?"

Saul's throat constricted. Babbling? Hardly. "Once. I got a nosebleed."

"Aspirin . . ."

". . . cures headaches," Saul replied, the code completed.

"Ten o'clock tonight." The man groaned. "Goddamn storm. Who figured it'd screw things up?"

The roar grew louder as the snowmobiles stopped outside the shed. The door jerked open. Three men from the Ski Patrol stepped in.

"You still okay?" one man asked Saul.

"I'm fine. But this guy's babbling."

2

Maintain a pattern. Every day, Saul kept the same routine, appearing at scheduled places at established times. Eight-thirty: breakfast at the coffee shop in his hotel. A half hour's walk, the route unchanging. Twenty minutes' browsing in a book store. Eleven o'clock: the slopes, again his route consistent.

For two reasons. First—in case somebody needed to get in touch with him, the courier would know where he was at any time and be able to intercept him, though it had just been demonstrated how an accident could jeopardize procedure. Second—if Saul was being watched, his schedule was so predictable it might bore his shadow into making mistakes.

Today, more than usual, he had to avoid suspicion. He helped take the injured man down to the ambulance. At the lodge, he chatted with the Ski Patrol in their office, waiting for his chance to slip away. He went to his room and changed from his ski suit to jeans and a sweater. He reached his customary bar exactly when he always did, sitting in the smoke-filled conversation pit, watching cartoons on the giant television screen, sipping a Coke.

At seven, he went to dinner, as always at the dining room in his hotel. At eight, he went to a Burt Reynolds car-chase movie. He'd seen the feature before and knew it ended at quarter to ten. He'd chosen the theater for its pay phone in the men's room. Making sure the stalls were empty, he put the proper change in the phone and dialed a memorized number precisely at ten o'clock as the man on the slope had instructed him.

A gruff male voice announced basketball scores. Saul didn't pay attention to the names of the teams. He cared only about the numbers, ten in all, a long-distance telephone number, mentally repeating them.

He left the men's room and, without being obvious, checked the lobby to see if he was being watched.

No indication of surveillance, though an expert shadow wouldn't let himself be noticed.

He stepped from the theater, pleased that the storm had persisted. Through the dark and confusion, he slipped down a side street, then another side street, waiting in an alley to make sure he wasn't being followed. With sight so restricted in the storm, a tail would have to follow him closely past this alley to keep up with him.

But no one did.

He crossed the street and chose a pay phone in an unfamiliar bar two blocks away. Near the din of electronic games, he dialed the numbers he'd been given.

A woman's sexy voice said, "Triple A Answering Service."

"Romulus," he said.

"You've got an appointment. Tuesday. 9 A.M. Denver. 48 Cody Road."

He set the phone back on its cradle. Leaving the bar, he walked through the cover of the storm to arrive at his hotel precisely when he would have if, after seeing the movie, he'd taken his usual thirty-minute walk.

He asked the desk clerk, "Any messages for Grisman? Room 211."

"Sorry, sir."

"No problem."

Avoiding the elevator, he walked upstairs to his room. The strand of hair at the bottom of his door remained exactly where he'd placed it when he'd gone out, assuring him no one had entered in his absence. One more routine day.

With two exceptions.

14

3

Follow standard procedure. In the morning, Saul bought his ticket at the last possible moment. When the driver started the engine, Saul got on the bus. He sat in back and watched for anyone boarding after him.

But no one did.

As the bus pulled from the station, he eased back, nodding with satisfaction, staring at the condominiums of Vail and the far-off dots of skiers on the snow-covered mountains.

He liked buses. He could see out the back if he was being followed. He could buy a ticket without getting logged in a computer, the reason he didn't fly or rent a car—he didn't want to leave a paper trail. What's more, a bus made several stops along its route. He could get off at any of them without attracting attention.

Though his ticket was for Salt Lake City, he never intended to go there. He left the bus at Placer Springs an hour west of Vail. After waiting to see if anyone else got off, he bought a ticket for Denver, boarded the next bus heading east, and slumped in the back seat. Analyzing what he'd done, he decided he'd made no errors. Certainly if someone had been watching him, his shadow would be puzzled now, soon nervous, making urgent phone calls. Saul didn't care. He'd gained his freedom.

He was ready to do his work.

4

Tuesday, 9 A.M. The Denver wind brought tears to his eyes. Gray clouds hulking over the mountains made the morning seem like dusk. Despite his down-filled coat, he shivered, standing on a suburban corner, squinting toward a building in the middle of the block.

Long, low, and drab. Counting from the address on the corner, Sal guessed the building was 48 Cody Road. He walked through slush to reach it. Though he'd used local buses to get here, transferring often, he nonetheless glanced behind him, just in case. He saw few cars and none that looked familiar.

Turning forward, he stopped in surprise, gaping at a Star of David above the door. A synagogue? Himself a Jew, he wondered if he'd misheard his instructions. Granted, he was used to meetings in uncommon places.

But a synagogue? His spine felt numb.

Uneasily he entered. He faced a shadowy vestibule. His nostrils flared from the smell of dust. As he shut the door, its rumble echoed.

Stillness settled over him. He chose a yarmulke from a box on a table, put the small black cap on the back of his head, and, lips taut, pulled another door.

The temple. He felt a pressure. The air seemed heavy and dense. It seemed to squeeze him. He stepped forward.

In a front seat, an old man stared at the white curtain that hid the Ark, his skullcap shiny from years of worship. The old man lowered his eyes toward his prayer book.

Saul held his breath. Except for the old man at the front, the temple was deserted. Something was wrong.

The old man turned to him. Saul tensed.

"*Shalom,*" the old man said.

Impossible. The man was—

5

Eliot.

He stood. As always, he wore a black suit and vest. A matching overcoat and homburg hat lay on the seat beside him. A gentile, he was sixty-seven, tall and gaunt, gray-skinned, dark-eyed, his shoulders stooped, his face pinched with sorrow.

Smiling warmly, Saul replied, *"Shalom."* His throat hurt as he approached.

They hugged each other. Feeling the wrinkled kiss on his cheek, Saul kissed the old man in return. They studied one another.

"You look well," Saul said.

"A lie, but I'll accept it. *You* look well, though."

"Exercise."

"Your wounds?"

"No complications."

"In the stomach." Eliot shook his head. "When I heard what happened, I wanted to visit you."

"But you couldn't. I understand."

"You received good care?"

"You know I did. You sent the best."

"The best deserves the best."

Saul felt embarrassed. A year ago, he *had* been the best. But now? "A lie," he said. "I don't deserve it."

"You're alive."

"By luck."

"By skill. A lesser man could not have escaped."

"I shouldn't have needed to escape," Saul said. "I planned the operation. I thought I'd allowed for every factor. I was wrong. A cleaning lady, for God's sake. She should have been on another floor. She never checked that room that early."

Eliot spread his hands. "Exactly my point. Random chance. You can't control it."

"You know better," Saul replied. "You used to say the word

accident had been invented by weak people to excuse their mistakes. You told us to strive for perfection."

"Yes. But—" Eliot frowned, "—perfection can never be attained."

"I almost had it. A year ago. I don't understand what happened." He suspected, though. He was six feet tall, two hundred pounds of bone and muscle. But he was also thirty-seven. I'm getting old, he thought. "I ought to quit. It's not just *this* job. Two others went bad before it."

"Random chance again," Eliot said. "I read the reports. You weren't to blame."

"You're making allowances."

"Because of our relationship?" Eliot shook his head. "Not true. I've never let it sway me. But sometimes failure can have a beneficial effect. It can make us try much harder." He took two slips of paper from the inner pocket of his suitcoat.

Saul read the neat handprinting on the first one. A telephone number. He memorized it, nodding. Eliot showed him the second sheet. Instructions, six names, a date, and an address. Again, Saul nodded.

Eliot took back the papers. Picking up his hat and overcoat, he left the temple to cross the vestibule toward the men's room. Thirty seconds later, Saul heard flushing. He took for granted Eliot had burned the pages and disposed of the ashes. If the temple had been bugged, their conversation alone would not have revealed the subject of the notes.

Eliot returned, putting on his overcoat. "I'll use the exit in the rear."

"No, wait. So soon? I hoped we could talk."

"We will. When the job's completed."

"How are your flowers?"

"Not just flowers. Roses." Eliot shook a finger at him in mock chastisement. "After all these years, you still enjoy baiting me by calling them flowers."

Saul grinned.

"Actually," Eliot said, "I've developed an interesting variation. Blue. No rose has ever been that color before. When you come to visit, I'll show it to you."

"I look forward to it."

Warmly they embraced.

"If it matters," Eliot said, "the job you'll be doing is designed to protect all this." He gestured toward the temple. "One more thing." He reached into his overcoat, pulling out a candy bar.

18

Saul's chest tightened as he took it. A Baby Ruth. "You still remember."

"Always." Eliot's eyes looked sad.

Saul swallowed painfully, watching Eliot leave through the back, listening to the echo of the door snicking shut. In accordance with procedure, he himself would wait ten minutes and go out the front. Eliot's cryptic remark about the purpose of this assignment troubled him, but he knew only something important would have caused Eliot to deliver the instructions in person.

He squeezed his fists, determined. This time he wouldn't fail. He couldn't allow himself to disappoint the only father he, an orphan, had ever known.

6

The man with a mustache munched a taco. Saul explained the assignment to him. They used no names, of course. Saul hadn't seen him before and wouldn't again. The man wore a jogging suit. He had a cleft in his chin. He wiped his mustache with a napkin.

Baltimore. Three days later, 2 P.M. The Mexican restaurant was almost deserted. Even so, they sat at the remotest corner table.

The man lit a cigarette, studying Saul. "We'll need a lot of backup."

"Maybe not," Saul said.

"You know the protocol."

Saul nodded. Established method. A team of fourteen men, the bulk of them working on surveillance, the others obtaining equipment, relaying messages, providing alibis, each of them knowing as little as possible about the others, all of them dropping out of sight an hour before the specialists stepped in. Efficient. Safe.

"All right," the man told Saul. "But this is *six* jobs. Times fourteen backup men. That's eighty-four. We might as well hold a convention, advertise, sell tickets."

"Maybe not," Saul said.

"So humor me."

"The key is all together—at one time, one place."

"Who knows when that'll be? We could wait all year."

"Three weeks from today."

The man stared down at his cigarette. Saul told him where. The man stubbed out his cigarette. "Go on," he said.

"We can keep surveillance to a minimum, simply making sure all six of them show up for the meeting."

"Possibly. We'd still need communications. Someone else to get the stuff."

"That's you."

"No argument. But getting the stuff in the building won't be easy."

"Not your worry."

"Fine with me. It's flaky. I don't like it. But if that's the way you want it, we can do the job with twenty men."

"You're right," Saul said. "That's how I want it."

"What's the matter?"

"Let's just say I had a few assignments with people who let me down. I'm losing my faith in human nature."

"That's a laugh."

"For this job, as much as I can, I want to depend on myself."

"And me, of course. You'll have to depend on me."

Saul studied him. The waitress brought the check.

"My treat," Saul said.

7

The estate spread across the valley—a three-story mansion, swimming pool, tennis courts, stables, a lush green pasture, riding trails through a parklike forest, ducks on a lake. He lay in tall grass on a wooded bluff a half mile away, the warm spring sun on his back, its angle such that it wouldn't reflect off the lens of his telescope and warn the bodyguards in front of the house that someone was watching them. He studied a dust cloud on a gravel road, a limousine approaching the

20

house, four other limousines already parked in front of a six-stall garage to the left. The car stopped at the house, a bodyguard stepping forward as a man got out.

"He ought to be there by now," a voice said from a walkie-talkie next to Saul, the raspy tone of the man he'd talked to in Baltimore. The walkie-talkie had been adjusted to a seldom-used frequency. Even so, there was always a chance of someone accidentally overhearing the conversation, so the walkie-talkie had been equipped with a scrambler. Only someone with another scrambler tuned to the same uncommon frequency could receive a clear transmission. "That's the last of them," the voice continued. "Eyeball I.D. Counting the guy who lives there, all six targets are in the zone."

Saul pressed the "send" button on the walkie-talkie. "I'll take it from here. Head home." He stared through the telescope at the house. The visitor had gone inside, the limousine joining the others in front of the garage.

He checked his watch. Everything on schedule. Though the mansion was closely guarded now, its security force had been minimal a week ago, just a man at the gate, another patrolling the grounds, a third in charge of the house. With a Starlite nightscope, he'd studied the estate three nights in a row, learning the guards' routine, when they were relieved and when they were careless, choosing four A.M. as the best time to infiltrate the grounds. In the dark, he'd crept through the forest toward the back. Precisely at four, two members of his team had created a diversion on the road that ran past the gate by pretending to be kids revving loud jalopies in a drag race. While the guards were distracted, Saul had picked the lock on a storm door, entering the basement. He hadn't worried about a warning system since he'd noticed that the guard in charge of the house never took precautions to shut off an alarm when he entered. In the basement, he used a shielded penlight, hiding plastique explosive in a furnace duct, attaching a radio-activated detonator. Taking his equipment, he locked the door and disappeared into the forest, hearing the roar of the jalopies finishing the race.

Two days later, a full security force had sealed off the estate. When they searched the house, they might have found the explosive, but from his vantage, he'd seen no commotion. The guards had seemed concerned only with watching the perimeter of the house.

He'd soon learn if the explosive remained. Glancing at his watch again, he saw that twenty minutes had passed. Time enough for the man with the cleft in his chin to have got away. Putting the walkie-talkie and the telescope in his knapsack, he concentrated on a single blade of grass, focusing on it, narrowing his vision till the grass absorbed his mind. Free of emotion, achieving a stillness, he picked up a radio transmitter and pressed a button.

The mansion blew apart, from the basement upward, outward, its walls disintegrating, rubble flying, spewing in all directions. The roof lifted, toppling, shrouded with dust, engulfed with flames. The shock wave hit him. Ignoring it, he shoved the radio transmitter in his knapsack. Hearing a rumble, he ignored it also, running from the bluff, approaching a car in a weed-covered lane.

Eight years old. The team member responsible for transportation had bought it cheap, using cash and an alias, from a man who'd advertised in the Baltimore want ads. No one could trace it here.

He obeyed the speed limit, calm, allowing no satisfaction, even though he'd achieved what his father had asked.

8

EXPLOSION KILLS SIX

COSTIGAN, VIRGINIA (AP)—An unexplained explosion Thursday evening destroyed the secluded mansion of Andrew Sage, controversial oil magnate and energy adviser to the president. The powerful blast killed Sage and five unidentified guests who, highly placed sources speculate, were representatives from various large American corporations, members of the Paradigm Foundation, which Sage had recently founded.

"Mr. Sage's family is too distraught to talk about it," an FBI official announced at a press conference. "As much as we can determine, Mr. Sage had convened a kind of industrial summit meeting in an attempt to solve the nation's economic crisis. The president, of course, is deeply shocked. He lost not only a trusted adviser but a cherished friend."

Sage's family was not present on his country estate at the time of the explosion. Several members of his security staff were injured by flying rubble. Investigators continue to search the wreckage for a clue to the cause of the blast.

9

Saul reread the front-page story, folded the newspaper, and leaned back in his chair. A cocktail waitress, breasts and hips bulging from her costume, passed his table. He glanced from the piano player in the lounge, across the noisy casino, toward the blackjack tables, watching a pit boss study the crowd.

He felt uneasy. Frowning, he tried to understand why. The job had gone smoothly. His getaway had been uneventful. After leaving the car at a Washington shopping mall, he'd taken a bus to Atlantic City. He'd made sure no one followed him.

Then why was he worried? As slot machines rang, he continued frowning.

Eliot had insisted on explosives. But Saul knew the job could easily have been done in a less dramatic way. Prior to the meeting, the six men could have died from apparent natural causes at different times in widely separate parts of the country: heart attack, stroke, suicide, traffic accident, a variety of other ways. The inner circle would have noticed the pattern, understanding what it meant, but there'd have been no publicity. Saul had to conclude, then, that publicity was the reason for the job. But why? Saul's instincts nagged him. Publicity violated the logic of his training. Eliot had always insisted on subtlety. Then why now had Eliot suddenly changed?

Another thing bothered him—his present location, Atlantic City. After a job, he always went to a predetermined neutral site—in this case, a locker at a Washington gym—finding money and instructions on where to disappear. Eliot knew the locations Saul preferred—the mountains, Wyoming and Colorado in particular—and as a favor, Eliot always agreed to them. So why the hell was I sent to Atlantic City? he thought. He'd never been here. He didn't like crowds. He tolerated them only as a necessary evil when he gratified his need to ski. Here, people swarmed around him like scavenging insects.

Something was wrong. The orders to use explosives, to go to Atlantic City—they were blatant violations of routine. As roulette wheels clattered, Saul's hands itched with apprehension.

He left the cocktail lounge, approaching the blackjack tables. He hated crowds, but in the locker at the gym, he'd found two thousand dollars and orders to play blackjack.

Accepting his cover, he found an empty chair and bought five hundred dollars' worth of chips. After betting a twenty-five dollar chip, he received a king and a queen.

The dealer won with blackjack.

10

"Goddamned bastards," the president said. He punched a fist against the palm of his hand. He hadn't slept. The news had aged him shockingly, much more than the recent assassination attempt. Fatigue made him tremble. Grief and anger pinched his face. "I want the man who killed my friend. I want those sonsofbitches—" Abruptly the president stopped. Unlike his predecessors, he understood the wisdom of silence. What he didn't say couldn't be used against him.

Eliot wondered if the president knew the tapes of his Oval Office conversations were being duplicated.

The director of the CIA sat next to Eliot. "The KGB got in touch with us at once. They flatly deny they had anything to do with it."

"Of course they deny it," the president said.

"But I believe them," the director said. "The job was too sensational. It's not their style."

"That's what they want us to think. They've changed their tactics to confuse us."

"With respect, Mr. President, I don't think so," the director said. "I'll grant you, the Soviets don't like the shift in our mideast policy— away from the Jews toward the Arabs. The Soviets have always counted on our pro-Israeli stance. They've used it to turn the Arabs against us. Now we do what they've been doing. They're upset."

"So it makes sense for them to interfere," the president said. "Our deal with the Arabs is simple. If we turn our back on Israel, the Arabs will sell us cheaper oil. The Paradigm Foundation was established to hide our negotiations with the Arabs—businessmen dealing with other businessmen instead of government with government. Destroy the Paradigm Foundation—you destroy the negotiations. You also warn us not to reopen them."

"Sure, it makes sense," the director said. "Too much sense. The Russians know we'd blame them. If they wanted to interfere, they'd hide their tracks. They'd be more clever."

"Who the hell did it then? The FBI found Andrew's arm a half a mile away from the wreckage. I want to get even with someone. Tell me who. Qaddafi? Castro?"

"I don't think so," the director said.

"We did," Eliot said. He'd been silent, waiting for the proper moment.

The president swung toward Eliot, stunned. *"We what?"*

"Indirectly at least. One of our men did. Naturally it wasn't authorized."

"I hope to God not!"

"We found out by accident," Eliot said.

The director, who was also Eliot's superior, stared at him indignantly. "You didn't tell *me.* "

"I didn't have a chance. I learned about it just before this meeting. We've been watching the man for several months. He's ruined several assignments. His behavior's erratic. We've been thinking of letting him go. Three weeks before the explosion, he dropped out of sight. Today he resurfaced. We managed to retrace his movements. We can put him in the area at the time of the blast."

The president's face turned pale. "Go on."

"He's under surveillance in Atlantic City. He seems to have a lot of money. He's losing at blackjack."

"Where'd he get the bankroll?" the president said, eyes narrowed.

"He's Jewish. The Mossad helped us train him. He fought in their October War in seventy-three. He's got expensive tastes, which he can't maintain if we let him go. We think the Israelis paid him to turn."

"That *does* make sense," the director said grudgingly.

The president clenched a fist. "But can you prove it? Can you give me something to raise hell with Tel Aviv?"

"I'll speak to him. There are ways to stimulate conversation."

"After that, do we have procedures for dealing with double agents?"

The president's evasive language made Eliot wonder again if he knew the Oval Office tapes were being duplicated.

Tactfully Eliot nodded.

"I suggest you implement them," the president said. "It doesn't make a difference, but for my satisfaction, what's his name?"

11

As he left the casino's restaurant, Saul saw a man in the crowd who suddenly turned to walk the other way. A man with a cleft chin and a mustache. *No, it couldn't be.* From the back, the man had the same narrow build. The color and style of his hair were the same. The man Saul had spoken to in Baltimore. The man who'd helped on the job.

Saul's muscles hardened. He had to be wrong. When a team disbanded after a job, the agency never sent two men to disappear in the same place. For the sake of caution, the team wasn't supposed to see each other again or be connected in any way. Then what was this man doing here?

Relax, Saul told himself. You've made a mistake. Go after the guy and take another look. Satisfy your mind.

The man had blended with the crowd, moving along a corridor, going through a door. Saul slipped around two women, passing a row of clattering slot machines. He recalled the moment when he'd seen the man—the sudden turn to walk the other way, as if the man had forgotten something. Maybe. Or had the man turned because he didn't want Saul to recognize him?

Grabbing the door, Saul pulled it open and saw a theater, dimly lit, deserted. The entertainment wouldn't start for several hours. Empty tables. A curtain hid the stage.

The right edge of the curtain trembled.

Saul ran down plush stairs. He reached the lowest tables and vaulted to the edge of the stage, creeping toward the right edge of the curtain, silently cursing himself because he'd left his automatic in his room. There'd been no choice. In Atlantic City, the quickest way to draw attention was to carry a handgun, no matter how well concealed.

The curtain stopped trembling. He stiffened as a door banged open —to his right, below the stage, past the tables, beneath an Exit light. A waiter came in, carrying a pile of tablecloths.

The waiter squinted at Saul and braced his shoulders. "You're not supposed to be here."

Random chance again. Another version of the cleaning lady coming in the room when she wasn't supposed to. Christ.

Saul made his choice, dropping to the floor, rolling beneath the heavy curtain.

"Hey!"

He heard the waiter's muffled shout beyond the curtain. He ignored it, continuing to roll, springing to a crouch beside a grand piano. Dim light from the wings cast shadows on the stage. Drums, guitars, microphones, musicians' stands. His eyes adjusted to the shadows. He crept toward the right wing of the stage. A space between angled partitions led him to a table, a chair, a rack of costumes, a wall of levers and switches.

No one.

"He went through there!" the waiter shouted beyond the curtain.

Saul stepped toward a fire door. He'd trained himself to ignore distractions, staying alive this long because of his concentration. Again, it saved him. As he touched the knob on the door, he paid no attention to the quick steps on the stage beyond the curtain. He was preoccupied by something else—the whisper of cloth behind him. He dodged. A knife rebounded, clattering off the metal door. A shadow lunged from behind a crate, the only corner Saul had deliberately failed to check. Don't go to your enemy. Make him come to you.

As adrenaline quickened his instincts, Saul crouched, bending his knees for balance, ready to meet the attack. The man struck, surprising Saul by using the heel of his palm as a weapon, his fingers upright, thrusting straight ahead. Trained to defend himself against this form of combat, Saul blocked the hand. He used the heel of his own palm, slamming the man's ribcage, aiming at his heart.

Bones cracked. Groaning, the man lurched back. Saul spun him, grabbed from behind, and pushed the fire door, dragging him out.

Five seconds had passed. As he closed the door, he glimpsed two waiters on the stage. He spun toward a hall of doors. At its end, a guard had his back turned, making a phone call.

Saul tugged the injured man in the opposite direction, shoving open a door marked Stairs but not going through, instead rushing farther down to a door with a large red star. He turned the knob. It wasn't locked. He went into a dressing room, dropped the man, and shut the door. Flicking the lock, he swung to protect himself. The room was deserted.

He held his breath, listening at the door.

"Hey!" a waiter shouted. "Anyone pass you down there?"

Saul didn't hear the guard's response.

"The door to the stairs!" a second waiter shouted.

Saul heard them running. The sound of their footfalls receded.

He stared at the man on the floor. Unconscious, the man breathed shallowly, expelling red foam from his nostrils and mouth. The splintered bones from the shattered ribcage caused extensive internal bleeding. Death from lung and heart congestion would occur in minutes.

A man with a mustache. The man Saul had talked to in Baltimore. No doubt about it. He must have followed me here, Saul thought.

But how? He'd been confident he wasn't shadowed. Conclusion— the man was good at his work.

Too much so. When the man had turned abruptly outside the restaurant, his motive hadn't been to keep Saul from recognizing him. Exactly the opposite. The man had wanted to confuse Saul into following him—to lead Saul to a quiet place and . . .

Kill me. *Why?*

Something else disturbed him. Method. The knife would have done the job if I hadn't been alert. But the way he came at me, lunging straight ahead with the heel of his palm, aiming toward my rib cage. It's unique. Only someone trained in Israel knows how to do it.

The Mossad. The Israeli intelligence network. The best in the world. Saul had been taught by them. So had the man on the floor.

But why would they—?

No professional assassin works alone. Somewhere close, other members of the death team waited.

He stepped from the dressing room, glancing along the hall. The guard was gone. Wiping his fingerprints off the doors, he left the way he'd come—past the stage and its curtain, through the empty theater.

In the casino, the noises from the crowd swept over him. Slot machines jangled. He glanced at his watch. A voice crackled from the public address system, asking Princess Fatima to pick up a service phone. Translated, the announcement meant the casino had an emergency. All security personnel were ordered to contact the office at once.

He tried not to hurry as he left the casino's glitter and reached the boardwalk, his eyes not used to twilight. Tourists leaned against a rail, a cool breeze tugging their clothes as they gazed past the beach toward whitecaps. Passing them, his footsteps rumbling on the boardwalk, he glanced at his watch again.

The man would be dead by now.

12

The lights of the greenhouse reflected off its glass, concealing the night. Pacing the aisles, Eliot tried to distract himself with his roses, savoring their fragrance. Different varieties—myriad sizes and colors. Complicated, delicate, they required perfect care and cultivation.

Like the men he controlled, he thought. Indeed he'd always believed that his men were as sensitive as his roses and as beautiful. With thorns.

But sometimes even the best of his creations had to be culled.

He paused to study a rose so red it was crimson. It seemed to have been dipped in blood. Exquisite.

He concentrated on the rose he'd mentioned to Saul in Denver. Blue.

Frowning, he glanced at his watch. Near midnight. Outside, the April night was chilly and dry. But the greenhouse was warm and humid. Though he sweated, he wore his black vest and suitcoat.

He pursed his lips. His wizened forehead narrowed. Something was wrong. An hour ago, he'd been told of the mission's failure. Saul had survived. The death team had removed the assassin's body, but not before an Atlantic City security guard had found it. That sloppy detail had to be taken care of. To quell his nervousness, Eliot amused himself by imagining the startled look on the Atlantic City headliner's face if he'd entered his dressing room and found a corpse on the floor. After the many gangster movies the superstar singer had appeared in, real life might have been an education for him. But how would *that* sloppy detail have been taken care of?

His amusement died when he heard the phone. The special phone —green, appropriate for a greenhouse, next to the black phone on the potting table. Only a handful of people knew its number. He hoped one man in particular would be calling.

Though he'd waited anxiously, he forced himself to let the phone ring two more times. Clearing his throat, he picked it up. "Hello?"

"Romulus," the strained voice said. "Black flag." The man sounded out of breath. Eliot took for granted the greenhouse and its phones were bugged. He and his men used prearranged codes. Romulus was Saul. Black flag meant an emergency—specifically that his cover had been blown and someone was dead.

Eliot answered, "Give me a number. I'll call you back in fifteen minutes."

"No," Saul blurted.

Eliot bit his lip. "Then tell me how you want to do it."

"I've got to keep moving. You give *me* a number."

"Wait ten seconds." Eliot reached in his suitcoat, pulling out a pen and note pad. He wrote down a number he knew Saul had memorized.

967–876–9988

Below it, he wrote the number of a pay phone he knew was safe.

703–338–9022

He subtracted the bottom from the top.

264–538–0966

He read Saul the remainder.

Saul in turn would subtract that number from the one he'd memorized.

967–876–9988
− 264–538–0966
703–338–9022

30

He'd then have the number of the pay phone Eliot planned to use.

"In thirty minutes," Saul said abruptly.

Eliot heard a click as Saul hung up. He set the phone down. Tense, he forced himself to wait till he had control. Saul's insistence that he call Eliot, not the other way around, was unexpected but not disastrous. He'd have needed to leave here and reach a safe phone, no matter what. But if Saul had given him a number, he could have used it to locate the phone Saul was calling from. He could then have sent a team to that location.

Now he had to think of another way. He concentrated on his roses, nodding as the solution came to him.

He checked his watch, surprised that ten minutes had elapsed since Saul had hung up. But he still had time to drive to the phone he planned to use outside a local supermarket—after midnight, no one would be in the area—and make a hurried call to set up the trap. A minute to explain instructions. Then he'd wait for Saul to get in touch with him again.

All the same, as he turned off the lights in the greenhouse, he felt a moment's hesitation. Standing in the dark, he thought that Saul was so superior he regretted having to terminate him. But then again, Eliot had many superior men. One less wouldn't matter, given the stakes.

But something else troubled him. The way Saul had avoided the trap in Atlantic City. What if Saul was even better than Eliot thought?

13

The bowling alley rumbled from strikes and gutterballs. Only a third of the lanes had players. Ricky's Auto Parts was beating First-rate Mufflers.

Saul sat with his swivel chair turned so his back was to the luncheon counter. He tried to look preoccupied by the games, but actually he studied the entrance to the bowling alley.

Stay off the streets—too great a risk of being seen. Choose a public place—the cops won't bother you. Pick a spot that isn't crowded—you've got to have room to maneuver. And an exit—the service door behind the counter.

"Refill?" the waitress said behind him.

He turned to the tired woman in the wrinkled uniform. She held a pot of coffee. "No, thanks. I guess my friend won't be coming."

"Closing time." She glanced at the clock above the milk dispenser. "In five minutes."

"What do I owe you?"

"Eighty cents."

He gave her a dollar. "Keep the change. I'd better call and find out what happened to him."

"Over there." She pointed to a pay phone near a glassed-in display of bowling balls for sale.

Distressed, he hoped his smile looked convincing as he walked to the phone. He'd told Eliot he'd call back in thirty minutes. On schedule, he shoved a coin in the slot and pressed the button for the operator. He told her the number Eliot had given him. A Virginia area code. The corresponding pay phone would have to be near Falls Church, where Eliot lived. Eliot didn't have time to drive far.

The operator told Saul the charges for three minutes. He inserted the coins, listened to the different tones as they dropped through the slots, and heard a buzz.

Eliot answered quickly. "Yes?"

Though these phones weren't tapped, the operator might overhear the conversation. Saul used indirect references, quickly explaining what had happened. "Our friends from Israel," he concluded. "I recognized their style. They don't want me working for the magazine. Why?"

"I'll ask the editor. Their accounting office must be confused."

"It's something to do with the last article I wrote. One of my researchers wanted to stop me from writing another one."

"Maybe he thought you were working for a rival magazine."

"Or maybe *he* was."

"Possibly. It's a competitive business," Eliot said.

"It's cutthroat. I need job security."

"And health benefits. I agree. I know where you can go to relax. An executive retreat."

"Not far, I hope. It's late. On foot, I might get mugged."

"There's a hotel in your neighborhood." Using code, Eliot told Saul the address. "I'll make a reservation for you. Naturally I'm upset. You have my sympathy. I'll find out why they're angry."

"Please. I knew I could count on you."

"That's what fathers are for."

Saul put the phone back on its hook. He'd been watching the entrance to the bowling alley. He heard the rumble of another gutter-ball. An opposing player laughed. Beyond an open door marked Office, a bald man flicked some switches on a wall. The lights went dim.

"Closing time!" the waitress said.

Saul glanced through the glass door toward the parking lot. Arc lights gleamed. Behind them, shadows loomed. No other choice. Skin prickling, he crossed the lot.

14

From the dark at the end of the deserted block, he saw his destination. A hotel. Eliot had said he'd make a reservation, but Saul hadn't guessed he was being literal. A kind of joke. Saul almost smiled.

The only light on the street was the glowing neon sign above the dirty concrete steps leading up to the dilapidated wooden structure.

AYFARE HOTEL

Saul decided the burnt-out letter on the sign was either an M or a W. Mayfare. Wayfare. It didn't matter which. The important thing was one of the letters was missing, a signal to him that all was ready, the place secure. If every letter had been working, he'd have been warned to stay away.

He scanned the neighborhood. Seeing no one, he started down the street. The district was a slum. Broken windows. Garbage. The tenements looked deserted. Perfect. Alone, at three o'clock in the morning, he wouldn't draw attention here. No police cars would bother patrolling this district, stopping to ask where he was going and why he was out so late. The local residents would mind their own business.

His footsteps echoed. Unwilling to risk getting trapped in a taxi, he'd been walking for several hours, his legs stiff, shoulders aching. He'd backtracked, often going around a block, to check if he was being followed. He hadn't seen a tail. That didn't mean there wasn't one.

But soon it wouldn't matter. He was almost home.

The neon sign grew larger as he neared it. Though the night was cool, sweat trickled down his chest beneath his turtleneck sweater and the bulletproof vest he always wore for a few days after a job. His hands felt numb. He subdued the urge to hurry.

Again, he glanced behind him. No one.

He approached the hotel from the opposite side of the street, tempted to go around the block, to scout the neighborhood, to reassure himself everything was as it should be. But since no opponent could have known he was coming here, he didn't see the need for further evasive tactics. All he wanted was to rest, to clear his mind, to learn why he was being hunted.

Eliot would care for him.

He stepped from the curb to cross the street. The dingy hotel, its windows darkened, waited for him. Past the door, a rescue team would have food and drink and comfort ready. They'd protect him.

Though his heart raced, he walked steadily, seeing the warped cracks on the wooden door.

But he felt uneasy. Procedure. Eliot had always said, no matter what, don't violate procedure. It's the only thing that guarantees survival. Always circle your objective. Check the territory. Make extra sure.

Obeying the impulse, he pivoted, shifting abruptly toward the sidewalk he'd just left. If in spite of his caution he'd been followed, this final unexpected change in direction might confuse a tail and make him show himself.

The blow jerked him sideways, its impact stunning, unanticipated, high on his left side near his heart against his bulletproof vest. He didn't know what had happened. Then he realized. He'd been shot. A silencer. He gasped, the wind knocked out of him.

His vision blurred. He fell to the street, absorbing the jolt as he rolled to the gutter. The bullet had come from above him, from a building opposite the hotel. But the vest should have stopped it. Why was he bleeding?

Confused, he groped to his feet, bent over, stumbling across the littered sidewalk. His chest felt on fire. He lurched down an alley, pressing himself against its wall, peering through the dark. Shadowy objects hulked before him. At the far end, he saw another street.

But he couldn't go down there. If he'd been followed, it wouldn't have been by just one man. There'd be backup—other members of the death team watching the nearby streets. When he came to the end of the alley, he'd be shot again, maybe in the head or the throat. He'd trapped himself.

He staggered past a fire escape and the stench of overflowing garbage cans. Behind him, silhouetted by the hotel's neon sign, a man approached the alley, his footsteps echoing in the eerie quiet. The man walked with his knees bent, stooped, aiming a small automatic with the tube of a silencer projecting from its barrel.

The Mossad, Saul thought again. The characteristic, flat-footed, seemingly awkward crouch that insured an assassin could keep his balance, even if wounded. He himself had been trained to maintain that posture.

The assassin entered the alley, pressing himself against the dark of the wall, inching forward, blending with the night.

He's being careful, Saul thought. He doesn't know I left my hand-gun behind. He'll come slowly.

Whirling, Saul stared toward the other end of the alley. A second figure entered. No way out.

But there had to be. The fire escape? No good—as he struggled up, he'd attract their fire. He sensed them pressing closer.

The door beneath the fire escape? He lunged, twisting the knob, but it was locked. Using an elbow, he smashed a window next to the door, knowing the crash would alert his hunters, rushing, feeling the glass lance through his jacket. Blood soaked his arms. His shoes scraped as he thrust himself through the window, wincing from pressure on his chest, tilting, falling.

He struck a floor. Darkness surrounded him. Soon, he thought. The men in the hotel. They'll charge out to help me. Stay alive till they get here.

He scrambled forward, bumping against an unseen bannister, jarring his chest. Sweat slicked his face. Feeling around, he touched two stairways, one up, one down. Stifling a groan, he staggered up. The hall stank from urine. He sprawled on a landing, squirmed ahead, and cracked his skull against the spoked wheels of a baby carriage.

He touched its greasy side. As blood dripped off his arms, he shoved the carriage toward the top of the stairs. The wheels creaked. He froze. Don't make a sound. Outside the window, a shadow crept near.

He sensed what his hunter felt. The only entrance to this building was the broken window. But the window might be a trap.

The shadow paused.

But Saul had been shot. He was on the run. The shadow might feel confident.

He did. With amazing speed, the shadow dove through the window, thudding on the floor, rolling quickly, stopping in the dark.

The assassin would find the two sets of stairs. But up or down? Which way had Saul gone? The rule was up. The high ground was easier to defend.

The problem was, had Saul remained consistent, obeying the rule, or had he gone to the basement, hoping to fool his enemy? A mental toss of a coin.

The tenement was silent. All at once, the gunman charged the stairs. Pushing the baby carriage, Saul struck him in the face, hearing the carriage clatter as the gunman toppled. Lunging down, Saul kicked, feeling the jaw give way.

He heard a moan and grabbed the gunman's sweater. Jerking it down with one hand, he rammed his other arm up toward the throat. The larynx snapped. The gunman fell, convulsing, suffocating. His pistol thumped.

Saul bent in pain to find it. The feel was familiar, palm-sized. He'd used the weapon often—a Beretta, this one equipped with a barrel long enough to accommodate a silencer. A customized .22, so precisely remachined that what it lacked in power it gained in accuracy. The handgun preferred by the Mossad—another of their calling cards.

He peered through the shattered window. Down the alley, the second gunman stalked through the shadows. Saul squeezed the trigger, jerking from repeated spits, continuing to shoot as the gunman fell and heaved.

He leaned against the wall, trying to keep his balance. There'd be other hunters. He had to assume it. His survival depended on assumptions. Get away. He hurried up the stairs.

A baby cried in an apartment. He reached the top of the stairs, pushed a metal door, and came out crouching on the roof, his pistol aimed at air vents, clotheslines, pipes, TV aerials. No one. Move. He crept through shadows, biting his lip from pain as he eased to a lower level. Stars glinted coldly.

Abruptly he faced the edge. The next building was too far away for him to reach with a jump. Glancing around, he saw a rectangular structure projecting from the roof, opened its door, and stared toward the black of a stairwell. Dear God, the pain!

One floor, then another, then another. At last on the bottom, he peered toward an exit. Someone might be waiting, but he had to take the risk. The street was dark. He eased out. Holding his breath, he reached the sidewalk. No shots. No figures lunging at him.

He'd made it. But where could he go? He didn't know how badly he was hurt. He couldn't show himself much longer or they'd find him.

He thought of the hotel. The gunmen had intercepted him, trying to stop him from reaching it. He didn't understand why help wasn't here. The gunmen had used silencers. Maybe the rescue team didn't know he'd been shot.

But he'd been hit on the street outside the hotel. Surely the rescue team had been watching. Why had they failed to rush out, to help him?

Because they didn't know where he'd gone. They didn't want to jeopardize the integrity of the hotel. They were keeping their position in hope that he'd reach them. Get there.

He saw a rusty Plymouth Duster parked at the curb, its battered shape the only car on the shadowy block. If it wasn't locked. If it would start.

If.

He pulled the door. It opened. The keys weren't in the ignition switch. Chest aching, he bent down, fumbling beneath the dash, finding what he needed. He joined two wires. The Duster started.

Clutching the wheel, he stomped the accelerator. The Duster roared from the curb. He screeched around a corner. Buildings blurred. The street seemed to shrink as he squealed around another corner.

Ahead, he saw the hotel and veered toward the curb. In the light from the neon sign, his hunters couldn't use a nightscope. Its lens would magnify the light so much a gunman would be blinded.

He jerked from the impact as the Duster hit the curb and shuddered across the sidewalk. Skidding to a stop before the grimy concrete steps, he shouldered open his door. The car was positioned so it gave him cover. He charged up the steps, hitting the entrance, slamming through. At once he dropped to the floor and spun to aim his handgun toward the street.

He'd reached the hotel. He was safe.

The silence stunned him. The rescue team? Where were they?

Peering behind him, he saw only darkness. "Romulus!" he shouted, heard an echo, but received no answer.

He crawled around, smelling dust and mildew. Where the

hell—? The place was empty. Confused, he searched the murky lobby. No one. He checked the office and the rooms along the hall, darting glances toward the entrance, straining to listen for anyone coming.

Completely deserted. Nothing had been prepared for his arrival. Not a secure location. Christ, this hotel had been the bait to lure him into a trap! They'd never expected him to get inside!

He understood now that the men who'd waited here had indeed come out. But not to rescue him. Instead to track him down and kill him. They were out there searching for him. And the car outside would tell them where he was.

He ran toward the door. Hurrying down the steps, he saw a gunman appear at the corner, aiming a short-barreled submachine gun, unmistakably an Uzi.

Saul shot as he ran, seeing the gunman grab his arm and jerk behind the corner.

He hadn't bothered to waste time reaching for the wires beneath the dash to turn off the Duster's engine. The driver's door hung open. He yanked the gearshift. Squealing, the car jolted off the sidewalk, fishtailing, roaring down the street. A volley of bullets shattered the rear windshield. Glass exploded over him. Slumping, he steered, trying to hide himself.

On the corner ahead, another gunman stepped out. Saul swung the steering wheel in his direction, pressing the accelerator, racing toward him. Thirty feet, twenty. The gunman aimed a pistol. Ten feet. Suddenly the gunman broke his stance, diving in panic toward a doorway.

Saul veered, avoiding a fire hydrant, speeding past the gunman, screeching down a side street. A cluster of bullets whacked the Duster.

He skidded through an intersection, listing, racing down another side street. Checking his rearview mirror, glancing ahead, he saw no other gunmen.

He was safe. But blood streamed down his chest where he'd been shot, and from his elbows where he'd cut himself breaking the window. Safe. But for how long?

Despite his urgency, he eased his foot off the accelerator. Don't run traffic lights. Obey the speed limit. Bleeding, in a stolen car with a shattered rear window and bullet holes in the body, he didn't dare get stopped by the police. He had to ditch this car.

And do it fast.

15

He drove past a truck stop, squinting at the bright lights of a gas station and a restaurant. Two pickup trucks, three semis. Heading a quarter mile farther, he turned toward a trailer court. Four-thirty. No lights were on in the trailers. He parked between two cars on a strip of gravel, shut his headlights off, and disconnected the ignition wires beneath the dash.

Pain made him wince. After glancing around to make sure he hadn't attracted attention, he wiped the clammy sweat from his brow. Straining to take off his jacket, he lifted his turtleneck sweater, touched the Velcro straps on his bulletproof vest, and tugged them, pulling the vest off.

Eliot had always insisted, never violate procedure. After a job, take precautions. Wear your vest. In case of complications from the job. Established methods keep you alive.

The vest was somewhat bulky. A quarter-inch thick, weighing a pound and a half, it was made from seven layers of Kevlar, a synthetic nylonlike fiber five times stronger than steel. But Saul was big-boned, rugged, and the extra girth made him seem merely overweight. At the casino, though he hadn't risked carrying a gun, he'd felt confident the vest would be unobtrusive. Once again, a habit had saved his life.

But the bullet should only have stunned him. It shouldn't have gone through the vest. It shouldn't have wounded him. Frowning, he fingered the blood on his chest, probing for the bullet hole. Instead he touched the bullet itself, embedded a quarter-inch into his chest, sticking out between two ribs, its impact slowed by the vest.

He gritted his teeth and pulled it free, exhaling, stifling the urge to vomit. For a moment in the dark, the car seemed to swirl. Then the spinning stopped, and he swallowed bile.

He wiped the bullet, troubled. Nothing made sense. It shouldn't have gone through the vest. The bullet was slim and pointed, but its tip should have been blunted by its impact against the vest.

He took a chance and opened the car door, using the interior light to study the bullet, more troubled by what he saw.

The bullet was green. Teflon streamlined its shape, making it capable of piercing the vest. A special item favored by elite intelligence networks. Including the Mossad.

He studied the silencer on the Beretta. Possession of one was as illegal as having a machine gun or a rocket launcher. Rather than risk getting caught with one or trying to buy one on the black market, operatives assembled their own, using parts easy to obtain and innocent-looking if distributed in a toolkit. In this case, the gunman had bought a plastic tube, wide enough to fit over the Beretta's muzzle. The tube had been filled with an alternating series of metal and glass-wool washers, the holes in the washers wide enough to allow for the passage of a bullet. The tube had a hole in the end, small enough to prevent the washers from falling out, large enough to let the bullet escape. Three holes had been drilled a quarter-inch down from the tube's open mouth. Set screws through these holes braced the silencer over the pistol's barrel. Quickly assembled, it was effective for seven shots before the glass wool lost its muffling power. It could then be swiftly taken apart, its components thrown away with no sign of what they'd been used for. Simple. The method preferred by the Mossad.

What the hell was going on? How had his opponents known he was going to that hotel? He himself had known only a few hours before. It wasn't a question of his having been followed. The assassins had anticipated his movements. They'd been *waiting* for him.

Eliot had made the arrangements. Eliot must have done something wrong. Perhaps he'd used an unsecured phone.

But Eliot didn't make mistakes.

Then Eliot must have been followed, his conversations picked up by a directional microphone.

But Eliot knew better. He always carried a jamming device that interfered with microphones.

Maybe one of Eliot's men was a double agent. But for whom? The Mossad?

Saul shut the door. The light went off. He used a handkerchief to wipe the blood from his chest. In the night, he felt tired and cold.

He didn't like coincidences. Eliot had sent him to Atlantic City, a location that seemed unusual, where a member of the disbanded team had tried to . . . Saul began to shiver. Eliot had also sent him to the abandoned hotel, where again Saul had almost been killed.

The common denominator. Eliot.

The implication was unthinkable. Eliot—Saul's foster father—had put out a contract on him?

No!

Saul pulled down his turtleneck sweater and stepped from the car, tugging on his sportcoat. Five o'clock—the eastern sky was turning gray.

He left the trailer court, walking in pain along the highway. At the truck stop, he waited in the shadow of a semi till its driver left the restaurant.

The driver stiffened when he saw him.

"Fifty bucks for a ride," Saul said.

"Against the rules. You see that sign? No passengers. I'd lose my job."

"A hundred."

"So you mug me when you get the chance. Or your buddies hijack the truck."

"Two hundred."

The driver pointed. "Blood on your clothes. You've been in a fight, or you're wanted by the cops."

"I cut myself shaving. Three."

"No way. I've got a wife and kids."

"Four. That's my limit."

"Not enough."

"I'll wait for another driver." Saul walked toward a different truck.

"Hey, buddy."

Saul turned.

"That kind of money, you must really need to get out of town."

"My father's sick."

The driver laughed. "And so's my bank account. I hoped you'd offer five."

"Don't have it."

"Ever seen Atlanta?"

"No," Saul lied.

"You're going to." The driver held out his hand. "The money?"

"Half now."

"Fair enough. In case you get any funny ideas, I'd better warn you. I was in the marines. I know karate."

"Really," Saul said.

"Assume the position while I search you. I'd better not find a gun or a knife."

Saul had thrown away the silencer and put the small Beretta in his underwear, against his crotch. The gun felt uncomfortable, but he knew only naked body searches were accurate. The driver would frisk the contours of Saul's body—the arms, up the legs, and along the spine. But Saul was doubtful the driver would feel his privates or reach inside his underwear. If the driver did . . .

"All you'll find is four hundred dollars," Saul told him. "In Atlanta, if the cops come looking for me, I'll know who to blame. I'll phone your boss and tell him about our arrangement. It'll be a comfort to me to know you lost your job."

"Is that any way to talk to a pal?" The driver grinned. As Saul expected, the frisk was amateurish.

Through the gleaming day, as the truck roared down the highway, he pretended to sleep as he brooded over what had happened. Eliot, he kept thinking. Something was horribly wrong. But he couldn't keep running. He couldn't hide forever.

Why does Eliot want to kill me? Why the Mossad?

This much was sure—he needed help. But who to trust?

The sun glared through the windshield.

Clutching his chest, he sweated, feverish, thinking of Chris.

His foster brother.

Remus.

CHURCH OF THE MOON

1

Among the surge of Orientals on noisy, acrid Silom Road, the tall Caucasian somehow avoided attention. He moved with purpose, smoothly, steadily, blending with the rhythm of the crowd. As soon as someone sensed him, the man was already gone. An untrained observer could not have guessed his nationality. French perhaps, or English. Maybe German. His hair was brown, but whether dark or light was hard to say. His eyes were brown, yet blue and green. His face was oval yet rectangular. He wasn't thin but wasn't heavy either. Ordinary jacket; shirt and pants of neutral color. In his thirties, maybe older, maybe younger. Without scars or facial hair. Unusual in only one respect—he seemed to be invisible.

In fact, he was an American. Though he traveled under many identities, his real name was Chris Kilmoonie. He was thirty-six. His scars had been disguised by plastic surgery. Indeed, his face had been reconstructed several times. He'd cut the labels from his clothes. He'd stitched the equivalent of five thousand dollars in large bills of various currencies beneath the lining of his jacket. The rest of his fifteen-thousand-dollar emergency fund had been converted into gold and gems—an eighteen-karat Rolex watch, for example, and a precious necklace—which he wore out of sight. He had to be able to move from country to country as quickly as possible, freed from dependence on banks. He didn't worry that a thief who suspected his wealth would try to take it from him. Beneath his jacket, behind the belt at his spine, he carried a Mauser HSc, 7.65-mm automatic pistol. But more than the weapon, Chris's eyes discouraged confrontation. Deep within them, past their shifting colors, lurked a warning confidence that made a stranger want to keep his distance.

Halfway down the street, Chris paused among bamboo-awninged stalls where vendors shouted to be heard above one another, waving elaborate kites, silk scarves, and teak statuettes. Ignoring a pushcart salesman who offered him a piece of roasted monkey, he glanced beyond the cacophonous rush of bicycles and mopeds toward a thin, peaked, two-story church, enmeshed with vines, between the Oriental Hotel and a mission. From this angle, he saw the rectory, a two-story bungalow attached to the rear of the church. Beyond it, he saw the graveyard and the pepper garden that sloped down to the muddy, crocodile-infested river. In the distance, rice paddies merged with the jungle. What interested him most, though, was the six-foot stained glass window beneath the church's peak. He knew that years before, a one-foot slice of glass had been broken during a storm. Because this parish in Sawang Kaniwat, old town, Bangkok, was poor, the slice—which resembled a crescent moon—had been replaced by a cheap piece of galvanized steel. The crescent, stark beneath the peak, accounted for the nickname: Church of the Moon.

Chris also knew that, at the request of the Russian KGB, the church had been converted into an Abelard-sanctioned safe house in 1959, available for use by operatives from any agency, no matter their differences in politics. As he waited for a break in traffic, then crossed the street, he took for granted that agents from various intelligence networks watched from nearby buildings. They didn't matter. Within the church and the surrounding area, he was guaranteed immunity.

He opened a listing wooden gate and walked along a soggy gravel path beside the church. In back, the blare of the street was muffled. He tugged his shirt away from his sweaty chest, the temperature ninety-five, the humidity smothering. Though the rains weren't due for another month, thick black clouds loomed over the jungle.

He walked up the creaky unpainted steps and knocked on the rectory door. An Oriental servant answered. Speaking Thai, Chris asked to see the priest. A minute passed. The old priest came and studied him.

Phonetically, Chris said, "Eye ba."

In Thai, this phrase is an expletive, referring to a dirty or large monkey. It can also mean guerrilla. It was all Chris had to say to gain asylum here.

The priest stepped back and nodded.

Chris went in, squinting while his eyes adjusted to the shadows in the hallway. He smelled pepper.

"You speak—?"

"English," Chris replied.

"Are you familiar with our arrangements?"

"Yes, I've been here once before."

"I don't recall."

"In 1965."

"I still don't—"

"I looked different then. My face was crushed."

The old priest hesitated. "Ruptured appendix? Fractured spine?"

Chris nodded.

"I remember now," the old priest said. "Your agency should be complimented. Its surgeons were meticulous."

Chris waited.

"But you're not here to recall old times," the priest continued. "My office is more convenient for conversation." Turning left, he entered a room.

Chris followed him. He'd read the old man's file and knew that Father Gabriel Janin was seventy-two. His white whisker stubble matched the bristle of his close-cropped hair. Emaciated, stooped and wrinkled, the priest wore muddy canvas shoes and dingy pants below a shapeless mildewed surplice. Both his age and slovenly appearance were misleading. From 1929 to 1934, he'd been a member of the French Foreign Legion. Bored by the challenge he'd met and exceeded, he'd entered the Cistercian Order of monks at Citeaux in 1935. Four years later, he'd left the order and, during the war years, trained to become a missionary priest. After the war, he'd been transferred to Saigon. In 1954, he'd been transferred again, this time to Bangkok. In 1959, he'd been blackmailed by the KGB, because of his preference for young Thai girls, to be the housekeeper for this internationally sanctioned safe house. Chris was well aware that, to protect his guests, the priest would kill.

The office was narrow, cluttered, musty. The priest shut the door. "Would you like some refreshment? Tea perhaps, or—?"

Chris shook his head.

The priest spread his hands. He sat with a desk between them. A bird sang in the pepper garden.

"How may I help you?"

"Father—" Chris's voice was hushed as if he were going to confession, "—I need you to tell me the name of a dentist who'll extract teeth and stay quiet about it."

Father Janin looked troubled.

"What's the matter?"

"Your fine organization should not need this information," the old priest said. "It has dentists of its own."

"I need the name of yours."

The priest leaned forward, frowning. "Why does this concern you? Why come here? Forgive my bluntness. Has this dentist wronged someone or destroyed the cover of someone? Are you returning a favor by removing him?"

"No favor," Chris assured him. "My employers worry about information leaks in our network. Sometimes we have to go outside our sources."

Father Janin considered. He kept frowning as he nodded. "Understandable. But all the same . . ." He tapped his fingers on his desk.

"When you make inquiries, my cryptonym is Remus."

The priest stopped tapping his fingers. "In that case, if you'll stay the night, I'll try to have your answer by the morning."

That's not soon enough, Chris thought.

2

In the dining room, he sat at a table eating chicken and noodles laced with hot peppers, as the Thais preferred it. His eyes watered; his nostrils flared. He drank warm Coke, glancing out the window toward the back. The clouds had reached the city, rain falling densely, like molten lead. He couldn't see the crosses in the graveyard.

Father Janin's reluctance disturbed him. He was sure that at this moment the priest was making phone calls, investigating his background. The phone, of course, would not be bugged. Neither would the safe house. The place was neutral territory. Anyone who violated its sanctity would be exiled from his network, hunted by the world's intelligence community, and executed.

All the same, Chris felt troubled. As soon as the agency learned he was here, the local bureau chief would wonder why. He'd contact his superior. Since cryptonyms gained their significance from their first two letters—AM, for example, referred to Cuba; thus AMALGAM would be the cryptonym for an operation in that country—the bureau chief's superior would check the first two letters in Chris's cryptonym REMUS and learn that RE meant Chris was answerable only to headquarters in Langley, Virginia, and in particular to Eliot. Soon Eliot would be informed that Chris had arrived unexpectedly at the Bangkok safe house. Eliot, of course, would be puzzled since he hadn't directed Chris to come here.

That was the problem. Chris didn't want Eliot to follow his movements. Given what Chris intended to do, he didn't want Eliot to know the consequences, didn't want Eliot to grieve or feel embarrassed.

He tried not to show impatience. At the earliest opportunity, he'd go to the priest and get the dentist's name.

Preoccupied, he turned from the dismal rain beyond the window. Wiping his sweat-blurred eyes, he gaped in disbelief at a man whom he had last seen seventeen years ago.

The man, a Chinese, had entered the dining room. Slender, round-faced, genteel, he wore an impeccable khaki suit, the jacket of which was buttoned to his collar in the Mao style. His youthful face and his thick black hair belied his sixty-two years.

The man's name was Chin Ken Chan. I.Q.: one hundred and eighty. Multilingual in Russian, French, and English in addition to Chinese. Chris knew his background. Chan had received his formal education from Dame Sahara Day-Wisdom, O.B.E., at Merton College, Oxford University, from 1939 till the war had ended. During that time, he'd been influenced by the Communist members of clubs at both Oxford and Cambridge, easily recruited by the mole Guy Burgess to help Mao after the war. Because Chan was a homosexual, he'd never risen higher than the rank of colonel in the intelligence arena of China. But he was a valuable idealist in the Maoist cause and, despite his effete appearance, one of its finest killers, particularly with the garotte.

Chan glanced dismissively at Chris and walked toward another table. He sat primly, reaching between the buttons of his jacket to pull out his own set of chopsticks.

Chris chewed and swallowed, hiding his surprise. "The Snow Leopard."

Chan raised his head.

"Does the Snow Leopard miss Deep Snow?"

Chan nodded impassively. "It's been thirteen years since we've had Deep Snow in the Orient."

"I was thinking of *seventeen* years ago. I believe it snowed then in Laos."

Chan smiled politely. "There were only two Americans in the snow that year. I recall they were brothers—but not by birth."

"And this one is eternally grateful to you."

"Chris?" Chan said.

Chris nodded, throat tight. "Good to see you, Chan."

His heart raced as he grinned and stood. They crossed the room and embraced.

3

Father Janin felt apprehensive. As soon as a servant had taken the American to the dining room, he grabbed the phone on his desk and dialed quickly.

"Remus," he said.

He hung up, gulped a glass of brandy, frowned, and waited.

Coincidences bothered him. Two days ago, he'd given sanctuary to a Russian, Joseph Malenov, the director of the KGB's opium traffic into Southeast Asia. Malenov had stayed in his room, where, by agreement, the priest supplied him daily with 300 milligrams of the suppressant Dilantin to try to calm his outbursts of rage and hypertension. The treatment was working.

Yesterday, the priest had given sanctuary to a Chinese Communist operative, Col. Chin Ken Chan. Informants had told the priest that Chan was here to meet the Russian and perhaps become a double agent for the KGB. Such arrangements were not unusual. In an Abelard safe house, opposing operatives frequently took advantage of neutral territory to transact business, sometimes defecting. But the priest was not convinced of Chan's motivation. He knew that the Chinese Communists opposed Russia's opium smuggling into Southeast Asia, partly because they resented Soviet interference in the region, partly as well because they felt that opium undermined the character of the area. It made no sense that Chan, who for years had been sabotaging Russia's opium shipments, would defect to the very man who directed the smuggling.

Now, today, the American had arrived. His request for a dentist who would extract teeth and stay quiet about it could have only one purpose—to prevent someone's body from being identified. But whose? The Russian's?

His thoughts were interrupted when the phone rang.

The priest picked up the receiver and listened.

In a minute, he set it down, twice as puzzled.

REMUS, he'd learned, was the cryptonym for Christopher Patrick Kilmoonie, one-time lieutenant in the American Special Forces, who in 1965 had worked in conjunction with the CIA in an operation called Deep Snow, the purpose of which was to destroy the flow of Russian opium. In 1966, Kilmoonie had resigned from the military and joined the CIA. In 1976, he'd entered a Cistercian monastery. In 1982, he'd rejoined the CIA. The combination of religion and politics seemed unusual, but Father Janin could empathize since he himself had combined them. Still, what troubled him was that all three men were connected in different ways with the opium traffic.

And one other connection. When the American had mentioned that in 1965 he'd come here with a crushed face, ruptured appendix, and fractured spine, the priest had remembered the American's escort —the same Chinese now in this building—Chin Ken Chan.

Coincidences bothered him.

4

Chris stood on the rectory's porch as rain drummed on the corrugated metal roof. He still couldn't see the graveyard. Next to him, Chan leaned on the railing, facing outward. Though the safe house wasn't bugged, they used the noise from the rain to prevent their conversation from being overheard. They'd chosen a windowless corner.

"Two things," Chan said.

Chris waited.

"You must leave here quickly. Joseph Malenov is in a room upstairs," Chan said.

Chris understood. In their profession, what was said was seldom what was meant. Discretion was the rule. For Chan to speak even this directly was unusual. Chris quickly made the connection, filling the gaps between Chan's statements.

He was shocked. The basis of their way of life was adherence to strict codes, the most extreme of which was the sanctity of an Abelard safe house.

Chan intended to commit the cardinal sin.

"It's never been done," Chris said.

"Not true. While you were in the monastery—"

"You've been keeping tabs on me."

"I saved your life. I'm responsible for you. During your stay in the monastery, the code was broken twice. In Ferlach, Austria. Then again in Montreal."

Chris felt a chill.

Chan's gaze never wavered.

"Then the world's gone crazy," Chris said.

"Isn't that why you left it? Because the monastery offered a code with honor?"

"No. Back then, the profession still had rules. I left because I failed the profession. Not the other way around."

"I don't understand."

"I can't explain. I don't want to talk about it. If the sanction's lost its meaning, how can we depend on anything else?" He shook his head in dismay. "Nothing's sacred."

"Everything gets worse," Chan said. "Six years ago, what I plan would have been unthinkable."

"And now?" Chris asked.

"Since precedent has been established, I feel free from obligation. Malenov is mentally diseased. These past few months, he's increased the opium traffic beyond tolerance. He has to be stopped."

"Then kill him outside," Chris insisted.

"He's too well guarded then."

"But you'll be hunted."

"By them all." Chan nodded. "Everyone. The Snow Leopard has his tricks."

"The odds," Chris said.."If everyone's against you . . . Ferlach, and then Montreal? What happened?"

"To the violators? They were found, and they were killed. And so will I be killed. In time. But I will stretch the time."

"I ask you not to do this."

"Why?"

50

"Because I feel responsible to *you.*"

"The debt is mine. I interfered with what you understand as fate. But I must face my own. As I grow old, I must prepare to die with what you Westerners call dignity, what I call honor. I must face my destiny. Too many years I've waited for this chance. The opium is wrong. It has to be stopped."

"But the KGB will only send another man to replace him."

Chan clutched the rail. "Not Malenov. The man is evil." Sweat drenched his face. "He has to die."

Chris felt distressed by Chan's directness. "In the morning, I will leave."

"But I can't wait that long. The Russian leaves tomorrow."

"I need important information from the priest."

"Then get it soon. When I act, our friendship won't be overlooked. The coincidence of our meeting after all these years will seem suspicious. Fate, my friend. I didn't save your life so long ago to have you lose it due to me now. Get out of here. I beg you."

The rain fell harder.

5

Something wakened Chris. He lay in his room in the dark, squinting at the luminous dial on his watch. Three-thirty. Puzzled, he kept still and concentrated. The storm had passed. Occasional drops of water trickled off the eaves. As moonlight glimmered through his open window, he smelled the sordid odor of the river and the fertilized soil of the garden below. He listened to the songs of the birds beginning to stir.

For a moment, he thought he'd wakened from habit and nothing more. His six years in the monastery had trained him to use the hours before dawn for meditation. Normally he would have wakened shortly anyhow.

But then he glanced toward the hall light filtering through the crack below his door. A shadow passed. Whoever it was, he thought, the person knew how to walk like an animal, carrying the weight of his body along the outsides of his feet. He imagined a cat stalking silently toward its prey.

It might have been a servant patrolling the hall. Or Chan. Or someone after Chan. Or after me, Chris thought, because of my friendship with Chan.

He grabbed the Mauser by his side and threw off his sheet, lunging naked in the dark toward the protection of a chair. His testicles shrank. He held his breath and waited, cautious, aiming toward the door.

Beyond it, he heard a noise like a fist slamming into a pillow. Muffled, it nonetheless carried a great deal of force.

As someone groaned, an object thudded to the floor out there.

Chris left the cover of the chair, creeping toward the wall beside his door. With his ear to the wall, he listened to the rattle of a latch as a door came open in the hall.

Someone spoke, alarmed, in Russian. *"What have you done?"*

Chris heard the old priest answer, also in Russian. "He was going in your room. You see his garotte. He meant to strangle you. I had no choice. I had to kill him."

Chris opened the door. If he didn't, if he stayed in his room, the priest might wonder why the noise hadn't wakened him. Suspicious, the priest might decide Chris was somehow involved in this.

Chris squinted from his open door toward the light in the hall.

The priest swung toward the sound he'd made, aiming a Russian Tokarev automatic pistol with a silencer.

Chris froze. He raised his hands, the Mauser high above his head. "Your voices woke me." He shrugged. "I can see this is none of my business."

Waiting for a nod of dismissal from the priest, Chris stepped back in his room and closed the door.

He stared at the dark. He'd seen a man in another doorway. Middle sixties. Shrunken, pale. Dark circles under his eyes. Rumpled hair. Nervous twitches. Wearing sweat-stained silk pajamas. Joseph Malenov, Chris thought. He'd never met the man, but he'd seen photographs of him and knew that Malenov was addicted to the opium he smuggled.

On the floor, between the priest and Malenov, Chris had seen Chan's body, the base of his skull shattered by the Russian pistol's 7.62-mm bullet. The floor had been dark with blood and urine. There'd been no point in checking to see if Chan was alive.

Chris seethed. Other shadows blocked the light at the base of the door. He recognized the sound of someone unfolding a blanket. He heard men, more than two, quietly, but not as quiet as Chan had been, lift the body, wrap it, and carry it away. He smelled acrid sandalwood, then the resin odor of pine. Someone must have lit a pot of incense and thrown sawdust on the floor to absorb the body's fluids.

Chris stepped toward the window, careful not to show himself. The birds erupted from the trees, alarmed by intruders. Silhouetted by the moonlight, two Oriental servants left the rectory's porch, hunched over, carrying a heavy object wrapped in a blanket between them. A third servant led the way, flashing a light toward the path through the crosses in the graveyard and the pepper plants in the garden.

They went down the slope toward the river—to feed Chan to the crocodiles, or else to boat him across to the jungle.

Friend, Chris thought. His throat felt tight.

He clutched his Mauser.

6

Father Janin made the sign of the cross. In the church, he'd been kneeling at the altar rail, reciting his daily prayers. He stared at the votive candles he'd lit, enveloped by the fragrance of beeswax and frankincense. They flickered in the dark.

5 A.M. The church was quiet.

Sanctuary.

Pushing from the altar rail, the old priest stood and genuflected to the tabernacle. He had prayed for God's forgiveness. Having vowed to guard this safe house, he believed he'd lose his soul if he didn't fulfill his obligations. Though the KGB had recruited him, he felt allegiance to every network. Every operative in the world was his parishioner. Their differences in politics—or religion, or lack of it—didn't matter. Even atheists had souls. Cold, tired men came here for refuge. As a priest, he had to offer them the corporal works of mercy. If he had to kill to protect the sanctity of this safe house, then he prayed for God to understand. What justification could be more compelling? In the dark, the candles flickered in commemoration of the dead.

The old priest turned from the altar, stiffening as he saw a shadow move.

From the dark of the nearest pew, a man stood, walking toward him.

The American.

The priest reached through the slit in the side of his surplice, pulling the pistol from his belt, aiming it under the loose folds of his garment.

The American stopped at a careful distance.

"I didn't hear you come down the aisle," the priest said.

"I tried to be quiet, to respect your prayers."

"You came to pray as well?"

"The habit dies hard. You must have been told by now that I too was a Cistercian."

"And your friend? You feel no need for retribution?"

"He did what he had to. So did you. We know the rules."

Nodding, the priest clutched the pistol beneath his surplice.

"Did you get the name of the dentist?" the American said.

"Not long ago. I have it written down for you."

The priest set his prayer book in a pew. With his free hand, he reached through the other slit in his surplice, pulling out a piece of paper. After setting it on the prayer book, he stepped carefully back.

The church was still. The American smiled and picked up the message. In the dark, he didn't try to read it.

"The man you seek lives far away," the old priest said.

"So much the better." The American smiled again.

"What makes you say that?"

But the American didn't answer. Turning, he walked silently toward the back of the church, his shadow disappearing. Father Janin heard the creak of a door being opened. He saw the gray of early dawn outside. The American's figure blocked the gray. The door abruptly closed, its rumble eerie in the stillness.

He'd been holding his breath. Exhaling, he put the pistol back in his belt, his forehead slick with sweat. Frowning, he glanced at the stained glass window beneath the peak at the back of the church. Pale light filtered through, emphasizing the silhouette of the galvanized steel sickle moon.

7

The Russian, Chris thought.

He didn't blame the priest. What he'd told the priest was true. The priest had only been obeying the rules. More than authorized, the priest was *obligated* to insure the safety of a guest, even if he had to kill another guest who attempted to violate the sanction.

The Russian, though. As Chris left the church, skirting the pools of water in the morning twilight, heading toward the rectory in back, he thought about him, seething without showing it. From habit, he seemed more relaxed the more determined he became. His pace appeared leisurely, a stroll at dawn to appreciate the stillness, admiring the birds.

The Russian, he kept thinking.

He reached the back, pausing in half light, pretending to enjoy the view of the river, debating. For years, Chan had fought against the Russian, becoming so obsessed he sacrificed his life for this chance to kill him. Back in '65, Chris as well had fought the Russian, joining forces with Chan in a combined CIA–Communist Chinese operation to stop the flow of opium from Laos into South Vietnam. Following a failed attack on a Pathet Lao camp, while Chris was being tortured for information (face crushed, appendix ruptured, spine fractured), Chan had led a rescue mission, saving Chris's life. Chan had brought Chris to this safe house, caring for him, never leaving his side till the American surgeons arrived.

Now Chan was dead.

In the same place Chan had nursed Chris back to life.

Because of the opium.

The Russian had to die.

He knew the danger. He'd be an outcast, hunted by everyone. Regardless of his skill, they'd find him eventually. He'd soon be dead.

It didn't matter. Given his reason for wanting the dentist, given what he intended to do, he'd soon be dead regardless. What difference did it make? But this way, without losing anything he wasn't already prepared to lose, he could return a favor to his friend. That was paramount, more than the sanction, more than anything. Loyalty, friendship. Chan had saved his life. Obeying honor, Chris was obligated to repay his debt. If not, he'd be in disgrace.

And since the sanction had been violated twice already, the only meaning that remained was in his private code.

He squinted from the river to the graveyard. Mindful of the paper the priest had given him, he pulled it out, reading the dentist's name and address. His eyes hardened. Nodding grimly, he walked up the porch steps, entering the rectory.

In his room, he packed his small overnight bag. From a leather pouch, he removed a hypodermic and a vial of liquid. Carrying his bag, he left the room.

The hall was quiet. He knocked on the Russian's door.

The voice was tense behind it. "What?"

Chris answered in Russian. "You have to get out of here. The Chinese had a backup man."

He heard the urgent rattle of the lock. The door came open, Malenov sweating, holding a pistol, so drugged his eyes were glazed.

He never saw the web of skin between Chris's thumb and first finger streak toward him, striking his larynx, crushing his vocal cords.

The Russian wheezed, falling back.

Chris stepped in, closing the door. As Malenov lay on the floor, unable to speak, struggling frantically to breathe, his body convulsed, his feet turning inward, his arms twisting toward his chest.

Chris filled the hypodermic from the vial of liquid. Pulling down the Russian's pajama pants, he injected 155 international milliunits of potassium chloride into the distal vein of the Russian's penis. The potassium would travel to the brain, the chloride to the urinary tract, causing the body's electrolytes to depolarize, resulting in a massive stroke.

Already the Russian's face was blue, turning gray, about to turn yellow.

Chris put the hypodermic and the vial inside his overnight bag. Picking up the trembling body, he leaned it against a chair so the Russian's neck was in line with the chair's wooden arm. He tilted the chair so it fell across the Russian, making the injury to his neck seem the consequence of a fall.

For Chan, he thought.

He picked up his bag and left the room.

The hall was empty. Using the Russian's key to lock the door, he went downstairs, across the rectory's porch, toward the graveyard.

In the gray of dawn, he knew if he went out the front toward the street he'd be followed as a matter of course by agents from various intelligence networks, so he went down the slope toward the river. Smelling its stench, he found a boat that seemed less leaky than two others. Paddling from shore, he ignored the gaping jaws of a crocodile.

8

Two hours later, the priest (after knocking repeatedly on the Russian's door) instructed his servants to break it down. They stumbled in and found the body sprawled beneath the overturned chair. The priest gasped. As the guardian of this safe house, he was accountable to his guests' superiors. He could justify killing Chan, but now the Russian had died as well. Too much was happening at once.

If the KGB decides I failed . . .

Appalled, the priest inspected the body, praying the death was natural. He found no sign of violence, except for the bruise on the throat, but that could be explained by a fall against the chair.

He quickly calculated. Malenov had come here, distraught, in need of a rest, requesting drugs to treat his rage and hypertension. He'd nearly been assassinated. Possibly the added strain, combined with the drugs, had caused a heart attack.

But now the American had disappeared.

Too much was happening.

The priest rushed to a phone. He called the local KGB. The Bangkok bureau chief called his superior. An unexplained death in an Abelard safe house qualified as an emergency, requiring immediate investigation.

One hour after the priest's discovery of the body, a Soviet IL-18 cargo plane took off from Hanoi, North Vietnam, battling a headwind to fly the 600 miles to Thailand in slightly under two hours. The KGB's investigating officer, in tandem with a team of expert physicians, studied the position of the body, taking photographs. They rushed it to the cargo plane and took off for Hanoi, this time helped by a tailwind, returning in ninety minutes.

The autopsy lasted seven hours. Though the Russian's heart had not occluded, his brain had hemorrhaged. Cause of death: a stroke. But why? No embolisms. Blood tests showed the presence of Dilantin, which the Russian had been taking; also opium, which Malenov had been addicted to. No other unusual chemicals. After a microscopic examination of the body, the coroner discovered the needle mark in the distal vein of the Russian's penis. Though he couldn't prove it, he suspected murder. He'd seen a handful of cases like this before. Potassium chloride. The separation of the chemical into its two component parts would cause a stroke. A body normally contained potassium and chloride, so the evidence was hidden. He reported his suspicion to the investigating officer.

An hour after that, the KGB bureau chief for Bangkok was sent to the Church of the Moon. He questioned the priest at length. The priest admitted that an American, a friend of Chan, had been staying at the rectory.

"His name and particulars?" the bureau chief asked.

Afraid, the old priest answered.

"What did the American want?" the bureau chief asked.

The old priest told him.

"Where does this dentist live?"

When the bureau chief heard the reply, he studied the priest across the desk. "So far away? Our coroner in Hanoi has established the time of death as 6 A.M." The bureau chief gestured toward the night beyond the office window. He pointed at his watch. "That's fifteen hours ago. Why didn't you tell us about the American right away?"

The priest poured another glass of brandy, drinking it all at once. Drops rolled down his whisker-stubbled chin. "Because I was afraid. This morning, I couldn't be sure the American was involved. If I'd killed him for precaution's sake, I'd have been forced to explain myself to the CIA. But I didn't have any evidence against him."

"So you preferred to explain yourself to us?"

"I admit I made a mistake. I should have kept closer watch on him. But he convinced me he had no intentions toward your operative. When I found the body, I hoped the cause of death was natural. What point was there in admitting my mistake if I didn't have to? You can understand my problem."

"Certainly."

58

The bureau chief picked up the phone. After dialing and waiting for an answer, he spoke to his superior. "The Abelard sanction has been violated. Repeat: violated. Christopher Patrick Kilmoonie. Cryptonym: Remus. CIA." The bureau chief repeated the description the priest had given him. "He's on his way to Guatemala." The bureau chief gave the address. "At least, he claimed he was going there, but given what's happened, I don't think he'll do the expected. Yes, I know—he's fifteen hours ahead of us."

After listening for a minute, the bureau chief set down the phone. He turned to the priest and shot him.

9

"Are you sure?" the CIA director blurted into the phone.

"Completely," the KGB director answered on the emergency long-distance line. He spoke in English since his counterpart did not speak Russian. "Understand—I didn't call to ask permission. Since the rogue is yours, I'm merely following protocol by informing you of my intention."

"I guarantee he wasn't acting on my orders."

"Even if he were, it wouldn't matter. I've already sent the cables. At this moment, your communications room should be receiving yours. Under the terms of the Abelard sanction, I've alerted every network. I'll read the last three sentences. 'Find Remus. Universal contract. Terminate at your discretion.' I assume since your agency has been embarrassed, you'll go after him more zealously than all the other networks."

"Yes . . . you have my word." The CIA director swallowed, setting down the phone.

He pressed a button on his intercom, demanding the file on Christopher Patrick Kilmoonie.

Thirty minutes later, he learned that Kilmoonie was assigned to the paramilitary branch of Covert Operations, a GS-13, among the highest-ranking operatives in the agency.

The director groaned. It was bad enough to be embarrassed by a rogue, but worse when the rogue turned out to be a world-class killer. Protocol—and prudence—required that to execute this man the director would have to use a team of other GS-13s.

The file on Remus told the director something else. He stood in anger, stalking from his office.

Eliot was Remus's control.

10

"I don't know anything about it," Eliot said.

"Well, you're responsible for him! You find him!" the director said, completing the argument, storming from Eliot's office.

Eliot smiled at the open door. He lit a cigarette, discovered ashes on his black suit, and brushed them off. His ancient eyes gleamed with delight that the director had come to him instead of demanding that Eliot go to the director. The angry visit was one more sign of the director's weakness, of the power Eliot enjoyed.

He swung his chair toward the window, letting sunlight warm his face. Below, a massive parking lot stretched to the fence and the trees that buffered the agency from the highway at Langley, Virginia. From his perspective, he saw just a portion of the ten thousand cars surrounding the huge, tall, H-shaped building.

His smile dissolved. Already preoccupied by the hunt for Saul, he'd been troubled yesterday when told that Chris, Saul's foster brother, had arrived at the Abelard safe house in Bangkok. Eliot hadn't instructed him to go there. For the past several weeks, since Chris had abandoned his station in Rome, he hadn't been reporting in. Assumption: Chris had been killed.

But now he'd suddenly reappeared. Had he been on the run for all that time, finally able to reach asylum? Surely he could have found a way to contact Eliot before then, or at least have got in touch with him when he arrived at the Church of the Moon. It didn't make sense. To ask for a dentist not affiliated with the agency. To violate the sanction by killing the Russian. What the hell was going on? Chris knew the rule.

The best assassins from every network would be hunting him. Why had he been so foolish?

Eliot pursed his wrinkled lips.

Two surrogate brothers, both on the run. The symmetry appealed to him. As sunlight glared off the cars in the lot, his smile returned. He found the answer to his problem.

Saul and Chris. Saul had to be killed before he guessed the reason he was being hunted. So who knew where he would hide better than his counterpart?

But the dentist . . . Eliot shivered. Something troubled him about that detail. Why, before he killed the Russian, would Chris have wanted the name of a dentist?

Eliot's spine felt cold.

11

"Mexico City," Chris said. "The soonest flight."

Behind the airline's ticket counter, the Hawaiian woman tapped on a computer keyboard. "Sir, how many?"

"One," he answered.

"First class or coach?"

"It doesn't matter."

The woman studied the screen on the console.

Voices droned from speakers in the noisy crowded terminal. Behind him, Chris felt other customers waiting.

"Sir, Flight 211 has room in coach. It leaves in fifteen minutes. If we hurry, we can get you aboard. Your name?"

Chris told her the false name on his passport, paying cash when she asked for his credit card, avoiding a paper trail as much as possible.

"Any luggage?"

"Just this carry-on."

"I'll phone the boarding attendant and ask him to hold the flight. Enjoy your trip, sir."

"Thank you."

Though he smiled as he turned to hurry through the terminal, his muscles hardened. Carefully he scanned the crowd for anyone watching him. He reached the metal detector, a Sky Policeman studying him, but Chris had dropped his Mauser down a Bangkok sewer, knowing he'd be caught trying to carry the pistol on board a plane. He could have put it in a suitcase and arranged for the case to be stored beneath the plane. That luggage wasn't searched. But he couldn't risk waiting for it to be returned. He had to keep moving. He grabbed his overnight bag after it came through the scanning machine and rushed down the corridor toward the boarding dock.

A stewardess watched from the plane's open door as he ran down the passenger tunnel. His footsteps echoed.

"Thanks for waiting," he told her.

"No problem. They're late getting food on board." She took his ticket.

He passed the first-class passengers, going through the bulkhead toward the seats in back. Several were empty. The boarding attendant had asked him if he wanted smoking or nonsmoking. Chris didn't smoke, but since the smokers' section was in the rear, he'd chosen the seat that was farthest back. He needed to watch as many passengers as he could, the aisle, and especially the door.

His seat was between an overweight man and an elderly woman, near the washrooms. Squeezing past the man, he sat in the middle, smiling to the woman, sliding his compact bag beneath the forward seat. He buckled himself in and, looking bored, peered along the aisle.

He had to assume the worst—that the needle hole in Malenov's body had been discovered and a universal contract issued against him. Though his intention remained the same—to find a dentist—he couldn't go to the one the priest had recommended. The address the priest had given him was in Guatemala, but the priest would have told the KGB's investigators where he was going. In turn, the investigators would have radioed their people in Guatemala to watch for him. He had to choose another country, one he knew well, in which he could disappear and use his own resources to find a trustworthy dentist. Mexico appealed to him. But leaving Bangkok and then Singapore, he hadn't been able to get on flights as quickly as he needed them. The plane to Honolulu had landed forty minutes behind schedule. He'd missed the next flight to Mexico City and been forced to wait for this one. At the start, he'd hoped for a twelve-hour lead, but it was now sixteen hours since he'd killed the Russian.

He waited tensely. In Bangkok, it would be night, but eight thousand miles to the east, it was morning in Honolulu. The sun glared through the windows, making him sweat as he listened to the hiss of the cabin's air conditioning. He felt the vibration of the idling engines through the fuselage. A hatch thumped beneath him, probably last-minute baggage being stowed. Through the window, he watched two loading carts drive away.

He peered along the aisle. A stewardess pulled the passenger door shut, reaching to secure the locking bolt. In a minute, the jet would taxi toward the runway.

Breathing out, he relaxed. Abruptly his stomach burned; he stiffened. The stewardess opened the door. Two men stepped in. As she locked the door, the men came down the aisle.

He studied them. Midtwenties. Muscular yet lithe. Shirts and pants of muted colors. They seemed determined not to glance at the other passengers, concentrating on their ticket folders, then the numbers and letters above the rows of seats. They split up, ten rows apart, ahead of Chris.

He'd waited as long as he could before he'd bought his ticket, hoping to be the last passenger on board the plane. From the back, he'd been watching for anyone who hurried to get on even later than he had.

As they turned to take their seats, he leaned across the man beside him, staring down the aisle. Their shoes. He wasn't looking for extra-thick soles or reinforced caps that would make the shoes a weapon. Despite the myth of karate, an operative seldom struck with his feet. A kick was too slow. He looked for a more important characteristic. These men wore high-backed shoes snug above their ankles. Preferred by operatives, the high fit supplied the primary function of preventing them from slipping off in a chase or a fight. Chris wore the same design.

He'd been spotted, no way to tell by whom—the Russians, the English, the French, maybe even his own people. At this moment, someone was making urgent calls to Mexico City. When he landed, a team of assassins—maybe several teams—would be waiting for him.

The jet moved, backing from the dock. It turned, its engines roaring louder as it taxied past the terminal.

A bell rang in the cabin. A stewardess came along the aisle, checking that everyone's seatbelt was fastened.

He gripped the arms of his seat, swallowing hard, turning to the woman beside him. "Excuse me. Do you have any Kleenex?"

She seemed annoyed. Groping in her purse, she handed him several pieces.

"Thanks." He tore the Kleenex, shoving wads of it in his ears. The woman blinked in astonishment.

The sounds in the cabin were muffled. Across the aisle, he saw two men talking to each other, their lips moving, words indistinct.

The jet stopped. Through the window, he saw the takeoff strip. A plane streaked out of sight. Another plane took its place. There were only two more planes in front of this one.

He shut his eyes, feeling the plane's vibrations. His chest tightened.

The jet moved forward again. When he opened his eyes, he saw only one plane between this jet and the runway.

Suddenly he yanked his seatbelt. He jerked up, squeezing past the man next to him toward the aisle. A stewardess lunged to grab him. "Sir! You have to stay in your seat! Fasten your belt!"

He pushed her away. Passengers turned, startled. He heard a muffled scream.

The two men stared back, surprised. One scrambled to stand.

Chris grabbed the handle of the emergency door across from him, pulling.

The door flew open. Wind rushed in. He felt the deeper rumble of the jets.

The plane approached the runway. As the stewardess lunged again, he clutched the lower edge of the door frame, swinging out into space. He dangled, peering toward the cabin, the frantic passengers, the killer who darted toward him.

Chris let go of the moving plane. He hit the tarmac, rolling, his knees bent, his elbows tucked, the way he'd learned in jump school. Despite the Kleenex in his ears, he winced from the shriek of the engines. Exhaust roared over him, heat smothering. Another jet loomed close to him.

He ran.

12

The room was massive, antiseptic, temperature-controlled. Computer terminals lined the walls. Fluorescent lights hummed, glaring.

Eliot's wizened forehead narrowed in concentration. "Airline passengers," he told a clerk.

"Which city?"

"Bangkok. Departures. The last sixteen hours."

The agency clerk nodded, tapping on a keyboard.

Eliot lit another cigarette, listening to the clatter of printouts. The problem stimulated him. There was always the chance that Chris had stayed in Thailand, hiding somewhere. Eliot doubted it, however. He'd trained his operatives to leave the danger zone as soon as possible. Before the Russian's body was discovered, Chris would have wanted a good head start. He'd have used a cover name, possibly an independently acquired passport. Probably not, though. Freelance forgers were a security risk. More likely, Chris would have used a passport Eliot had supplied to him, hoping to go to ground before his trail was spotted.

When the clerk came back with several sheets of paper, Eliot leaned across the counter, drawing his bony finger down the list. He straightened excitedly when he found one of Chris's cover names on a United flight out of Bangkok to Singapore. He told the clerk, "Departures from Singapore. The last thirteen hours." Again he waited.

When the clerk brought the second list, Eliot lit another cigarette and concentrated. Chris would have used the same passport. After all, he couldn't risk a customs agent's discovery of other passports with different names in his luggage. He exhaled sharply. There—the same alias on a Trans World flight from Singapore to Honolulu. "Departures from Honolulu," he told the clerk. "The last five hours."

As the clerk brought the third list of names, Eliot heard the computer room's door hiss shut. Turning, he saw his assistant walking toward him.

The assistant was a Yale man, class of '70—button-down collar, club ring and tie, a black suit and vest in imitation of Eliot. His eyes crinkled with amusement. "MI-6 just called. They think they found Remus. The Honolulu airport."

Eliot turned to the new list of names. He found the alias on a Hawaiian Airlines flight. "He's on his way to Mexico City."

"Not anymore," the assistant said. "He must have noticed his babysitters on the plane. A half minute before takeoff, he popped an emergency door and jumped."

"On the runway?"

The assistant nodded.

"My, my, my."

"Surveillance couldn't catch him."

"I'd be surprised if they had. He's one of the best. After all, I trained him." Eliot smiled. "So he's on the run in Honolulu. The question is, what would I do if I were Remus? An island's a poor place to hide. I think I'd want to get out of there. Fast."

"But how? And to where? At least we know where he won't go. He'd be crazy to try for Guatemala or Mexico. He has to figure we'll be waiting for him there."

"Or maybe he'll figure we won't be waiting since those countries are so damned obvious," Eliot said. "It's check and countercheck. A fascinating problem. In Chris's place, how would I get out of Hawaii? A teacher ought to be able to outguess his student."

His smile died as he thought, then why haven't I outguessed Saul?

13

In Atlanta, the azaleas were in bloom, though the only view Saul had of them was from glaring headlights as the truck zoomed past a park, heading into the city. Their pink flowers, mixed with the white of dogwood, seemed like eyes along the road. His bleeding had stopped, though his chest still throbbed from the bullet wound. His fever remained.

"As far as you go," the driver said, stopping beneath an overpass, the semi's air brakes hissing. "My depot's a mile away. I can't let 'em see you. Like I said, taking riders I'd lose my job."

"This is far enough." Saul opened his door. "And thanks."

The driver shook his head. "Not good enough. You're forgetting something."

Saul frowned as he stepped to the road. "No, I don't think so."

"Think again. The money. Remember? Half at the start, and half when we got here. You owe me another two hundred bucks."

Saul nodded. Preoccupied with the problem of why his father was hunting him, he'd forgotten his deal with the driver. It hadn't seemed important.

The driver slid his hand beneath the seat.

"Relax," Saul told him. He needed all his money. But the driver had kept his bargain. Shrugging, Saul gave it to him.

"For a minute there." The driver brought his hand from under the seat.

"You've been on the road too long. Your nerves are shot."

"It's the speed limit."

"Buy your wife a fur coat."

"Sure. And go to McDonald's with the change." The driver grinned, putting the money in his pocket.

The air brakes hissed. The semi pulled from the curb. In the dark beneath the overpass, Saul watched the taillights disappear. Hearing traffic roar above him, he started along the shadowy road.

The last time he'd been to Atlanta, he'd checked on several hotels in case he ever needed them. His wound required attention. He wanted a bath. A change of clothes. He couldn't risk a place where they cared about the quality of the guests, as long as the bill was paid in advance. It had to be far from the luxury of Peachtree Street. He knew exactly where to go.

A train wailed in the distance. Old buildings flanked him. He hunched, easing the pressure in his wound, sensing them converge. Four, if his fever hadn't weakened his hearing.

Just after he crossed a river bridge. The current whispered below him. Past a burnt-out building, at a vacant lot, he braced himself. With blood on his clothes, hunched the way he was, he must have looked like an easy mark.

They came from the dark, surrounding him. For a moment, they reminded him of a gang who'd beaten Chris and himself outside the orphanage years ago.

"I'm not in the mood," he said.

The tallest kid grinned.

"I'm telling you," Saul said.

"Hey, all we want is your money. We won't hurt you. That's a promise."

The others giggled.

"Really," Saul said. "Back off."

They crowded him and snickered.

"But we need," the tall kid said.

"Try someone else."

"But who? There's nobody else. You see someone else around?" The tall kid flicked open a switchblade.

"You need lessons. You're holding it wrong."

The tall kid frowned. For a moment, he seemed to suspect. Then he glanced at the others. Pride made him lunge with the knife.

Saul broke their extremities.

"Like I said, a mistake."

He almost walked away. On impulse, he searched them.

Seventy dollars.

14

"That seat's reserved," the square-jawed man growled, pointing at the glass of beer on the counter before the bar stool.

Chris shrugged and sat, tapping his fingers to *The Gambler* by Kenny Rogers. "Your friend won't need it while he's in the men's room."

On a stage in back, a stripper did a slow grind to the rhythm of the country-western tune. "She'll hurt herself," Chris said.

The burly man scowled. "She's not the only one. You a masochist? That your problem?"

"Not me. I discriminate. I have sex only with women."

"I get it." The man wore a flowered shirt hanging loose over his faded jeans. He stubbed out his cigarette, stood, and glared down at Chris. "You want that stool so bad you want me to shove it up—"

"You tried to do that in Saigon once. It didn't work."

"But this is Honolulu. I could take you now."

"I don't have time for you to try." Chris turned to the barman. "Another beer for my friend. I'll have a Coke."

"Not drinking?" the man in the flowered shirt asked.

"Not today."

"Bad action?"

"It's not good. You look ridiculous in that shirt."

"A change from the uniform. On R and R, I go nuts for color. You'd be surprised. It attracts the women."

"Tell them you're a major. That'll impress them more than the shirt."

"Uncool."

Chris paid for the drinks.

The husky man sipped his beer. "You've been making the rounds of Special Forces bars?"

Chris nodded.

"Checking for friends?"

Chris nodded.

"Who owe you favors?"

Shrugging, Chris glanced at the doorway. "You've got a suspicious nature."

"And you've got the knee ripped out of your pants."

"I had to leave a place in a hurry. I haven't had time to buy another pair."

"You're safe in here. Nobody's going to bother you with several A-teams to back you up."

"But when I step outside. . . . In fact, I'd like to take a trip. Off the islands."

"Any special place?"

"I hoped you'd be my travel agent. As long as it's not the mainland."

The thick-necked man glanced toward the naked stripper. "We fly out of here tomorrow."

"Military transport?"

"The Canal Zone." The man glanced back at Chris. "Okay?"

"You can get me aboard?"

"No problem. A couple guys owe me favors."

"I owe *you* one now."

"Hey, who keeps score?"

Chris laughed.

"I got another problem, though," the major said.

69

"What is it?"

"The guy I'm with who was sitting there. He should've been back by now. He's so damned drunk he must've fallen in or passed out in the men's room."

A Waylon Jennings record started blaring. The stripper put her clothes back on.

15

Chris sweated, throwing more dirt to the side. He leaned on his shovel, squinting at the semitropical forest around him—sweet-smelling cedars, thorny laurel trees. Bright-colored birds, having adjusted to his presence, fluttered and sang in the boughs. Mosquitoes hovered, never settling on him. He didn't worry about fever since the major, en route here to Panama, had supplied him with the necessary suppositories. Standard equipment for Special Forces, their chemical was absorbed by the capillaries in his lower intestines, causing his body to emit a subtle, mosquito-repelling odor. Chris had known the chemical was working when his urine turned green.

In the humid sun, he resumed his work, shoveling more dirt to the side, enlarging the hole. He'd borrowed the idea from the "man traps" the Viet Cong had dug in the jungle during the war. A deep pit covered by a sheet of metal, with earth and ferns placed on the sheet to disguise it. Carefully balanced, the sheet would tilt down when an unwitting soldier stepped on it, impaling his body on the *pungi* stakes arranged below. Though Chris would not use stakes, the pit retained its deadly purpose.

He'd been digging throughout the morning. The pit was now seven feet long, three feet wide, and four feet deep. It resembled a grave. "Two more feet down," he told himself, wiping sweat from his forehead, continuing to shovel.

When he finished, he walked from the clearing to the forest, searching among ferns till he found four solid sticks, each four feet in length. He wiped his sweaty forehead again, walked back to the clearing, and eased down into the pit. In contrast with the sun, the pit felt cool. He reached for the sheet of plywood he'd set to the side. The sheet measured seven feet by three, a half-inch thick. He'd struggled through the forest to carry it here. Few people lived in this region. He'd made sure he wasn't followed.

Using the sticks, he supported each corner of the plywood so it covered the pit. Then he crawled from the dark through a burrow he'd dug. In light, he gently covered the plywood with dirt from the hole, dug up ferns, and planted them above the sheet.

Stepping back, he studied the camouflage. The freshly-turned earth was dark, in contrast with the light brown surface ground. By tomorrow, there'd be no difference. Satisfied, he placed a rock across the entrance to the burrow.

He was almost ready. Only one more thing to do. He'd have gone to the dentist first, but in his subsequent groggy condition, he wasn't sure he'd have had the strength to carry the plywood here and dig the hole. He had to arrange things properly. As soon as he came back from the dentist in Panama City, he wouldn't need the suppositories the major had given him. Malaria wouldn't matter.

16

"Mr. Bartholomew?" the nurse asked Chris. She was Panamanian, attractive, her dark skin stark against her white uniform. "The doctor's last appointment took longer than he expected. You'll have to wait a few more minutes."

Nodding, Chris thanked her. Panama was bilingual: Spanish and English. Chris spoke Spanish in addition to three other languages. Even so, he'd found it easier to use English when he'd come to the dentist two days ago, explaining what he wanted.

"But there's no reason to do it," the dentist had said.

"You don't need a reason. All you need is this." Chris had taken off his eighteen-karat gold Rolex watch, giving it to the dentist. "It's worth four thousand dollars. There'll be money too, of course. And this." Chris had shown him the precious necklace. "When you're finished."

The dentist's eyes had glinted avariciously. He suddenly frowned. "I won't be part of anything illegal."

"What's illegal for a dentist to take out teeth?"

The dentist shrugged.

"I'm eccentric. Humor me," Chris had said. "I'll come back in two days. You'll keep no record of my visit. You won't take X rays."

"Without X rays, I can't guarantee my work. There might be complications."

"It won't matter."

The dentist had frowned.

Now Chris sat in the waiting room, staring at cheap wooden chairs and a cracked plastic-covered sofa. There weren't any other patients. A fluorescent light sputtered. He glanced toward the magazines printed in Spanish. Instead of picking one up, he closed his eyes and concentrated.

Soon, he thought. Tonight, before returning to the forest, he'd come back here and destroy the office. After all, despite the dentist's promise, there was always the chance he'd make records and take X rays while Chris was unconscious from the anesthetic. It was important there be no evidence.

He'd return to the forest clearing and begin his fast. Sixty days would probably be how long it took, though once the mosquitoes began to attack him he'd no doubt get malaria, and that would speed the process. Thirty days maybe. Sixty at the most.

He would meditate, praying to God to forgive his sins—the countless people he'd killed, not like the Russian whose death had been justified because of the opium, because of Chan, but those whose crime had merely been that they existed. In anguish, he recalled their names, their faces, how most of them had begged for mercy. He'd beg now for mercy toward himself. He'd try to purify himself from shame, the sickness in his soul, the accusation of his emotions.

He would fast till his mind was filled with rapture. As his flesh shrank to his body, he'd hallucinate, his mind floating. For his final conscious act, while ecstasy transported him, he'd crawl down the burrow to his grave. In the dark, he'd kick and pull the sticks that supported the sheet of plywood. It would fall, the earth above it sinking, smothering.

His body would be hidden. Either it would decompose, or else scavenging animals would dig it up. They'd scatter his bones. Probably only his skull would remain intact, but without his teeth, the authorities wouldn't be able to identify him.

That was important. He had to die namelessly. For the sake of Saul and Eliot. They'd no doubt be shocked that he'd violated the sanction. But their embarrassment would be tempered by admiration that he'd never been caught. Of course, they'd wonder where he'd gone. They'd always be puzzled. But puzzlement was better than their grief and shame if they learned he'd committed suicide. He wanted to do this cleanly. He didn't want to be a burden to the two men he was closest to—surrogate brother, surrogate father.

Fasting is the only method of suicide permitted by the Catholic Church. All other ways imply despair, a distrust of God's wisdom, an unwillingness to bear the hardships with which God tests his children. An absolute sin, suicide's punishment is eternal damnation in the fires of Hell. But fasting is undertaken for the purpose of penance, meditation, and spiritual ecstasy. It purifies the spirit by denying the body. It brings a soul closer to God.

Considering his sins, it was the only way Chris could think of to go to Heaven.

"Mr. Bartholomew, the doctor will see you now," the nurse told Chris.

He nodded, standing, walking through an open door to a room with a dentist's chair. He didn't see the doctor, but behind a closed door, he heard water trickling in a sink.

"I'm qualified to administer the anesthetic," the nurse explained.

He sat in the chair. She prepared a hypodermic.

"What is it?" Chris said.

"Atropine and Vistaril."

He nodded. He'd been concerned that the anesthetic would be Sodium Amytal, the so-called truth serum that reduced a person to an unconscious, almost hypnotized condition in which his will was so impaired he'd answer the most forbidden of questions.

"Count backward, please," the nurse said.

When Chris reached ninety-five, his vision began to spin. He thought of the monastery, his six mute years with the Cistercians in which the only communication had been by means of sign language, in which each day had been blessedly the same—meditation and work. He thought of the white robe he'd worn, a white like the swirling in his mind.

If he hadn't been asked to leave, if he weren't thirty-six, one year beyond the age when he could apply for readmission, he could still find solace and redemption there.

Now, with the secular life unacceptable to him and the religious life unavailable to him, he had only one choice remaining—the fast of death, of purification, the journey toward ultimate perfection.

But the swirling in his mind intensified. His mouth felt dry. He struggled to breathe. "It isn't atropine," he murmured. "It's something else."

He fought to escape the dentist's chair. The nurse fought back, hands massive. "No," he mumbled, frantic.

But the swirling whiteness became another kind of whiteness. In the spinning blur, a door came open. A figure in white approached him, floating ghostlike.

"No."

The face loomed close—old, wrinkled, gray.

Chris gaped. The dentist. It couldn't be.

He thrashed. As his mind sank into blackness, it flashed a final lucid thought.

Impossible. The dentist was Eliot.

BOOK TWO

SEARCH AND DESTROY

"MY BLACK PRINCES"

1

Eliot brooded, his wrinkles deepening as he checked Chris's pulse. Finally nodding, he turned to the nurse. "The doctor's in a bar around the corner." His voice rasped. "I suggest you join him."

Wide-eyed, she backed to the door.

"One other thing." She froze as he reached beneath the dentist's coat, pulling out an envelope. "Your money. Lock the other door as you go out."

She swallowed, leaving the dentist's office, crossing the waiting room, fleeing.

Eliot listened to the click of the lock. He shut the door between the waiting room and this office, staring at a tray of dental instruments.

Chris slumped in the chair, breathing shallowly, unconscious from Sodium Amytal. The drug repressed inhibitions, allowing an interrogator to obtain information from an unwilling subject. For the subject to answer, though, he couldn't be totally unconscious, rather in a controlled half sleep, unaware of his surroundings but not oblivious to what he was asked. Since the nurse had been ordered to subdue Chris completely, Eliot had to wait for some of the drug to wear off.

He inserted a needle-tipped tube in a vein in Chris's arm, then opened a drawer, removing two full hypodermics next to the ampule in which the Amytal had been stored. Since it came as a powder, 500 milligrams of the drug had been mixed with 20 milliliters of sterile water. He inserted one hypodermic in the tube extending from Chris's arm. When he pressed the hypodermic's plunger, the flow of the solution could be controlled by a valve in the tube. He set the second hypodermic near him in case he needed it, though if the session took longer than thirty minutes he'd have to mix a new solution since Amytal decomposed quickly in liquid form.

Five minutes later, as Eliot expected, Chris's eyelids began to flutter. Eliot opened the valve in the tube, allowing a portion of the drug to enter the vein. When Chris's speech became garbled, Eliot would have to close the valve till Chris showed signs of becoming too awake, then open the valve again to subdue him. The procedure required care.

It was best to start simply. "Do you know who I am?" Receiving no answer, Eliot repeated the question.

"Eliot," Chris whispered.

"Very good. That's right. I'm Eliot." He studied Chris, for a moment reminded of the first time he'd seen him—thirty-one years ago. He recalled the boy clearly, five years old, dirty, thin, in rags, his father dead, his mother a prostitute who'd abandoned him. The row house in the slum in Philadelphia had been filled with tables. On each table, the boy had neatly arranged piles of flies he'd killed with a rubber band. "You remember," Eliot said. "I took care of you. I'm as close to you as a father. You're as close to me as a son. Repeat it."

"Father. Son," Chris murmured.

"You love me."

"Love you," Chris said tonelessly.

"You trust me. No one else has ever been as kind to you. You're safe. You've nothing to fear."

Chris sighed.

"Do you want to make me happy?"

Chris nodded.

Eliot smiled. "Of course you do. You love me. Listen carefully. I want you to answer some questions. Tell me the truth." He was suddenly conscious of the smell of peppermint in the dentist's office. "Have you heard from Saul?"

Chris took so long to answer Eliot thought he wouldn't. He breathed when Chris said, "No."

"Do you know where he is?"

Chris whispered, "No."

"I'm going to give you a sentence. What does it mean?" Four days ago, the message had been cabled from Atlanta to Rome, in care of Chris at the Mediterranean Flower Shop, the agency's office there. Till his disappearance, Chris had been the assistant bureau chief, on probation while Eliot studied the possible bad effects of the monastery on Chris's work. The message had not been signed, but that was not unusual. All the same, its arrival coincided with Saul's disappearance. Assuming Saul would try to contact Chris, Eliot had learned that this

78

message—in contrast with many others Chris had been sent—bore no relation to agency codes.

" 'There's an egg in the basket,' " Eliot said.

"A message from Saul," Chris answered, eyes closed, groggy.

"Go on."

"He's in trouble. He needs my help."

"That's all it means?"

"A safety-deposit box."

Eliot leaned closer. "Where?"

"A bank."

"*Where?*"

"Santa Fe. We both have keys. We hid them. In the box, I'll find a message."

"Coded?" Eliot's bony fingers clutched the dentist's chair.

Chris nodded.

"Would I recognize the code?"

"Private."

"Teach it to me."

"Several."

Eliot straightened, his chest tight from frustration. He could ask Chris to explain the several codes, but there was always the chance that, by failing to ask a crucial question, he might not learn all the information he required. No doubt Chris had taken precautions to stop an enemy from posing as himself and gaining access to the safety-deposit box. Where was the key, for example? Was there a password? Those questions were obvious. What troubled Eliot were the questions he *couldn't* imagine. Chris and Saul had been friends since they'd met in the orphanage thirty-one years ago. They must have hundreds of subtle private signals. All Eliot had to do was fail to learn one of them, and he'd miss this chance to trap Saul. Of course, the agency's computers could decipher the private code, but how long might the process take?

Eliot had to move *now*.

He rubbed his wrinkled chin, abruptly thinking of another question. "Why did you want your teeth removed?"

Chris answered.

Eliot shivered. He'd thought nothing could shock him.

But *this?*

2

Chris swelled with affection as he cradled the candy bar. "A Baby Ruth. You still remember."

"Always." Eliot's eyes looked sad.

"But how did you find me?" Chris's tongue felt thick from the Amytal.

"Trade secret." Eliot grinned, his lips taut as if on a shrunken skull.

Chris glanced out the jet's window, hearing the muffled roar of the engines as he squinted from the sun and studied the snowlike clouds spread out below him. "Tell me." He sounded hoarse, staring back at his foster father.

Eliot shrugged. "You know what I've always said. To guess an opponent's next move, we have to think as *he* would think. I trained you, remember. I know everything about you."

"Not quite."

"We'll discuss that in a moment. The point is I pretended I was you. Knowing everything about you, I became you."

"And?"

"Who owed you favors? Who could you depend on for your life? Who *had* you depended on? As soon as I knew what questions to ask, I calculated the answers. One of them was to have men watch the Special Forces bars in Honolulu."

"Clever."

"So were you."

"Not enough—since I was spotted in the bar. And followed, I assume."

"You have to remember you were playing against your teacher. I doubt anyone else could have guessed what you intended."

"Why didn't you order me picked up in Honolulu? I violated the sanction, after all. The other networks are hunting me. You'd have earned some points with them, especially the Russians, if you brought me in."

80

"I wasn't sure you'd let us take you alive."

Chris stared at him. Eliot's assistant, wearing a Yale ring and tie, brought a tray of Perrier, ice, and glasses, setting it on the table between them in this lounge section of the plane.

Eliot didn't speak till the assistant left. "Besides—" he seemed to choose his words, pouring Perrier in two glasses, "I was curious. I wondered why you wanted a dentist."

"Personal."

"Not anymore." Eliot handed him a glass. "While you were unconscious in the dentist's chair, I asked you some questions." He paused. "I know you intended to kill yourself."

"Past tense?"

"For my sake, I hope so. Why did you want to do it? You know your death would hurt me. Your suicide would hurt even worse."

"That's why I wanted my teeth removed. If my body was ever found, it couldn't be identified."

"But why ask the priest? Why go to the safe house?"

"I wanted a dentist who was used to working with operatives, who wouldn't ask questions."

Eliot shook his head.

"What's wrong?"

"That isn't true. With a little trouble you found a dentist on your own. You didn't need someone familiar with our profession. All you needed was sufficient money to bribe a man into silence. No, you had a different reason for asking the priest."

"Since you know all the answers . . ."

"You went to the priest because you knew he'd make inquiries before he gave you the information. I'd learn where you were. I'd be puzzled about your request and intercept you."

"What good would that have done? I didn't *want* to be stopped."

"No?" Eliot squinted at him. "Your request to the priest was the same as a cry for help. A suicide note before the fact. You wanted to tell me how much pain you were in."

Chris shook his head.

"Unconsciously? What is it?" Frowning, Eliot leaned forward. "What's wrong? I don't understand."

"I'm not sure I can explain it. Let's just say . . ." Chris debated in anguish. "I'm sick. Of everything."

"The monastery changed you."

"No. The sickness came before the monastery."

"Drink the Perrier. Your mouth will be dry from the Amytal."

Automatically Chris obeyed.

Eliot nodded. "What kind of sickness?"

"I'm ashamed."

"Because of what you do?"

"Because of what I feel. The guilt. I see faces, I hear voices. Dead men. I can't shut them out. You taught me discipline, but the lesson isn't working anymore. I can't stand the shame of—"

"Listen to me," Eliot said.

Chris rubbed his forehead.

"You're a member of a high-risk profession. I don't mean just the physical danger. As you've discovered, there's also a spiritual danger. The things we have to do can sometimes force us to be inhuman."

"Then why do we have to do them?"

"You're not naive. You know the answer as well as I. Because we're fighting to protect the way of life we believe in. We sacrifice ourselves so others can have normal lives. Don't blame yourself for what you've needed to do. Blame the other side. What about the monastery? If your need was spiritual, why couldn't the Cistercians help you? Why did they force you out? The vow of silence? After six years, was it too much for you?"

"It was wonderful. Six years of peace." Chris frowned. "Too much peace."

"I don't understand."

"Because of the strictness of the Order, a psychiatrist came to test us every six months. He checked for signs—tiny clues of unproductive behavior. The Cistercians believe in work, after all. We supported ourselves by farming. Anyone who couldn't do his share couldn't be allowed to live off the sweat of others."

Eliot nodded, waiting.

"Catatonic schizophrenia." Chris breathed deeply. "That's what the psychiatrist tested us for. Preoccupations. Trances. He asked us questions. He watched for our reactions to various sounds and colors. He studied our daily behavior. One day when he found me sitting motionless in a garden, staring at a rock—for an hour—he reported to my superior. The rock was fascinating. I can still remember it." Chris narrowed his eyes. "But I'd failed the test. The next time somebody found me paralyzed like that—catatonic—I was out. Peace. My sin was I wanted too much peace."

On the tray, beside the Perrier bottles, a long-stemmed crimson rose stood in a vase. Eliot picked it up. "You had your rock. I have my roses. In our business, we need beauty." He sniffed the rose and handed it to Chris. "Did you ever wonder why I chose roses?"

Chris shrugged. "I assumed you liked flowers."

"Roses, though. Why roses?"

Chris shook his head.

"They're the emblem of our profession. I enjoy the double meaning. In Greek mythology, the god of love once offered a rose to the god of silence, as a bribe, to keep that god from disclosing the weaknesses of the other gods. In time, the rose became the symbol for silence and secrecy. In the Middle Ages, a rose was customarily suspended from the ceiling of a council chamber. The members of the council pledged themselves not to reveal what they discussed in the room, *sub rosa*, under the rose."

"You've always liked playing with words," Chris said, returning the rose. "My trouble is, I can't believe in them anymore."

"Let me finish. Part of my delight in roses comes from the different varieties. The various colors and shapes. I have my favorites—Lady X and Angel Face. I used those names as cryptonyms for two of my female operatives. My ladies." Eliot smiled. "The names of other varieties appeal to me. The American Pillar. The Gloria Mundi. But the goal of every rose enthusiast is to create a new variety. We cut and layer and graft, or we cross-pollinate seed. The ripe seed is kept in sand till spring, when it's sown in pans. The first year produces only color. After that comes the full bloom and the merit. The new variety is a hybrid. Only a large, well-formed, singly grown blossom standing higher than the rest will do. To enhance the quality of the bloom, the side growth must be removed by a process called disbudding. You and Saul—you're my hybrids. Raised without families, in the orphanage, you had no side growth—you didn't need to be disbudded. Nature had already done that. Your bloom was developed through rigorous training and discipline. To give your characters substance, certain feelings had to be cut from you. Patriotism was layered onto your character. Military experience and, of course, the war were grafted onto you. My hybrids—you stand higher than all the rest. If your conditioning failed and you now feel, it shouldn't be guilt you feel but pride. You're beautiful. I could have given you a new name for a new species. Instead I think of you in terms of the particular rose I'm holding, so dark crimson it's almost black. It's called the Black Prince. That's how I think of you and Saul. As my Black Princes."

"But Saul didn't fail. He . . ." Chris's eyes changed. "Wait a minute. You're not telling me all this just for . . ."

Eliot spread his hands. "So you guessed."

"What's wrong? What's happened to Saul?"

Eliot studied him. "Because of your brother, I'm asking you not to try again to kill yourself."

"What is it?" Chris sat forward, tensing. *What about Saul?*

"Five days ago, he did a job for me. After, a member of the team tried to kill him. He got in touch with me. I arranged for him to go to a secure location. When he got there, he discovered the location had been compromised. Another team tried to kill him. He's on the run."

"Then, Jesus, bring him in!"

"I can't. He's afraid to get in touch with me."

"With *you?*"

"The mole. I've always said there was one. From the agency's beginning. Someone who infiltrated us at the start, who's been compromising us ever since. Someone close to me is using what Saul tells me, using it to try to get at Saul."

"But why?"

"I don't know why he's so important he has to be killed. What he's discovered, or whom he threatens. I *won't* know till I catch the mole. It isn't easy. I've been looking since 1947. I have to find Saul, though. I have to insure his safety."

"How? If he won't get in touch with you, if he's afraid the mole will intercept his message."

Eliot set the rose down. " 'There's an egg in the basket.' "

Chris felt the jet lurch.

Eliot said, "That message arrived in Rome four days ago. Addressed to you. I think from Saul."

Chris nodded.

"I don't know what it means," Eliot said. "For God's sake, don't tell me. Even this rose might have ears. But if it's from Saul and it tells you where to find him, use it. Go. Be careful. Bring him in."

"One Black Prince to rescue another?"

"Exactly. Your surrogate father is asking you to save your surrogate brother. If you're looking for a reason not to kill yourself, you've found it."

Chris turned to the window, eyes narrowed, more than just from the sun. He brooded—all thoughts of suicide canceled by concern for his brother. His heart quickened. Saul needed help. Beside that, nothing else mattered. His brother needed him. He'd found the only reason that could make him want to live.

He turned to Eliot, his voice grim. "Count on it."

"Ironic," Eliot said. "A hit team's chasing Saul, and everyone else is chasing you."

"You'll appreciate the complexity."

"I'll appreciate it more when Saul is safe. What country should I tell the pilot to fly to?"

"Home."

"What city?"

Chris considered. The safety-deposit box was in Santa Fe, but he couldn't go there directly. He had to land close to it, yet far enough away to lose a tail. He had to be evasive in case this conversation was being monitored. "Albuquerque."

Eliot straightened, his ancient eyes bright, signaling he recognized deception and approved.

"Has it occurred to you?" Chris said.

Eliot frowned. "I don't understand."

"That hybrids are usually sterile."

The jet descended through the clouds.

3

The Sangre de Cristo mountains loomed in the distance. Snow still capped the peaks, the slopes dark with oak and fir. Despite the blazing sun, the air felt dry.

Chris walked along the narrow street, passing flat-roofed adobe houses with red slate trim and walls around gardens. Through a gate, he saw a bubbling fountain. Piñon trees provided shade, the green of their needles contrasting with the earth tones of the houses.

Pausing at the end of the block, he glanced back down the street. He'd chosen this expensive residential section of Santa Fe because he knew it would be quiet—little traffic, few pedestrians. The isolation made it easy for him to check on anyone following him. He took for granted that, if the KGB or MI-6 or any of the other networks hunting him had spotted him, they'd never have let him wander the streets this long. They'd simply have killed him right away. He had to conclude, then, that they weren't close.

For Saul, though, he'd been willing to take the risk. His eyes gleamed. For his brother, he'd take *any* risk. He'd gladly make himself a target to draw out someone besides his hunters.

The mole. Whoever was intercepting Eliot's messages to Saul. Whoever wanted Saul dead. The questions nagged him. What had Saul done, or what did he know? This much was clear. Since Chris was not supposed to report to Eliot for fear of a leak, the only way the mole could get his hands on Saul was by following Chris. But so far Chris had seen no evidence of surveillance.

Glancing behind him again, he passed a house with a courtyard and veranda partly concealed by junipers. He peered toward the mountains, crossed a street, and approached a Spanish cathedral. Climbing the high stone steps, pulling the iron ring on a huge oak door, he entered a dark cool vestibule. The last time he'd been here was in 1973. In honor of its hundredth anniversary, the church had been extensively restored that year. Since then, as he'd hoped, it hadn't changed. The vaulted ceiling, the stained glass windows, the Spanish design around the stations of the cross remained as they had been. He walked to the marble holy water fountain, dipping his hand in, genuflecting toward the distant golden tabernacle on the altar. Crossing himself, he went to the row of confessionals on his left, beneath the choir loft, at the back of the church, his footsteps echoing on the smooth stone floor.

The confessional in the corner drew him. Nobody sat in the nearby pews. He heard no muffled voices from inside, so he opened the ornate door, stepped in, and closed it behind him.

The church had been shadowy, but the narrow penitent's cubicle was totally dark, its musty smell stifling. Out of habit, he silently recited, "Bless me, Father, for I have sinned. My last confession was . . ." He recalled the monastery, his sins, his plan to kill himself, and stopped. His jaw hardened. He couldn't be distracted. Saul alone mattered. Instead of kneeling to face the screen behind which a priest would normally be hidden, he quickly turned and reached toward the top right corner. In the dark, his fingers searched. All these years. He sweated, wondering if he'd been foolish. What if a carpenter, repairing the confessional, had discovered . . . ? He pulled the loose molding from the seam where the wall met the ceiling and grinned as he touched the key he'd wedged into the niche years before.

4

The bank had been designed to look like a pueblo: flat-roofed, square, with support beams projecting from the top of the imitation-sandstone walls. Two yucca plants flanked the entrance. Traffic blared. In a restaurant across the street, a businessman sat at a middle table, facing the window and the bank. He paid for his lunch and left, ignoring another businessman who came in and sat at the same middle table, facing the window and the bank. All along the street, other members of the surveillance team seemed a part of the normal pattern. A young man handed out advertisements. A truck driver carried boxes into a building. A woman browsed through a record store, close to a window. Lingering as long as seemed normal, they left the area, replaced by others.

In the restaurant, the businessman lit a cigarette. He heard a short muffled beep from the two-way radio in his pocket, no more obtrusive than a doctor's paging device, the signal that Remus had been sighted along the street. Peering through the heat haze toward the entrance to the bank, he saw a woman come out, her hand raised to shield her eyes from the sun. A man wearing tan clothes passed her, going in. As a waitress brought a menu, the businessman reached in his pocket, pressing the radio's transmitter button twice.

Remus was in the bank.

5

Chris passed the security guard and a row of cages with signs for Deposits and Mortgages, descending the stairs at the back. Indian sand paintings hung on the walls. He reached a counter, gave his key to a clerk, and wrote *John Higgins* on a bank form. He and Saul had opened an account here in 1973, depositing a thousand dollars, leaving instructions that the rent for the safety-deposit box should be deducted from the account. Chris hadn't been back here since, though he knew Saul contacted the bank each year to make sure the account and the box hadn't been put on inactive status. The clerk stamped the date on the bank form, initialed it, and pulled out a list of renters, comparing signatures.

"Mr. Higgins, I'm supposed to ask for a password."

"Camelot," Chris said.

Nodding, the clerk marked an X beside the name on the list. He opened the counter's gate and led Chris through the vault's massive door to a long high wall of safety-deposit boxes. Lights glared. As the clerk used both the bank's key and Chris's key to unlock a box, Chris glanced to the end of the hall toward a floor-to-ceiling mirror. He didn't like mirrors. Often they were also windows. Turning his back to it, he took the closed tray the clerk gave him and went to a booth.

As soon as he'd shut the door behind him, he checked the ceiling for a hidden camera. Satisfied, he opened the tray. The hand-written message was coded. Translated, it told him, *Santa Fe phone booth. Sherman and Grant.* He memorized a number. Shredding the message, putting it back in the box, he took a Mauser from the tray and tucked it beneath his jacket behind his belt at his spine. He pocketed the two thousand dollars he'd left here for an emergency.

6

While the businessman ate his salad, he stared through the window toward the bank. The blue cheese dressing tasted stale. A Ford van stopped before him at the curb, blocking his vision. Sunlight glinted off the windshield.

The businessman swallowed nervously. Come on. Hurry up. Get that damned thing moving.

Standing, he peered beyond the van, reached in his pocket, and pressed the transmitter button three times.

Remus was leaving the bank.

7

Chris put the Santa Fe map in his pocket as he stepped in the phone booth at the intersection of Sherman and Grant streets. Cars rushed by. Shoppers paused at the windows of trendy boutiques. He shut the door and muffled traffic noises. Though he didn't smile, he felt amused, assuming this location with its combination of street names— Civil War generals—had been chosen by Saul as a joke. We'll soon be together again, he thought. His chest swelled, but he couldn't allow his eagerness to distract him. Putting coins in the slot, he dialed the number he'd memorized. A recorded voice told him the time was 2:46. If an enemy had subdued Chris and forced him to reveal the message in the safety-deposit box, the man would have been baffled by the significance of hearing the time. Unless he'd kept Chris alive to question him further, he couldn't have learned that the specific time meant nothing. Any hour would have been important, the announcement a signal to Chris to study the walls of the phone booth. Among the graffiti, he found a message to Roy Palatsky, a boy he and Saul had known at the orphanage. He glanced away at once. In case, despite his precautions, he was being watched, he didn't want to betray his fascination with the graffiti. In code, the obscene message told him where to find Saul.

8

"He made a call," the businessman said on the scrambler-protected long-distance line. "He must have received directions. We could pick him up now."

"Don't. A call's too obvious." Eliot's voice sounded thin and brittle from his Falls Church, Virginia, greenhouse. "These two men have private codes dating back to when they were five years old. That call was likely a bluff to tempt you to show yourselves. What if all he learned was directions to go to another spot where he'd learn still other directions? Don't interfere with him. The only way to capture Romulus is to follow Remus. For God's sake, don't let him see you."

9

Chris flew higher, skirting a cloud bank, watching the mountains below him. Snow-capped peaks, connected by saddlelike ridges, stretched as far as he could see. Ravines splayed down in all directions. He put the rented Cessna on automatic pilot while he studied a topographical map, comparing its contour lines with the rugged terrain below him. Valleys alternated with mountains. Streams cascaded.

On the wall of the phone booth, the coded message had given him numbers for longitude and latitude, as well as instructions how to get there. He'd gone to the Santa Fe library, where he'd learned that the coordinates referred to a section of mountain wilderness to the north, in Colorado. Renting this plane at the Santa Fe airport had been easy. He'd used the alias on his pilot's license, had paid a deposit and bought insurance. He'd filed a flight plan to Denver, indicating he'd return in three days. But once in the air, he'd gradually veered from his flight plan, northwest, toward the coordinates in the wilderness.

The sky was brilliant. He felt good. The cockpit muffled the engine's drone. He compared a deep long valley to a similar pattern on the map and glanced ahead toward another valley, oval, with a lake. His coordinates met near the lake. He'd almost reached his destination. Checking the sky around him, pleased that he saw no aircraft, he smiled and thought of Saul.

At once he attended to business, slipping on his bulky parachute. The plane soared closer to the valley. Aiming toward a mountain beyond the lake, he locked his controls on target, opened his door, heard the roar of the engine, and felt the surge of the wind. He had to struggle to brace the door against its force.

Pressing his shoes against the lower section of the plane, he leapt out past the wing struts, twisting, buffeted. His stomach rose. Gusts of air pressed his goggles against his face. He couldn't hear the plane now. All he heard was the hiss as he fell—and a roar in his ears. His helmet squeezed against his skull. Clothes flapping, arms and legs stretched out for balance, he fell horizontally, facing the abrupt enlargement of the landscape. The lake grew. But he quickly achieved a sense of stasis, blissful, almost anesthetizing. If he closed his eyes, he no longer had the sense of falling. Rather he felt suspended, floating, relaxed. In jump school, his instructors had warned him about this deceptive, dangerous sensation. Hypnotized by the almost sexual massage of the wind, some jumpers waited too long before they pulled their ripcord.

Chris understood the attraction. He'd been apprehensive before his first jump, but from then on, he'd looked forward to the pleasure of the others. Now his pleasure was moderated by his need to be with Saul. Eagerly he pulled the ripcord, waited, felt the chute unfold from his back and the lurch as the nylon blossomed, supporting him. He hadn't worried about the chute. Last night, after buying it from the local jumpers' club, he'd spread it out, arranging the lines before he packed it. He'd never have trusted someone to do that for him any more than he'd have let someone clean a weapon and load it for him. Swaying in the wind, he glanced toward the peak beyond the lake and saw the tiny outline of his plane—on automatic pilot—approaching the mountain he'd aimed it toward. He gripped the parachute lines and leaned to the right, angling away from the lake, veering toward a meadow. He saw a cabin above a slope of pines, braced in the V between two cliffs.

The meadow enlarged abruptly. As he settled down, it seemed to swoop toward him. With a jolt, he hit, the impact shuddering through him as he bent his knees and toppled sideways, absorbing the shock along his hip, his side, and his shoulder. The chute billowed in the wind, dragging him across the meadow. He surged to his feet, tugging the chute lines, pulling them toward him while he rushed to meet the nylon hood and compact the chute, restraining the wind's resistance.

"You're out of practice," a husky voice said from the shelter of the pines.

Recognizing it, Chris turned, feigning irritation. "What the hell? You think you can do it better?"

"I sure can. I've never seen a crummier landing."

"The wind was against me."

"Excuses," the voice said. "The sign of an amateur."

"And criticism's the sign of an ungrateful sonofabitch. If you didn't have so much to say, you'd come out here to help me."

"Definitely not the tough guy I used to know."

"Tough or not, I'm the closest thing to a brother you've got."

"No argument. Even with your faults, I love you."

Chris's throat ached with affection. "If you're so damned sentimental, why don't you show yourself?"

"Because I can't resist making an entrance."

A husky dark-haired man stepped slowly from the forest. Six feet tall, solidly muscled, with chiseled chin and cheek and forehead, the man grinned, his dark eyes glinting. He wore high laced boots, faded jeans, and a green wool shirt that matched the pines. He carried a bolt-action Springfield rifle. "Eight years, Chris. God, what's the matter with us? We never should have separated."

"Business," Chris said.

"Business?" Saul answered, the word tinged with disgust. "We let it ruin us."

Eager, Chris hurried toward him, clutching his folded parachute. So much to know, to say. "What's happened? Why are they trying to kill you?"

"Business," Saul said again. "He turned against me."

"Who?" Chris had almost reached him.

"Can't you guess? The man we figured never would."

"But that's impossible!"

"I'll prove it to you."

But suddenly only one thing had significance. Chris dropped the parachute, staring at Saul's rugged handsome face. Hardly able to breathe, he opened his arms and hugged him. Straining, they seemed to want to crush each other's chest and back and muscles, to absorb each other's life.

He almost wept.

Their embrace was interrupted. Turning, they peered through a cleft in the pine trees toward the explosion that echoed through the valley as the plane Chris had flown disintegrated on the mountain.

10

"No, you're wrong! He's not against you!" Chris held his parachute, helmet and goggles, running up the game trail through the pines. "He asked me to find you!"

"Why?"

"To help you! To bring you in!"

"Why?" Saul asked again.

"It's obvious. The mole kept intercepting Eliot's instructions to you."

"Mole," Saul scoffed. "Is that what Eliot told you?"

"He said the only way to bring you in safely was for me to act alone."

"He couldn't find me, but he knew I'd try to get in touch with you. He set you up to lead him to me."

From the shadowy woods, Chris saw the cabin brilliant in the sun, small, its long walls chinked with mud, its roof slanting up toward the merging V of the cliffs behind it. "How'd you find this place?"

"I built it. You chose the monastery. I prefer this cabin."

"But it must have taken you—"

"Months. Off and on. After every assignment, when Eliot sent me to Wyoming or Colorado, I slipped away and came back here. I guess you could say it's home."

Chris followed across the scrub-grass clearing. "You're sure no one knows about this place?"

"I'm positive."

"But how?"

"Because I'm still alive." Saul glanced toward the valley's far horizon. "Hurry. We don't have much time."

"For what? You're not making sense." Puzzled, Chris left the sun's glare, entering the musty shadows of the cabin. He had no chance to appreciate the simple handmade furniture. Saul led him past the sleeping bag on the floor toward the back wall, opening a roughly planed door. Chris felt the cool dank air of a tunnel.

"It's a mine shaft." Saul pointed toward the dark. "That's why I built the cabin here. A den ought to have two holes." He turned to the fireplace. Striking a match, he lit the kindling beneath the logs in the hearth. The kindling was dry, but the logs were wet with sap. The flames spread, sending thick smoke up the chimney. "I probably don't need the smoke. No harm in being sure, though. Leave your chute," he told Chris. "Here's a flashlight." Saul led him into the tunnel.

In the flashlight's beam, Chris saw his frosty breath. Timbers supported the roof of the tunnel. An old pick and shovel lay against the wall to the left. A rusted wheelbarrow leaned on its side. Saul touched a dull glint of metal in the moist cold stone. "Silver. Not much left."

The flashlight showed the end of the tunnel. "Here. We have to climb." Saul squeezed through a niche in the rock. He reached up, wedged his boot in a crack, and scrambled out of sight.

Chris followed, scraping his back in the narrow cleft. The stone felt slimy. He had to put the flashlight in his pocket. Then he realized he didn't need it. Above, a narrow beam of light attracted him in the dark—a long way up. Saul leaned toward an outcrop above him, blocking the light. When Saul shifted, Chris could see the light again. "You think I was followed?"

"Of course."

Chris reached for a rock. "I'm sure I wasn't."

"The surveillance team would have been the best."

The rock broke from Chris's hand, rumbling down the niche. He froze. "But nobody knew I was looking for you."

"Eliot did."

"You keep blaming Eliot. Next to you, he's the only man I trust."

"Exactly. Your mistake. Mine too." Saul's voice was bitter. His silhouette disappeared beyond the narrow shaft of light.

Chris scrambled higher. The beam of light became larger, brighter. Sweating, he squirmed from the niche and lay on a funnel of weathered rock, its smooth slope warmed by the sun. He peered toward Saul, who crouched above him, shielded by sagebrush, concentrating on the valley. "But I saw no other planes."

"Around you," Saul said. "Sure. But above you? A spotter plane at forty thousand feet? The pursuit team would have held back, flying slowly, out of sight. Till they got instructions."

Chris crawled to him, hunching beneath the sagebrush. "You set me up," he blurted angrily. "You could have met me anywhere."

"That's right. But here, with elaborate precautions, you'd be convinced. I had to prove it to you."

"Prove what?"

"I think you know."

Chris heard a far-off drone—then another and still others, louder, amplified by the echo of the towering cliffs. Through a distant pass, he saw glinting specks swoop nearer. Choppers. Hueys. Four of them. He flashed back to Nam and muttered, "Jesus."

Below him, smoke swirled from the cabin's chimney. Across the valley, the Hueys roared closer, assuming attack formation. The lead chopper fired a rocket. Exhaust whooshing, the missile streaked down, exploding in the clearing before the cabin. Earth flew, blast stunning. The other choppers soared nearer, releasing rockets.

Above their rush, Chris heard the repeated cracks of fifty-caliber machine guns. The cabin blew apart. Concussions thundered through the valley. The choppers swooped closer, strafing the crater where the cabin had stood. Even on the bluff, Chris's ears throbbed.

"Two failed attempts against me. This time they've got to make sure." Saul clenched his teeth.

The choppers pivoted from the flaming wreckage, skimming the tips of the pine trees, hurrying toward the meadow beside the lake. Blades glinting, they hovered twenty feet above the meadow. A rope flipped from each, dangling toward the grass. A man wearing pale outdoor clothes, an automatic rifle slung across his back, appeared at an open hatch. He gripped the rope, rappelling to the ground. Other men, like spiders from dragonflies, slipped down from other ropes. In the meadow, they unslung their rifles, spreading in a semicircle, their backs to the lake. "By the book," Chris said.

"They're not sure we were in the cabin. They have to assume we're still a threat. How many?"

"Sixteen."

"Check." Saul pointed. Chris saw a man in one chopper lower a dog in a sling. A German shepherd. A second dog descended from another chopper. On the ground, two men stopped aiming their rifles and squirmed back to free the harnesses from the dogs. Relieved of their cargo, the choppers retreated to the far end of the valley.

Every elite corps preferred a different breed. The Navy Seals used hunting poodles. The Rangers liked Dobermans. "German shepherds. Special Forces." Chris's throat felt dry.

The dogs ran with the two men toward the trees. The other men aimed, ready to provide covering fire. A group of four darted toward the trees, then five and another five.

Chris scanned the trees, waiting for the men to appear. "We don't have a chance. All I've got is this Mauser. You've got just that bolt-action Springfield. Even if we were properly armed—"

"We won't have to fight."

"But those dogs'll track us into the tunnel." Chris turned toward the basin behind him, watching the niche from which he'd climbed. "The men'll find where we went. They'll order the choppers to strafe this bluff. Then they'll climb up here and finish the job."

"Believe me, we're covered."

Chris opened his mouth to object, then froze as Saul gestured abruptly toward the trees. A man stepped out, presumably inviting shots so the other men would have a target. As the decoy approached the smoking wreckage, a second man showed himself, then a third. "They're feeling confident. The dogs must have followed our scent directly to the cabin." Saul watched the lead man point toward the wall of rock behind the shattered logs. "He's found the tunnel."

"We have to get out of here."

"Not yet."

"For Christ's sake—"

Five men joined the first man. Cautious, they came near the cliff. From the top, Chris couldn't see them now. Droning, the choppers continued hovering in the safety of the far end of the valley. Saul squirmed back, pausing at the smooth rock funnel that sloped down to the niche. Careful not to show himself, he listened. Chris frowned, puzzled.

Saul abruptly grinned and pointed toward sounds from the niche. Chris didn't understand why Saul seemed pleased. Then he did as Saul pulled a radio transmitter from his pocket, pushing a button.

Bracing himself, Chris felt the earth shake. A roar burst up from the tunnel. Spinning, he peered toward the cabin's wreckage below the cliff. Chunks of rock flew across the clearing. Dust swirled.

"Six down, ten to go," Saul said.

"You rigged explosives in the tunnel."

"Eliot always said make sure you protect your escape route. Now I'm turning his rules against him. Have I convinced you he wants to kill me?"

Chris nodded sickly, staring toward the trees below him. The other men ran from the pines toward the rumble of falling rock in the tunnel.

"No one else knew I was looking for you. He used me." The implications made his stomach feel like ice. "He tried to kill me too. Goddamn it, why? He's like—"

"I know. He's the closest we have to a father."

In the clearing, a man blurted instructions into a field radio. The choppers suddenly left their safe position at the far end of the valley and rushed toward the clearing, their roar growing louder. Chris saw the German shepherds on guard at the rim of the trees.

"All right," Saul said. "Those men are close enough to the tunnel. Let's get out of here." He scrambled back. Chris followed, watching Saul push the radio transmitter again. "Another surprise." Chris barely heard him in the sudden explosion from the cliff behind him. The shockwave pushed him forward, pressing his ears. A rumble came next, a swelling crash of rocks and earth as the cliff fell toward the men in the clearing. He heard their screams.

"That ought to take care of the rest of them," Saul said. Running, he dropped the transmitter.

"What about the choppers?"

"Trust me."

They raced through sagebrush. Chris tasted dust, squinting from the sun. In the rapidly approaching roar of the choppers, he wondered if the other side of the bluff would end at another cliff. Instead Saul led him down a wooded slope toward a different valley. In the shadowy cover of trees, Chris felt the sweat cool on his forehead.

"The choppers'll take a minute to work out their strategy," Saul said, breathing quickly. "One'll probably land to look for survivors."

"That leaves three." The fallen pine needles muffled Chris's steps.

"They'll have to guess we were on that bluff. They'll head for this valley."

"On foot, we can't get away before they bring in reinforcements. They'll use other dogs to track us."

"Absolutely right." Saul reached the bottom, splashing through a stream, charging up its bank. Chris followed, his wet pants clinging cold to his legs. Ahead, Saul stopped in a thick stretch of timber. He tugged at fallen logs and tangled underbrush. "Quick. Help."

Chris heaved the logs. "But why?" Then he understood. He pulled a rotten stump away and saw a sheet of plastic wrapped around a bulky object. Before he could ask what it was, Saul unwrapped the sheet.

Chris almost laughed. A trail bike—thick wide tires and heavy suspension. "But how'd you—?"

"I use it to get in and out of here. I don't take chances by leaving it around the cabin." Saul raised it, guiding it past the deadwood they'd pulled away. He pointed through the trees. "Over there. A game trail cuts across the valley." He glanced toward the increasing roar of the choppers. "They'll separate to search different sectors of the valley."

Chris helped him. "But the noise from their engines'll stop them from hearing the bike. They'll never spot us if we stay beneath the trees."

"Get on." Saul turned the key and kicked the throttle. The bike coughed. He kicked the throttle again, and the bike droned smoothly. "Here, take the rifle."

"It's no help against a chopper."

Saul didn't answer. He flicked the clutch, toed the gearshift, and twisted the accelerator. The bike lurched forward, jolting on the bumpy ground. Chris crowded against him, grinning as they swerved through a maze of trees. Shadows flickered. At the game trail, Saul drove faster. Feeling the rush of wind on his face, reminded of when they were kids, Chris almost laughed.

He froze when he heard a thunderous roar directly above him. Glancing up, he saw a grotesque shadow swoop past a break in the trees. The game trail sloped up. At the top, as Saul raced through a tiny clearing, Chris stared back across the valley. He saw two choppers diverging to search the far and middle sectors. At this other end, the chopper that had just surged past had apparently failed to see them.

The game trail angled down now. Steering, Saul followed the twists and turns. Chris heard the chopper again. "It's doubling back, rechecking something!"

The game trail reached a swath of grass that stretched from one side of the valley to the other.

Saul stopped the bike. "They'll see us if we try to cross. But we can't stay here. If we wait till night, they'll have time to bring in another team with dogs."

Overhead, the wind from the chopper rustled the nearby trees. Chris braced himself for the impact of fifty-caliber machine gun bullets.

Saul took the Springfield from him. "I wasn't sure how they'd come for me. On foot or with choppers." He pulled the Springfield's bolt, catching the round he ejected, replacing it with a round he took from his pocket. He shoved the bolt in place again.

Then he revved the accelerator, urging the bike from the trees, racing across the meadow. Glancing back, Chris saw the chopper pivot, darting in their direction. "They've seen us!"

Saul twisted the handlebars, veering back toward the trees. Machine gun bullets tore at the ground. The chopper swept over them, its obscene silhouette blotting out the sun. At once, the glare came back. Saul raced the bike into the forest. Jumping off, he aimed through branches toward the chopper as it twisted sharply above the meadow.

Chris said, "A Springfield can't shoot that chopper down."

"This one can."

Belly exposed, the chopper began a strafing approach to the trees, zooming larger. Saul pulled the Springfield's trigger, absorbing the recoil. In wonder, Chris saw the chopper's gas tank explode. He leapt for cover, shielding his eyes. Chunks of fuselage and canopy, of struts and blades erupted amid a roaring fireball in every direction across the meadow. The bulk of the fuselage hung perversely. It suddenly crashed.

"I drilled the core from the bullet, filled it with phosphorus, and put a plug in to keep the air from setting it off," Saul said.

"The other choppers . . ."

"They'll head this way. They'll search this end of the valley. We'll go back the other way. Where they've already searched."

Saul grabbed the bike. Chris quickly got on. They rushed back along the game trail. Twenty seconds later, the remaining choppers roared past toward the flaming wreckage in the meadow.

11

Eliot clutched the greenhouse phone, his tall gaunt body stooped, his forehead aching. "I understand," he said impatiently. "No, I don't want excuses. You weren't successful. That's what matters, not why you failed. Clean up the mess you made. Use other teams. Keep after them." He still wore his black suit and vest, a chest-high apron draped over them. "Of course, but I assumed your team was equally good. It seems my judgment was wrong. Believe me, I'm sorry too."

Setting down the phone, he leaned against a potting table, so tired he thought his knees would buckle.

Everything was going wrong. The hit on the Paradigm Foundation should have been simple, one man to blame, a man who couldn't say he was following orders if he was killed when he tried to fight off his captors. Simple, Eliot thought. Meticulously planned. He'd chosen Saul because he was Jewish, because the hit had to be blamed on someone other than Eliot, so why not the Israelis? He'd arranged for Saul's previous jobs to go badly—a cleaning lady coming into a room when she shouldn't have, for example—to make Saul seem as if he was out of control. Sending Saul to gamble in Atlantic City had been another way of compromising him. Saul had to fit the behavior of an agent who'd gone bad, a rogue beyond salvage. A brilliant, careful plan.

Then why had it gone wrong? After a career of avoiding mistakes, have I finally started to make them? he thought. Have I finally gotten too old? Did I delude myself into thinking that, because I sabotaged Saul's three previous jobs, he was in fact no longer resourceful?

For whatever reason, the plan was almost a disaster now. Saul's escape had jeopardized everything, creating new problems, drawing more attention to the Paradigm hit. An hour ago, the White House had called—not an aide but the president himself, enraged that his best friend's murder was still not avenged. If everything had gone as planned, if Saul had been silenced, the president would have been satisfied, turning his attention to the Israelis, blaming them for engineering the assassination. Now, instead of getting the answers he wanted, the president was asking more questions, digging, probing. If he ever learned who'd actually ordered the hit . . .

An irony struck him. Chris, by violating the sanction, had committed the cardinal sin. But Saul—though he didn't know it—had committed an even greater sin.

Its secret had to be maintained. He picked up the phone and dialed his assistant at Langley. "Put this on the wire. Every network. KGB, MI-6, all of them. 'Subject: Abelard sanction. Reference: Church of the Moon, Bangkok. Violator Remus sighted by CIA in Colorado, USA.' " Eliot told his assistant the coordinates. " 'Remus has evaded execution. Request assistance. Remus helped by rogue CIA operative Saul Grisman, cryptonym Romulus. Agency requests Romulus be terminated with Remus.' "

"Perfect," his assistant said.

But hanging up, Eliot wondered if it was. Cursing the news from Colorado, he felt threatened, apprehensive. Not only had Saul escaped. Worse, Chris was with him. Eliot blanched. Since no one else had

known what Chris was doing, they'll suspect me, he thought. They'll
want to know why I turned against them.

They'll come after me.

His hand shook as he dialed again. The phone buzzed so often he
feared he'd get no answer. The buzzing stopped, a husky voice responding.

"Castor," Eliot said. "Bring Pollux. Come to the greenhouse." He
swallowed thickly. "Your father needs you."

12

When the moon came out, they left the ravine where they'd buried
the trail bike under rocks and earth and fallen branches. They wouldn't
need it anymore. As twilight turned to dark, they hadn't been able to
steer it safely through the trees. Of course, another hit team using dogs
would find the bike, but Saul and Chris would be far away by then. In
the moonlight, they worked their way across a meadow, staying low to
hide their furtive silhouettes. They reached the upward draw they'd
chosen at dusk when, studying Chris's terrain map, they'd planned
their route. They climbed the rocky chasm, never speaking, never
glancing behind them, always listening for uncharacteristic sounds
from the valley below them. Since the attack on Saul's cabin, they'd
traveled twenty miles through three connecting valleys. Chris's spine
ached from the shock of the trail bike's wheels on bumps and branches.
He enjoyed the exertion of climbing, the release of tension in his muscles.

At the top, they rested, sprawling out of sight in a rocky basin, the
moon illuminating their sweaty faces.

"If this were Nam, we wouldn't have a chance." Saul kept his voice
low, catching his breath. "They'd send a surveillance plane with a heat
sensor."

Chris understood—the trouble with a heat sensor was it picked up
animal as well as human body temperature. In Nam, the only way to
make a sensor practical had been to spray poison from planes and kill
all the wildlife in the jungle. That way, if a sensor registered a blip, the

heat source had to be human. Chris recalled the unnatural silence of a jungle without animals. But here there was too much wildlife for a heat sensor to be useful. The forest sounds were constant, reassuring, the brush of leaves, the whisper of branches. Deer grazed. Porcupines and badgers scavenged. But if the noises ever stopped, he'd know something had spooked them.

"They'll bring in other teams," Chris said.

"But only to flush us out. The real trap's in the foothills. They'll watch every ranger station, every road and town around here. Sooner or later we have to come down."

"They can't surround the entire mountain range. They'll have to be selective. The nearest foothills are south and west of here."

"So we'll go north."

"How far?"

"As far as we have to. We're at home up here. If we don't like the way things look, we'll just keep moving farther north."

"We can't use the rifle to hunt. The shot would attract attention. But we can fish. And there'll be plants—stonecrop, mountain sorrel, spring beauties."

Saul grimaced. "Spring beauties. Well, I needed to lose weight anyhow. At least the dogs can't track us up sheer cliffs."

"You're sure you're in condition for this?" Chris grinned.

"Hey, what about you? That monastery didn't make you soft, I hope."

"The Cistercians?" Chris laughed. "Make me soft? They're the toughest order in the Catholic Church."

"They really don't talk?"

"Not only that. They believe in brutal daily work. I might as well have spent another six years in Special Forces."

Saul shook his head. "The communal life. Did you ever think about the pattern? First the orphanage, then the military, next the agency and the monastery. There's a common denominator."

"What?"

"Segregated disciplined cadres. You're addicted."

"Both of us. The only difference is you never took the extra step. You were never tempted to enter a Jewish monastic order."

"Didn't those Cistercians teach you anything? There's no such thing as a Jewish monastic order. We don't believe in retreating from the world."

"That's probably why you stayed in the agency. It's the nearest thing to monasticism you could find."

"The quest for perfection." Saul frowned in disgust. "We'd better get moving." He pulled a compass from his pocket, studying its luminous dial.

"Why does Eliot want to kill you?"

Even in the night, Chris saw the angry glow on his brother's face. "Don't you think I keep asking myself? He's the only kind of father I've got, and now the bastard's turned against me. Everything started after a job I did for him. But why?"

"He'll make sure he's protected. We can't just go to him and ask."

Saul clenched his teeth. "Then we'll go around him."

"How?"

They swung toward a sudden far-off rumble. "Sounds like something blew up," Saul murmured.

"Dummy." Chris laughed.

Saul turned to him, confused.

"That's thunder."

Thirty minutes later, as they climbed to the bottom of a jagged ridge, the stormclouds scudded overhead, obscuring the moon. In a sudden stinging wind, Saul found a protective lip of rock. Chris squirmed beneath it as the rain hit.

"Go around him? How?"

But Saul's reply was drowned by more thunder.

CASTOR AND POLLUX

1

Saul tensed. Crouching on a roof, concealed by the dark, he stared toward the street below him. Cars flanked the curbs; lamps glowed behind curtains in apartments. He watched a door come open in a building across the street. A woman stepped out: midthirties, tall, trim, elegant, with long dark hair, wearing navy slacks, a burgundy blouse, and a brown suede jacket. Saul studied her features in the light above the door. Her skin was smooth and tanned, her high strong cheeks accentuated by a beautiful chin, an exquisite forehead, a sensual neck. She'd often been mistaken for a model.

Saul knew better, though. He crawled back from the waist-high wall at the edge of the roof, then stood and opened the maintenance door that led to a ladder and finally stairs. For an instant, he recalled his escape from the tenement in Atlantic City, racing from the roof down the stairs to the street where he'd stolen the Duster. This time, after he hurried unnoticed down the stairs of this attractive apartment building, he glanced both ways along the street and passed the parked cars to follow the woman.

She walked to his left, reached a streetlight, and turned the corner. Saul heard the echo of her high-heeled shoes as he crossed the street and went around the corner after her. A cruising taxi made him nervous. An old man walking a dog aroused his suspicion.

Halfway down the block, the woman entered a doorway. Saul came nearer, glancing through a window toward red-checked tablecloths in the booths of a small Italian restaurant. He paused as if to study the menu on the wall beside the entrance. He could wait close by for her to come out, he thought, but he saw no acceptable hiding places. All the buildings on this street were businesses. If he stayed in an alley or jimmied a lock to get up on another roof, the police might find him. As well, he didn't want to confront her on the street. Too dangerous. In a way, by going in the restaurant, she'd solved a problem for him.

When he entered, he heard an accordion. Candlelight glowed off polished oak. Silverware clinked amid muted conversations. He scanned the busy room, smelling garlic and butter. Peering past a waiter carrying a tray, he concentrated on the corners in the rear. As he expected, she sat with her back to a wall, facing the front but near an exit through the kitchen. Her waiter had taken the other place settings. Good, Saul thought, she planned to eat alone.

The maître d' came over. "Do you have a reservation, sir?"

"I'm with Miss Bernstein. In that corner." Smiling, Saul passed him, crossing the room. His smile dissolved as he stopped before the table. "Erika."

She glanced up, confused. Abruptly her brow contorted in alarm.

He pulled out a chair and sat beside her. "It isn't polite to stare. Keep your fingers on the edge of the table. Away from the knife and fork, please."

"You!"

"And please don't raise your voice."

"Are you crazy coming here? Everybody's hunting you."

"That's what I want to talk to you about." Saul studied her face —the smooth dark cheeks, the deep brown eyes and full lips. He fought the urge to draw his finger across her skin. "You keep getting lovelier."

Erika shook her head, incredulous. "How long has it been? Ten years? Now out of nowhere you suddenly show up—in the worst kind of trouble—and that's all you can say?"

"You'd prefer to hear you're getting uglier?"

"For Christ's sake—"

"That's no way for a nice Jewish girl to talk."

She raised a hand in dismay.

He stiffened. "Please keep your fingers on the edge of the table," he repeated.

She obeyed, breathing deeply. "This can't be coincidence. You didn't just happen to choose this place."

"I followed you from your apartment."

"Why? You could have come up."

"To find a roommate or someone waiting in case I tried to get in touch with you?" He shook his head. "I figured neutral ground was better. Why are they after me?"

She frowned in surprise. "You actually don't know? Because of

Bangkok. Chris violated the sanction." Her voice was low but tense. The noises from the nearby kitchen kept the other customers from hearing her.

"But Bangkok was after. What's that got to do with me?"

"After *what?* You don't make sense."

"Just tell me."

"Chris killed a Russian. The KGB issued a contract against him. Because of the rules of the sanction, the other networks have to help."

"I know all that. But what's it got to do with *me?* Atlantic City happened *before* Bangkok."

"What are you talking about? Five days ago, we received a message from your agency—a revision of the contract. Chris had been seen in Colorado. You were helping him, the message said. The CIA declared you a rogue and asked for you to be killed with Chris."

Saul murmured, "Eliot."

"For God's sake, would you tell me what—?" Nervous, she glanced at sudden stares from nearby customers. "We can't talk here."

"Then where?"

2

In the dark, Saul gazed through the window toward the distant lights of the Washington Monument. "Nice location."

"Ten blocks from our embassy," Erika said behind him.

He didn't give a damn about the view. His reason for staring out the window was to test her. On guard, he waited for her to try to kill him. When she didn't, he closed the draperies and turned on a corner lamp, angling it so he and Erika would cast no shadows on the drapes.

He nodded in approval of the living room, its furniture simple, carefully chosen, elegant. He'd already searched the bedroom, the kitchen, and the bathroom. As she'd promised, he'd found no roommate, no one waiting for him. "Microphones?"

"I checked this morning."

"This is tonight." He turned on the television, not because he wanted its noise to muffle their conversation, instead because he needed a constant sound for a test. He'd seen a portable radio in the kitchen. Now he got it and turned it on, switching to the FM band. He divided the room into quadrants, checking each section for bugs by slowly moving the radio's dial. A hidden microphone was normally tuned to an FM number not used by a station in the area. All an eavesdropper had to do was wait in a nearby safe location, adjust a radio to the FM number he'd chosen, and listen to whatever was said near the mike he'd planted. Similarly, Saul could use a radio to pick up the same transmission. As he moved the dial, if he heard the noise from the television come from the radio—often as squawky feedback—he'd know the room was bugged. In this case, no matter which FM station he tried, he didn't pick up the laugh track from the sit com. He scanned the ceiling, the walls, the furniture, the floor. Satisfied, he turned the TV and radio off. The room seemed unnaturally still.

"The sanction?" he said as if their conversation in the restaurant hadn't been interrupted. "That's the only reason your people are after me? Because I'm helping Chris?"

"What other reason could there be?" Erika raised her eyebrows, troubled. "We hate to help the Russians, but the sanction has to be maintained. Abelard's the cardinal rule. If it's destroyed, we sink toward chaos."

"Then if you had the chance, you'd kill me? A fellow Jew, a former lover?"

Erika didn't answer. She took off her jacket. The two top buttons of her blouse were open, spread by the swell of her breasts. "You gave me the chance a few minutes ago when you looked out the window. I didn't take it."

"Because you knew I did it deliberately—to see how you'd react."
She grinned.

The gleam of amusement in her eyes made him grin in return. He felt as attracted to her as he'd been ten years ago, wanting to ask how she was, what had happened to her since he'd last seen her.

But he had to deny himself. He couldn't trust anyone except his brother. "For what it's worth, Chris is out there. If you killed me . . ."

"I assumed you'd have backup. He'd come after me to get revenge. I'd be foolish to try unless I had you both together."

"On the other hand, maybe you'd feel lucky. I don't have time for this. I need answers. Eliot's hunting me, but not because of Chris. That's merely Eliot's excuse. Hell, he asked Chris to find me—*after Chris had already violated the sanction.*"

"That's insane."

"Of course." Saul gestured with frustration. "If the Russians knew Eliot had asked Chris for help instead of killing him, they'd put out another contract. Eliot risked his life to try to find me."

"Why?"

"To kill me."

"You expect me to believe this? Eliot's like a father to you."

Saul rubbed his aching forehead. "Something's more important than his relationship with me, more important than the sanction, so important he has to get rid of me. But dammit, I don't know what. That's why I came to you."

"How would I—?"

"Atlantic City. *Before* Chris violated the sanction. Even then, the Mossad came after me. I have to assume your people were helping Eliot."

"Impossible!"

"It's not! It happened!"

Erika's eyes flashed. "If we helped Eliot, I'd know about it. A lot of things have changed since the last time I saw you. I'm supposed to be a clerk in our embassy, but I'm a colonel in the Mossad now. I control our intelligence teams on the eastern seaboard. Unless I approved it, none of our people would have tried to kill you."

"Then whoever ordered it lied to you and covered it up. Someone in the Mossad works for Eliot."

Erika continued glaring. "I can't accept it! If what you say is true—" She shuddered, raising her hands. "Just wait a minute. This is senseless. I'm arguing with you when I don't even know the details. Tell me about it. Exactly what happened."

Saul slumped in a chair. "Ten days ago, Eliot asked me to do a job. The Paradigm Foundation."

Erika's eyes widened. "Andrew Sage's group. The president's friend. That was you? The president's blaming *us.*"

"But why?"

"The Paradigm Foundation worked for the president. A group of American billionaires who negotiated with the Arabs to get cheaper oil if the State Department abandoned its loyalty to Israel. The president thinks we protected our interests by destroying the foundation."

108

"And stopping the negotiations," Saul said. "For once, the president's being logical."

"Go on. What happened?"

"You mean I've finally got your attention? You see the point? If you help me, you'll be helping yourselves."

"You mentioned Atlantic City."

"After the job, Eliot sent me there to drop out of sight."

"Absurd. That's no place to hide."

"Damn right it isn't. But I always do what Eliot tells me. I don't argue. Someone from the Mossad tried to kill me in a casino. I called Eliot for protection. He sent me to a hotel where a Mossad team set up another trap. Only Eliot knew where I was going. The team must have worked for Eliot."

"I tell you it's impossible!"

"Because you didn't know about it? You're being naive."

"Because of something else. Whoever helped Eliot was also helping whoever wanted Sage's group destroyed. We'd never be stupid enough to kill the president's friend, no matter how badly we wanted those negotiations stopped. We'd be the first country the president accused, exactly what's happened. The hit didn't help us—it hurt us! What Mossad team would turn against Israel?"

"Maybe they didn't know why Eliot wanted me killed. Maybe they didn't know the connection between me and the hit."

"I still don't understand what makes you sure they were Mossad."

"You figure it out. They used the heels of their palms in hand-to-hand combat. They used Berettas and Uzis. They walked with that flat-footed, half-crouched stance for balance. No one else is taught to do that. They even made silencers the way your people do."

She stared in disbelief.

3

Chris crept up the stairs, his rubber-soled shoes touching the concrete softly. Close to the wall, out of sight from anyone peering past the railing down the stairwell, he approached each landing. Fluorescent lights hummed as he listened for other sounds above him. Checking all five levels, he found no one, then came down one level to open a fire door, studying the fourth floor hall. Numbered apartments flanked both sides. Directly to his right, he saw an elevator, pushed its button, and waited. A light above its door showed 5, then 4. A bell rang as the door slid open. With his hand on the Mauser beneath his jacket, he discovered no one.

Good, he thought. As much as possible, the building was secure, though he didn't like the flimsy locks on the outside doors or the absence of a guard in the lobby. He debated whether he should have continued to watch the building from the street. The problem had been that from his vantage he couldn't see the back, nor could he determine if someone entering the building belonged here or was hunting Saul. Besides, he couldn't know if trouble was already inside. He had to assume that agents from various networks—especially from Eliot—were watching the people he and Saul would likely ask for help, and Erika certainly qualified as their friend, though they hadn't seen her since '73. It was possible no one knew how close the friendship was, but since they needed her help, Chris believed in being thorough. Now that he'd checked the building, he felt more confident, knowing that Erika's apartment—on the left, halfway down the hall—was protected. A hunter couldn't reach the fourth floor, by either the elevator or the stairs, without his knowing it. He went back to the stairwell, left its door slightly open, and listened for the elevator's bell or footsteps below him.

Earlier, he'd smiled from a roof near Saul, recognizing Erika's figure as she left her apartment to walk down the street, enjoying the memory of the first time he'd met her, when he and Saul had gone for special training to Israel in 1966. Then as now her elegance deceived. A veteran of the Israeli Six-Day War in '67 and the October War in '73, she was as capable—indeed as deadly—as any man. Ironic, he thought. In America strong women were considered threats whereas in Israel they were treasured, since their nation's survival left no room for sexual prejudice.

The creak of a door coming open below him troubled him. He turned to the rail, seeing shadows at the bottom of the stairs. As the door snicked shut down there, he took advantage of its echo to shift to the level above him, drawing his Mauser, easing to his stomach on the chilly concrete.

The shadows might belong to people who lived in the building and preferred climbing the stairs for exercise instead of using the elevator.

If they came all the way up, they'd panic at the sight of his Mauser. He'd have to run.

The lights hummed, almost obscuring the gentle brush of footsteps climbing higher.

Second floor, he thought. No, third. They're stopping. He almost relaxed, then corrected his guess.

The fourth, directly below him. The footsteps paused. He clutched the Mauser, staring at the distorted silhouettes projecting up.

He aimed. Were they tenants? They seemed to inch higher. In a moment, he'd see their faces. He pressed his finger on the trigger, braced for an instant's judgment.

The shadows stopped. The door creaked open down there, then shut.

He rose to a crouch and pointed the Mauser down the stairs. Seeing no one, he hurried down. Cautious, he opened the door and squinted out.

Two men stood halfway down the hall, facing left toward Erika's apartment. One man held a submachine gun, short-stocked, stubby-barreled, unmistakably an Uzi, while the other man tugged a pin from a grenade.

Chris saw them too late. The first man fired. In a continuous deafening roar, the Uzi's bullets splintered the door to Erika's apartment. Ejected casings flew through the air, clinking against each other on the carpet. The acrid stench of cordite filled the hall. The gunman shifted his aim, continuing to squeeze the Uzi's trigger, spraying the wall beside the door. The second man released the lever on his grenade and kicked the door's shattered lock, preparing to throw as the door burst in.

Chris fired twice. The second man spun from the impact to his skull and shoulder, dropping the grenade. The first man pivoted, shooting at Chris. Despite the noise, Chris heard a bell. He ducked to the stairwell. Footsteps charged from the elevator. The gunman kept shooting. Amid a roar of bullets, people screamed, their bodies ripped, falling.

The grenade exploded, amplified by the hall, shrapnel zinging. The stench of cordite flared Chris's nostrils. He fought to overcome the ringing in his ears, to listen for sounds in the corridor.

On guard, he peered from the stairwell. To his right, in front of the elevator, two men with Uzis lay motionless in a pool of blood.

Of course. Two pairs covering both routes to this floor. But their timing was off. The elevator arrived too late. The second pair heard the shots and charged out but got killed by the man they wanted to help.

He turned to his left. The gunman who'd shot at Erika's apartment sprawled beside his dead companion, his face blown off.

Hearing panicked voices in apartments, Chris raced down the hall. Erika's door was shattered. Dangling open, it showed the living room. The Uzi's spray of bullets had mangled the furniture, blowing apart the television. Drapes hung in tatters.

"*Saul?*" But he saw no bodies.

Where the hell were they?

4

As the first roar of bullets had erupted through the door, Saul dropped to the rug, hearing Erika do the same. His impulse had been to crawl to the kitchen or the bedroom. But then the bullets burst through the wall instead of the door, beginning at waist level, angling down. The rug across which he'd have to crawl toward either room heaved from their impact. Chunks of carpet flew in a systematic pattern, marching back and forth from the far end of the room toward the middle where he lay. He and Erika had to roll in the opposite direction, away from the bullets toward the wall beside the door. He felt it shudder above him. Fragments of plaster pelted him. The rug heaved closer. If the gunman dropped his aim much lower . . .

The door crashed in. Saul aimed his Beretta, hearing two pistol shots, a body falling, screams, an explosion, silence.

Close to the wall, he rose to his feet, sensing Erika do the same. He heard shouting out there and aimed toward a shadow in the doorway.

"Saul!" someone yelled. The shadow entered.

Saul eased his finger off the trigger.

Chris turned, peering anxiously along the wall. "Are you hit?"

Saul shook his head. "What happened?"

"No time. We have to get out of here."

Doors opened along the hall. A woman screamed. A man yelled, "Call the police!"

Chris froze, staring past Saul toward something in the room.

"What's wrong?"

Saul spun toward Erika, afraid she'd been hit. She faced the two of them, backing away from a chair beneath which she'd drawn a hidden pistol, another Beretta.

"No!"

She aimed at Chris. Saul remembered what she'd told him earlier. She'd be foolish to try to kill Saul unless she also had a chance at . . .

"No!"

Too late. She fired. Saul heard the sickening whack of a bullet hitting flesh. A groan. He whirled. Beyond Chris, a man with a pistol lurched back against the corridor's wall, his throat spurting blood.

Chris clutched the side of his head. "Jesus!"

"I missed you," Erika said.

"By a quarter-inch! The bullet singed my hair!"

"You'd prefer I let him kill you?"

Past the shattered windows, sirens wailed in the night.

Erika hurried toward the door. Saul quickly followed. "Where did that guy come from?"

As he reached the corridor, rushing past the bodies on the floor, he saw his answer. Down the hall, from the apartment next to Erika's, a man aimed an Uzi. Erika fired. Saul and Chris shot one second afterward. The man wailed, doubling over, his finger still pressed on the trigger, spraying the floor. The Uzi jerked from his hands.

Erika ran toward the elevator.

"No," Saul told her. "We'll be trapped in there."

"Don't argue, dammit!" Avoiding the pool of blood around the bodies, she pressed the elevator button. The door slid open. She pushed Saul and Chris inside, touched number 5, and the door slid shut.

Saul's stomach sank as the elevator rose.

"We can't go down," she said. "God knows who's in the lobby. The police or—" Reaching up, she tugged a panel from the elevator's roof.

Saul straightened when he saw the trapdoor beyond the panel. "Emergency exit."

"I checked the day I rented the apartment," she said. "In case I needed a private escape route."

Saul pushed the trapdoor to raise it. The elevator stopped. As his stomach settled, he saw Chris press the button that kept the door closed. Jumping up, Saul grabbed the trapdoor's edge and climbed through the narrow exit, kneeling in the dark. He reached down for Erika's hands, smelling the grease on the elevator cables beside him.

"They didn't need to bug my apartment or watch the building from outside." She climbed up next to him. "You saw. They had two men in the apartment next to mine. As soon as you arrived, they sent for help."

From the elevator, Chris handed them the panel. Squirming up, he leaned down, sliding the panel back in place. He shut the trapdoor. "Now what? God Almighty, the dust. I can hardly breathe."

"Above us. On the roof, there's a superstructure for the elevator. It's the housing for the gears." Erika's voice echoed in the dark shaft. She climbed, her shoes scraping against the concrete wall.

Saul reached up, touching a metal bar. The moment his shoes left the elevator's roof, he heard a rumble. No! The elevator was going down! He dangled. "Chris!"

"Beside you!"

Saul's fingers almost slipped from the greasy bar. If he fell, if the elevator went all the way to the bottom . . . He imagined his body crashing through the elevator's roof and squirmed to get a better grip on the bar. Erika's hand tightened on his wrist. He scrambled up.

"Keep your head low," she ordered. "The gears are directly above you."

Saul felt the speeding cables, the rush of air from the whirring gears. He hunched on a concrete ledge.

"My jacket," Chris said. "It's caught in the gears."

Their rumble was magnified by the echo in the shaft. Saul spun to him, useless, blind. The rumble stopped. The cables trembled in place. The silence smothered him.

He heard the rip of cloth. "My sleeve," Chris said. "I have to get it out before—"

The rumble began again, muffling Chris's words. Saul reached for him, almost losing his balance, straining not to fall.

"I did it," Chris said. "My jacket's out."

The elevator stopped below them. As silence returned, Saul heard the door slide open. A sickened voice moaned, someone gagging. "It's worse than they told us! A goddamn slaughterhouse! Call the station!

114

On the double! We need help!" Footsteps rushed from the elevator. The door slid shut. The rumble began once more as the elevator descended.

"They'll seal off the building," Erika said.

"Then let's get out of here."

"I'm trying. There's a maintenance door to the roof. But it's locked."

Saul heard a rattle as she tugged at a latch. "We're stuck in here?"

The elevator stopped. He heard the scrape of metal.

"The hinge pins. One of them's loose." Erika kept her voice low. Saul heard more scraping. "There. I've got it out."

"What about the other one? Use my knife."

"It's moving. Okay, I've got it." She pulled the hatch. Through a crack, Saul welcomed the glow from the city. He leaned close, gasping fresh air.

"They'll check the roof," Erika said. "We'll have to wait till they've finished." Despite Saul's eagerness to leave, he knew she was right; he didn't argue. "I can see the door to the roof," she added. "If it opens, I'll have time to shut the hatch and slide the pins back in."

The elevator rumbled again, rising. A male voice drifted up, muffled. "The coroner's on the way. We're searching the building. Who lives in that apartment?"

"A woman. Erika Bernstein."

"Where the hell is she? I searched the apartment. I didn't see any bodies."

"If she's still in the building, we'll find her."

Ten minutes later, two policemen came through the door to the roof, aiming revolvers and flashlights. Erika shut the maintenance hatch, silently replacing the pins in the hinges. Saul heard footsteps and voices.

"Nobody up here."

"What about the hatch to the elevator?"

A flashlight glared through the grill in the hatch. Saul pressed back with Chris and Erika, deep in the shadows.

"There's a lock."

"Better check it. Maybe it's been jimmied."

The footsteps came closer.

"Be careful. I'll stay back and cover you."

Saul heard a rattle as the lock was jerked.

"You satisfied?"

"The captain said to be thorough."

"What difference does it make? He always double-checks everything himself. Then he sends us back to *triple*-check."

The footsteps drifted away. The door to the roof creaked shut.

Saul breathed out sharply. Sweat stung his eyes. Double-check and triple-check? he thought, dismayed. We're trapped in here.

5

All night, the elevator kept going up and down, raising dust that smeared their faces and clogged their nostrils, making them gag. After Erika reopened the maintenance hatch, they took turns straining for fresh air through the gap. Saul kept checking the luminous hands on his watch. Shortly after six, he began to see Chris and Erika, their haggard features becoming more distinct as the morning sun filtered through the grill.

At first he welcomed the light, but as he sweated more intensely, he realized the shaft was getting warmer, baked by the sun's glare on the elevator's superstructure. He felt suffocated. Taking off his jacket, he pried his gritty shirt away from his chest. By eleven o'clock, he'd removed his shirt as well. They slumped in a stupor, wearing only their underwear. Erika's flesh-toned bra clung to her breasts, sweat forming rivulets between them. Saul studied the exhaustion on her face, worrying for her, at last concluding she was tougher than Chris and he. She'd probably outlast both of them.

By noon, the elevator went up and down less often. The ambulance crew and the forensic squad had come and gone. In the night, the bodies had been taken away. From muffled conversations in the elevator, Saul learned that two policemen were watching Erika's apartment, two others watching the lobby. Still it wasn't safe to leave. Grimy, they'd attract attention if they showed themselves in daylight. So they continued to wait, struggling to breathe. When the sun went down, Saul's vision was blurred. His arms felt heavy. His stomach cramped from dehydration. They finally reached the limit they'd agreed on—twenty-four hours from the attack.

Crawling wearily from the narrow hatch, they stumbled to stand on the roof. Fingers slack, they put on their clothes, gulping the cool night air, swallowing dryly. Dizzy, they stared toward the far-off gleam of the Capitol building.

"So much to do," Chris said.

Saul knew what he meant. They needed transportation, water, food, a place for them to bathe and find clean clothes and rest. Above all, sleep.

And after sleep, the answers.

"I can get us a car." Erika pushed her long dark hair behind her shoulders.

"Your own or from the embassy?" Chris didn't wait for an answer. He shook his head. "Too risky. The police know who you are. Since they didn't find your body, they have to figure you're involved. They'll watch your parking spot beneath the building. They'll find out where you work and watch the embassy."

"I've got a backup car." Her breasts arched as she put on her blouse. She buttoned the sleeves. "I used a different name to buy it. I paid cash—a slush fund from the embassy. The car can't be traced to me. I keep it in a garage on the other side of town."

"That still leaves us with the other problem—a place to go," Chris said. "The police have our descriptions from the neighbors who saw us outside your apartment. We can't risk going to a hotel. Two men and a woman—we'd be obvious."

"And whoever's hunting us will check your friends," Saul added.

"No hotel. No friends," she said.

"Then what?"

"Stop frowning. Don't you like surprises?"

6

The captain of homicide clutched the phone in his office, staring bleakly at the half-eaten Quarter-Pounder on his cluttered desk. As he listened to the imperious voice on the phone, he suddenly lost his appetite. His ulcer began to burn. Past the screen of the open window, sirens wailed in the Washington night. "Of course." The captain sighed. "Sir, I'll take care of it. I guarantee no problem."

Curling his lips in disgust, he set the phone down, wiping his sweaty hand as if the phone had contaminated him. A man appeared in the doorway. Glancing across his desk, the captain saw his lean-faced lieutenant—jacket off, tie loosened, wrinkled shirtsleeves rolled up— light a cigarette.

Beyond the lieutenant, phones rang; typewriters clattered. Weary detectives searched files and questioned prisoners.

"That scowl on your face," the lieutenant said. "You look like you just heard the department's forcing you on another exercise program."

"Shoveling shit." The captain sagged in his creaky chair.

"What's wrong?"

"That bloodbath last night. Six men with enough weapons to invade a small country, blown away in an apparently ordinary apartment building."

"You ran out of leads?"

"You could say that. It never happened."

The lieutenant choked on his cigarette smoke. "What the hell are you talking about?" He stalked past filing cabinets into the room.

"The call I just got." The captain gestured with contempt toward the phone. "It came from high up. I mean so high I'm not even allowed to tell you who. It makes me sick to think about it. If I don't handle this thing right, I'll be back in a squad car." Wincing, the captain pressed his burning stomach. "This damn town—sometimes I think it's the ass-end of the universe."

"For Christ's sake, tell me."

"The men who got killed. The government's impounded their bodies." The captain didn't need to explain what "government" meant. Both he and his lieutenant had worked in Washington long enough to recognize the synonym for covert activities. "For security reasons, those corpses won't be identified. Official business. No publicity. The government's handling almost everything."

"Almost?" The lieutenant jabbed his cigarette in an overflowing ashtray. "You're not making sense."

"Two men and a woman. We've got the woman's name—Erika Bernstein. We've got detailed descriptions. If we find them, I've got a number to call. But we can't let them know they've been seen, and we can't pick them up."

"That's crazy. They shot six men, but we can't arrest them?"

"How the hell can we? I told you the government impounded the bodies. Those corpses don't exist. What we're looking for are three nonkillers for a mass murder that never happened."

7

Erika left the building first. One at a time, Chris and Saul followed shortly afterward, using different exits, scanning the dark before they retreated along shadowy streets. Making sure they weren't pursued, they each hailed a taxi as soon as they were out of the neighborhood, giving the drivers instructions to take them to separate districts on the other side of Washington. While Erika went to the parking garage to get her car, Chris waited at a pizza parlor they'd agreed on. Saul in turn went to a video-game arcade where he played Guided Missile while he glanced through the window toward the street they'd chosen.

Just before the arcade closed at midnight, he saw a blue Camaro stop at the curb, its engine idling. Recognizing Erika behind the wheel, he went out, automatically scanning the street as he opened the passenger door.

"I hope the two of you won't feel cramped in back."

He wondered what she meant. Then he noticed Chris hunched down out of sight behind the driver's seat. "The elevator shaft, now this?" Groaning, he climbed in back. As Erika pulled from the curb, he hunkered on the floor near Chris.

"You don't have to be chummy too long," she said.

Saul noticed the periodic glow of streetlights as she drove. "How long exactly?"

"An hour."

He groaned again, shoving Chris. "Hey, move your big feet."

She laughed. "The cops want two men and a woman. If they saw us together, they might pull us over, just on a hunch."

"I'm not so sure," Chris said.

"But why take chances?"

"That's not what I mean. While I waited at the pizza parlor, I got a look at a newspaper. The killings weren't mentioned."

"It must have been yesterday's paper," Erika said.

"No, today's. Six men dead. Your apartment shot up. I expected a front-page story, descriptions of us, the works. I checked some other papers. I found nothing."

"Maybe they got the story too late to run it."

"The shooting happened at quarter after ten last night. There was plenty of time."

She turned a corner. Headlights flicked past the Camaro. "Someone must have convinced the papers not to run it."

"Eliot," Saul said. "He could've impounded the bodies and asked the police to stay quiet for the sake of national security. The papers would never have known what happened."

"But why?" Chris said. "He's hunting us. He could have our pictures on every front page in the country. With so many people searching for us, he'd have a better chance to catch us."

"Unless he doesn't want publicity. Whatever this is all about, he wants to keep it private."

"What, though?" Chris clenched a fist. "What's so damned important?"

8

Saul felt the Camaro turn. In the night, the smooth highway suddenly changed to a bumpy side road. On the back floor, he gripped the seat. "Don't you have any shocks in this thing?"

Erika grinned. "We're almost there. It's safe to sit up now."

Grateful, Saul raised himself to the seat. Easing back, stretching his cramped legs, he peered through the windshield. The Camaro's headlights showed dense bushes on both sides of a narrow dirt lane. "Where are we?"

"South of Washington. Near Mount Vernon."

Saul tapped Chris's shoulder, pointing toward a grove of trees. Beyond them, moonlight glimmered on an impressive red brick mansion.

"Colonial?" Chris said.

120

"A little later. It was built in eighteen hundred." Erika stopped the car where the lane curved from the trees toward the lawn before the extensive porch. She aimed her headlights toward the forest beyond.

"You know who lives here?" Chris said. "We agreed we couldn't risk going to friends."

"He's not a friend."

"Then who?"

"This man's a Jew. I fought beside his son in Israel. I've been here only once—when I came to tell him his son died bravely." She swallowed. "I gave him a photograph of the grave. I gave him the medal his son never lived to receive. He told me if I ever needed help . . ." Her voice sounded hoarse.

Saul felt what she hadn't said. "You knew the son well?"

"I wanted to. If he'd lived, I might have stayed in Israel with him."

Saul put a comforting hand on her shoulder.

The house stayed dark. "Either he's asleep," Chris said, "or he isn't home."

"He's cautious. Unexpected visitors this late—he wouldn't turn the lights on."

"Sounds like us," Chris said.

"He survived Dachau. He remembers. Right now he's probably staring out here, wondering who the hell we are."

"Better not keep him waiting."

She stepped out, walking past the headlights toward the house. From the car's back seat, Saul watched her disappear behind a flowering dogwood, absorbed by the night. He waited five minutes. Suddenly nervous, he reached for the door.

Her tall slim figure emerged from shadows. She got back in the car.

Saul felt relieved. "He's home? He'll help us?"

She nodded, driving past the front of the house. A lane curved toward the murky forest in back. "I told him some friends and I needed a place to stay. I said it was better if he didn't know why. He asked no questions. He understood." The Camaro bumped along the lane.

Saul turned around. "But we're leaving the house."

"We won't be staying there." Her headlights glared through the trees.

With the windows open, Saul heard the predawn songs of birds. Mist swirled. He hugged his arms against the dampness.

"I hear frogs," Chris said.

"The Potomac's up ahead." She reached a clearing and an old

stone cottage, partly covered with vines. "He says it's his guest house. There's power and water." Stopping, she got out, studied the cottage, and nodded approvingly.

As she went in with Saul, Chris walked around to the back, instinctively checking the perimeter. Wooden steps angled down a steep slope to the misty river. In the dark, he heard waves lap the bank. Something splashed. He smelled decay.

A light came on behind him from a window in the cottage. Turning, he watched Saul and Erika open cupboards in a rustic kitchen. With the window closed, he couldn't hear what they said, but he was struck by their ease with one another—even though they hadn't been lovers in ten years. He'd never experienced that kind of relationship. His inhibitions nagged at him. His throat felt tight as Saul leaned close to Erika, gently kissing her. Ashamed to be watching, he turned away.

He made a warning noise when he entered. The living room was spacious, paneled, with a wooden floor and beams across the peaked ceiling. He noticed a table to his left and a sofa before a fireplace to his right, the furniture covered with sheets. Across from him, he saw two doors and the entrance to the kitchen. He smelled dust.

"We'd better open the windows," Erika said as she and Saul came into the living room. She took the sheets off the furniture. Dust swirled. "There's some cans of food in the cupboards."

Chris felt ravenous. He lifted a window, breathing fresh air, then checked the doors across from him. "A bedroom. A shower. Tell you what. I'll cook. You can have the bathroom first."

"You won't get an argument." She touched her hair, already unbuttoning her blouse as she stepped in, closing the door behind her.

They heard the sound of the shower and went to the kitchen, where they cooked three cans of beef stew. The steam made Chris's stomach growl.

The water soon stopped. When Erika came back, she wore a towel around her hair and a robe she'd found in the bathroom closet.

"You look beautiful," Saul said.

Mocking, she curtsied. "And you look like you need a bath."

Saul rubbed the dirt on his face and laughed. But nothing was funny. While they ate their first few spoonfuls, no one spoke. Finally Saul set down his spoon.

"Those men in the apartment next to yours would have known it was me, not Chris, who came home with you. Even so, they sent for a hit team. Sure, I'm helping Chris, but he's the one who violated the sanction. He should have been the primary target, but he wasn't. *I* was. Why?"

"And Colorado had nothing to do with the sanction either," Chris said. "Whatever their reason, they didn't attack till I found you. It wasn't me they wanted. It was *you.*"

Saul nodded, troubled. "Atlantic City. The Mossad."

"Those men at my apartment weren't Mossad," Erika insisted. "I'd have been told about the hit. They'd have made sure I was safe before they tried to kill you."

"But they handled themselves like Israelis."

"Just because they used Uzis and Berettas?" she said.

"All right, I grant you. Even the Russians sometimes use those weapons. But the other things. The heel of the palm in hand-to-hand combat."

"And the way they made silencers, and their flat-footed crouch for balance when they stalked you. I know," Erika said. "You told me. Those tactics don't prove a thing."

Saul's face turned red with impatience. "What are you talking about? Nobody else is trained like that."

"Not true."

They stared at her.

"Who else?" Chris said.

They waited.

"You say they seemed to be cooperating with Eliot," she continued, "but trained by the Mossad."

They nodded.

"Think about it," she said.

"My God," Chris said. "You just described *us.*"

9

The implications kept Chris awake. He lay on the sofa and stared toward dawn beyond the window. Past the closed bedroom door, he heard a muted gasp—Saul and Erika making love. He closed his eyes, struggling to ignore what he heard, forcing himself to remember.

1966. After he and Saul had finished their tour in Nam and their stint in Special Forces, Eliot had wanted them to receive extra training, "final polish" he'd called it. Flying separately to Heathrow Airport outside London, they'd rendezvoused at the baggage area. With keys they'd been given, they'd opened lockers and taken out expensive luggage filled with French clothing. Each suitcase had also contained a yarmulke.

During the flight to Tel Aviv, they'd changed clothes in the washroom. A stewardess put their discarded outfits in shopping bags and stuffed them in an empty food container at the rear of the plane. At the airport, once past customs, they were greeted by a heavy middle-aged woman who called them affectionate nicknames. In their skullcaps and French clothing, they looked like typical Parisian Jews embarking on their first kibbutz experience, and so it would have seemed when they boarded a bus designated for travel outside the city.

A few hours later, they were given rooms in a gymnasium–residence complex similar to a YMCA in America. Instructed to go at once to the main hall, they and twenty other students were met by an old man who introduced himself as Andre Rothberg. His casual appearance belied the deadly legend he'd created for himself. Bald and wrinkled, dressed in white shoes, white trousers and a white shirt, he resembled a genteel sportsman. But his history told of a very different man. His father, the fencing instructor for the last Russian czar, had taught Andre the quickness and coordination of hand and eye that had propelled him through the sports activities of Cambridge in the thirties, British naval intelligence during the Second World War, and finally the Israeli intelligence community after the '48 truce. Though Jewish, he'd remained a British citizen and thus had never been given access to the inner circles of power in Israel. Undaunted, he'd made his own valuable contribution by devising a system of self-defense training unequaled for its precision. Rothberg called it "killer-instinct training," and the performance Chris and Saul witnessed that day stunned them.

Using a trolley suspended by a chain from the ceiling of the vast room, an assistant pushed in the naked cadaver of a male, six feet tall, robust, recently deceased, in his twenties. Before the corpse had been harnessed and hooked in an upright position, it must have been stored on its back, where blood had settled, for the posterior side was blue-black while the front was yellow. It hung in a standing posture, feet on the floor, next to Rothberg. He took a large scalpel and made a ten-inch slash on each side of the chest, then across the bottom. With additional strokes, he separated the subcutaneous tissue from the rib cage and lifted the flap to expose the bones. He waited while his students inspected his work, drawing their attention to the undamaged ribs. He put the flap back in place and sealed the incisions with surgical tape.

Chris never forgot. Rothberg turned so his back was to the corpse. He stood flat-footed, legs spread apart, holding his arms out, palms down, parallel to the floor. His assistant placed a coin on the back of each hand. The assistant counted to three. In a blur, Rothberg flipped his hands over and caught the coins. But at the same time the corpse jerked back, its harness snapping against the hook that suspended it. Rothberg showed the coins he'd caught. He put them in his pocket and turned to the corpse, stripping the surgical tape, raising the skin flap. The ribs on both sides had been shattered. Not only had Rothberg flipped his hands to catch the coins with eyeblink speed. At the same instant, he'd also rammed his elbows back to strike the corpse, a movement so swift it was undetectable. The agility would have been remarkable in anyone, let alone a man in his sixties. As the other students murmured their surprise, Chris glanced around him, for the first time noticing Erika.

"So you see," Rothberg explained, "if our friend were still alive, his shattered ribs would have punctured his lungs. He'd have died from asphyxiation due to foam produced by the blood and air in his lungs. Cyanotic in three minutes, dead in sixteen—plenty of time to inject a drug if called for. But most important, an irreparable wound that results in little damage to your own ability to defend yourself against others. For the three major weapons your body offers you, which do not lose their ability to function even under the most serious impact, are the tip of your elbow, the web of skin between your thumb and first finger, and the heel of your palm. In the future, you will learn to use these weapons with speed, coordination, and the proper stance for balance. But for now we'll adjourn to dinner. Tonight I shall demonstrate the proper use of the garotte and the knife. For the next few days, it's all show and tell."

A "few days" turned out to be seven weeks. From dawn till sunset, every day except for the Jewish Sabbath, Chris and Saul went through the most intensive training they'd ever received, Special Forces included. Demonstrations were followed by practice sessions and then by grueling exercise. They learned fencing and ballet.

"For agility," Rothberg explained. "You must understand the need for refinement. Endurance doesn't matter, nor does strength. It makes no difference how huge and sturdy your opponent may be in comparison to yourself. A well-placed blow to the proper spot will kill him. Reflex—that's the most important factor, hence the fencing and the ballet. You must learn to control your body, to feel at home with it, to make your mind and muscle one. Thoughts must be transmitted instantly into action. Hesitation, faulty timing, and misplaced blows allow your opponent the chance to kill you. Speed, coordination, and reflex—these are your weapons as much as your body. Practice till you're too exhausted to move, till your prior training—as brutal as it was—seems like a holiday. Then practice more."

When not in the classrooms or the gym, Chris and Saul spent hours in their room, developing their skills. In imitation of Rothberg, Chris held out his arms, palms down. Saul put a coin on the back of each hand. Chris jerked his hands away and tried to turn his palms to catch the falling coins. Then it was Saul's turn to try. For the first week, they thought the trick was impossible. The coins would strike the floor, or Chris and Saul would catch the coins too low and awkwardly. "You just got killed," they'd tell each other. By the end of the second week, their reflexes had improved sufficiently for them to catch the coins in one smooth blur. The coins seemed suspended in the air, captured before they began to fall.

But the coins were merely a device, not the final purpose. Once the skill of catching them had been mastered, another difficulty was added. As Rothberg explained, they had to learn not only how to deliver blows backward, with their elbows, instantly—but also how to do it forward, with the heels of the palms, equally fast. Practicing this second method of attack, Chris and Saul put pencils on a table. When they jerked their hands from the coins, they had to jab the pencils off the table before they caught the coins. Again the trick seemed impossible. They failed to catch the coins, or they missed the pencils, or they moved so clumsily that again they told each other, "You just got killed."

Miraculously, by the end of the third week, they could manage both tricks at once. But jabbing the pencils wasn't the final purpose either. To their speed and coordination, they now added accuracy, spreading ink on the palm of each hand, then dropping the coins and striking at a circle on a sheet of paper tacked to the wall. At first they either failed to leave an inky palmprint in the circle or else failed to catch the coins, but by the beginning of the fifth week, they could study the well-placed ink stains, glance down at the coins in their hands, and congratulate themselves. "The other guy got killed." Eventually Rothberg judged them skilled enough to practice on cadavers. But the last week he insisted on the final test. "Put the coins in your pocket. Slip on these padded vests," he told them. "Practice on yourselves."

Chris lay on the sofa in the cottage, watching sunlight glint off the window. The Potomac whispered along its bank. A breeze nudged branches. Birds sang. He remembered, on that kibbutz in Israel there'd been no birds. Only heat and sand and seven weeks of sweat and concentration and pain. But when his killer-instinct training had been completed, he'd been as close as he would ever come to the goal of perfection Eliot constantly recommended—among the chosen few, the best, the most disciplined, capable, deadly, a world-class operative about to begin his career. In 1966, he thought. When I was young.

Now after successes, defeats, and betrayals, Chris mused on the years that had intervened. The agency, the monastery, the agency again, his probation in Rome, the Church of the Moon, the grave he'd dug in Panama. The pattern seemed predetermined. At the age of thirty-six, he considered everything he'd learned. He analyzed those seven weeks in Israel, recalling what Erika had said—that the description of the men who'd hunted Saul in Atlantic City also matched Saul and himself—men affiliated with Eliot but trained by the Mossad. Still, as hard as Chris tried, he couldn't remember any other Americans at Rothberg's school. The implication made his stomach sink. Had Eliot lied about that as well? Had he sent others to Rothberg at different times, even though he'd promised Chris and Saul they were unique? Why would Eliot lie about that?

Chris remembered something else. As Erika moaned in sexual climax beyond the closed door of the bedroom, he relived the moment sixteen years ago in Israel when he'd first seen her. Shortly afterward, Saul had been taken from Chris's group and put with Erika's. Despite the intensive schedule, they'd somehow found the time to become lovers. Chris felt a weight on his chest. In those days, his need to please Eliot had been so great he'd denied all emotion except loyalty to his father and his brother. He'd purged himself of any wish for gratification and fulfillment—unless his father permitted it. Sex was allowed for therapeutic purposes. But a love affair was unthinkable. "It compromises you," Eliot had said. "Emotion's a liability. It prevents you from concentrating. In a mission, it gets you killed. Besides, a lover might turn against you. Or an enemy might hold her hostage to force you to turn against the agency. No, the only people you can love and trust and depend on are myself and Saul." The weight pressed harder on his chest. Bitterness scalded him. For despite his conditioning, Chris had eventually experienced emotion—not love for a woman, but guilt for the things he'd done, and shame for having failed his father. Confusion tore at him. He'd sacrificed what he now realized were basic human needs in order to please his father. Now his father had turned against him. Among his deceptions, had Eliot lied about love as well? Chris seethed with regret for the life he might have known, a life his shame and guilt would not allow him now. If not for his need to help Saul, he'd have killed himself to stop the agony of self-disgust. The things Eliot made me do, he thought. He clenched his fists. And the normalcy I was never granted. Incapable of anger toward Saul, he nonetheless felt envious, for Saul had managed to stay true to Eliot and yet find self-fulfillment. He felt capable of rage toward Eliot, though. He shuddered, squeezing his eyes shut, wincing with regret. If things had been different, he wondered, rigidly shaking his head, if he and not Saul had been put in Erika's group in Israel—his throat clamped shut—would *he* now be the one to hold her as she shuddered?

10

Erika studied herself in the dressing room's mirror. Through the louvers in the door, she heard two saleswomen talking. She'd arrived at ten, as the department store opened. Few customers had been waiting to get in, so her grimy skirt and blouse hadn't attracted much attention. Walking quickly through the women's department, she'd chosen bras and panties, a corduroy jacket, a paisley blouse, jeans, and high leather boots. She changed in the dressing room.

Clutching her discarded clothes, she opened the door and peered out cautiously, seeing no other customers. The saleswomen turned as she approached.

"Don't ever try to change a flat tire in a brand new outfit," Erika said. "I should have called Triple A."

"Or your boyfriend," the younger woman said, apparently noticing Erika didn't wear a wedding ring.

"I just broke up with him. To tell the truth, he was useless."

The saleswomen laughed.

"I know what you mean," the younger one said. "My boyfriend's useless too. Except for—"

They laughed again.

"I wish I had your figure," the older one said. "Those clothes fit you perfectly."

"After the flat tire, something had to go right. Would you mind taking care of these?" She held up the grimy slacks and blouse.

"I've got just the place." The younger woman dropped them in a wastecan behind the counter. While the older woman cut off the tags on the new clothes, Erika paid for them, smiling to herself at the name on the receipt she was given. Goldbloom's. Might as well stay kosher, she thought.

In the men's department, she glanced at the paper on which Saul and Chris had written their sizes, choosing poplin slacks, a tennis shirt, and a lightweight windbreaker for Saul, a tan oxford shirt and pale blue summer suit for Chris. Her timing was perfect. At precisely ten-thirty, she paused at the pay phone near the lost-and-found counter by the exit. She told the Alexandria operator the Washington number, inserted the proper coins, and listened as the phone buzzed once before a woman's voice replied, "Good morning, Israeli embassy."

"*Ma echpat li?*"

11

In English, the phrase meant, "I should care?" It corresponded with the Hebrew lettering on a poster of a Jewish washerwoman with her arms raised in either surrender or disgust that hung on the wall directly above the switchboard in the embassy's communications center. The operator knew at once to relay the call to an emergency switchboard in the basement.

Misha Pletz, a harried man of thirty-five with a mustache and a receding hairline—chief of logistics for the Mossad on the United States eastern seaboard—plugged in his jack. "One moment please." He turned on a meter next to his desk and watched a dial. The device measured the electrical current on the phone line. If the line had been tapped, the drain of electricity would have caused the dial to veer from its normal position. The needle showed a normal current. *"Shalom,"* Pletz said.

A woman's attractive husky voice spoke slowly to him. "Don't take any outside calls. Fourteen-thirty."

A bell rang abruptly, indicating the line had been disconnected.

Pletz unplugged his jack. He drew his finger down the index on the wall to the left of his switchboard. Pulling out this day's card, he stared at a list of numbers. The call had come through at ten-thirty. Beside that number, he found the name of the operative assigned that time for checking in during emergencies. BERNSTEIN, ERIKA.

Pletz frowned. For the past thirty-six hours—since the attempted assassination at her apartment—no one at the embassy had known where Erika was or if she was still alive. The police had come to the embassy early yesterday morning, explaining what had happened, wanting information about her. They'd been greeted by the personnel director, who expressed dismay at the killings and offered to help in every way. His help amounted to showing the police the embassy's file on Erika, a carefully edited document that established her cover as a clerk and completely obscured her actual function as a colonel in the Mossad. She kept to herself, the personnel director explained. She had few friends. He provided the names. Having learned a lot but in effect nothing, the detectives left, dissatisfied. Pletz assumed they'd watch the embassy in case Erika showed up, though his informants had told him last night that the investigation had inexplicably been terminated. Since then, Pletz had waited. Because she should have called him as soon as possible, her thirty-six hours of silence suggested she was dead.

But now she'd made contact. Pletz's relief changed quickly to alarm. She'd told him, "Don't take any outside calls," a code phrase instructing him to abandon all collaboration with any foreign intelligence service, even the United States. She'd mentioned "fourteen-thirty," military time for 2:30 P.M., the signal for when she'd call back, presumably from a safer phone. Four hours from now. Pletz hated waiting.

What the hell was going on?

12

"They'll stay together," Eliot said. "Both of them with the woman."

"Agreed," his assistant said. "Together they'd have a better chance to protect themselves."

"And use her contacts." For security reasons, Eliot avoided his office as much as possible. Using his greenhouse as a distraction, he studied the hint of blight on an American Beauty Rose. "We have to assume she'll call her embassy. Its scrambler system's too sophisticated for us to intercept her conversations."

His assistant glanced toward the square-faced muscular sentry at each entrance to the greenhouse. Eliot could have had his pick of regular agency personnel to guard him. Instead he'd chosen a pair the assistant had never heard of, introducing them only as Castor and Pollux, unfamiliar cryptonyms. The house, the grounds, and the street were also being guarded, but those teams had been chosen by the assistant himself. The sanctum, though—Eliot apparently trusted only these men to guard him here. The assistant was puzzled.

"But we can guess what she says to her embassy." Eliot's hand trembled slightly as he treated the rose's blight with a chemical. "In her place, I'd need money and identification—passports, drivers' licenses, credit cards, presumably under several different names. The Israelis don't trust outside help. They do that kind of job in their embassy."

The assistant handed Eliot a cloth to wipe his hands. "So they'll have to deliver a package to her."

Eliot studied him with uncustomary approval. "Good. You see my point. Arrange to have anyone who leaves the embassy followed."

"We'll need a lot of people."

"Use the sanction as your excuse. Tell the KGB and the other networks that the courier might lead them to Remus. Tell them we're close to finding the violator."

Now it was the assistant's turn to say, "Good."

"Amazing, the way things get out of control. If Romulus had been killed in Atlantic City, none of the other problems would have happened."

"Remus would still have violated the sanction."

"He doesn't matter. Romulus does. The Paradigm Foundation had to be destroyed. The president had to be convinced the Israelis did it." Eliot winced; the blight had spread to another rose. "But after Colorado, once we assumed which friends they'd ask for help, we shouldn't have failed at the woman's apartment. We're a step behind them, but we shouldn't be. I chose Saul because he's past the age of maximum ability, like an athlete on the decline. I never dreamed he'd—"

"—make a comeback?"

Eliot shrugged. "The same with Chris. I was sure he'd use his special knowledge of Saul to find him. But after the monastery, and particularly after what happened in Bangkok, I never dreamed he'd stay alive this long. It's going bad." Eliot frowned. "If they learn the truth . . ."

"How could they?"

"Two weeks ago, I'd have said they couldn't. But with the luck they've been having . . ." Eliot's face seemed pinched. "Or maybe it's more than luck."

13

"I can have you in Israel by tomorrow," Pletz told Erika from the scrambler-protected phone in his office. "You'd be secure while we sort this out."

"I can't." Erika's husky voice was worried. "I have to stay with Chris and Saul."

"We can't protect your friends. If the other agencies found out we were helping someone who violated the sanction—"

"That's not the issue. Yes, they're friends, but they're involved in something besides the sanction, something important enough that to kill them it didn't matter if I got killed as well. I want to find out what. I can tell you this. It's related to the Mossad."

Pletz stiffened. "How? You know we didn't try to kill you."

"Someone wants to make it look as if you did."

"But that's crazy. Why?"

"That's what I want to find out. I can't talk longer. I've got to assume this call is being traced. Get me the identification papers I asked for—the drivers' licenses, the credit cards. And something else."

"I know. The money."

"Something more important."

Pletz asked, "What?" He gasped when he heard the reply.

14

As the well-dressed man stepped from the embassy, squinting from the sun, carrying a briefcase, he took for granted he was being watched. All day, the embassy's security team had been noticing an unusual amount of surveillance. Anyone leaving the premises, no matter if on foot or in a vehicle, was being followed. In turn the security team, cooperating with Pletz, had arranged for an unusual number of couriers to leave the building. Given the intense activity, this particular courier had a good chance of completing his mission.

He stopped at a bookstore first and bought Stephen King's new novel. He walked another block and stepped in Silverstein's Kosher Market, buying matzos and chicken-liver pâté. Next he went to a liquor store and chose white wine. In another block, he arrived at his apartment building, soon to be greeted by his girlfriend.

He'd substituted his briefcase for an identical one in the kosher market. Already the grocer had hidden the original after removing a package from it. Wrapped in butcher's paper, labeled "smoked salmon," the package lay now at the bottom of a large cardboard box, covered by kosher meats and gourmet canned goods. While the grocer's wife watched the store, Silverstein carried the box to his delivery truck in the alley. He loaded several other boxes in front of the first one and drove across town to the Marren Gold Catering Service.

The following morning, Gold's Catering delivered the boxes to the Georgetown home of Dr. Benjamin Schatner, where guests soon arrived from the synagogue to congratulate Schatner's son on a brilliantly performed Bar Mitzvah. After the reception, one of the guests, Bernie Keltz, decided to drive his family down to George Washington's estate at Mount Vernon. The mansion was only twenty miles away, Keltz's children had never seen it, and the flowers would be in bloom.

Keltz parked the car in the visitors' lot. He walked with his wife and two young daughters along a path till they stopped at a gate. Smiling in the pleasant breeze, they gazed along a sweeping lawn toward the mansion at the far end of the grounds. As they strolled beneath soaring trees past glorious gardens, Keltz explained to his daughters about the smaller buildings: the spinninghouse, the smokehouse, the warehouse. "The estate was like a village. Completely self-sufficient." His daughters played a jumping game on the weathered brick path.

At half-past three, Keltz's wife set her large burlap purse on the floor in front of a display case in the Washington's Home Is Your Home gift shop. Next to her, Erika studied a rack of colorful slides. While Keltz bought a cast-metal replica of the Washington Monument, insisting it be gift-wrapped, Erika picked up the purse and left the estate.

15

Beside the drivers' licenses and credit cards, the computer printout stretched across the dining table in the cottage near the Potomac. As the river whispered beyond the sunset-tinted screen of an open window, Saul, Chris, and Erika stared down at the paper. It showed a list of names—all Americans who, though not affiliated with the Mossad, had nonetheless received killer-instinct training at Andre Rothberg's school in Israel. Though Erika's request had puzzled him, Misha Pletz had gathered the information from the embassy's computers.

1965 Sgt. First Class Kevin McElroy, U.S.A., S.F.
       Sgt. First Class Thomas Conlin, U.S.A., S.F.
1966 Lt. Saul Grisman, U.S.A., S.F.
       Lt. Christopher Kilmoonie, U.S.A., S.F.

1967 Staff Sgt. Neil Pratt, U.S.A., Rangers
     Staff Sgt. Bernard Halliday, U.S.A., Rangers
1968 Lt. Timothy Drew, U.S.A., S.F.
     Lt. Andrew Hicks, U.S.A., S.F.
1969 Gunnery Sgt. James Thomas, U.S.M.C., Recon
     Gunnery Sgt. William Fletcher, U.S.M.C., Recon
1970 Petty Officer Arnold Hackett, U.S.N., Seals
     Petty Officer David Pews, U.S.N., Seals

The list continued—nine years, eighteen names.

Chris said, "I don't believe it."

Erika glanced at him. "You thought you were unique?"

"Eliot told us we were. He said he wanted to make us special. The only operatives in the world with our particular combination of skills."

She shrugged. "Maybe he thought you turned out so well he decided to repeat the idea."

Saul shook his head. "But we went to Israel in '66. This list shows two other men went there before us. Eliot lied when he said we were the only ones."

"Even later," Chris said. "In the seventies. After the rest of those men had killer-instinct training, he still kept telling us we were the only two of our kind."

Erika glanced back toward the list. "Maybe he wanted you to feel unique."

"My ego isn't tender," Chris said. "I wouldn't have cared how many other men were trained the same as I was. All I wanted was to do my job well."

"And please Eliot," Saul said.

Chris nodded. "That's why we wanted to do our jobs well. Why the hell would he lie about these other men?"

"We're not sure Eliot's the one who arranged for these other men to study with Rothberg," Erika said.

"We have to assume he did."

"Not yet we don't," she answered. "We can't afford assumptions. Maybe somebody else had the same idea Eliot did. For now, we know just what's on this list. So what does it tell us?"

"Patterns," Saul said. "The men were sent in pairs."

"Like us," Chris said.

"Each member of a pair had the same rank. In '65, McElroy and Conlin were sergeants. In '66, Saul and I were lieutenants. In '67, Pratt and Halliday were staff sergeants." Saul drew a finger down the list, noting other paired ranks: gunnery sergeants and petty officers.

"Each member of a pair came from the same military branch," Chris said. "McElroy and Conlin belonged to Special Forces."

"Like us," Saul said, echoing Chris's remark.

"Pratt and Halliday were in the Rangers. Thomas and Fletcher were from Marine Reconnaissance. Hackett and Pews were Navy Seals."

"But the pattern isn't consistent," Erika said. "In that respect, the pairs are different from each other. Four different military units—Special Forces, Rangers, Recon, Seals."

"They're different, but they're the same," Chris said.

Erika frowned in confusion.

Saul explained, "They're elite. Those units are the best-trained cadres we've got."

"Of course," she said.

Saul didn't need to elaborate. She knew as well as he did that the U.S. military was structured like a pyramid. The better the training, the fewer soldiers received it. Near the top were the army's Rangers and the Marine Corps' Recon unit—small, extremely well prepared. But the army's Special Forces stood above them, even smaller and better prepared. At the summit, the smallest, best-prepared group was the navy's Seals. This hierarchy was part of a system of checks and balances that the U.S. government imposed on the military. If the Rangers or Recon attempted a coup, Special Forces would be called in to stop them. In turn, if Special Forces attempted a coup, the Seals would be brought in to stop them. The question remained—who would stop the Seals if *they* tried a coup?

"It doesn't matter if those units are different from one another," Chris said. "Compared to conventional military forces, they're in a class by themselves. The best."

"Okay, it makes sense," Erika said. "Take soldiers from exclusive American cadres. Give them even more sophisticated training in Israel. But why?"

"And why those particular men?" Saul asked. "And why so few of them? What's the principle of selection?"

Erika frowned. "I know I said we shouldn't make assumptions, but I'm going to make one anyhow. Those men were sent to Israel from 1965 to 1973. Do you suppose—?" She studied their faces. "Maybe they distinguished themselves in combat."

"Where? In Nam?" Chris said. "Like us?"

"The years fit. By '65, America was deeply involved in the fighting. By '73, America had left. Maybe those men were war heroes. The best of the best. Once they proved their ability under fire, how much better could they get? Only killer-instinct training would be higher."

"You're describing men who'd eventually be better prepared than the Seals."

"I'm describing yourselves," she said.

Chris and Saul stared at each other.

"Something's missing," Chris said. "I can feel it. Something important. We've got to find out more about these men."

16

Sam Parker left the glass and chrome structure, enjoying the sweet smogless Sunday breeze. As senior computer programmer for the National Defense Agency, he spent most of his days in windowless, temperature-controlled, antiseptic rooms. Not that he minded. After all, the computer had to be protected. But despite the intellectual stimulation of his work, he did mind coming here on Sunday. The trouble with being an expert was that underlings kept passing their mistakes to him.

He glanced from D.C. across the river toward Virginia and the Pentagon. Its parking lot, like the defense agency's, was almost deserted. Sure, they're at home drinking martinis, grilling steaks the same as I should be, he thought as he walked toward his drab brown, fuel-efficient, made-in-America car. Martinis? In truth, Parker didn't drink, though he didn't object if others did, in moderation. Even on Sunday, he wore a jacket and tie to go to work. He admired propriety and was constantly embarrassed by the way his freckles and red hair made him stand out in a crowd. At fifty-five, he hoped the red would soon turn diplomatic gray.

Driving from the parking lot, he didn't notice the Pinto that began to follow him. Nor five minutes later did he notice the other car, a Toyota, till it weaved from the passing lane, scraping his left front fender, cutting him off. Sunday drivers, he raged. Probably a tourist. He pulled to the side of the road. His fury cooled as he shut off his engine and saw the Toyota's driver get out. An absolutely gorgeous woman, tall and lithe, with long dark hair, wearing jeans and boots. She approached him, smiling. Well, he thought, if he had to have an accident, he might as well enjoy it.

He stepped out, trying his best to look stern. "Young lady, I hope you've got insurance."

She touched his shoulder. "I'm so scared. I don't know how it happened." She embraced him. As he felt her breasts against his chest, he heard a car stop. Two men suddenly flanked him, a muscular Jew and, Jesus, the other guy looked like an Irishman.

"Anybody hurt?" the Irishman said.

The Jew leaned close. Parker flinched, feeling something sting his arm.

His vision blurred.

17

They did it quickly. Saul leaned Parker's limp body back in his car, then slid beside him and drove toward a break in traffic before any curious motorists had a chance to stop. Erika followed in the Toyota, Chris in the Pinto. They soon split up, each taking a different exit. Making sure no one followed them, they headed south and rendezvoused at the cottage.

Parker was alert by then. He struggled as Saul tied him to a chair in the living room.

"I've seen your faces," Parker said foolishly. "I saw some of the roads you used to get here. Kidnapping's a federal offense. You'll go to jail for this."

Saul squinted at him.

"Oh," Parker said, his eyes bleak with understanding. "Please, don't kill me. I promise I won't say a word."

Chris approached him.

"My wife's expecting me home at four," Parker warned. "When I'm late, she'll call Security."

"She already has. It's *after* four. But how can they find you?"

"Oh," Parker moaned again. He strained at the ropes around him. "What do you want?"

"It's obvious, isn't it? Information."

"Promise you won't hurt me. I'll tell you anything."

"You'll tell us lies."

"No, I'll cooperate."

"We know you will." Chris rolled up Parker's sleeve. Parker gaped as Chris rubbed his arm with alcohol, then filled a hypodermic from a vial. "It feels like Valium," Chris said. "Since you've got no choice, you might as well stop fighting and enjoy it." He slid the needle in Parker's arm.

The interrogation lasted thirty minutes. The Israeli embassy had supplied all the information it could. Chris needed another source. Because the men he was interested in had all been in the U.S. military, he knew he'd find the background he wanted in the National Defense Agency's computers. The trick was to gain access to the computers, and the first step was to learn the codes that would make the computers responsive to questions. The wrong codes would trigger an alarm, alerting the NDA's security force that someone without clearance was trying to infiltrate the databank.

Torture was an obsolete method of interrogation. It took too long, and even when a subject seemed to have been broken, he sometimes lied convincingly or told only part of the truth. But Sodium Amytal—the same drug Eliot had used on Chris in the dentist's office in Panama—was quick and reliable.

Voice slurred, Parker told Chris everything he wanted to know. The codes were changed weekly. There were three of them: a numerical sequence, an alphabetical sequence, and a password. The numerical sequence was a joke of sorts, a variation on Parker's social security number. Satisfied they could communicate with the computers, Chris drove Parker back to Washington.

En route, Parker wakened, complaining that his mouth felt dry. "Here, sip this Coke," Chris told him.

Parker said it helped. He sounded groggy. "You're letting me go?"

"Why not? You did your part. We've got what we wanted."

The Coke had been mixed with scopolamine. By the time they

arrived in Washington, Parker had become hysterical, flailing at hallucinations of spiders that tried to smother him. Chris let him out in
a porno district where prostitutes backed away from Parker's wails and
insane gesticulations.

The scopolamine would wear off by the next day. Parker would
find himself in a psychiatric ward. Though his hallucinations would
have disappeared, another effect of the drug would persist. His memory
of the last two days would have been erased. He wouldn't recall being
kidnapped. He wouldn't recall his interrogation or the cottage or Chris,
Saul, and Erika. The authorities, having been warned by Parker's wife
about his disappearance, would feel relieved to have found him. They'd
conclude he wasn't the saint he pretended to be. A porno district. Sure,
the hypocrite had gotten more fun than he bargained for. By the time
the authorities investigated further, Saul and Erika would have finished
the job.

18

The Haven Motel was half hidden behind a steak house, a movie
theater, and a bar on the outskirts of Washington. "All the comforts,"
Saul said as he parked near the office. He and Erika had chosen the
place because it looked sleazy enough so a clerk wouldn't question why
they'd rent a room for just a few hours. But it wasn't sleazy enough that
the police would make a habit of rousting it.

While she waited in the car, Saul went in the office. The soft drink
machine had an Out of Order sign. The Naugahyde sofa was cracked.
The plastic plants were dusty. Behind the counter, a woman barely
turned from a Clint Eastwood movie on television. Saul registered as
Mr. and Mrs. Harold Cain. The only time the woman looked interested
was when she took his money.

Back in the car, Saul drove to the unit assigned to him. He turned
the Pinto around, noting a driveway that led to a side street. Checking
the room, they found a black and white television, a bureau with glass
stains, a bed with wrinkled sheets. The faucet dripped in the bathtub.

They carried several boxes in. Using one of the credit cards Misha

Pletz had supplied, they'd gone to a Radio Shack and bought a computer, printer, and telephone modem. Working quickly, they unpacked the components, integrated, and tested them. Saul went outside, chose a concealed vantage behind a garbage bin, and studied the entrances to the motel's parking area. If he saw trouble approaching, he could warn Erika, using a small walkie-talkie he'd also bought from Radio Shack.

In the room, Erika picked up the phone and touched a sequence of numbers Parker had mentioned. The sequence put her in contact with the NDA. She heard a beep from the phone. The computer had answered its number, awaiting instructions. She touched an alphabetical sequence—SUNSHINE, the name of Parker's cocker spaniel—and heard another beep; the computer was primed to gather information. This method of dealing with the computer had been designed to allow the efficient exchange of data over long distance. Parker's equivalent in San Diego, for example, didn't have to come to Washington to use the NDA's computer, nor did he have to contact Parker and explain what he needed. All he had to do was phone the computer directly. The method was simple and secure, but to make it work, you had to know the codes.

Erika set the phone in the modem, a small receptacle for the ear- and mouth-piece, linked to the computer. She sat at the keyboard, typing instructions. The message passed through the modem and the phone to the NDA's databank. Parker had explained that his computer wouldn't release information unless it received the code word FETCH. She typed this now. The printer next to her began to clatter, translating the electronic signals received through the phone. She waited, hoping the NDA's security force wouldn't trace the phone call.

The printer stopped. Nodding, she typed GOOD DOG, the sign-off code Parker had given her, turned the computer off, put the phone on its cradle, and grabbed the printouts.

19

Chris slumped discouraged on the sofa. The night's rain added to his gloom, drumming on the cottage's roof. Drops trickled down the chimney, landing on the burnt wood in the fireplace, raising the bitter smell of ashes. He felt damp. "If there's another pattern, I don't see it."

Saul and Erika frowned at the printouts on the table. She'd asked only for essential data: place and date of birth, religious affiliation, education, special skills, commanding officers, battle commendations.

"None of them was born at the same time or place," she said. "They're a mixture of religions. They're each specialists in different things. They had different commanding officers and served in different areas of Southeast Asia. What's the connection? Unless we're wrong, there has to be *something* that links them together."

Chris stood wearily, crossing the room toward the table. He paused beside Erika, reading the printouts again. "There." He pointed down the left side of the page. "Each pair was educated in the same city, but the cities are different from each other. Omaha, Philadelphia, Johnstown, Akron. It doesn't make sense. And over here." He pointed to the right. "They each had cryptonyms, but I don't see any other pattern. Butes and Erectheus. What the hell does *that* mean?"

He ignored the data he'd already eliminated, focusing on the information that puzzled him.

Omaha, Neb. Kevin McElroy. Castor.
Omaha, Neb. Thomas Conlin. Pollux.

Philadelphia, Pa. Saul Grisman. Romulus.
Philadelphia, Pa. Christopher Kilmoonie. Remus.

Johnstown, Pa. Neil Pratt. Cadmus.
Johnstown, Pa. Bernard Halliday. Cilix.

Akron, Ohio. Timothy Drew. Amphion.
Akron, Ohio. Andrew Wilks. Zethus.

Shade Gap, Pa. James Thomas. Butes.
Shade Gap, Pa. William Fletcher. Erectheus.

Gary, Ind. Arnold Hackett. Atlas.
Gary, Ind. David Pews. Prometheus.

The list continued—nine pairs, eighteen names.

"Pennsylvania's mentioned often," Saul said.

"But what's it got to do with Nebraska, Ohio, and Indiana?"

"Let's try the cryptonyms," Erika said. "The names are foreign. Greek and Roman, right? From myth."

"The category's too general. That's like saying Omaha and Philadelphia are in the United States," Chris said. "We've got to find a more specific connection. Cadmus and Cilix? Amphion and Zethus? I don't know who they were or what they did, let alone what they've got to do with each other."

"Then start with the pair you do know," Erika said. "Yourselves. Romulus and Remus."

"Common knowledge. They're the brothers who founded Rome," Saul said.

"But we never founded anything, and we're not brothers," Chris said.

"We might as well be." Saul turned to Erika. "Castor and Pollux. They sound familiar. Something to do with the sky. A constellation."

Erika nodded. "When I learned night navigation, my instructor said to let the ancient warriors guide me. Castor and Pollux. They're called the Gemini—the morning and evening stars."

"Gemini," Chris said. "Twins."

"What other names look familiar?" Saul asked. "Here—at the bottom. Atlas."

"The strong man who holds the sky above the earth."

"Prometheus."

"He stole fire from the gods and gave it to humans."

"But there's no connection between them."

"Maybe," Erika said.

Chris and Saul looked at her.

"What we need is an index to myth," she told them. "I think I know the pattern now, but I have to find out who Cadmus and Cilix and the others were."

"There's a dictionary over here," Chris said, checking several shelves of books beside the fireplace. "A lot of old paperbacks. Here. A desk encyclopedia." Two volumes. He picked up the first, turning its dog-eared pages. "Atlas," he said and started reading. He glanced up abruptly. "Shit."

"What is it?" Saul looked startled.

"What's the other cryptonym that begins with A?"

Saul quickly scanned the printout. "Amphion. He's paired with Zethus."

Chris urgently flipped pages, reading. "Jesus, I don't believe it. Tell me the other names."

"Alphabetically? Butes is paired with Erectheus, and Cadmus is paired with Cilix."

Chris kept flipping pages, reading anxiously. "I know the pattern. I know how they're related."

The room was still. "They're related in the most basic way there is," Erika said.

"You figured it out."

"I wasn't really sure till I saw the look on your face."

"Atlas and Prometheus were brothers. Amphion and Zethus were twins."

"Like Castor and Pollux," Saul said.

"Butes and Erectheus? *Brothers.* Cadmus and Cilix? *Brothers.* Romulus and Remus . . ."

"But where's the parallel?" Saul spun to the printouts. "Castor and Pollux were twins, but the men assigned those cryptonyms are McElroy and Conlin. They sure as hell don't sound like twins."

"That's true," Erika said. "And here, farther down, Pratt and Halliday don't sound related, but they've been given cryptonyms that refer to brothers. It's the same with all the other names. Drew and Wilks, Thomas and Fletcher, Hackett and Pews—if they're not related, why give them cryptonyms that refer to brothers?"

"Maybe they came from broken homes," Chris said. "If their parents got divorced and married someone else, McElroy and Conlin could have different names but still be related."

"Maybe in one case," Erika said. "But all of them from broken homes with parents remarried?"

"I know. It's stretching," Chris agreed.

"Besides, you and Saul don't come from a broken home. As you said, you're not related." Suddenly her eyes became wary. She turned

144

to Saul. "Then *you* said something else. You said, 'We might as well be.' Why did you say that?"

Saul shrugged. "We've known each other almost as long as if we'd been brothers. Since we were five. Right, Chris?"

Chris smiled. "You're the best friend I've got."

"But why?" Erika said, her voice strained with confusion. "I don't mean why you're friends. I mean why you've known each other so long. Did you grow up in the same neighborhood?"

"In a way. We met at the school," Saul said.

"*What* school?" Erika frowned.

"The Franklin School for Boys in Philadelphia. Where we were raised. We didn't come from a broken home. Hell, we didn't come from any home at all. We're orphans."

Chris stared toward the rain beyond the window.

"That's the other puzzling detail in the pattern," Erika said. "Each pair of men was educated in the same city. McElroy and Conlin in Omaha. You and Chris in Philadelphia. The others in Akron and Shade Gap and so on. Since all their cryptonyms form a pattern, you'd think those cities would form a pattern as well."

"They do," Chris said. In anger, he turned from the rain at the window. "Boys' Home."

"What?" Saul stared in dismay.

"It's in Akron." Trembling with rage, Chris walked toward Saul and Erika. "The Haven for Boys is in Omaha. Pennsylvania has the Johnstown Boys' Academy and the Shade Gap Boys' Institute, not to mention our own Franklin School for Boys in Philadelphia. The cities on these printouts read like the top ten boys' schools in the country. But don't let the titles fool you," Chris told Erika bitterly. "Haven for Boys, or School for Boys, or Boys' Institute. They all mean the same damn thing: orphanage." He clenched his teeth. "The men on this list all share one thing in common with Saul and me. They're orphans. Each pair was raised in the same institution. That's why their cryptonyms suggest they're brothers, even though their last names are different." Chris breathed painfully. "Because when each member of a pair met the other, their loneliness forced them into a bond. They formed so strong a friendship they became the emotional equivalent of bloodbrothers. Goddamn him, Saul! Do you understand what he did to us?"

Saul nodded. "Eliot lied to us in the most fundamental way I can think of. He never loved us. All along—from the start—he used us."

Erika clutched Saul and Chris strongly by the arms. "Would one of you mind telling me what in God's name you're talking about?"

"It takes a lifetime," Chris said. He slumped on the sofa and moaned.

20

The rain fell harder, making the morning seem like dusk. Eliot stood at his office window, brooding, unaware of the stormy Virginia landscape. His skin looked as gray as the rain. Behind him, someone knocked on his door. He didn't turn to see who entered.

"Something strange, sir. I don't know what to make of it, but I thought I'd better let you know." The voice belonged to Eliot's assistant.

"It's not good news, I gather," Eliot said.

"They had a security leak over at the National Defense Agency. Yesterday their chief programmer was found in a porno district. Hallucinations, fits. The police thought he was high on something, so they put him in the psychiatric ward to dry out. Well, this morning he's all right, but he can't remember going to the porno district, and he doesn't remember taking any drugs. Of course, he could be lying, but—"

"Scopolamine," Eliot said and turned to him. "Get to the point."

"Last night, while he was in the psych ward, someone used his code to get in the NDA's computer bank. They've got a system over there to find out who asked for what information. That's where we come in. Whoever used that programmer's code didn't want classified information. All he wanted was the major statistics on eighteen men. Since you supervised their training, the NDA thought you ought to know about the leak. The thing is, sir, two of the names were Romulus and Remus."

Eliot sat wearily behind his desk. "And Castor and Pollux, and Cadmus and Cilix."

"Yes, sir, that's right." The assistant sounded puzzled. "How did you know?"

146

Eliot thought about Castor and Pollux standing guard outside his office door. Then he thought about Saul and Chris. "They're getting closer. Now that they've guessed what to look for, they won't take long to figure the whole thing out."

Mournfully he swung toward the rain streaking down the window. "God help me when they do."

He silently added, *God help us all.*

BOOK THREE
BETRAYAL

THE FORMAL EDUCATION
OF AN OPERATIVE

1

At 1700 hours on December 23, 1948, United States military intelligence at Nome, Alaska, picked up the evening weather forecast from the Russian ports of Vladivostok, Okhotsk, and Magadan. The air force used these reports in conjunction with forecasts from Japanese ports to schedule night testing flights for its B-50s. The Russian forecast told of unseasonably warm weather. Nothing to worry about.

Seven minutes later, all frequencies were jammed by an amplified signal from the Russian naval base at Vladivostok to one of its submarines at sea. Coded and exceedingly lengthy for a Soviet communique, the message was sufficiently unusual for American military intelligence at Shepherds Field in Nome to concentrate on deciphering it rather than pay attention to the Japanese weather reports. They routinely cleared four B-50s for a high-altitude flight to test de-icing systems.

At 1900 hours, all four planes were hit by a Siberian cold front with wind gusts of over seventy knots. All de-icing systems failed. None of the planes returned to base. The lead plane, *Suite Lady,* had been piloted by Major Gerald Kilmoonie. When news of his loss arrived at the Eighth Air Force base (SAC) in Tucson, Arizona, General Maxwell Lepage called Roman Catholic chaplain Hugh Collins in Philadelphia to deliver the news to Mrs. Dorothy Kilmoonie and her three-year-old son, Chris. He told the chaplain to tell Gerry's wife that the country had lost the finest skeet shooter he'd ever known.

2

Two years later—1950. On Calcanlin Street in Philadelphia stood thirty rowhouses. It was a miserable place for a child to play. The street was dark and narrow. The coal ashes and sandlots held concealed traps of rusty nails, broken glass, and rat droppings. The weed-choked cracks in the sidewalk widened to crevasses at the curb and craters in the road. Toward the middle of the block, at its darkest, stood the dilapidated home of Dorothy Kilmoonie.

The house overflowed with tables: a card table with mother-of-pearl inlay; end tables; three-legged parlor tables; a coffee table with cigarette burns all over its top; a high tea table wedged against the Maytag wringer-washer in the bathroom; a dining table; a kitchen table with a chrome border and a Formica top supporting a plastic bowl of wax fruit. There were piles of dead flies beside the imitation fruit. There were similar piles on every table in the house. Also on every table, next to the flies, were pieces of old dry bologna, curled like shavings of cedar wood.

The first thing Chris had done that hot August morning was slide the screen from the parlor window and place a fat headless oily sardine on the window sill. When his mother had left him alone in the house in July while she went to spend the summer in Atlantic City, she'd put a roll of bologna in the icebox as well as several cans of soup and sardines and boxes of crackers in the cupboard. She'd given money to the neighbors, telling them to look after Chris, but by the end of July, the neighbors had spent the money on themselves and left Chris to survive alone with the food he had. He hated bologna. He'd used it for days to lure the flies into the house. But their distaste for bologna was equal to his. And the rat droppings from the street, though the flies enjoyed them, dried even faster than the meat. The sardines worked perfectly, however. By nine that morning, he could nod with pride at a new heap of flies on the coffee table, killed with a long rubber band from one of his mother's garters.

At the most exciting moment of the hunt, as he perched fighting for balance on an end table, aiming his rubber band toward a clever fly that always took off a moment before he shot at it, he sensed an unfamiliar movement in the street and glanced out the window toward a large ominous black car parked in front of his house. At the age of five, he prided himself on knowing the difference between Hudson Hornets and Wasps, Studebakers and Willys and Kaiser-Frazers. This was a 1949 Packard, and its bulk took up most of the width of the street. From the driver's seat, a heavy man in a military uniform with a body like a punching bag seemed almost to roll from the car to the road. He straightened and, while surveying the cluttered neighborhood, smoothed the rear of his pants. With his shoulders hunched and his body stooped slightly forward, he rounded the back fenders of the Packard and opened the front passenger door. A tall slim gray-faced man in a badly wrinkled trenchcoat slowly got out. The man had slender cheeks, thin lips, a downward bend in his nose.

Chris didn't hear what they said to each other, but the way they stared at this house made him nervous. He crept from the table near the window. As the men left the car, walking up the crumbly sidewalk, he turned in panic, running. He dodged past a tea table and the kitchen table toward the listing door to the cellar. It creaked when he closed it leaving a finger-wide gap that allowed him to see through the kitchen to the parlor. In the dark, on the cellar steps that smelled like rotten potatoes, he felt afraid that the strangers would know where to catch him because they could hear the drumming of his heart.

The front door rattled as they knocked. He held his breath and reached for the rope that stretched from the parlor through the kitchen to these stairs. There hadn't been time for him to lock the front door, but he had other ways to protect himself. He clutched the rope. The front door scraped open. A man's deep voice asked, "Anybody home?" Heavy footsteps rumbled, coming down the hall. "I saw the boy at the window." Their shadows entered the parlor. "What's with all these tables? My God, the flies."

Chris hunched on the stairs, peering through the crack in the door across the dirty linoleum toward the net on the parlor floor. When not killing flies, he'd been making the net since his mother had left, taking kite string from Kensington Park, cord from vacant lots, rope and shoelaces from trash cans, wool and thread from neighbors' bureau drawers, twine from the mill down the street, and clotheslines from nearby yards. He'd tied them all together—long pieces, short pieces, thick and thin—to form a huge intersecting pattern. His mother had

153

promised to come back. She'd said she'd bring saltwater taffy and seashells and photographs, lots of photographs. And the day she did come back, he'd capture her in the net and keep her trapped till she promised never to go away again. His eyes stung as he watched the two men enter the parlor, standing on the net. If it could trap his mother . . .

"And what's with all this twine and stuff on the floor?"

Chris yanked the rope. He'd attached it to chairs perched on tables in the parlor. When they fell, they pulled twine through the chain in the ceiling light and raised the corners of the net.

As the chairs clattered, the two men shouted. "What the—? Jesus!"

Chris puffed his chest, wanting to cheer, then suddenly scowled. The men were laughing, doubled over. Through the crack in the door, he saw the one in the uniform grab the net and rip the knots apart, breaking the string, stepping out of the twine.

Tears burned his cheeks. Furious, he scrambled down the cellar steps, swallowed by darkness. His hands shook from rage. He'd make them sorry. He'd get even with them for laughing.

The cellar door creaked open. Light struggled to reach the bottom of the stairs. Through a knothole in the wall of the coalbin, he watched their shadows come down. Their laughter continued. Someone must have told them everything about him, he thought—how he'd stolen the clothesline, the thread, and the twine; even where he'd hide. The cellar's light switch didn't work, but they seemed to know that also, for they had a flashlight, aiming it around the musty basement, stalking him.

He crept back toward the deepest corner of the coalbin. It was empty in summer. Even so, grit scraped beneath his sneakers. The flashlight swung his way. Dodging it, he stepped on a chunk of coal. His ankle twisted. Losing balance, he banged against a wall.

The flashlight came closer. Footsteps scurried. No! He slipped from a hand, but as he scrambled from the bin, another caught his shoulder. No! Weeping, he kicked, but he touched only air, flailing as the hands spun and lifted him.

"Let's get you up in the light."

He struggled frantically, but the hands pinned his arms and legs, allowing him only to squirm and bang his head against a chest as the men took him up the cellar stairs. After the dark, he blinked from the sunlight through the kitchen window, crying.

154

"Take it easy," the heavy man in the uniform said, puffing from his exertion.

The one in the trenchcoat frowned at Chris's tar-coated sneakers, filthy pants, and grimy hair. He took out a handkerchief, wiping the tears and coal dust from Chris's face.

Chris pushed the arm away, trying to seem as tall and strong as his tiny frame would allow. "Not funny!"

"What?"

Chris glared at the net in the parlor.

"Oh, I see," the civilian said. Despite his cold eyes and sickly face, his voice sounded friendly. "You heard us laughing."

"Not funny!" Chris said louder.

"No, of course not," the man in the uniform said. "You've got us all wrong. We weren't laughing at you. Why, the net seemed a good idea. Course you could've used some better material and a few lessons in design and camouflage. But the idea . . . Well, that's why we laughed. Not at you but *with* you. Sort of in admiration. You've got spunk, boy. Even if you didn't look like him, I could tell from the way you handle yourself—you're Gerry's son."

Chris didn't understand a lot of the words. He frowned as if the man in uniform was trying to trick him. A long time ago, he vaguely recalled, someone had told him he'd once had a father, but he'd never heard of anybody named Gerry.

"I can tell you don't trust me," the man said. Spreading his legs, he put his hands on his hips, like a cop. "I'd better introduce myself. I'm Maxwell Lepage."

Like "Gerry," this name meant nothing. Chris stared suspiciously.

The man seemed puzzled. "*General* Maxwell Lepage. You know. Your dad's best friend."

Chris stared even harder.

"You mean you never heard of me?" The man was astonished. He turned to the tall gray-faced civilian. "I'm no good at this. Maybe you can get him to—" He gestured helplessly.

The civilian nodded. Stepping ahead, he smiled. "Son, I'm Ted Eliot. But you can call me just Eliot. All my friends do."

Chris glared with mistrust.

The man called Eliot pulled something from his trenchcoat. "I figure every boy likes chocolate. Especially Baby Ruths. I want to be your friend." Eliot put his hand out.

Fidgeting, Chris pretended not to care, refusing to look at the candy bars.

"Go on," the man said. "I ate one already. They're good."

Chris didn't know what to do. The only advice his mother had ever given him was not to take candy from strangers. He didn't trust these men. But he'd eaten nothing except stale crackers all week. His head felt light. The growling in his stomach persisted. Before he knew it, he grabbed the candy bars.

The man called Eliot smiled.

"We've come to help," Lepage said. "We know your mother left."

"She's coming back!"

"We're here to take care of you." Lepage glanced at the flies in disgust.

Chris didn't understand why Eliot closed the windows. Was it going to rain? As Lepage gripped Chris's arm, he realized he'd dropped his weapon, the slimy rubber band. They took him to the porch, Lepage holding him while Eliot locked the door. He noticed Mrs. Kelly squinting from her window next door, then suddenly ducking away. She'd never done that before, he realized—and suddenly felt afraid.

3

He sat in the front seat of the car between the two men and stared first at Lepage's heavy shoes, next at Eliot's gray-striped tie, and finally at the door handle. The thought of escape passed quickly once the car began to move and he became fascinated watching Lepage shift gears. He'd never ridden in a car before. The indicators on the dashboard, the movement of people and vehicles outside held him enthralled till, before he could anticipate their arrival anywhere, Lepage parked in front of a huge building with pillars that reminded Chris of the post office. Directed by Lepage's firm grip on his shoulders, Chris walked between the two men through marble halls lined with benches. Men and women dressed as if to go to church went by, carrying stacks of paper and what looked like small suitcases.

Behind a frosted glass door, a young woman sat at a desk. She spoke to a box beside a phone, then opened another door where Chris and the two men went through. In the inner office, an old man with white hair and a pencil-thin mustache sat at another desk, but this one was larger, before an American flag and a wall lined with thick leather-covered books.

As Chris stopped before the desk, the man looked up. He searched through some papers. "Let's see now. Yes." He cleared his throat. "Christopher Patrick Kilmoonie."

Afraid, Chris didn't answer. Lepage and Eliot both said, "Yes." Chris frowned in confusion.

The man studied Chris, then spoke to Lepage and Eliot. "His mother abandoned him . . ." He ran his finger down a sheet, his voice astonished, disapproving. "Fifty-one days ago?"

"That's right," Eliot said. "His mother went away with a male companion for the Fourth of July weekend. She hasn't been back."

Chris kept turning his head from one man to another, waiting for what they'd say next.

The man glanced at a calendar, scratching his cheek. "Soon be Labor Day. Has he got any older brothers or sisters, any relatives who'd take care of him?"

"No," Eliot said.

"For the whole summer? How'd he survive?"

"He ate sardines and bologna and killed flies."

The man looked stunned. "Killed . . . ? His mother? Is she employed?"

"She's a prostitute, your honor."

It was yet another word Chris didn't understand. Curiosity overcame him. For the first time in the office, he spoke. "What's a prostitute?"

They turned away and didn't answer.

"What about his father?" the man said.

"He died two years ago," Lepage replied. "It's all in his file. You can understand why the Welfare Department recommends he become a ward of the city."

The man tapped his fingers on his glass-topped desk. "But I'm the one who has to make the decision, and I don't understand why the Welfare Department sent you to this hearing instead of its own representative. What's the government's interest in this matter?"

Lepage answered, "His father was a major in the Air Force. He died in the line of duty. He was my friend. Mr. Eliot and myself, we've sort of—well, we've unofficially adopted the boy, you might say. Discounting his mother, we're the nearest thing to a family he's got. Since our work prevents us from raising him ourselves, we want to make sure someone else does it properly."

The man nodded. "You know where he'll be sent."

"We do," Eliot said, "and we approve."

The man studied Chris and sighed. "Very well." He signed a piece of paper, put it in a folder with a lot of other papers, and handed the folder to Lepage. "Chris . . ." The man struggled, unable to choose his words.

"I'll explain it to him," Eliot said. "When we get there."

"Explain what?" Chris began to tremble.

"Thank you," Lepage told the man.

Before Chris knew what was happening, Lepage turned him to the door. Confused, Chris was taken out again into the hall past the green glass doors that reminded him of the bank and the telegraph office around the corner from the five-and-dime. But where was that now? he thought. And where was he going?

4

The metal gate was high and wide and black. Its bars looked as thick as Chris's wrist, the space between them so narrow he knew he could never squeeze through. To the left, a large iron plaque said,

BENJAMIN FRANKLIN SCHOOL FOR BOYS

To the right, another plaque said,

TEACH THEM POLITICS AND WAR
SO THEIR SONS MAY STUDY MEDICINE AND MATHEMATICS.
JOHN ADAMS

Beneath this plaque, built into the high stone wall that seemed to stretch forever in both directions, a heavy door led to a sentrylike room filled with stacks of newspapers, mail sacks, and packages. A man in a sweater vest tipped a conductor's cap, smiled, and continued sorting the packages. Lepage and Eliot didn't say a word but, with Chris in hand, went directly through the room, out into the sun, across a lawn toward a huge brick building.

"That'll be your high school some day," Lepage told Chris. "But for now it's only where we'll sign you up."

Carved in stone, above the entrance to the building, were the words:

WISDOM THROUGH OBEDIENCE,
PERFECTION THROUGH HUMILITY.

It was only half-past noon, so they waited on an old refectory bench, its oak thickly varnished and waxed. The bench felt hard, and the contour of its seat made Chris slide back while his feet dangled over the floor. Uneasy, he stared at the clock on the wall, tensing every time the second hand jerked forward. Its dull snick seemed to grow louder; it reminded him of the sound in a butcher shop.

A woman arrived at one. She wore low heels, a plain skirt and sweater. Unlike his mother, she didn't use lipstick, and her hair instead of being curly was combed straight back in a bun. She barely glanced at Chris before she went with Lepage to her office.

Eliot stayed on the bench with him. "I bet those two hamburgers we bought you didn't begin to fill you up." He smiled. "Eat those Baby Ruths I gave you."

Chris hunched his shoulders, staring stubbornly at the wall across from him.

"I know," Eliot said. "You figure it's smarter to save them for when you get hungry again. But you'll be fed here—three times a day. And as for the candy bars, the next time I see you I'll bring you some more. Do you like any other kinds?"

Chris slowly turned, bewildered by this tall thin man with gray skin and sad-looking eyes.

"I can't promise I'll visit you often," Eliot said. "But I want you to know I'm your friend. I want you to think of me as . . . let's call me a substitute father, someone you can count on if you get in trouble, someone who likes you and wants what's best for you. Some things are hard to explain. Trust me. One day you'll understand."

Chris's eyes felt hot. "How long will I be here?"

"Quite a while."

"Till my mother comes to get me?"

"I don't think . . ." Eliot pursed his lips. "Your mother's decided to let the city take care of you."

Now Chris's eyes felt swollen. "Where is she?"

"We don't know."

"She's dead?" Chris was so desperate to hear the answer he took a moment to realize he was crying again.

Eliot put an arm around him. "No. But you won't be seeing her anymore. As far as we know, she's alive, but you'll have to get used to thinking of her as dead."

Chris wept harder, choking.

"But you're not alone." Eliot hugged him. "I care for you. I'll always be close to you. We'll see each other often. I'm the only family you've got."

Chris jerked from Eliot's arms as the door came open. Lepage stepped out of the office, shaking hands with the woman, who now wore glasses and held Chris's folder. "We appreciate your help." He turned to Eliot. "Everything's taken care of." He looked at Chris. "We're going to leave you with Miss Halahan now. She's very nice, and I'm sure you'll like her." He shook Chris's hand. Chris winced from the pressure. "Obey your superiors. Make your dad proud of you."

Eliot bent down, touching Chris's shoulders. "More important, make *me* proud of you." His voice was soft.

As the two men walked down the hall, Chris blinked in confusion through his tears, feeling the security of the candy bars in his pocket.

5

Too much to sort out. The forty-eight acres of the school were divided by a solitary road. To get to the dormitory from the high school building, Miss Halahan told Chris they had to walk quite a way. He had trouble keeping up. The road was completely empty, as if a parade were about to begin, but there were no barricades along the route, no spectators, only the immense trees on either side, like umbrellas shielding Chris from the sun.

Despite her explanations, he felt disoriented. Across from the high school was a cluster of buildings that made up the "residence halls and refectory," she said. To the left was the immense stone "chapel," and across the road from it, the "infirmary." The wind had been light, broken by the mass of buildings, but as he followed Miss Halahan past the "gymnasium" at the center of campus, he was suddenly struck by a fierce hot gust that surged across playgrounds on either side of the road. He saw goalposts and track hurdles and baseball backstops, but what surprised him was the lack of earth. Everything around him was a huge expanse of concrete.

The sun now blazed as Chris passed the "armory" and the "energy plant" with its smokestacks and hills of coal. His legs ached when he finally reached the end of the road. Staring at the bleak gray building she called the "dormitory," he became apprehensive. She had to tug his resisting hand, leading him down an echoing stairwell, taking him to a large basement auditorium that smelled of wax, where he peered uneasily at a dozen other boys, some older, some younger, all wearing dingy clothes as he was.

"You arrived just in time," Miss Halahan said. "For the weekly initiation. Otherwise we'd have had to do it all over again just for you."

Chris didn't understand. "Initiation" was yet another word he'd never come across. He didn't like its sound. Nervous, he sat in a creaky seat and realized that all the other boys had followed his instincts, staying apart from each other. The auditorium was unnaturally quiet.

An old man dressed in khaki pants and shirt with an olive drab tie marched to the center of the stage. He stood before a podium, and again Chris noticed an American flag. The old man held a baton beneath one arm and introduced himself as Colonel Douglas Dolty, director of admissions and headmaster of the dormitory. He began his speech with animal and sports jokes. A few boys laughed. The colonel ventured to guess that many heroes of the sports world knew about the school and on occasion would visit the boys. Though anxious, Chris was surprised to find himself interested. His cheeks felt tight from his now-dried tears. The colonel told a story (incomprehensible to Chris) about a place called ancient Greece and three hundred soldiers called Spartans who died heroically trying to hold off an army of Persians at

161

a pass called Thermopylae. "Gentlemen," he concluded, "I'm going to show you what this school is all about."

He formed the boys in two lines and led them outside, down the road to the vocational arts building. There, the *newbies*, as they learned they were called, were shown the foundry, where boys filled cast-iron molds. In the print shop, other boys were setting type for the next issue of the school's paper. Chris saw the carpentry and machine and auto mechanics shops. He went to the tailor shop, the shoe shop, and the laundry. Even there, his group was impressed by the noise and activity and the importance of children like themselves doing the work. They wanted to try out the machines.

But the colonel saved the best for last. With a smile of pride, he took them to the armory, showing Chris and the others the 1917 Enfield rifles, polished to a gleam, that they soon would carry, as well as the sabers, the dress uniforms of gun-metal gray, and the snap-on white collars they would wear in their student platoons. Here especially Chris was awestruck. No boy spoke up or clowned around. Chris inhaled the sharp sweet smell of gun oil, Brasso, and bore cleaner. The respect he and the other boys gave this old man was the same respect they would show him on the day in their senior year when they signed up for Army Airborne or the Second Marine Division. Respect indeed would turn to love. Nurtured in a male system, in the Spartan atmosphere of Franklin, love would turn to patriotism and pride. Fear, through prolonged punishment, would soon become commonplace and would finally be unknown. The glitter of saber scabbards, the charisma of rifles, insignias, and chevrons would create excitement, fusing all the needed alloys of heroism and loyalty to produce the men Franklin passed on to the outside world.

"We can't have you looking the way you do now, can we?" the colonel said. Continuing to reassure them with his smile, he took them to another building where he gave each boy two pair of lace-up high-cut black shoes, similar to combat boots. He handed each a white dress shirt and three plain shirts of various colors, four pair of pants, socks and underwear, four handkerchiefs—all wrapped in a tight bundle by a long bilious cotton nightshirt. With their shoes tied around their neck and their bundle of clothes clutched to their chests, they looked like miniature airborne troops as they ventured out into the dry hot wind again and trotted at double time back along the road to the dormitory.

6

The barber was waiting. When he finished, two inches of scalp showed above Chris's ears. With the back of his head shaved bare, he looked like a boot camp recruit. He felt nervous and shy, but as he studied the other boys and they studied him, he straightened, glancing at himself in a mirror, seeing his newly acquired rugged features, feeling unexpectedly athletic, strangely confident.

But the showers were next: a small tiled room with fixtures that had no handles, the flow of water controlled by a governess who peered through a window and manipulated dials. A male attendant told them to take off their clothes and stuff them in a large canvas bag at the end of the room. Chris felt ashamed. He'd never been naked in front of any person except his mother. His eyes felt swollen again as he remembered her. He tried to cover himself with his hands and saw other boys do the same. But it puzzled him that the male attendant and the governess didn't seem to notice they were naked.

Herded into the small shower, they tried hard not to touch each other, an impossible task as they struggled with bars of soap and cringed beneath the powerful steaming nozzles. The spray was so thick Chris barely saw the other boys. The water abruptly stopped. Disconcerted, Chris left the shower room with the others. They dripped on the tile of a locker room, huddling, feeling cold now. The attendant handed each of them a towel and pointed toward a large metal pail filled with something gooey and sweet-smelling he called cold cream, telling them to rub it on their faces, their arms and legs, and any spots that were red and raw. Chris suddenly noticed that the large canvas sack where he and the others had stuffed their clothes was gone. He never saw his tar-stained sneakers and grimy shirt again.

Or his candy bars.

He wanted to moan, feeling tricked and betrayed. Eating them had been all he'd had to look forward to.

But there wasn't time for self-pity. The attendant took their towels and led them shivering, naked, from the locker room up the stairwell

163

to a huge room where bunk beds lined the walls. Each bed had two shelves and a storage locker. The windows were barred. Demoralized, Chris put on his gray wool socks and pants and shirt. But though uncomfortable in the itchy new clothes, he glanced at the other boys in amazement. Except for their differences in hair color and complexion, all looked alike. He didn't know why, but somehow that reassured him.

The attendant explained their schedule. Wake-up at 6, breakfast at 7, school from 8 to 12, lunch till 12:30, rest till 1, school till 5, play till 6, then supper and study hall, in bed by 8. "Any discomfort, itchiness, bloody gums, or illness of any kind, report it to me at once. Tomorrow I'll teach you how to make your bed so I can bounce a quarter off it. The first few weeks, you'll sleep with a rubber sheet—in case."

The attendant marched them from the dormitory to the mess hall, where they were joined by hundreds of other children, all sizes, all ages, all dressed in gray with their hair cut severely. They'd been in classes till now, but despite the crowd, the room was oddly silent as the boys filed past the counters with their trays to receive their food.

Chris gagged when he saw the first meal he would eat here. One boy had mentioned tuna casserole. Another had grumbled about brussels sprouts. Chris had never heard of that before. All he knew was that this green stuff was covered by white guck and the whole thing smelled like spit-up. He sat with his group at a plastic-covered table, staring at the salt shaker, refusing to eat, when he felt a shadow loom over him. "Everybody eats, or everybody's punished," a deep voice growled. Chris had to think about what the man had said. He gradually understood. He saw the other boys staring at him and realized that, if he didn't eat, the other boys would be blamed because of him. He debated with himself, stifling the pressure in his throat. Slowly he picked up his fork. He stared at the creamy white stuff. He didn't breathe as he chewed and swallowed, and somehow not breathing seemed to help.

They were told after supper they'd get a treat. A movie. Just as Chris had never had a car ride before, he'd never seen a movie. As he crowded with the other boys, his eyes expanded with delight. The black and white images flickered magically on the screen. He watched an actor named John Wayne—the rest of the boys seemed to know who he was and applauded with delight—in a war story called *The Fighting Seabees*. His chest pounded. Shooting and explosions. The other kids cheered. He loved it.

That night, as he lay in his bottom bunk in the dark of the dormitory, he wondered where his mother was. He tried to understand what he was doing here. He recalled what Lepage had said about his father dying in something called the line of duty. Frightened and puzzled, he heard a boy across from him begin to sob. Chris felt his own tears hot and bitter at the corners of his eyes as an older boy yelled, "Quit yer cryin'! I wanna sleep!"

Chris stiffened, embarrassed. When he realized the older boy had been yelling at the new boy across from him, he swallowed his sorrow, squeezing his eyes shut, determined to avoid attention, to be one of those who didn't cry. But he wished he'd made Lepage tell him why his mother was called a prostitute, and he wished with all his heart that his mother would return from Atlantic City and take him away from here. Grief strangled him. But in his dream, he saw Eliot handing him a Baby Ruth candy bar.

7

"I root for the Phillies," a boy to Chris's right said.

Chris knelt with his group at the back of the first-grade room, putting puzzles together—mostly maps of the United States with cartoons of corn and apples, factories, mines, and oil wells drawn on various sections, though sometimes the maps were of countries Chris had never heard of, China, Korea, and Russia, for example. The puzzles were brightly colored, and he quickly learned how to put them together. He'd never been to school before, but despite the complaints he'd heard from the older boys, he thought he was going to like it. For a little while, at least. Despite what Eliot had told him, Chris was sure his mother would come to take him home.

The boy who'd said he rooted for the Phillies looked even thinner than Chris, his face so lean his eyes bulged. When the boy smiled, waiting for approval from the others, Chris noticed he had several missing teeth. But when the boy got no response, his smile quickly vanished, replaced by humiliation.

Another boy spoke. To Chris's left. Though the same age as the other boys in the group, he was bigger—not just taller but heavier—than the rest. He had the darkest hair, the tannest skin, the squarest face, the deepest voice. His name was Saul Grisman, and last night in the dorm, Chris had heard an older boy whisper that Grisman was a Jew. Chris hadn't known what he meant. "What's the matter with ya?" the other boy had said. "Where ya been? A Jew." Chris still hadn't known what he meant. "Aw, for Pete's sake," the other boy had said, "I didn't know Micks could be so dumb." When Chris had asked what a Mick was, the older boy had walked away in disgust.

Now Saul said, "I root for *all* the teams! And I got the baseball cards to prove it!" He reached beneath his shirt and pulled out two handfuls of them.

The other boys blinked, astonished. They stopped putting together the puzzles and quickly glanced toward the governess, who sat at the front desk, reading a book. Assured, they leaned forward guiltily, staring in awe at the baseball cards. Saul showed the cards one at a time: pictures of men in uniform swinging bats or running or catching balls, Yogi Berra, Joe DiMaggio, Jackie Robinson, names Chris had never heard of, with their life story on the back of each card, how many home runs they'd hit or outs they'd made. Saul enjoyed watching the other boys admire his treasures, but he wouldn't let them handle one card, which he raised with reverence. "He played before those other guys, and he was better," Saul said.

Chris squinted at the heavy man in the picture, then down at the name—Babe Ruth. Feeling nervous because he didn't know anything about these players, he tried to think of something to say that would make the other kids accept him. "Sure," he nodded wisely. "They named a candy bar after him." For an instant, he thought of the gray-faced man named Eliot.

Saul frowned. "A what?"

"A candy bar. Babe Ruth."

"That's *Baby* Ruth."

"That's what I said."

"It's not the same. It's *Babe.* Not Baby."

"So what?"

"The candy bar's named after some guy's baby named Ruth."

Chris blushed. The other boys sneered at him as if they'd known the secret all along. The governess glanced up from her book, sending a shock through the room. Saul fumbled to put the cards beneath his shirt while the other boys ducked quickly down to put more puzzles together. The governess stood, walking ominously over to them. She towered, making Chris nervous as she watched for a long time before she returned to her desk.

"How'd you get to keep the cards?" one boy asked Saul as the class walked in double file to lunch. The other boys strained to hear Saul's answer. Not only did Saul have something none of the rest of them had, but he'd actually managed to smuggle the cards into school. Chris remembered that everything the boys had brought here with them had been taken from them the first day, including (he recalled bitterly) his candy bars, which he wished he'd eaten right away instead of saving. So how had Saul kept the baseball cards?

"Yeah, how'd you get to keep them?" another boy asked.

Instead of answering, Saul only smiled.

"Can I sit next to you at lunch?" a third boy asked.

"Me too. Can I sit next to you? Can I look at the cards again?" another boy asked. Though they had to walk in ranks, they nonetheless seemed to crowd around Saul as they entered the refectory for lunch.

When Chris carried his tray of weiners and beans to their table, he found that the only empty seat was the farthest from Saul. The other boys sat proudly next to Saul or across from him, a few even daring to whisper more questions about the cards till a supervisor stopped and glared them all into silence.

Outside the refectory, they were allowed to speak as they went to their room for rest period, but Chris couldn't get a word in. All anybody wanted to talk about was where Saul had gotten the cards and how he'd managed to keep them. Because of Chris's disastrous remark about Babe Ruth and the candy bar, the other boys treated him as the dummy of the group, and Chris wished harder for his mother to come and rescue him. He decided he didn't like school after all.

He disliked it even more when, late in the afternoon, the governess marched them to the swimming pool in the basement of the gymnasium. An instructor told them to strip and shower, and again Chris felt ashamed to be naked in front of other people. His shame soon turned to fear when the instructor ordered them to jump into the pool. Chris had never seen so much water. He was afraid of his head going under and choking as he had one time when his mother was giving him a bath. But the instructor nudged him toward the pool, and Chris finally jumped in willingly because the water would hide his nakedness. Splashing down through the cold sharp-smelling water, he landed abruptly, surprised the water came up only to his waist. The other boys entered as reluctantly as Chris, except for Saul, who considered the pool a thrilling challenge and even sank down so his head was under water.

"You!" The instructor pointed. "What's your name?"

"Saul Grisman, sir." The "sir" was an absolute rule. They'd learned whenever a boy spoke to a grownup he had to say "sir" or "ma'am," depending.

"You look like you've gone swimming before."

Saul answered, "No, sir."

"Never had lessons?"

"No, sir."

The instructor rubbed his chin, impressed. "Maybe you're a natural."

With their admiration of Saul reinforced by the instructor's approval, the boys competed with each other to get close to Saul as they held the edge of the pool and the instructor showed them how to kick their legs.

"That's right. Watch Grisman," the instructor said. "He's got the idea."

At the farthest place from Saul, sputtering, struggling to keep his head above water, kicking awkwardly, Chris had never felt so lonely. Back on Calcanlin Street, he'd spent the summer alone waiting for his mother, but in the familiar house in the familiar neighborhood with friends to play with, he hadn't felt alone. In fact, that hadn't been the first time his mother had left him alone; he was almost used to living by himself, though he always missed his mother when she was gone. But now in these strange surroundings, shivering in the water, excluded by the other children, envying Saul, he felt the bitter ache of loneliness and decided he hated this place.

The only time he mustered interest was the next night, Saturday, when after a day of practice making his bed, learning to lace, tie, and polish his shoes, to knot and adjust his tie to the proper length, he went with every boy in the school to see another movie. Chris eagerly recalled the first one he'd seen here, *The Fighting Seabees.* This one was called *Battleground.* Everyone cheered as it began, and again the action was exciting, lots of shooting and explosions. Chris loved the plot about a group of American soldiers fighting as a team in war. The music— blaring trumpets, pounding drums—made his stomach feel warm.

But after, none of his group cared what he thought about the movie. Everybody wanted to know what *Saul* thought. Chris almost broke his rule by crying himself to sleep. Instead he clenched his teeth in the darkness, planning to run away.

8

The sudden glare of the overhead lights woke him at six. Someone said it was Sunday. Blinking sleepily, he shuffled with the other boys to the washroom, where with his toothbrush in his left hand he held out his right hand for the supervisor to pour him some tooth powder. As he cleaned his teeth, making sure he reached all the way to the back the way the supervisor had shown him, the peppermint taste of the Colgate made him feel slightly sick. He listened to the flushing of urinals and toilets and tried not to look at the boys getting off the seats. The toilets were in the open—no walls or doors—and his shyness prevented him from relieving himself till he absolutely had to. He surprised himself by sitting, not caring who watched him, his need too great. In fact, no one seemed to care. And the relief he felt afterward, combined with the confidence he'd acquired by overcoming this further taboo of shyness, made him anticipate the day with unexpected optimism. He even enjoyed the milky scrambled eggs he washed down with orange juice, and he felt a little like the soldiers in their uniforms in *Battleground* when he put on his stiff dress shirt and his cadet clothes before the supervisor marched his group to chapel.

It had colored windows, but no crosses or other religious symbols could be seen anywhere. As every boy sat at his assigned place in the pews, the chaplain, Mr. Applegate, stepped up to a podium and led the boys in song—first "The Star-Spangled Banner," then "God Bless America." Next the chaplain pulled out a dollar bill (which gained Chris's interest right away) and read the words on the back of Washington's picture. "The United States of America!" he said loud enough to be heard at the back of the chapel. "In God We Trust! Remember those two statements! We trust in God! He trusts in us! That's why this country is the greatest, richest, most powerful on earth! Because God trusts us! We must always be willing to be His soldiers, to fight His enemies, to preserve our God-ordained way of life! I can think of no greater honor than to fight for our country, for its greatness and glory! God bless America!" The chaplain held up his hands, demanding a response. The boys shouted it back to him. "God bless America!" he repeated. Again they shouted it back. As the chapel gradually became quiet, Chris felt the echo of the shouts linger in his ears. He felt excited in a frightened way, not understanding what the chaplain meant but responding to the emotion in his words.

"The Biblical text this morning," the chaplain said, "is from the Book of Exodus. Moses, leading God's chosen people, is pursued by the Pharaoh's soldiers. Helped by God, Moses parts the Red Sea, allowing His People through, but when the Pharaoh's men attempt to cross, God returns the Red Sea and drowns them." The chaplain opened the Bible, drawing a breath to read. Then he hesitated. "Considering today's politics, I suppose the Red Sea is not the most apt image for drawing a parallel with our country against the Communists. Perhaps Red-White-and-Blue Sea would be more appropriate." Chris didn't know what he meant, but the instructors sitting in the front row laughed discreetly, mindful they were in chapel. The chaplain pushed his glasses back on his nose and read. The service concluded with "God Bless America" again, then "The Battle Hymn of the Republic," and finally another chorus of "The Star-Spangled Banner."

Hoping for a chance to play, Chris was dismayed to learn that at the close of what was called the nondenominational service all the boys had to divide into their own religious groups, Lutheran with Lutheran, Anglican with Anglican, Presbyterian with Presbyterian, for further worship. He was confused, not knowing where to go because he didn't know if he had a religion or what it was. Glancing uneasily around him as he left the chapel with the other boys, he felt a hand on his shoulder and whirled to a red-haired freckled supervisor who looked as if he had a sunburn. "Kilmoonie, you come with me." The supervisor's voice had a lilt. He said his name was Mr. O'Hara. "Yes, Kilmoonie, I'm Irish like you. We're both R.C.s." When Chris frowned, the supervisor explained, and that was the day Chris learned he was something called a Roman Catholic. That was also the day he learned a little about what it meant to be Jewish. As the different religious groups walked toward separate buses that would take them to various churches, Chris glanced across the concrete that led toward the dormitory and saw a boy walking all alone. Without thinking, he blurted, "But why doesn't Saul have to come?"

The supervisor apparently didn't notice Chris hadn't said *sir.* "What? Oh, that's Grisman. He's Jewish. His Sunday's on Saturday."

Chris frowned as he boarded the bus. Sunday on Saturday? What sense did that make? He thought about it as the bus drove past the big iron gates at the entrance to the school. He'd been here only a few days, but already he'd lost track, and though as recently as the night before he'd fallen asleep making plans to run away, now the outside world seemed foreign and scary. His eyes widened nervously at the crowded sidewalks and the busy streets. The sun hurt his eyes. Car horns blared. The boys were under strict orders not to say a word while they were on the bus and especially not to make faces or do anything else that would attract the attention of people on the street. In the strange silence of the bus (except for the muffled roar of its engine), Chris stared ahead as did the other boys and felt unsettled, incomplete, eager to get back to the school and its routine.

The bus stopped in front of a church whose towers made it look like a castle. A cross loomed over it. Bells droned. A lot of people wearing suits and dresses were going in. Mr. O'Hara lined the boys up two by two and marched them in. The church was dark and felt cool. As Mr. O'Hara led the boys down a side aisle, Chris heard a woman whisper, "Don't they look cute in their uniforms? Look at that young one. Isn't he sweet?" Chris wasn't sure if the woman meant him, but he felt self-conscious. All he wanted was to be invisible within the group.

The church made him feel even smaller than he was. He stared at the peaked roof (the highest he'd ever seen) with its crisscrossed beams and hanging lights. He peered at the front where a red light flickered above the altar. Candles glowed. The altar was covered with a stiff white cloth. A small shiny golden door on the altar looked as if it held a secret.

But beyond the altar hung the most disturbing sight of all. His chest shrank, suffocating him. Kneeling, he had to grip the seat ahead of him tightly to control his trembling hands. He'd never felt so scared. Beyond the altar hung a statue—a lean, twisted, agonized man whose hands and feet were nailed to a cross, whose head was pierced by what looked like spikes, whose side had been cut open, blood streaming down.

He glanced around in panic. Why didn't the other boys seem shocked by the statue? Or the other people (the "outsiders," as he'd begun to think of them)—why weren't *they* gaping in horror? What

171

kind of place *was* this? Subduing himself, trying to understand, he heard Mr. O'Hara snap his fingers twice, and at once the older boys stopped kneeling. They sat in the pews. Chris followed their lead. He felt even more afraid when an organ began to blare, its eerie chords filling the church. A choir began singing, but the language was foreign, and he didn't understand. Then a priest wearing a long colorful robe came to the altar, followed by two boys in white cloaks. They faced the small gold door, their backs to the people, speaking to the statue. Chris hoped for an explanation—he wanted someone to tell him why the man was nailed up there.

But he couldn't understand what the priest was saying. The words seemed gibberish. They made no sense. *"Confiteor Deo omnipotenti . . ."*

All the way back to school, Chris felt confused. The priest had spoken briefly to the people in English, talking about Jesus Christ, who apparently was the man nailed above the altar, but Chris hadn't learned who Jesus was. Mr. O'Hara had mentioned that next week Chris would be starting something called Sunday school—maybe, Chris thought, I'll find out then. In the meantime, he sighed as the bus returned through the open gates of Franklin School, heading up the single road toward the dormitories. After the disturbing experience of being on the outside, in the scary church with the awful statue, he welcomed being back. He recognized some of the boys. He looked forward to sitting on his bunk. Knowing what he was supposed to do and when he was supposed to do it, he felt secure, pleased not to be confused. And lunch was served exactly on time. Hungry, he swallowed huge mouthfuls of hamburger and potato chips, drinking glass after glass of milk. It was good to be back home, he thought, then abruptly stopped chewing as he realized the word that had flashed through his head. Home? But what about the house on Calcanlin Street? And what about his mother? Confused again, he understood—without knowing why—that he was going to be living here for a long time. Peering along the table toward Saul in his honored center place, he told himself if this was going to be his home he'd better learn how to get along. He needed friends. He wanted to be Saul's friend. But how, when Saul was bigger and stronger and faster, and above all had the baseball cards?

172

9

The answer came to him the next day in swimming class. By now, he was less ashamed of being naked in front of the other boys. As the instructor told the class to kick their legs the way Saul was, Chris felt his heart race with satisfaction. I'm doing it! he thought. I'm really doing it!

"That's right, Kilmoonie," the instructor said. "Keep those legs out straight. Kick strong and steady. Just the way Grisman does."

The other boys looked astonished at Chris as if they hadn't known he existed till the instructor said something good to him. Chris blushed, kicking harder, his chest filled with pride. He glanced down the line and noticed Saul turn his way as if curious to see who Kilmoonie was and whether he kicked as well as the instructor said. For a moment, while the other boys splashed, Chris and Saul stared into each other's eyes. Chris might have been wrong, but Saul seemed to grin as if the two of them shared a secret.

After class, they all hurried shivering to the dressing room, where their gray shirts and pants hung on pegs. Chris hugged himself, hopping from one bare foot to the other on the cold tile floor as he grabbed a towel from a pile in the corner, drying himself. An angry voice startled him.

"Where's my cards?"

Chris turned, bewildered, seeing Saul paw frantically through his clothes. The other boys gaped.

"They're gone!" Saul swung accusingly toward the group. "Who stole my—?"

"No talking," the instructor warned.

"But my cards! They were in my pocket! Somebody must have—"

"Grisman, I said no talking."

But Saul's anger made him lose control. "I want my cards back!"

The instructor stalked toward him, stopping with his feet spread apart, his hands placed threateningly on his hips. "I want my cards back, *sir!*"

Distraught, Saul opened and closed his mouth, no sound coming out.

"Go on and say it, Grisman. *Sir!*"

Saul blinked toward the floor, confused, angry. "Sir!"

"That's better. What cards are you talking about?"

"My baseball cards." Saul quickly added, "Sir. They were in my—"

"Baseball cards?" The instructor curled his lip. "We don't issue baseball cards. Where'd you get them?"

Saul's eyes looked swollen and misty. "I brought them to school with me." He swallowed. "Sir. I had them in my pants pocket and—"

"You weren't supposed to keep anything you brought here. You don't have toys here, Grisman. You don't *own* things. All you're supposed to have is what you're *told* you can have."

Chris felt a snake uncoil in his stomach, embarrassed for Saul, who nodded, staring toward the floor, beginning to cry. The other boys gasped.

"Besides, Grisman, what makes you so sure one of your classmates stole these precious baseball cards? *Illegal* baseball cards. How do you know it wasn't me?"

Tears streaming down his cheeks, Saul peered up, sniffling, struggling to speak. "Did you, sir?"

The silence made Chris squirm.

"I ought to claim I did, just to keep peace around here," the instructor said at last. "But I didn't. If I had these ridiculous cards, I certainly wouldn't give them back to you. It was one of your friends."

Eyes red, squinting, Saul turned to the other boys, face tense with hate. Though Chris hadn't taken the cards, he nonetheless felt guilty when Saul's gaze stabbed him before continuing to the next boy and the next. Saul's lips shook.

"A lot of rules have been broken," the instructor growled. "You shouldn't have had the cards. But since you did, you should've kept another rule—if you've got a secret, make sure no one else knows it. There's an even more important rule, and this one's for everybody. You never steal from a teammate. If you can't trust each other, who *can* you trust?" His voice became low and hard. "One of you is a thief. *I intend to find out who.* All of you," he snapped, "line up."

They trembled. He scowled as he searched their clothes.

But he didn't find the cards. "Where are they, Grisman? Nobody's got them. You made trouble for nothing. You must have lost them outside."

Saul couldn't stop weeping. "But I know they were in my pants."

"Say *sir.*" Saul jumped. "And if I ever see those cards or hear about them again, you'll be the sorriest wretch in this school. What's the matter with the rest of you? Move it! Finish dressing!"

The boys scrambled to do what they were told. Chris pulled on his pants, watching Saul stare angrily at everyone as he buttoned his shirt. Chris guessed what Saul was doing—looking for bulges in somebody's clothes—as if he didn't think the instructor had searched hard enough. While the instructor locked the door to the swimming pool, Saul moved next to a boy and studied a lump in his shirt pocket. The boy pulled a handkerchief from that pocket and blew his nose.

The instructor turned from locking the door, shouting, "Aren't you dressed yet, Grisman?"

Saul hurried, tugging on his pants, tying his shoes. Tears dripped on his shirt.

"Fall in," the instructor said.

The boys lined up, two by two. Fastening his belt, Saul ran to his place. As they marched to the dormitory, the world seemed to change. A few boys were sympathetic. "Gee, that's too bad. What a dirty trick. Who'd be mean enough to steal your cards?" But the group didn't have the same eagerness to be close to Saul and get his attention.

Saul, for his part, didn't want to be close to them either. He stayed to himself in the dormitory. At supper, he gave up his honored central place, preferring to sit at the end of the table, not talking to anyone. Chris understood. If they were excluding Saul, *he* was excluding them. Though only one boy had stolen the cards, Saul couldn't tell which one. As a consequence, Saul was blaming everybody. The boys in turn had discovered Saul was vulnerable. He'd even cried, and that made him just another kid in the group. His cards had made him special. Without them, he'd still be taller and stronger and faster—but he had no power. Worse, by breaking down, he'd embarrassed them.

Soon the class had other heroes of the moment. In swimming class, a few kids even managed to equal Saul's performance, possibly because he showed no enthusiasm. He'd lost his joy. But Chris never went to the pool without feeling troubled by what had happened in the locker room that day. Who'd stolen the cards? he wondered, noticing the angry flare in Saul's eyes each time the group dressed, as if Saul relived his loss and humiliation.

Another question equally troubled Chris. How had the cards been stolen? The instructor had searched each boy's clothes. So how had the cards disappeared? He felt excited as a sudden thought occurred to him.

Eager, he couldn't wait to tell Saul, but then he remembered what had happened when he confused Babe Ruth with the candy bar, and he stopped himself, afraid of being laughed at if he was wrong. He waited for his chance to prove what he suspected, and the next day when his class walked from the school building to the dormitory, he hung back. Out of sight, he hurried to the changing room in the basement of the gym. After searching beneath the benches and behind the equipment locker, he found the cards wedged between a pipe and the wall beneath the sink. He shook as he held them. Whoever had stolen the cards must have been afraid the class would be searched. To protect himself, the boy had hidden them in the changing room, planning to come back when it was safe. Chris shoved the cards in his pocket, breathless as he ran from the gym to the dormitory to give them to Saul. He imagined how delighted Saul would be. Now Saul would be his friend.

Unlike the group, Chris had never stopped wanting to be close to him. From the start, he'd felt attracted as he would to a brother, and he'd never forgotten that afternoon in swimming class when the instructor had praised him for kicking as well as Saul did and Saul had turned to him grinning as if they shared a bond. But Saul now had built a wall around himself, and without the gift of the cards, Chris didn't know how to break through.

As he reached the dormitory, though, Chris suddenly felt uncertain. The cards had been stolen a week ago. Why hadn't the boy who hid them come back to get them? Pausing on the stairs, Chris knew the answer. Because the boy had realized he couldn't show them to anyone or play with them except in secret. Otherwise word would get around —Saul would find out, and there'd be trouble. The bulge of the cards in Chris's pocket made him worried. Though he hadn't stolen the cards, it would seem as if he had. Saul would blame him. After all, how else would Chris have known where they were?

Panicked, Chris had to get rid of them. In the dormitory's basement washroom, he thought of hiding them under a sink as the thief had done. But what if a janitor cleaned beneath the sinks and found them, or what if a boy dropped his comb and happened to glance beneath the sink as he picked the comb up? No, he needed somewhere out of reach. Glancing above him, he noticed the steam pipes covered with grimy asbestos liners suspended along the ceiling. Climbing on the shoeshine stands, then across the cast-iron towel racks attached to the wall, he wedged the cards above a steam pipe. Nervous, he climbed back down, sighing in relief that he hadn't been caught. Now all he had to do was figure out how to return the cards to Saul without being blamed for stealing them.

He couldn't sleep all night, thinking about it. There had to be a way.

The next day, Saul was still sulking when Chris came over to him outside the refectory after lunch. "I know who stole your cards."

Saul angrily demanded, "Who?"

"The swimming instructor."

"He said he didn't take them."

"He lied. I saw him give them to our teacher. I know where she put them."

"Where?"

A supervisor came over. "You guys are supposed to be in your room for rest period." He followed them into the dormitory.

"I'll tell you later," Chris whispered to Saul when the supervisor wasn't looking.

After school, Saul hurried to Chris. "So tell me where."

In the school building, Chris told Saul to watch the corridor while he snuck back in the classroom. "She put them in her desk."

"But her desk is locked," Saul said.

"I know a way to open it." Chris left Saul in the corridor. He'd seen their teacher go outside, so he guessed it was safe to be in the classroom. He didn't try to open the desk, but he waited long enough to make it seem he had. Finally he joined Saul in the corridor.

"Did you get them?" Saul asked anxiously.

Instead of answering, Chris made Saul follow him down the stairs. With no one around, he quickly reached beneath the front of his pants, pulling the cards out. Earlier he'd retrieved them from the pipe in the dormitory's basement washroom.

Saul looked delighted. Then his brow contorted, mystified. "But how'd you get in her desk?"

"I'll show you sometime. You got your cards back. I'm the one who found them. Just remember who helped you—that's all." Chris started toward the exit.

Behind him, Saul said, "Thanks."

Chris shrugged. "It was nothing."

"Wait a minute."

Chris turned. Coming toward him, Saul frowned as if trying to decide on something. Pained, he fumbled among his cards and handed Chris one. "Here."

"But—"

"Take it."

Chris looked at the card. Babe Ruth. His knees felt weak.

"Why'd you help me?" Saul asked.

"Because." The magic word said everything. He didn't need to add, "I want to be your friend."

Saul glanced self-consciously at the floor. "I guess I could show you a better way to do that kick in swimming class if you want."

Heart pounding, Chris nodded. Then it was his turn to frown. He groped in a pocket. "Here." He handed Saul a candy bar. Baby Ruth.

Saul's eyes widened in amazement. "Candy's not allowed. Where'd you get this?"

"How'd you bring the cards into school without getting caught?"

"A secret."

"Same with me and the candy bar." Chris scuffled his feet. "But I'll tell *you* if you tell *me.*"

They stared at each other and started grinning.

10

Chris had a secret all right. Earlier that day, when the governess had taken Chris out of class and marched him to the administration building, he'd been afraid he was going to be punished for something. His legs shaky, he entered an office. At first it looked empty. Then in confusion he noticed a man by a window, peering out. The man was tall and thin. He wore a black suit, and when he turned, Chris blinked in surprise, recognizing the gray face of the man who'd brought him here.

"Hello, Chris." The man's voice was soft. He smiled. "It's good to see you again."

Behind him, Chris heard the door shut as the governess left the office. He tensed, gazing up at the man, who continued to smile.

178

"You do remember me, don't you? Eliot?"

Chris nodded.

"Of course you do. I came to find out how you're getting along." Eliot approached him. "I know the school must seem strange to you, but you'll get used to it." He chuckled. "At least the food must agree with you. You look as if you've put on a couple pounds." Still chuckling, he crouched so Chris didn't have to strain to look up at him. "I had another reason for coming here." He peered directly into Chris's eyes.

Chris shifted from one leg to the other.

"I told you I'd come back to see you." Eliot put his hands on Chris's shoulders. "I want you to know I keep my promises." He reached in a pocket. "And I promised to bring you more of these." He held out two Baby Ruth candy bars.

Chris's heart beat fast. By now, he knew how valuable candy was in the school. The only way to get it was by smuggling it in. He studied them eagerly.

Slowly, formally, Eliot gave them to Chris. "I promise something else. I'll bring them every time I come to see you. Count on that. I want you to know you've got a friend. More than a friend. I'm like your father. Trust me. Depend on me."

Chris put one of the bars in his pocket, vaguely sensing a way to use it, uncertain how. He glanced from the other bar toward Eliot, who smiled again. "Oh, by all means, eat it. Enjoy it." Eliot's eyes twinkled.

Tearing off the wrapper, his mouth watering as he bit into the chocolate, Chris suddenly felt hollow. His chest ached. Unable to stop himself, he threw his arms around Eliot, sobbing convulsively.

11

Eliot sometimes visited twice in a week. Other times he was gone for half a year. But true to his promise, he always brought Baby Ruth candy bars. Chris learned that no matter how stern the school could be there was one adult whose kindness and interest he could always depend on. Eliot arranged to take Chris from school to see boxing and tennis. They went to Howard Johnson's for chocolate sundaes. Eliot taught Chris how to play chess. He took Chris to his large home in Falls Church, Virginia, where Chris marveled at the huge chairs and sofas, the enormous dining room, and the spacious bedrooms. Eliot showed him the brilliant roses in the greenhouse. Intrigued by the suburb's name—Falls Church—Chris smelled the roses, reminded of the fragrance of Easter service, feeling as if the greenhouse indeed were a church.

As his relationship with Eliot grew, so did his friendship with Saul. The two boys seemed inseparable. Chris shared his Baby Ruths with Saul, and Saul for his part shared his physical skills, teaching Chris the secrets of baseball and football and basketball. But Saul, the natural athlete, had trouble with mathematics and languages, so Chris, the natural scholar, helped Saul to study and pass his exams. They complemented each other. What the one couldn't do, the other could, together unbeatable. Saul again became the envy of his group. But so did Chris.

Only one thing was lacking to make it all perfect.

Eliot's next visit was the first weekend in July. "Tomorrow's the Fourth, Chris. Tell you what. Why don't I take you to the big fireworks show downtown?"

Chris got excited.

But Eliot seemed troubled. "I've been wondering. Now tell me the truth. You won't hurt my feelings."

Chris didn't know what he meant.

"These trips we go on."

Chris felt afraid. "You're going to stop them?"

"No. Good Heavens, they mean too much to me." Eliot laughed and mussed Chris's hair. "But I've been thinking. I bet it must get boring for you with only a grownup to talk to. You must get tired of seeing the same old face. What I've been wondering—well, would you like to share these trips with someone else? Have you got a friend, a *special* friend, you'd like to bring along? Someone you're really close to, who's almost family? I won't mind."

Chris couldn't believe his luck—the chance to be with the two most important people in his world at once. He'd always felt bad, not being able to share his fortune with Saul. In turn, he felt so proud of being friends with Saul he wanted Eliot to know him. His eyes beamed, excited. "You bet!"

"Then what are you waiting for?" Eliot grinned.

"You won't go away?"

180

"I'll stay right here."

Bursting with anticipation, Chris ran from the bench near the armory where they'd been sitting. "Saul! Guess what?" Behind him, he heard Eliot chuckle.

Thereafter Saul was always included. Chris felt overjoyed at Eliot's approval of his friend. "You're right. He's special, Chris. You made an excellent choice. I'm proud of you." Eliot brought candy bars for both of them now. He took them for Thanksgiving to his home. He let them go on a plane ride. "Chris, there's one thing that bothers me. I hope you're not jealous when I give Saul candy bars or show him attention. I wouldn't want you to think I was ignoring you or treating him with more importance than you. You're like a son to me. I love you. We'll always be close. If I make Saul feel good, it's because I want to make *you* feel good—because he's your friend, because he's family."

"Gosh, I couldn't be jealous of Saul."

"Then you understand. I knew you would. You trust me."

Every Saturday night, in the many years to come, the school showed a different movie, but in one way, they were all the same. *Battle Cry, The Sands of Iwo Jima, Guadalcanal Diary, Francis Goes to West Point, Francis in the Navy*. "That talking mule sure makes the military seem a lot of fun," the boys said. *The Frogmen, Back to Bataan, Combat Squad, Beachhead, Battle Zone, Battleground, Battle Stations.* In ancient history, they learned about Alexander's conquests and Caesar's Gallic wars. In American history, they learned about the War for Independence, the War of 1812, the Civil War. In literature classes, they read *The Red Badge of Courage, For Whom the Bell Tolls, The Thin Red Line*. They didn't mind the repeated theme, for the books were filled with heroics and action, always exciting. As well, the boys liked rifle practice, tactical maneuvers, precision marching, and the other training they received in the school's militia. They enjoyed the war games. In class as well as in sports, they were encouraged to compete against the other boys, to see who was smarter, stronger, faster, better. And they couldn't help noticing the strangers who often appeared silently at the back of the gym or the football field or the classroom, sometimes in uniform, sometimes not. With dark narrowed eyes, the strangers watched, comparing, judging.

12

Candy. Because of it, Saul saved Chris's life in 1959. The boys were fourteen—though they didn't know, they were about to end one set of adventures and begin another. With money Eliot had given them, they'd gone into business, smuggling candy into school in exchange for kitchen detail and similar nuisance jobs the other boys did for them. On December 10, after lights out, they snuck from the dormitory across the snowy grounds to a secluded section of the high stone wall. Saul stood on Chris's shoulders and climbed. Chris grabbed his arm, squirming up after him. In starlight, they saw their frosty breath escape from their mouths as they lay on top and studied the dark street below them.

Seeing no one, they eased over. Dangling, Saul let go first, but Chris suddenly heard him groan and peered down, startled. Saul had landed on his back, sliding in a blur to the street.

Chris didn't understand. He quickly jumped to help, bending his knees to absorb the impact, but the moment he landed, he realized something was wrong. Like Saul, his legs shot out from under him. Falling, he cracked his head on the sidewalk and slid out into the street. Dimly he became aware that the snow had melted during the day but now at night had frozen to a slick sheet of ice. Frantic, he failed to stop himself as he continued skidding toward Saul. His boots struck Saul where he lay and knocked him farther into the street.

The sudden clanging paralyzed him. A streetcar swung around a corner, approaching them, its headlight glaring. Its wheels scraped on the icy tracks. Chris saw the driver shouting behind the windshield, tugging the rope that rang the bell, and yanking a lever. The brakes squealed, but the wheels continued sliding ahead. Chris tried to stand. Dizzy from his injured skull, he lost his balance, falling again. The streetcar's headlights blinded him.

Saul dove across him, grabbed his coat, and dragged him toward the curb. The streetcar's shadow passed with a wind that made Chris shiver. "You damn crazy kids!" the driver shouted from his window. The bell kept clanging as the streetcar rumbled down the street.

Chris sat on the icy curb, breathing deeply, his head between his knees. Saul checked his skull.

"Too much blood. We've got to get you back to the dorm."

Chris almost didn't manage the return climb over the wall. A supervisor nearly caught them as they crept up a stairwell. In a shadowy washroom, Saul cleaned Chris's wound as best as he could, and the next day when a teacher asked about the scab on Chris's head, Chris explained he'd tripped down some stairs. That should have been the end of the matter, except because Saul had saved Chris's life, their bond was closer. But neither boy anticipated repercussions or realized what else had almost happened to them.

Ten days later when they next went over the wall, a gang confronted them as they headed toward the stores on the other side of Fairmont Park.

The biggest kid demanded their money, grabbing at Chris's pockets.

Angry, Chris pushed him and never saw the fist that struck his stomach. Through blurry eyes, he saw two other kids grab Saul's arms from behind. A fourth kid punched Saul's face. Blood spattered.

Unable to breathe, Chris tried to help Saul. A fist split his lips. As he fell, a boot cracked his shoulder. Other boots rammed his chest, his side, his back.

He rolled from their impact, writhing. Muffled punches threw Saul on him.

Mercifully, the beating stopped. The gang took the money. On bloody snow, Chris peered through a swirl as they ran away. Delirious, he nonetheless felt mystified about . . .

He wasn't sure what—something about . . .

He sorted it out only after a police car found them staggering back to school and took them first to the emergency ward at the hospital, then to the infirmary at school.

The gang had looked more like adults than kids, their hair too short and neat, their boots and jeans and leather jackets strangely new. They'd driven away in an expensive car.

Why had they been so sure we had money? Chris thought. He remembered the last time he and Saul had gone over the wall—when Saul had pulled him away from the streetcar—and wondered if the gang had been waiting then.

His thoughts were interrupted. In the infirmary bed, aching, he smiled through swollen lips when he saw Eliot hurry in.

"I came as soon as I could." Eliot sounded out of breath, tugging off his black topcoat and homburg hat, snowflakes melting on them. "I wasn't told till—oh, dear God, your faces!" He glanced appalled from Chris to Saul. "You look like they beat you with clubs. It's a miracle you weren't both killed." He studied them, sickened.

"They used just their fists," Saul answered, weak, his face bruised and puffy. "And their boots. They didn't need clubs."

"Your eyes. You'll have shiners for weeks." Eliot winced. "You can't know how sorry I am." His voice became stern. "In a way, I suppose, you invited it, though. The headmaster told me what he discovered you'd been up to—sneaking from school, buying candy. Is that what you do with the money I give you?"

Chris felt embarrassed.

"Never mind. It's not the time to raise the subject. Right now, you need sympathy—not a lecture. As long as it happened, I hope you gave them some lumps in return."

"We never touched them," Saul murmured.

Eliot looked surprised. "But I thought the school gave you boxing class. You guys are tough. I've seen you on the football field. You mean you didn't land even one punch?"

Chris shook his head, stiffening from pain. "They hit me before I knew what was going on. Boxing? I never had a chance to raise a fist. They were all over us."

"They moved too quick for me," Saul added. "Boxing's a joke. They were better than that. They were—" He struggled for the proper word.

"Experts?"

Aching, Saul nodded.

Eliot studied them and frowned. Lips pursed, he seemed to consider something. "I assume you've learned not to sneak out of school anymore." He didn't wait for an answer. "Even so, you ought to be prepared for an emergency. You should be able to defend yourselves. I certainly don't like seeing those handsome faces of yours turned into ground beef." He nodded thoughtfully as if making an important decision.

Chris wondered what.

13

Saul's fifteenth birthday occurred on January 20, 1960. On that occasion, Eliot drove up from Washington to take the boys out on the town. They went first to a Horn and Hardart automat for baked beans and coleslaw, then to an Elvis Presley movie, *G.I. Blues*. When Eliot returned them to the school, he gave them a set of books filled with stop-action photographs of men in white uniforms throwing or kicking each other. At that time, the only thing Americans knew about martial arts came from stories about Japanese soldiers in World War Two. The boys thought the pictures showed a form of professional wrestling. The next week when Eliot came to see them, they'd had a chance to study the books. He spoke of patriotism and courage and offered them the opportunity to forfeit all high school sports, instead to train privately for three hours a day, seven days a week till their graduation.

Both boys jumped at the chance. For one thing, it was a wonderful way of escaping the routine at Franklin. For another, more important, they still showed signs of the beating they'd received, and they were determined not to suffer like that again. Neither boy realized how extreme their determination would become.

The second weekend in February, Eliot took them to meet their instructors. The boys had known for some time that Eliot worked for the government, so they weren't surprised when he told them that seven years earlier, in 1953, the CIA had recruited Yukio Ishiguro, a former Japanese world judo champion, and Major Soo Koo Lee, a one-time senior karate instructor for the South Korean army. Both Orientals had been brought to the United States to train operatives in what, prior to killer-instinct training, were the finest forms of hand-to-hand combat. The base of operations consisted of a large gym, called a *dojo,* located on the fifth floor of a warehouse in downtown Philadelphia, about a mile from the orphanage.

The elevator to the fifth floor looked like a rusty shower stall. It barely accommodated the three passengers and stank of urine and sweat. Graffiti covered the walls. The *dojo* itself was a large loft with

185

steel girders in the ceiling and rows of harsh floodlights. Most of the floor was covered by green three-inch-thick *tatami* mats. Beyond them, a border of oak gleamed before mirrors on all the walls.

When Chris and Saul entered with Eliot, they noticed several gaming tables between the dressing room and mat area. At one of these tables, they found Lee and Ishiguro using black and white stones to play an oriental game that Eliot explained was called Go. Both instructors wore suits, Ishiguro's made of blue silk, Lee's of gray sharkskin. Both men were shoeless. Their socks were clean and white, their shirts heavily starched, their striped ties carefully knotted and pressed.

With no hair on his head and his belly protruding, Ishiguro looked like an oversized Buddha. But when he stood, his six-foot-three-inch height and two hundred and ninety pounds presented an awesome figure. In contrast, Lee stood five foot four inches tall on a small frame and still had his shiny ebony hair as well as a black thin mustache. His musculature suggested springy steel.

The game stopped at once. The two orientals gave short bows of respect to Eliot, then shook hands with the boys.

"I do hope our mutual friend, Mr. Eliot, has explained that we are not here to teach you a sport," Ishiguro said in flawless English. "Sensei Lee and I hope you will accept our service. If you do, we promise you will learn to perceive rapid movement as if it were slow. That much alone will place you above most men. Here, everything you learn will become second nature, as it must, for you will not have time to think if death approaches—instead you will have only a moment to prove that you should live. You may tell your school friends what you learn, but you will soon discover they don't understand. What you must never do is *show* them. Since you can't predict a future enemy, isn't it better if no one else has the knowledge you do?"

Lee said nothing, neither smiled nor frowned. While Ishiguro went to boil water for tea, Eliot broke the silence by asking Lee about the game of Go. Lee immediately came to attention.

"Appearance is deception," he said with a smile. "As you see, the board is made up of half-inch squares. The spaces are not important. The lines mean everything. By placing a stone on the board and building a pattern from there, I hope to enclose as much territory as possible. The object is simple—to offset my opponent with the suspicion that I'm establishing a network to entrap him. Which of course I am." Lee laughed. He demonstrated how to handle a stone using two fingers like a claw. Ishiguro returned with the tea, and eventually the meeting

186

concluded with the orientals admonishing the boys to consider the proposition and decide in private.

It was all too brief. Puzzled, they listened to Eliot's explanation as the creaky elevator descended.

"When you were little, you were interested in sports. As you got older, you idolized heroes in war movies. You've just met two middle-aged men in a sleazy Philadelphia warehouse. Two men who are recognized as great, as having superior skill, by over two-thirds of the world. Perhaps humility is the only visible sign of wisdom. I don't know. But they've accepted the responsibility of training men in specific areas of security for our government. Both are paid well, but I don't think they're interested in money. I believe their interest involves the opportunity to teach young men to become the best fighters in the world. Today was just an introduction, a chance for you to see what's involved. If you decide to participate, the program must be carried out to its conclusion. Never break a promise. They accept you as men. They won't appreciate little kids who stand around with their mouths open in wonderment or who give up. So make your choice wisely and call me collect before next Sunday. Oh, and by the way, if you do decide to join, there'll be no more evening meals at Franklin. But don't expect to be eating hoagies and steak sandwiches. They've got a special diet for you: flank steak, heart, fish for protein, rice to fill you up, tea occasionally, grapefruit juice always. No more Baby Ruths for a while, I'm afraid. Keep to their menu, it'll do you good. But if you tire of the food, you mustn't stop drinking the juice. Lee and Ishiguro swear by it. They say it takes all the cramps and stiffness away. This isn't the Marine Corps—you're gonna have to work your ass off for these guys."

When the boys phoned Eliot to say they wanted to join, he told them he'd pick them up on Sunday. "Dress up, wear clean underwear, be prepared for a ceremony. Think along the lines of a Bar Mitzvah or a confirmation."

On their second visit to the *dojo,* Chris and Saul were initiated into manhood through a ritual called *gempuku.* Instead of the traditional short sword and long sword, they were given a judo *gi* and a karate *gi.* The uniforms caught their attention. The first was heavily woven cotton, the second lightweight serge. Called *haori,* the coats reached down to the knees. The pants were *hakama,* and the purpose of their wide flaring sides was to give no suggestion of the build of the wearer.

Ishiguro noticed the boys' curiosity. "Mr. Lee and I have decided to accept you as *shizoku,* which means descendants of samurai. It has

187

special meaning to us and to your friend Mr. Eliot. It places the added responsibility on you to protect yourself against humiliation. If you accept that duty, you may need to dispose of yourself some day. That is why this ceremony of manhood tells you how to use the sword. True manhood is challenged when a decision of this type is needed. I must tell you of *jijin,* the proper use of the sword to end one's life."

Ishiguro sat down on the floor with his legs crossed before him. He took the small sword whose blade was only fourteen inches long and moved it from right to left horizontally across his abdomen.

"The pain will be intense. Your final act will be to rise above the pain by remaining still with your head bowed. Your assistant will finish the procedure."

Standing beside him, Lee took a sword whose blade was forty inches long and dramatized the final act of beheading. "Be careful not to cut completely through the neck but instead to leave a flap so the head will remain attached to the body."

Ishiguro looked up and smiled. "That is *seppuku,* and it means disembowelment—death with honor. Anything by other means is *jisai* or mere self-disposal. It is all a part of an honorable tradition, the initiation into a divine way of manhood we no longer have in this century. The instruction you receive will have no mystery, no glamor. It will train you to kill or, if you fail, to die with honor."

The boys were stunned.

"There is no longer time in your life to idolize others," Ishiguro continued. "Now there is only the self—without the approval of others. That is important, for to fascinate others with your skill places your personality in their stereotype of you, a stereotype at one time accepted, at another time unaccepted, depending on current fashion. You will rise above this. When you are through with us, your black belt will tell everyone only that you are a serious student. You will never officially pass beyond *shodan* or the first degree, though you'll go far beyond that. To reveal the true extent of your training would expose you to national and international competition. But the way of the samurai makes you more than a mere technician of swordplay or a specialist with the knife for the amusement of others. Your destiny is profound."

The boys learned how to sit properly, to bow, to show respect, and to release an opponent in distress. Ishiguro took Chris aside; Lee worked with Saul. The next day, the instructors switched partners. The first two weeks were devoted to learning proper falls, the *katas* or dance steps, and the means to unbalance an opponent. Once these basics were understood, the boys began the advanced training commonly reserved for black belts. They learned to choke an opponent, to lock his arms, to break his extremities.

"For men with instincts as quick as your own," Lee explained, "you will see a kick coming as if it were suspended. All you must do is step back or to the side and watch your assailant lose his balance. Never allow yourself to be cornered. Instead keep moving forward to corner your man. At the same time, wait for him to attack. Defend yourself so surely that your one and only blow serves its purpose. Never square off with him within the length of his legs. Never allow him to grab you from the front. To do so is merely to wrestle with him, to create a sport with him. I will show you how to protect yourself against an attacker who grabs you from the rear, who clutches your neck, your arms. You will learn to bend at the knee, to use the fulcrum of your hip. These tactics must be automatic."

They came to understand profoundly that the ability to overpower an opponent did not belong to the young or the athletic but to those with secret knowledge. The skills they learned gave them the confidence to relax and recognize danger. Their power made them humble.

Lee told them stories. "I went to missionary school. I learned your Bible—both books. I will tell you something that has always interested me. In the old book, Isaiah, your God said, 'I created day; I created night. I created good; I created evil. I, the Lord, did all these things.' I have always wondered how a Westerner can judge evil as wrong when his own God created it and permitted Lucifer to protect it. Strange how the warrior who has seen death and miracles either remains in the military or else joins a monastery—for the sake of the discipline. Meanwhile, those safe at home, who know nothing, talk of the bad, the wrong, the sinful. How wonderful that the history of the warrior does not allow the contemplation of good and evil but only of duty, honor, and loyalty."

Ishiguro allowed the boys to make a game of *shinigurai*. In Japanese, the word meant being crazy to die. He hoped that someday this horseplay would allow the boys to leap into the jaws of death with no hesitation. The game involved jumping over each other and objects, falling from heights and landing flatly on their chests.

Lee said, "There is nothing more exciting than to know that a friend is somewhere in the dark facing death. Such exhilaration!"

Ishiguro said, "I will read to you from the *Hugakure*. The title means hidden among leaves. It explains the classic code of ethics for

189

the samurai. The way of the samurai is death. In a fifty-fifty life-or-death crisis, simply approach the crisis, prepared to die if necessary. There is nothing complicated about it. Merely brace yourself and proceed. One who fails in a mission and chooses to continue living will be despised as a coward and a bungler. To be a perfect samurai, you must prepare yourself for death morning and evening, day in, day out. Hell is to live in uneventful times when you have no choice except to wait for valor."

On the day they finished their training, Ishiguro gave them their final lesson. "For many years in Japanese history, a commander held respect from his people. He was called a shogun, something like your president. Beneath him were his masters of skill, such as your Pentagon and CIA. Under the care and command of these masters were the *hatamoto*, who as samurai served their masters in the shogun's camp. The masters were intermediaries—they guaranteed honor to the chief and justice to the men. In turn, the samurai promised gratitude, bravery, and obligation. Their responsibility was known as *giri*. If a samurai developed a monastic conviction or sustained a crippling blow, he was dismissed from the service of the shogun. When a master died, the shogun released the master's samurai from service. These samurai would travel the country alone—they showed no allegiance to a wife —but because their skills were so precise and deadly, they were often hunted, certainly challenged often. Many formed teams. A few became bandits, but most became monks. Isn't it strange how the power to kill often makes a warrior monastic? But in your case, the shogun is not your president. Such a man passes in and out of favor by the whim of popular opinion. No, your shogun is Eliot. He may retire you, or he may die. But without him, you are only wanderers."

14

The rain kept drumming on the cabin's roof. Outside, the morning was as bleak as dusk.

Erika blinked in dismay. Taking turns, Chris and Saul had explained. "How long did you say you received instruction?" she asked.

190

"Three years," Saul answered. "Three hours every day."

She inhaled. "But you were only kids."

"You mean we were young," Chris said. "The way we were raised, I'm not sure we were ever kids."

"We enjoyed those classes. We liked making Eliot proud of us," Saul said. "All we wanted was his approval."

Chris pointed to the computer printouts on the table. "Given the other parallels, my guess is the men on this list grew up in the same kind of atmosphere we did."

"Conditioned," Erika said.

Saul's eyes were grim. "It worked. The spring we graduated from high school, Special Forces and the 82nd Airborne each sent recruiters to the school. They spent a week competing to convince our class which unit had more to offer." His voice became bitter. "The same way IBM and Xerox recruit at a college. The boys in our class chose one military unit or the other, but as a group, they enlisted one hundred percent. In doing so, they continued a tradition. No boy ever graduated from Franklin without joining the military. They wanted to prove their courage so much that six years later, in '68, by the time of the Tet offensive in Nam, eighty percent of our class had been killed in combat."

"Jesus," Erika said.

"But for us, the process still wasn't finished," Chris continued. "Eliot called it layering. After the school and the *dojo,* after Special Forces and Nam, we went through Rothberg's killer-instinct training. Then we went to the agency's farm in Virginia. Eliot had long since recruited us. In a sense, our training had begun when we were five. But after the farm, we were finally ready to work for him."

"He made you the best."

"He made us. Yes." Chris pursed his lips in anger. "And these other men as well. He programmed us to be absolutely dedicated to him."

"Never to question anything. Like the Paradigm job," Saul said. "I never dreamed of asking him why he wanted it done. If he ordered something, that was good enough."

"We were so naive he must have been tempted to laugh. When we snuck from school that night and the gang beat us up . . ." Chris glared. "I only now realized. Something about them always bothered me. They looked too neat. Their leather jackets were new. They drove an expensive car." He shivered. "They must have been operatives. He sent them to work us over, to make us angry so we'd grab the chance to learn at the *dojo*. God knows how many other ways he manipulated us."

"Those Baby Ruth candy bars. He gave me one in Denver when he set me up to be killed."

"The same when he asked me to hunt for you," Chris added. "We're Pavlov's dogs. Those candy bars are the symbol of his relationship with us. He used them to make us love him. It was easy. No one else ever showed us kindness. An old man giving candy to kids."

The rain drummed harder on the roof.

"And now we find out everything he said was wrong. A trick. A lie," Saul said. "He never loved us. He used us."

"Not only us." Chris seethed. "These other men must have felt he loved them too. He lied to everyone. We were all just part of a group. I could almost forgive his lies—the things he made me do!—if I thought we were special to him. But we're not." He listened to the storm, his words like thunder. "And for that, I'll see him die."

NEMESIS

1

Two minutes after the bootlegger opened, Hardy stepped back on the street, clutching two bottles of Jim Beam in a paper sack. He prided himself on his choice of brand. His government pension allowed him few frills, but he'd never debased himself by drinking unaged, bottom-of-the-price-list whiskey. Nor had he ever been tempted to try the cheap pop wines or the sick-sweet fruity rum concoctions preferred by the other drunks in his building. He had standards. He ate once a day, whether hungry or not. He washed and shaved daily and wore fresh clothes. He had to. In the Miami humidity, he sweated constantly, the alcohol oozing from his pores as fast as he tossed it down. Even now, at five after eight in the morning, the heat was obscene. His sunglasses shielded the glare and hid his bloodshot eyes. His flower-patterned shirt stuck to him, soaking the paper bag he held against his chest. He glanced toward his stomach, appalled by the pale puffy skin protruding from an open button on his shirt. With dignity, he closed it. Soon, in two more blocks, he'd be back in the dark security of his room, the blinds shut, the fan on, watching the last half-hour of "Good Morning, America," toasting David Hartman.

The thought of the day's first drink made him shake. He glanced around in case a cop was watching, then veered toward an alley, feeling sheltered beneath a fire escape. As traffic roared past the entrance, he reached in the paper bag, twisted the cap off one of the bottles, and pulled the neck out, raising it to his lips. He closed his eyes, luxuriating in the warmth of the bourbon trickling down his throat. His body relaxed. His tremors stopped.

Abruptly he stiffened, hearing the blare of music throbbing, coming closer. Puzzled, he opened his eyes and gaped at the tallest Cuban he'd ever seen, wearing a shiny purple shirt and mirrored glasses, gyrating to the raucous beat of the ghetto box strapped around his shoulders. Husky, cruel-lipped, the Cuban crowded him against the wall beneath the fire escape.

Hardy shook again—from fear this time. "Please. I've got ten bucks in my wallet. Just don't hurt me. Don't take the whiskey."

The Cuban only frowned. "What're you talking about? A dude said to give you this." He stuffed an envelope in the paper bag and walked away.

"What? Hey, wait a minute. Who? What'd he look like?"

The Cuban shrugged. "Just a dude. What difference does it make? You all look alike. He gave me twenty bucks. That's all I cared about."

As Hardy blinked, the Cuban disappeared from the alley, the music from his ghetto box fading. Hardy licked his lips and tasted a residue of bourbon. Nervous, he reached for the envelope in the bag. He felt a long thin object sealed inside. Awkwardly tearing the envelope, he dumped a key in the palm of his hand.

It looked like the key to a safety-deposit box. It had a number: 113. And letters: USPS. Groggy, he tried to concentrate, finally guessing what the letters referred to. United States Postal Service. A mail drop.

Like the old days. The notion disturbed him. He hadn't worked for Intelligence since 1973, when Watergate had resulted in a massive house-cleaning of the agency. Despite his drinking, he'd still been valuable enough that he'd hoped to cling to his job as director of South American operations till he reached the age for retirement. But the political scandals after the break-in had required scapegoats, and a boozer made a good one. At sixty-two, he'd been forced to resign—at least he'd received his full pension—and with an alcoholic's hatred of cold, he'd headed toward Miami.

Now he thought, Hell, I'm too old for games. A mail drop. What a crock. First they kick me out. Then they figure they can snap their fingers and I'll work for them again. He stuffed the key in the paper bag and stepped from the alley. Well, they'd better figure one more time.

He walked half a block before he questioned his assumption. Maybe the key didn't come from the agency. He frowned and paused. It might be from the other side. His head ached. Which other side, though? More important, why? Who needs a boozer? Even if I was sober, I'm out of practice. After nine years, I don't know anything about the agency's operations. What the hell?

The fierce sun stabbed through his tinted glasses, making him squint. His spine itched with the sense he was being watched. He glanced around him. Stupid, he thought. Pal, you're not kidding you're out of practice. An obvious move like that could have got you killed in the old days.

Not that it mattered anymore. Whatever game was being offered, he didn't intend to play. Someone had wasted time and twenty bucks. All he wanted was to get back home, turn the fan on, and drink his toast to David Hartman. Drink a lot of toasts. And have a few more when his good old pal Phil Donahue came on.

He soon saw the entrance to his apartment building. The owner called it a condominium, but a tenement would have been more accurate. The wreck was fifteen stories high—the concrete so substandard it crumbled from the salty air, the glass so thin it shuddered from the noisy traffic. The halls smelled of cabbage. The plumbing knocked. Through the thin walls, Hardy heard every time his neighbor took a leak. Retirement Villa, the sign said. Premature burial, Hardy thought.

He reached the building and stared at the seagull dung mixed with feathers on the sidewalk before the cracked glass door. His stomach soured as he analyzed the pattern of his days—the bourbon, the game shows, the soaps, at last the news if he could keep himself awake that long, the midnight nightmares, the 3 A.M. sweats. Hell, David Hartman can wait, he thought and turned from the entrance, continuing down the block. He admitted to being a fool. The trouble was, in spite of his bitterness toward the agency and his premonition of trouble, he couldn't stifle his curiosity. He hadn't felt this interested since he'd watched last season's hurricane.

Which postal station? Since he had to start somewhere, he chose the nearest one, stopping in alleys along the way to strengthen his courage with bourbon. The station was glass and chrome, long and low, flanked by palm trees that seemed to stoop from the heat. He walked through the hissing automatic door and smelled the pungent industrial cleaner the janitor used on the concrete floor. The postal boxes lined both sides of a corridor. He found 113 on an oversized door on the right-hand bottom row. Of course, every postal station in the city probably had a box numbered 113. The key might not fit, but when he drew it from the paper bag, he found the key turned smoothly in the lock. The box was so low that when he opened it he had to kneel to look inside. Because of the box's size, he'd expected a package. But he found nothing. Hollow with disappointment, angry at being fooled, he almost stood before his instincts warned him. Why a bottom box? Because, even kneeling, you can't see the top. To see the whole inside, you have to bend down toward the floor. If something's attached to the top, the clerk inserting mail from the other side can't see it. Not unless the clerk bent down to the floor, as Hardy did, and there it was, a small flat plastic container with a magnet sticking it to the top of the box.

His face red from bending over, Hardy pried the magnet free. Unsteadily, he got up. He glanced along the corridor of boxes. No one in sight. Instead of going to a safer location, he took a chance and yanked the flap on the container.

He frowned at another key. What the—?

Not a postal box key. It did have a number: 36.

He turned it over. Atlantic Hotel.

2

Saul tensed when he heard the key scraping in the lock. He crouched behind a chair, clutching his hidden Beretta, staring toward the gradually opening door.

He'd made sure the room was dark, tugging the drapes shut. The light from the hall streamed narrowly across the floor, then widened. A shadow obscured the light. An overweight man stepped slowly in, nervous, clutching something in a paper bag.

"Shut the door and lock it," Saul said.

The man obeyed. In the dark, Saul switched on a swivel-necked desk lamp, aiming it toward him. There wasn't any question now. From behind the lamp, shielded from its glare, he recognized Hardy. The man took off his tinted glasses, raising a hand to protect his eyes. Saul hadn't seen him in thirteen years. Hardy had looked bad then. Now, at the age of seventy-two, he looked worse—puffy fishbelly skin, red blotches on his wrinkled cheeks, a distended abdomen from his swollen liver and the fluid an alcoholic's body retains. His hair was gray, dull, lifeless. But at least it was combed. He'd shaved. He gave off no odor, except from bourbon. His clothes—a hideous flower-patterned shirt and electric-blue polyester pants—looked clean and pressed. His white shoes were freshly polished.

Hell, Saul thought, if I was a lush, I doubt I'd pay as much

196

attention to my appearance. "Hardy, it's good to see you. The light switch is to your left."

"Who—?" Hardy's voice trembled as he groped for the switch. Two lamps—on a bureau and over the bed—came on. Hardy squinted, frowning.

"You don't recognize me? I'm insulted."

Hardy continued frowning. "Saul?" He blinked in confusion.

Still keeping the Beretta hidden, Saul grinned and reached across the chair to shake hands with him. "How are you? What's in the bag?"

"Oh . . ." Hardy shrugged, embarrassed. "Just a few things. I had an early errand."

"Booze?"

"Well, yeah . . ." Hardy wiped his mouth self-consciously. "I'm having some friends over. I didn't realize the liquor cabinet was empty."

"Looks awful heavy. Set it on the dresser. Give your arm a rest."

Bewildered, Hardy did what he was told. "I . . . what's this all about?"

Saul raised his shoulders. "A reunion I guess you could say."

The phone rang. Hardy flinched and stared. It rang again. "Aren't you going to answer it?" But Saul didn't move. The phone stopped ringing. "For Christ's sake," Hardy said, "what's going on? That Cuban—"

"Impressive, wasn't he? I had to look for quite a while before I found him. Just the right sneer."

"But why?"

"We'll get to that. Are you armed?"

"You're kidding. With all these Cuban refugees?"

Saul nodded. Hardy was legendary for never going anywhere without a handgun, including to the bathroom. Once, to the dismay of the Secret Service, he'd worn a revolver to a White House conference with the president. Another time, during a prestigious dinner party, he'd fallen asleep from overdrinking, slumping in his chair till his handgun slipped from his shoulder holster, thumping on the floor in front of two congressmen and three senators. "Put it next to the booze on the dresser."

"Why?"

Saul raised the Beretta from behind the chair. "Just do it."

"Hey, come on." Hardy's eyes widened. He tried to laugh as if convincing himself this was a joke. "You don't need that."

Saul didn't laugh, though.

Hardy pursed his lips. Nervous, he stooped to lift his right pantleg, showing a snub-nosed Colt .38 in an ankle holster.

"Still like those revolvers, huh?"

"You know what they used to call me."

"Wyatt Earp." Saul tensed. "Use just two fingers."

"You don't have to tell me." Hardy sounded indignant. "I still remember the drill." He set the handgun on the dresser. "You satisfied?"

"Not quite." Saul picked it up. "I have to search you."

"Oh, for Christ's sake."

"I won't tickle." After frisking him, Saul showed particular interest in Hardy's buttons.

Hardy blanched. "Is *that* what this is all about? A microphone? You thought I was wired? Why would I—?"

"The same reason we used the Cuban. We're not sure if you're being watched."

"Watched? But why would anybody want to—? Wait a minute. We? Did you say we?"

"Chris is working with me."

"Kilmoonie?" Hardy sounded confused.

"Good. The booze hasn't ruined your memory."

"How could I forget what you guys did for me in Chile? Where—?"

"That phone call was him from the lobby. Two rings meant he doubts you were followed. If he spots any trouble, he'll phone again— one ring—to warn me."

"But I could've told you I wasn't followed." He noticed Saul avoid his stare. "I get it." He nodded grimly. "You figure I'm in no condition to spot a tail."

"Out of action, a person's skills get blunted."

"Especially if he's a lush."

"I didn't say that."

"Hell, you didn't have to." Hardy glared. "What made you sure I'd even come?"

"We weren't. When the Cuban gave you the key, you could've dropped it down a sewer."

"And?"

"We'd have left you alone. You had to prove you were ready to get involved—not just with us but with anything. You had to show you wanted some action."

198

"No."

"I'm not sure what—"

"You had another reason."

Saul shook his head.

"The Cuban," Hardy said. "I can see why you needed him. The key makes sense."

"Well, then—?"

"But the postal box and the second key?"

"Added precautions."

"No, you wanted to give me plenty of time in case I had to slip away and make a phone call. Chris would have seen me do it. He'd have called and warned you to run." Hardy seethed. "So who the hell did you think I'd be working for?"

Saul debated. It was possible Hardy had been approached. On the other hand, Saul didn't know where else to turn. He weighed the possibilities.

And told him.

Hardy looked stunned. For a moment, he didn't seem to understand. Abruptly his face turned red. The veins in his neck bulged. *"What?"* His voice cracked. *"Eliot?* You thought I'd cooperate with that sonofabitch? After what he did to me, you figured I'd help him?"

"We weren't sure. It's been a lot of years. Maybe you'd changed. Sometimes a person forgets to be angry."

"Forgets? Never! That bastard got me fired! I'd like to get my hands around his throat and—"

"Care to prove it?"

Hardy laughed.

3

Saul finished explaining. Hardy listened, eyes harsh, face even redder, feverish with hate. At last he nodded. "Sure. He turned against you, too. I'm not surprised. He turned against everybody else. The wonder is he took so long."

"Keep talking."

"I don't know what—"

"Eliot always said if you want to learn a man's secrets, ask someone who hates him."

"You know more about him than anybody does."

"I thought I did. I was wrong. But you were his rival. You investigated him."

"You heard about that?"

Saul didn't answer.

Hardy turned to the paper bag on the dresser. Yanking out a half-empty bourbon bottle, he twisted off the cap and raised it to his lips. He suddenly stopped, glancing self-consciously. "I don't suppose you've got a glass."

"In the bathroom." Saul took the bottle from him. "But I've got something else for you to drink."

"What is it?"

"Get the glass."

Suspicious, Hardy obeyed. When he came back from the bathroom, his fingers tightened on the glass. He gaped at the bottles Saul had taken from a drawer and swallowed sickly. "No."

"I need you sober. If you have to drink—"

"Vermouth? Is this a joke?"

"Am I laughing?"

"That's disgusting."

"Maybe you won't drink so much. In case you get tempted, though . . ." Saul took the whiskey bottles into the bathroom and emptied them down the sink.

Hardy moaned. "Sixteen bucks they cost me!"

"Here's a twenty. Keep the change."

"Sadist!"

"Think of it this way. The sooner we're finished, the sooner you can buy more bourbon." Saul went to the dresser and opened both kinds of vermouth—red and white—pouring them in Hardy's glass. "In case your stomach's stronger than I thought."

Hardy scowled at the pink concoction. He reached, drew back his hand, then reached again—and drained the glass in three swallows. Gasping, he clutched the dresser. "Jesus."

"You okay?"

"It tastes like Kool-Aid." Hardy shuddered. "I'll never forgive you for this." But he poured another glassful. "All right, I've got to know. So how'd you find out I investigated him?"

"I didn't."

"But you said—"

"I had a hunch—given the way you felt about him. But I wasn't sure. I figured if I asked, you might get scared and deny it. So I claimed I already knew, hoping you'd agree."

"I *have* been down here too long." Hardy sighed. "Okay, it's true. But you had me scared for a minute. Nobody should have known. Believe me, I was careful. A job like that, I didn't trust anybody for help. A little digging here, a little there. No obvious pattern. No time I couldn't account for." Hardy scowled. "Just my luck, Watergate came along. I wasn't involved in the break-in. But Eliot and I had been rivals quite a while. He convinced the director to dump me. As an example. I can see the logic. Hell, I was—still am—a lush. But I can't shake the feeling he saw it as a chance for a final victory."

"You think he knew you were investigating him?"

"Obviously not."

"What makes you sure?"

"He'd have had me killed."

Saul stared. "You learned that much?"

"I was close. There was something. I could feel it. Some days I thought all I needed was one more fact. Just one more—" Hardy shrugged. "But he won. Outside, with no way to continue the investigation, I let the booze control me." He held up his glass. "This is really awful."

"Maybe you'd like some coffee?"

"God, no, that's worse than the vermouth. Retirement." Hardy brooded. "You get lazy down here. How was I supposed to finish what I started? I couldn't get at the computers."

"You wanted to stay alive."

"Or I deserved to be fired. If I'd had any balls, I'd still have kept after him." His forehead broke out in sweat. "It's awful hot."

Saul crossed the room, turning on the air conditioner beside the drapes. It rattled, sending a musty breeze through the room. "What made you want to investigate him?"

Hardy sipped in disgust. "Kim Philby."

4

Back in 1951, Kim Philby had been a high-ranking member of Britain's foreign intelligence network, MI-6. Earlier, during the Second World War, he'd helped to train the inexperienced recruits of America's fledgling espionage network, the OSS. He'd offered advice when the OSS became the CIA in 1947. He'd come to Washington in 1949 to help the FBI investigate Soviet spy rings, and indeed he'd been responsible for proving that a well-respected British diplomat, Donald Maclean, was a Communist agent. Before Maclean could be arrested, however, Maclean had been alerted by another British diplomat, Guy Burgess, himself an unsuspected Communist agent, who fled with Maclean to Russia.

The revelation of such deep Soviet infiltration shocked the Western intelligence community. Equally disturbing was the mystery of how Burgess had known Maclean was under suspicion. Preoccupied by that question, Hardy, then a junior officer in the CIA, had sat in his car in a Washington parking lot, waiting for a sudden rainstorm to end so he could run to his favorite bar for lunch, when a startling thought occurred to him. Foregoing his thirst, he quickly drove back to his office in one of the Quonset buildings that had crowded the Washington Mall since the war. Throwing his rain-drenched topcoat over a chair in his cubicle, he searched through several files, scribbling notes to document the pattern he suspected.

Burgess had warned Maclean. Burgess knew Philby, the man who accused Maclean. Indeed Burgess had once been a guest in Philby's home. Had Philby made an inadvertent slip, letting Burgess know Maclean was in trouble?

That explanation made no sense. Philby had too much experience to reveal sensitive information to a friend of the man he planned to accuse.

Then what was the connection? Burgess, Maclean, and Philby. Hardy made a drastic leap in logic. What if Philby too was a Communist agent? What if Philby had accused Maclean but first had sent Burgess to warn him?

Why, though? Why would Philby accuse a fellow Communist agent? Hardy could think of only one reason—to protect a more important Communist agent who was close to being uncovered. But who'd be more important than Maclean? Hardy's breathing quickened. Philby himself? By accusing Maclean, Philby would raise himself above suspicion. Perhaps, in his work with the FBI, Philby had discovered he was close to being identified as a spy.

Assumptions, Hardy thought. But where's the proof? He suddenly recalled a Communist defector named Krivitsky who, years before, had warned about three Soviet agents in the British diplomatic corps. Krivitsky had identified one man by his last name, King (subsequently arrested), but Krivitsky had been vague about the other two: a Scotsman attracted to Communism in the thirties, and a British journalist in the Spanish Civil War. The Scotsman had now been identified as Maclean. But who was the British journalist?

Hardy studied the small details in Philby's dossier, almost laughing when he found what he wanted: Philby had once been a journalist —in the Spanish Civil War. Abruptly everything fit. Philby and Burgess had known each other as students at Cambridge. Maclean had also gone to Cambridge. In the thirties, each of them had been sympathetic to communism but then had undergone a drastic change, all at once preferring capitalism, joining the British diplomatic service.

Of course, Hardy thought. They'd been approached by the Russians and agreed to become deep-cover Soviet agents.

5

"That made my reputation," Hardy said. The sour vermouth tainted his breath. "People forget I'm the man who unmasked Philby."

"Some of us know who the legends are," Saul said.

"Me and Eliot." Hardy drank. "The golden boys. Eliot scored his points by using ex-Nazis and ex-Fascists who rebuilt their intelligence networks after the war, this time working for us. It seemed we couldn't do anything wrong."

"What's his background?"

"He didn't tell you even that much? Boston. His family was in the social register. His father went to Yale, then worked for the State Department. Shortly after Eliot was born in 1915, his father died when the Germans sank the *Lusitania*. His mother died in the 1918 flu epidemic. You understand what I'm saying?"

"Eliot's an orphan?" Saul felt a chill.

"Like you and Chris. Maybe that explains his interest in the two of you."

"He went to an orphanage?"

"No. He didn't have any grandparents or uncles and aunts. There were some distant relatives who might have taken him in. His inheritance was large enough that supporting him wouldn't have been a problem. But a friend of his father offered to raise him—a man with influence in the State Department. Eliot's relatives agreed. After all, this man could train Eliot as his father would have wanted. The man had wealth and power."

"Who?"

"Tex Auton."

Saul's eyes widened.

"That's right," Hardy said. "One of the designers of the Abelard sanction. Eliot got his training from Auton, who helped to establish the ground rules for modern espionage. You could say Eliot was there at the start of everything. Of course, before the war, America had no separate intelligence network. The military and the State Department did it all. But after Pearl Harbor, the OSS was formed, and Auton encouraged Eliot to join. Eliot went to England to receive his training. He ran some effective operations in France. He liked the work, so after the war he made the shift when the OSS became the CIA. Auton had retired by then, but Eliot often went to him for advice, and the most important thing Auton told him was not to try for the top positions in the agency."

"But for an ambitious man, that advice makes no sense."

"It does if you think about it. How many directors and deputy directors has the agency had over the years? So many I can't remember them. Those positions are political appointments. They change with whoever's in the White House. The real power in the agency—by which I mean the consistent power—lies just below the deputy director and

204

his subordinate: the number four position, nonpolitical, nonappointed, based on merit, on experience within the agency."

"So Eliot took Auton's advice."

Hardy nodded. "He rose as high as he dared. Hell, one president even offered him the directorship, but Eliot turned it down. He wanted to keep his job secure. But he also wanted more power, so he broadened his base, arranging for more and more agents to be responsible to him, spreading his influence into operations in every hemisphere. Chief of counterintelligence. He got that title in 1955, but he had considerable clout even in the forties. Senators, congressmen, presidents, they depend on elections. Eventually they have to leave office. But Eliot never had to worry about elections. Year after year, regardless of whether the Democrats or the Republicans ran the country, Eliot kept the number four slot in the agency. Only one other man ever managed the trick of holding power so long."

"J. Edgar Hoover."

"Right. But Hoover's dead now, so it's no exaggeration to say that Eliot's been the most consistent influence in American government since the forties. Mind you, Eliot always faced the danger of another ambitious man coming along to bump him out of his number four position. To give himself an edge, he investigated anyone who might be a threat to him. Presidents, cabinet members, the various directors of the agency, it didn't matter who. Maybe he learned that tactic from Hoover, or maybe Auton taught it to him. But he put together the best-documented collection of scandals you can imagine. Sex, booze, drugs—you name a vice, he found out about it. Tax evasion, conflict of interest, kickbacks, bribery. If someone threatened to take away Eliot's power, Eliot simply showed that person his file, and all threats stopped. That's why he's still in the agency even though he's past the age for retirement. Because of those files."

"Where are they?"

"Anybody's guess. Maybe a bank vault in Geneva. Maybe a locker at the local Y. Impossible to tell. Believe me, people have tried to find them. He's been followed, but he always loses a tail."

"You still haven't told me why you investigated him."

Hardy thought about it. "Another hunch. You remember how Eliot always insisted there were other Communist agents, not just Philby, Burgess, and Maclean, but a lot more, hidden here and in Britain, high in the government? In particular, he felt sure we had a Russian spy in the agency. He used this theory to explain the U-2 incident, the Bay of Pigs disaster, the JFK assassination. Whenever we started a new operation, the Russians seemed to know about it beforehand. Eliot's theory had seemed paranoid. Now it sounded convincing. Everybody in the agency started checking on everybody else. We got so busy looking behind our backs, suspecting each other, no work got done. We never found the spy. It didn't matter. Eliot's theory did as much damage as any spy could have done. In effect, he paralyzed the agency, and that's what started me thinking. Maybe Eliot protested too much. Maybe Eliot himself was the spy, cleverly disrupting the agency by insisting there was a spy. That was Kim Philby's tactic. Accuse someone else, and no one suspects the accuser."

"You suspected, though."

Hardy shrugged. "Let's say I was jealous. We started our careers together. At first, we were equally brilliant. But over the years, he had more successes. He rose higher while I stayed where I was. If things had been different, maybe I could have equaled him." He raised his glass. "I guess I wanted to bring him down and in the process pull myself up. I kept remembering my first big success. Maybe I could repeat it—exactly the same. I told you Eliot went to England for his OSS training during the war. We didn't know much about espionage, but the British did. The man in MI-6 who taught him. You'll never guess who he was."

Saul waited.

Hardy drained his glass. "Kim Philby."

Saul stopped breathing. *"Eliot's a mole?"*

"I didn't say that."

"Why the hell mention Philby if you're not accusing—?"

"It's only what I thought. I can make assumptions, but they're meaningless without proof."

"And you don't have the proof."

"I told you I never got that far. When Eliot had me sacked, my office was sealed. My apartment, my car, my safety-deposit box were searched. Every scrap of paper even vaguely related to the agency was taken from me."

"Including your research?"

"I never wrote it down, thank God. If Eliot had seen a file on him, if he thought I was dangerous . . . well, he wouldn't trust a drunk. I'd have had a sudden heart attack or fallen off a building."

"You remember what you learned?"

Hardy straightened indignantly. "Of course. I'm not—look, he's a man of habit, so I have to become suspicious when I find variations in his routine. In 1954—his travel vouchers tell an interesting story— he made several unexplained trips to Europe. For a week in August, he dropped completely out of sight."

"Vacation?"

"Without leaving an address or a phone number where the agency could reach him in an emergency?"

"I see your point."

"I can trace him to Belgium. After that . . ." Hardy lit a cigarette, exhaling smoke.

"And no one questioned his disappearance?"

"Not only wasn't it questioned, the next year he got promoted. For all I know, he'd been sent on a mission, and his promotion was a reward for success. All the same, that missing week . . ."

"If he's a mole, he could have been meeting with his KGB control."

"That suspicion occurred to me. But it's sloppy tradecraft. I can think of too many other less mysterious ways for the KGB to get in touch with him. Why invite attention by having him disappear like that? Whatever the reason for his disappearance, it was obviously necessary—something that couldn't be done any other way."

Saul frowned. As the air conditioner rattled, he shivered but not from the chill.

"Something else," Hardy said. "In 1973, he disappeared again— this time for the last three days in June."

"To Belgium again?"

"Japan."

"So what's the connection?"

Hardy shrugged. "I've no idea what he did on those trips. But I keep going back to my first assumption. Let's say during the war, when he went to England, he joined Philby, Burgess, and Maclean in becoming a Soviet double agent."

"Or a triple agent."

"Could be." Hardy scratched his chin. "I never thought of that. He could have pretended to go along with Philby, planning to use his relationship with the Soviets to the advantage of the United States. He always liked complexity, and being a triple agent's the most complex role of all. The difference is the same. Whether a double or a triple agent, he'd have been in contact with the KGB. Someone had to pass messages to him, someone so much a part of his routine no one would question if they regularly got in touch with each other, someone with freedom of movement, preferably with European connections."

"And you found him?"

"Roses."

"What?"

"As much as complexity, Eliot loves roses. He structures his day around them. He exchanges letters with other enthusiasts. He sends and receives rare varieties."

Saul felt a jolt. "And goes to flower shows."

"In Europe. Particularly a show in London every July. He hasn't missed that show since the first one in '46, right after the war. A perfect meeting place. He always stays with a friend who owns an estate near London . . . Percival Landish Junior."

Saul inhaled sharply.

"So you recognize the name?" Hardy asked.

"His father represented England's intelligence network at the Abelard meeting in '38."

"An interesting pattern, don't you think? Auton, who was also at that meeting, became friends with Landish Senior. Eliot—Auton's foster son—became friends with Landish's son. By the way, the senior Landish was Philby's supervisor."

"Jesus," Saul repeated.

"So I have to wonder," Hardy said. "Was Landish Senior a mole as well? The trouble with believing in a conspiracy is that after a while you can make anything fit your theory. Have I got too much imagination? Let's put it this way. If Eliot works for the Soviets, Landish Junior would be my candidate for the courier passing messages. He's perfect. He occupies the same position in MI-6 that Eliot does in the CIA. Like Eliot, he's been insisting there's a mole in MI-6. If Landish Senior worked for the Soviets, maybe Landish Junior continued the job after his father died."

"The question is how to prove it."

7

Erika stopped halfway down the aisle and leaned toward a passenger in a window seat. "Sir, fasten your seatbelt, please." She wore an attractive El Al stewardess uniform. Because of the hurried arrangements, she'd been given a limited choice of women for whom she could substitute. Her height, hair color, and facial structure had been similar to a scheduled member of the flight crew. But the woman whom Erika had replaced and who was now driving south from Miami toward Key West on a sudden all-expenses-paid vacation was a bit smaller than Erika, so the uniform fit tightly, emphasizing the contour of her breasts. The males on board looked pleased instead of puzzled.

Continuing down the aisle, she made sure everyone else's seatbelt was fastened. After asking a woman to slide her bulky purse into the space beneath the forward seat, she scanned the passengers. No one was smoking. The seats were locked in their upright position, the food trays folded up and secured. She nodded to another stewardess and walked toward the front, where she turned to survey the passengers again. As much as she could determine, none of them reacted strangely to her. No eyes tensed when she looked at them. No passenger avoided her gaze. Of course, a well-trained operative wouldn't have made those mistakes. All the same, she went through the formality—to fail to do it would have been her own mistake.

She knocked on the cockpit door and opened it. "Anybody up here want some coffee?"

The pilot turned. "No, thanks. The ground crew loaded the baggage. We're cleared to taxi."

"How's the weather look?"

"Couldn't be better. Blue skies all the way," Saul answered beside her. He and Chris—looking handsome in their pilots' uniforms—carried documents authorizing them to be supervisors on this flight. They sat at the rear of the cockpit, watching the crew, who had no reason to doubt they were what they claimed. With Erika, they'd boarded early, via the private stairs to the service entrance in the passenger tunnel, avoiding surveillance in the terminal. Their credentials had been beautifully forged. Again the Israeli embassy's Misha Pletz had worked his magic.

As the jet backed from the boarding platform, Erika returned to the passengers, double-checking for signs of recognition in anyone's eyes. A man seemed captivated by her figure. A woman looked apprehensive about the takeoff. Passing them, she decided they were nothing to worry about, though now that the jet was in motion it didn't matter if a hit team had come on board. El Al excelled in security precautions. Three of the passengers—at the front, the middle, and rear—were plainclothes airline guards. Beyond the windows, two heavy cars abruptly appeared, flanking the jet as it left the terminal toward the runway. In the cars, she noticed large grim men licensed to carry the automatic weapons they held out of sight—standard protection for this airline so often victimized by terrorists. When the plane touched down in London, two more cars would appear and escort the jet to the terminal. Inside the airport, the El Al section would be discreetly but effectively guarded. Under these conditions, a hit team foolish enough to move against Erika, Saul, and Chris would have to be suicidal.

Her sense of relief passed quickly. As she made sure the food lockers in back were securely locked, she remembered with dismay that she'd have to pass out cocktails and meals, mothering the passengers through the flight.

The senior attendant picked up a microphone. "Good evening." Static crackled. "Welcome to El Al's Flight 755 to—"

8

London. Despite the blue sky forecast, gray drizzly clouds hung over the city. Though burdened by her duties during the flight, Erika had nonetheless found time to consider the implications of what she'd learned.

The story Chris and Saul had told her about the Franklin School for Boys disturbed her. She herself had been raised on an Israeli kibbutz and as a consequence had been conditioned as well. But though like

210

them she was skilled as a soldier and an operative, she sensed a difference.

Granted, she'd been separated from her mother and father and raised by foster parents. Still, the entire community had given her love. Every Israeli was a member of her family. In a country so often attacked that many children lost both their natural and foster parents, grief became bearable if the nation as a whole was the ultimate parent.

But Saul and Chris had been shown no love except by Eliot, a love that had been a lie. Instead of the healthy atmosphere of a kibbutz, they'd endured an austere youth of rigid discipline and deprivation—not for the sake of their country, but instead for the secret motives of the man who claimed to be their benefactor. What kind of mind could have imagined such a plan?

Twisted. Perverted.

Like Saul and Chris, she'd been trained to kill. But she did it for her country, for the survival of her people, and with sadness, grieving for her enemy, whereas Saul and Chris had been purged of distracting emotion, denied their dignity, made into robots at Eliot's command. No noble principle justified what had been done to them.

Now their conditioning had failed. Though Erika enjoyed being reunited with them—especially Saul, for whom an affection she'd thought was dead had been revived as strongly as ever—her principal objective had to be idealistic: to help her country, to repair the damage Eliot had done to Israel when he'd made it seem responsible for killing the president's friend. Saul and Chris, though, had a different motive. Personal, and under the circumstances ironic, because emotional. They'd reached the limit of a lifetime's abuse. They'd been betrayed.

Now they wanted revenge.

9

At the London airport, the three of them passed through a private customs area set aside for airline personnel. The escorts Pletz had arranged to meet them waited inconspicuously on the other side. Avoiding the busy passenger section of the terminal, they left through a rear exit reserved for airport employees, their escorts first checking outside, then forming a phalanx through which Erika, Chris, and Saul stepped out to a bulletproof car. They drove past an airport guard at an open metal gate, then merged with the noisy London-bound traffic.

Chris set his watch for the English time zone. The morning sky was bleak. As dampness crept over him, he glanced out the back and frowned. "We're being followed."

"That blue car a hundred yards back?" the driver asked. He studied his rearview mirror, seeing Chris nod. "It's one of ours. But there's something else bothers me."

"What's that?"

"The orders we got. From Misha in Washington."

"What's the problem?"

"I don't get it. We're supposed to make sure you arrive okay, but then we're supposed to scram. It makes no sense. Whatever you're up to, even you three have to need backup. There's got to be a mistake."

"No, that's what we asked for."

"But—"

"That's how we want it," Saul said.

The driver shrugged. "You're the customer. I was told to get you a flat that's safe. The equipment you wanted's in the trunk. They call that a boot over here. I'll never get used to the way these people talk."

10

Pretending to settle in, they stopped unpacking their bags the moment the escorts left. Saul glanced at Chris. On signal, they scanned the room. The place was small, more homey than rented rooms in America—doilies, lace curtains, flowers in a vase. Like the car, it smelled of dampness. Though the escorts had vouched for the safety of the place, Saul didn't know if he could trust them. On the one hand, he saw no reason not to. On the other, too many people had become involved, too many chances for further betrayal.

As if they heard his suspicions, Chris and Erika nodded. Since the room might be bugged, they didn't say a word but quickly changed from their uniforms. The men paid no more attention to Erika's naked-ness than she did to theirs. In nondescript street clothes, they took apart, tested, and reassembled the weapons the escorts had given them. The other equipment they'd requested functioned perfectly. Leaving nothing behind, they crept down the musty back stairs of the rooming house. In the rear, they crossed a mews toward a maze of alleys, using complex evasion procedures to lose a tail in the London rain. Not even Misha Pletz knew why they'd come to England. Now on their own, they'd become invisible again, their destination undetectable.

Except, Saul thought uneasily. One other person knew—the man who'd supplied the address and description of their target. Strict secu-rity would have required silencing Hardy to protect themselves. But how could I justify it? Saul asked himself. Hardy helped. I like the sonofabitch too much.

All the same, he kept repeating. Loose ends bothered him.

11

They were waiting, and he hadn't thought to take even such an elementary precaution as avoiding his apartment. Of course he'd been drinking heavily, the familiar excuse. Not only had it clouded his judgment. It also had stunned his reflexes, so when he staggered into his apartment and turned to lock the door, he didn't move fast enough from the footsteps charging toward him. Maybe sober he could have yanked the door back open and rushed down the hall, but as adrenaline hit the alcohol in his stomach and made him want to throw up, the man who'd been hiding in the closet twisted his arm, slamming him hard against the wall, spreading his legs in a frisk position.

The second man, darting from the bathroom, pawed along his body, checking his buttocks and privates. "Snub-nosed thirty-eight. Right ankle," he told his partner, pocketing the weapon.

"Sofa," the partner told Hardy.

"Lawn chair," Hardy told him.

"What the—?"

"You guys practice hard enough, you'll soon get up to verbs."

"Just do what the hell you're told."

Hardy's forehead throbbed from its impact against the wall. He sat. His heart skipped a beat, but his mind stayed surprisingly calm, no doubt the effect of a day spent at the corner bar. Indeed since Saul had left, he'd been drinking harder than ever. Despite his determination never to let his drunkenness make him undignified, he'd let his pants become wrinkled, his shoes scuffed. Though he'd begged to go along, Saul had refused. "You've helped enough." But Hardy had understood. He thinks I'm too old. He figures he can't depend on a . . .

Lush? Hardy had stupefied himself to forget that Saul now did what he himself—if he'd had any guts—should have done years ago.

The two men were in their early thirties. Hardy smelled their sick-sweet aftershave. He glanced at their all-American anonymous features. Short neat hair and Brooks Brothers suits. He recognized them. Not that he'd seen them before, but in his prime he'd often used their counterparts.

GS-7s. The agency's drones. Their rank made him angry, aggravated by his drunkenness, telling him he wasn't considered dangerous enough for a shakedown by a first-class team. They represented contempt.

He seethed but didn't show it, bourbon making him brave. "Well, now that we're nice and comfy—"

"Shut your fucking mouth," the first man said.

"I told you."

"What?"

"You'd get up to verbs."

The two drones glanced at each other. "Make the call," the first one said. The second picked up the phone, and even through a blur, Hardy noticed he touched eleven digits.

"What? Long distance? I hope to God it's collect."

"I'm gonna love this," the second one said and spoke to the phone. "We've got him. No, it was easy. Sure." He stared at Hardy. "Guess what?" He grinned. "It's for you."

Reluctant, Hardy took the phone. Though he knew what was coming, he pretended he didn't. "Hello?"

The voice from the other end was as dry as chalk, as crisp as dead leaves—brittle, ancient, without a soul. "I trust my associates treated you well."

"Who—?"

"Come now." Phlegm obscured the voice. "No need for games."

"I said—"

"Very well. I feel like being amused. I'll play along."

Hardy fumed when he heard the name. "I hoped I'd never hear from you again, you bloodsucker."

"Name-calling?" Eliot clicked his tongue. "What happened to your manners?"

"I lost them with my job, you jack-off."

"Not at my age." Eliot laughed. "I believe you may have had some visitors."

"You mean apart from Tweedledum and Tweedledee here? Visitors? Who the hell would want to visit me?"

"Two very naughty children."

"The son and the daughter I'll admit to won't even talk to me."

"I'm referring to Saul and Chris, of course."

"Refer all you want. Whatever this is about, I haven't seen them. Even if I had, I'd never tell you."

"That's the problem, isn't it?"

"No, something else is. What's gone wrong?"

"That's very good. Answer a question with a question. It helps to avoid mistakes."

"It gives me a pain. I'm hanging up."

"No, wait. I'm not sure what they told you. They're in trouble."

"They told me nothing. They weren't here. For God sake, I'm trying to enjoy my retirement. Take your drones. Stay out of my life."

"You don't understand. It's Chris. He violated the sanction. Saul's helping him escape."

"So the first thing they do is come to me? Oh, sure. For what? A lot of good I'd be. Against the Russians? Bullshit." Hardy winced.

"Perhaps you're right. May I speak to one of my associates, please?"

Hardy felt too sick to answer. He handed the phone to number one.

"What is it? Yes, sir, I understand." He gave the phone back to Hardy.

"You made a mistake," Eliot said.

"Don't rub it in. I know."

"I have to admit you were doing quite well before that. Especially considering you're out of practice."

"Instinct."

"Habit's more reliable. Really, the Russians. Why did you have to mention them? I hoped you'd be a better opponent."

"Sorry to disappoint you."

"You wouldn't have mentioned the Russians unless you knew they claimed the violation. Apart from our differences, I was right to have you fired. Sloppy tradecraft. When you're interrogated, you ought to know you never volunteer information, no matter how seemingly irrelevant."

"I don't need a lecture, for Christ's sake. How'd you know they'd come to me?"

"I didn't. Actually—no offense—I thought of you only this morning. After I'd tried all their other contacts. You were my last resort."

That insult may have been why Hardy made his choice.

Number two put a briefcase on the coffee table. Opening it, he took out a hypodermic and a vial of liquid.

"I'm surprised they didn't use the chemicals sooner," Hardy said.

"I wanted to talk to you first. To reminisce."

"To gloat, you mean."

"I don't have time for this. It's my turn now. Hang up."

"No, wait. There's something I want you to hear." Hardy turned to number one. "In that cabinet." It was plastic-coated plywood, from the K-Mart. "Excuse the expression. There's a shot left in a fifth of Jim Beam. Would you bring it to me?"

The drone looked uncertain.

"For God's sake, I'm thirsty."

"Lush." Lips curled, the drone opened the cabinet and gave him the bottle.

Hardy stared at it. As if caressing a woman he loved, he slowly turned the cap. He swallowed the inch of liquid, savoring its wonder. On balance, it was the only thing he'd miss. "Still listening?"

"What was that about?"

"Hang on."

I'm seventy-two, he thought. My liver's a miracle. It should have killed me long ago. I'm a goddamn remnant, a fossil. Thirty minutes after the chemicals had been administered, he knew he'd have told the drones everything Eliot wanted. Saul and Chris would be killed. Eliot would have won again.

The sonofabitch kept winning.

Not anymore.

216

A lush? Saul wouldn't take me along because he couldn't depend on me. Eliot sent two drones because he didn't respect me.

"I've got a confession to make," Hardy said.

"We'll still use the chemicals."

"It doesn't matter. You're right. Saul came to see me. He asked questions. I gave answers. I know where he is. I want you to understand that."

"Why so direct? You know I won't make a deal."

"You'll have me killed?"

"I'll make it as pleasant as possible. Alcohol poisoning. I doubt you'll mind."

"Keep listening."

He set the phone on the coffee table and glanced beyond the drones toward the window. He weighed 220 pounds. In his youth, he'd been a tackle on Yale's football team. With a wail, he surged from the sofa, ramming past them, charging toward the window. For an instant, he feared the closed blinds would hold him back, but he should have expected they were as cheap as everything else in this goddamn cracker-box.

His head struck the window, shattering the glass. But his girth jammed in the window frame, his stomach sinking on jagged shards. He moaned, but not from pain, instead because the drones were grabbing his feet, straining to pull him back. He kicked, struggling, hearing the blinds rattle as the shards rammed deeper into his stomach. Desperate, tilting forward, he wrenched his feet away and suddenly hurtled bleeding into space. More glass went with him, glinting from the sun. He saw it vividly, feeling suspended. Gravity insisted. Plummeting, he left the splinters above.

Objects fall at an equal rate, provided their mass is the same. But Hardy had a great deal of mass. Faster than the shards of glass, he swooped toward the sidewalk, praying he wouldn't land on someone. Fifteen stories. The drop made his stomach swell. Toward his testicles. After all, he was upside down. Before he hit, he blacked out. But a witness later said his body exhaled on impact.

Almost as if he laughed.

12

The estate was huge. Saul crouched in the dark on a wooded bluff, peering down a murky slope toward the lights of the English manor house below him. Three stories high, its rectangular shape made it seem even higher. Long and narrow, it had a large middle section flanked by smaller wings to the right and left. Its clean straight lines were broken only by the row of dormer windows projecting from the slight slope in the roof and by the confusing array of protruding chimneys, stark against the rising moon.

Saul aimed a nightscope toward the wall enclosing the estate. In its earliest form, a nightscope had been based on the principle of projecting an infrared beam to illuminate the dark. This beam, invisible to the unaided eye, could be easily detected through special lenses in the scope. The device worked well, though the objects it revealed were necessarily tinted red. Nonetheless it did have a crucial drawback. After all, an enemy using the same kind of scope could detect the infrared beam from your own. In effect, you'd advertised yourself as a target.

A better principle was obviously needed, and during the late sixties, in response to the escalated fighting in Vietnam, an undetectable nightscope was finally invented. Known by the trade name Starlite, it illuminated the dark by magnifying whatever minuscule light source, such as the stars, was available. Since it projected no beam, it couldn't draw attention to the person using it. In the seventies, the scope had become commercially available, mostly in sporting goods stores. There'd been no difficulty in obtaining this one.

Saul didn't use it to study the manor, however, because the lights from the windows would have been so magnified they'd stab his eyes. But the wall was in darkness, and he saw it clearly. It seemed to be twelve feet high. He focused on its weathered rocks, its vivid chinks of ancient mortar.

But something about it troubled him. He felt as if he'd knelt here before and studied the wall. Struggling with recollection, he finally understood. The estate in Virginia. Andrew Sage and the Paradigm

218

group. The beginning of the nightmare. At once he corrected himself, for the wall down there reminded him of someplace else, the orphanage, and that was where the nightmare had really started. With eerie vividness, he imagined Chris and himself sneaking over the wall. In particular, he recalled the night . . .

The screech of crickets stopped. The forest became unnervingly quiet. As his skin prickled, he sank to the ground, drawing his knife, his dark clothes blending with the gloom. Controlling his breath, he kept his face down, straining to listen.

A bird sang, paused, then repeated its cadence. Exhaling, Saul rose to a crouch. Still cautious, he huddled against an oak, pursed his lips, and mimicked the song of the bird.

Directly, Chris stepped from the dark. A second figure emerged like the rustle of wind through bushes. Erika. She glanced back down the slope, then crouched beside Saul and Chris.

"The security's primitive." Chris kept his voice low.

"I agree," Erika added. She and Chris had separated down the slope, checking the estate's perimeter. "The wall's not high enough. There ought to be closed-circuit cameras. There's no electrified fence at the top."

"You sound like that disappoints you," Saul said.

"It bothers me," she answered. "England's in a recession. Its lower class resents its upper class. I'd be frantic for security if I were Landish. Given his position in MI-6, he ought to know how to protect his estate."

"Unless he wants to make it seem there's nothing to protect," Chris said.

"Or hide," she added.

"You think the security's not as primitive as it seems?"

"I don't know what to think. And you?" She turned to Saul.

"I scanned the grounds," he said. "I saw no guards, though there must be some in the mansion. We were right, though."

"Dogs?"

Saul nodded. "Three of them. Maybe others I didn't see. They're roaming freely."

"Breed?"

"All Dobermans."

"The marines would feel at home," Chris said. "Thank God, it isn't shepherds or standard poodles."

"You want to forget about it?"

"Hell, no," Erika said.

The two men smiled.

"Then let's do it. We were worried about timing—how to get our hands on him. He might have solved the problem for us. Take a look." Saul pointed toward the rear of the manor. "See the greenhouse?"

"The lights are on."

The long glass structure glinted in the night.

"Like Eliot, he worships roses. Would he let a servant in there? Or a guard? In his holy of holies? I don't think so. Only the high priest enters the sanctum."

"Maybe he's showing his roses to guests," Chris said.

"And maybe not. Just one way to tell."

Again the two men smiled at each other.

13

They crept down the slope through mist and bracken toward the rear of the estate. Clouds drifted across the moon. The night was chilly and damp. Chris braced his hands against the wall and bent a knee so Erika could climb to his shoulders, grip the top of the wall, and pull herself up. Saul went up next, climbing to Chris's shoulders, but when he clutched the top, he dangled, allowing Chris to use his body as a ladder. At the top, Chris and Erika helped Saul squirm beside them.

Flat, they scanned the estate. Lights gleamed. Below them, dark objects loomed.

Chris raised a tiny cylinder to his lips and blew. Though the night stayed quiet, Saul imagined the ultrasonic tone. The dogs would hear it, though. But what if they'd been trained to ignore its appeal?

They weren't. The massive Dobermans came with such deceptive softness Saul would never have heard them if he hadn't been prepared. Their paws didn't seem to touch the grass. Their dark shapes streaked through the night, abruptly materializing at the bottom of the wall. Even then, Saul wasn't sure he saw them till their white teeth suddenly glinted, flashing savagely. Despite their obscene sneers, they didn't growl.

They couldn't, Saul realized. Their vocal cords had been cut. A dog that barked was useless for protection. Growls alerted an intruder and gave him a chance to defend himself. These Dobermans weren't intended to be a burglar alarm. They served one purpose only—to surprise an intruder.

And kill him.

Erika reached in a knapsack. Pulling out a fist-sized canister, she twisted its top and dropped it among the dogs.

The canister hissed. The dogs attacked it. Suddenly backing off, they blinked in confusion, then slumped unconscious.

Saul held his breath as he squirmed off the wall and dropped to the grass, rolling in a parachutist's pose. Retreating from the fumes toward the cover of a hedge, he waited for Chris and Erika. In the moonlight, he studied the lawn before the house. Shrubs had been trimmed to form geometric shapes: pyramids, globes, and cubes, their shadows grotesque. "Over there." Saul pointed.

Chris nodded at a tree, whispering, "I see the glow. An electric eye."

"There'll be others."

"But the dogs had the run of the grounds," Chris whispered. "They'd have passed through the lights and triggered the alarms."

"The lights must be higher than the dogs."

Saul sank to his stomach on the dew-wet grass, crawling forward, squeezing beneath the almost invisible beam of the electric eye.

The greenhouse gleamed before him, gemlike. More spectacular were the roses, their various sizes, their brilliant colors. He watched a lean, stooped, white-coated figure walk among them, recognizing Landish from Hardy's description, especially the shrunken face. "He looks mummified," Hardy had said. "It's like he's dead, but his hair's long as if it kept growing."

Saul crept to the greenhouse, waiting while Chris and Erika slipped behind bushes, one on each side of the path between the manor and the greenhouse, on guard for anyone coming. He stood and walked inside.

14

The lights hurt his eyes.

The roses smelled oversweet, cloying.

Landish stood at a table, his back to Saul, mixing seed in trays of sand. He heard the door and turned, but he must have guessed it was a servant because his movement was calm. Only when he saw who'd entered did he react, stepping back against the table, his mouth open in surprise.

Saul was ten feet away. That close, Landish looked ill, his pinched skin waxy, jaundiced. Even so, as his shock diminished, his sunken eyes gleamed. "I wasn't expecting company." His voice sounded frail, but his British accent made it seem urbane.

Saul aimed his pistol. "Don't move. Keep your hands and feet where I can see them."

"You're surely not frightened of an old man harming you."

"I'm more concerned about this." Saul pointed toward a wire leading up beneath a grafting table. He stepped across, took pliers from his pocket, and snipped the wire. Feeling under the table, he yanked an alarm button free.

"My compliments." Landish bowed slightly. "If you're a burglar, I have to tell you I carry no money. Of course, you'll find silverware and crystal in the house."

Saul shook his head.

"You intend to kidnap me for ransom?"

"No."

"Since you don't have the lunatic's glare of a terrorist, I confess to—"

"Information. I don't have time. I'll ask you once."

"Who are you?"

Saul ignored the question. "We debated using chemicals."

"*We?*"

"But you're too old. The strain. We thought you might die."

"Considerate."

"We discussed torture. The problem's the same. You could die before you told us what we want."

"Why go to such extremes? Perhaps I'll tell you freely."

"Hardly. Anyway, we wouldn't know if you told the truth." Saul lifted a pair of shears from a bench. "We finally agreed on the way to persuade you." He crossed to a bed of roses, glanced at their first-prize ribbons, and snipped the stem off an exquisite dwarf Yellow Princess.

Landish groaned, swaying off balance. "That rose was—"

"Priceless. Sure. But not irreplaceable. You've still got four others. On the other hand, this scarlet Tear Drop over here is rarer."

"No!"

Saul clipped it, watching the bloom fall on a plaque it had won.

Landish clutched a table. "Have you lost your mind? Don't you realize what—?"

"I'm killing your children. This pink Aphrodite here. Beautiful. Truly. How long does it take to grow it to perfection? Two years? Five?" Saul hacked the bloom in half, its petals tumbling over a trophy.

Landish clutched his chest. His eyes bulged in horror.

"I told you I'd ask only once. Eliot."

Landish gaped at the ruined petals, swallowing tears. "What about him?"

"He works for the Soviets."

"What are you talking about?"

Saul slashed at a Gift from God, its purple theoretically impossible.

Landish shrieked. "No more!"

"He's a mole, and you're their courier."

"No! Yes! I don't know!"

"What the hell does *that* mean?"

"I delivered messages. It's true. But that was ten years ago. I'm not sure he was a mole."

"Then why did the KGB get in touch with him?"

"I haven't any—"

Saul stepped toward the masterpiece of Landish's collection. A Harbinger of Joy. Incredibly it was blue. "Eliot was wrong. When I saw him in Denver, he told me no rose has ever been blue."

"Don't!"

Saul raised the snips, pausing with the stem between the blades. The lights glinted off their edges. "If he wasn't a mole, what was he? What was in the messages?"

"I didn't read them."

Saul squeezed the blades against the stem.

"It's the truth!"

"Since when is MI-6 the delivery boy for the CIA?"

"I did it as a favor to Eliot!" Landish glanced back and forth from the mutilated roses to Saul, swallowing nervously. "I swear! He asked me to mediate!"

"Keep your voice down."

Landish shuddered. "Listen to me. Eliot said the messages identified a spy in the agency." His voice was strained. "But the informant was nervous and insisted on a courier he trusted. Since I knew the courier, I was the logical choice to act as relay."

"You believed this?"

"He's my friend." Landish gestured frantically. "Our networks often cooperate. If you want to know what was in the messages, ask the man who gave them to me."

"Sure. Just hop on a plane to Moscow."

"No. Much closer."

"Where?"

"In Paris. He works for the Soviet embassy there."

"You're lying." Saul clipped a leaf.

"I'm not! Don't you understand how delicate that rose is? Even injuring a leaf can—!"

"Then you'd better convince me you're telling the truth because I'm about to cut off another one."

"It's the only rose like that in the world."

Saul poised the shears.

"Victor Petrovich Kochubey."

"A name means nothing."

"He's their cultural attaché. He arranges tours for Soviet orchestras and dance troupes throughout France. He's also a master violinist. Sometimes he plays at the concerts. Sometimes he goes on tours by himself."

"But of course he's KGB."

Landish spread his hands. "He disclaims them. Fifteen years ago he was captured attempting to defect to the West. It was clear he'd try again. As a compromise, the Soviets allowed him to live in Paris, provided he used his talents for the good of the Motherland. They reminded him his children would stay in Moscow, where their excellent jobs and living conditions depended on his cooperation."

"That doesn't answer my question. Is he KGB?"

"Of course. His attempt to defect was a sham. But it served his purpose. His cover's excellent."

"And I'll bet you attend a lot of concerts."

"Not so much anymore." Landish shrugged but still glanced nervously at his roses. "Ten years ago, however . . . it wasn't difficult to meet privately with him. While discussing the fine points of Russian music, he passed me messages. On occasion, I gave him one. But they were sealed. I never read them. If you want to know what was in them, you'll have to speak with Kochubey."

Aiming the shears at the pale blue rose, Saul studied him.

"I've told you all I know." Landish sounded sad. "I realize you have to kill me to stop me from warning him. But I beg you not to destroy another rose."

"Suppose you're lying? What if your information's worthless?"

"How can I offer guarantees?"

"You can't, and if you're dead, I can't get revenge. What use would destroying more roses be? A corpse wouldn't care."

"Then we've reached an impasse."

"No. You're coming with me. If I find out you've lied, you'll see what gasoline and a match can do to this greenhouse. Think about it as we go. In case you want to change your story."

"You'll never get me past the guards at the gate."

"I won't have to. We'll leave the way I came in. Over the wall."

Landish scoffed. "Do I look like an athlete?"

"Then we'll lift you."

"I'm too brittle. My arms and legs would break."

"All right, no lifting."

"How then? It's impossible."

Saul pointed toward the rear of the greenhouse. "Simple."

"What?"

"We'll use that ladder."

15

Curtains billowed at the open window. Chris squinted toward the bullet-gray sky, his nostrils flaring from the salty air, his shoulders hunched from the damp. An angry wind chased waves across the Channel. He sounded troubled. "I'll take your place."

"I told you no," Saul said. "We agreed. One of us has to stay here with Landish while the other two get Kochubey. We cut cards to decide who took the risk. You won with the lowest card. You stay."

"But I don't want to."

"All of a sudden you feel like being a hero?"

"No. Of course not."

"Then what is it? I can't believe it's just because you want to go with Erika." Saul turned to where she had tied Landish to a chair. "No offense. You've got a wonderful sense of humor."

She stuck out her tongue.

He turned back to Chris. "What's wrong?"

"It's crazy." Chris shook his head, confused. "It's this feeling I've got. I know it means nothing. The trouble is I can't get rid of it."

"What's it about?"

Chris walked from the window. "You. I've got this sense, this . . . call it a premonition. Something's going to happen to you."

Saul studied him. Neither he nor Chris was superstitious. They couldn't afford to be. Otherwise they'd look for omens everywhere and as a consequence become paralyzed. Logic and skill were what they depended on. Even so, they'd each had experiences in Nam that made them respect "funny" feelings—buddies due to be sent back home who wrote letters to wives or girlfriends or mothers and gave them to teammates, saying, "Make sure she gets this. I won't make it." And the day before they left, they got a bullet through the head. Or other teammates due to go out on a routine surveillance mission, a piece of cake, they'd done it a hundred times, but this time they said, "I won't be seeing you." And they stepped on a mine.

Saul thought a moment. "When did it start?"

"At Landish's estate."

"When you saw the wall?"

Chris nodded. "How did you know?"

"Because I had a similar feeling."

"*What?*"

"I was sure I'd been there before. It took me a while, but I figured it out. The wall. Don't you get it? The same kind of wall we had at Franklin. Remember how we used to sneak over to bring in candy? The night we got beat up? Or the night I slipped on the ice, and you jumped down to help me, but you cracked your head? The streetcar? Remember?"

"You pulled me away and saved my life."

"That explains it. Both of us must have been reminded of that night. At Landish's estate, I got worried about you. I started thinking you were in trouble and I'd have to save you. The same thought happened to you, except reversed. Maybe you've always wanted to save *my* life."

"I have." Chris grinned. "A couple of times."

"But the wall made you want to do it again. Relax. Something's going to happen for sure. I'm going to Paris with Erika and get my hands on Kochubey. That's what'll happen."

"I want to believe that."

"Think of it this way. If I got in trouble, what could you do that Erika couldn't?"

She came over. "Be careful how you answer."

"And think about this," Saul said. "Suppose I let you go instead of me. Suppose something happened to you. I'd blame myself as much as *you* would if something happened to me. This second-guessing is useless. We made a bargain. You drew the lowest card. You got the easy job. You stay."

Chris hesitated.

"And as for your premonition, it and a load of manure'll fertilize a garden." Saul turned to Erika. "Ready?"

"Paris with a handsome escort? You've got to be kidding."

Chris wasn't satisfied. "It's almost ten. You ought to be in Paris this evening. Phone me at six and every four hours after that. Don't pick up Kochubey till you talk with me. As Landish thinks more about his roses, he might decide he gave the wrong information."

"I told the truth," Landish insisted from the chair.

"Just keep your mind on the only blue rose in the world."

227

The moment arrived. Unable to put it off, they shook hands and grinned self-consciously.

Saul picked up his bag. "Don't worry. I'll be careful. I want to make sure I'm around to pay back—" His eyes flashed.

"And I'll take care of your brother for you," Erika said. "For both of us." She kissed Chris on the cheek.

His heart felt swollen. He meant what he said. "Good luck."

Uncertainly they parted. Troubled, Chris watched from the open door, his throat tight as they got in the rented Austin, his brother and sister, and drove down the weed-covered lane, disappearing past the hedge-lined road.

When he couldn't hear the Austin's motor any longer, he stared at the rocks in the pasture, at last stepped in and closed the door.

"They'll be looking for me," Landish said.

"But they won't know where to hunt. We're sixty miles from your estate. But London's between, and that's where they'll guess we've gone."

Landish cocked his head. "This cottage must be on a cliff. I hear surf below us."

"Dover. I rented this place for a week. I told the realtor I needed a quiet vacation. This was perfect, he said. The nearest cottage is a half mile away. If you scream, no one'll hear you."

"Does my voice sound as if I'm strong enough to scream?"

"I'll try to make you comfortable. So you don't get bored, we'll talk about roses." Chris clenched his teeth. "If anything happens to Saul . . ."

16

They'd chosen Dover because it provided easy access by water to France. In a busy terminal that reminded Saul of an airport, he and Erika bought tickets separately and boarded the Hovercraft several minutes apart.

Uneasy, he went to a lounge in the stern, hoping to blend with the crowd. He knew that MI-6 and other intelligence agencies kept the

Hovercraft under surveillance the same as they did major airports and railway stations. Of course, in theory no enemies knew he'd left the United States. With the hunt against him concentrated in America, he had a good chance of not being recognized.

All the same, he didn't feel reassured. If someone spotted him, there wasn't room on board to run or hide. He'd have to fight, but even if he survived, he'd surely be killed by backup teams waiting for him to arrive in France. With no other choice, he'd have to yank open an emergency hatch and leap out into the Channel. If the undertow didn't suck him to his death, the cold rough water would soon exhaust him, draining his heat till he died from exposure.

It never came to that. The Hovercraft roared above the waves, crossing to Calais in twenty-two minutes. He felt it tilt as it rose from the water up a concrete ramp to the terminal. Stepping off, he merged with the other passengers. Though he hadn't spoken French in years, he understood most of what he read and heard. No one seemed to be watching for him. Customs was uneventful. But he'd left his handgun with Chris so he could get through customs, and he wouldn't relax till he replaced it.

He joined Erika at a seaside café they'd agreed on. They went at once to a black market munitions dealer Saul had worked with in '74, where they were overcharged a mere 200 percent for the equipment they needed. "A favor," the dealer said. "For a friend." Renting a car, they began the southeast drive to Paris 130 miles away.

17

"No," Chris said into the phone. "We've talked about roses till the thought of them makes me sick, but Landish still claims it's the truth."

"Then we'll grab Kochubey tonight." Saul's voice was distorted by long-distance static.

"You've got it set up?"

"With help from Erika's connections."

"Hang on." Chris stared at Landish tied to the chair. "Last chance. If anything goes wrong, you know the price."

"How many times do I have to tell you? He gave me the messages."

"All right," Chris told Saul. "Pick him up. But phone me as soon as you've gone to ground with him."

"Near dawn."

"Don't worry about waking me. Till you're safe, I won't be able to sleep."

"Still got that feeling?"

"Worse than ever."

"It's a walk-through. He'll be easy."

"For God's sake, don't get overconfident."

"I'm only trying to reassure you. Hold it. Erika wants to tell you something."

Interference crackled. Erika teased him. "We're having a wonderful time. The food's unbelievable."

"Spare me the gory details. I just had a peanut butter sandwich."

"How's your roommate?"

"Swell. When we're not talking about his stupid roses, I deal solitaire for him. His arms are tied, so he has to tell me which cards to turn over."

"Does he cheat?"

"No, I do."

She laughed. "I'd better run. What I wanted to say was not to worry. Everything's going smoothly. I'll take care of Saul. Depend on it."

"And don't forget yourself, huh."

"Never. See you tomorrow."

Aching with affection for both of them, he heard the click as she broke the connection. The doorstep creaked as he set down the phone.

18

He froze.

He'd locked the doors. The shutters were closed. No light showed to attract a stranger all the way here from the road in the dark. If someone who knew the cottage had come to welcome him, he'd have knocked instead of sneaking up.

They'd found him. He didn't know how. He couldn't think. No time. Grabbing the radio transmitter off the table, he dove to the floor and pressed a button.

Shockwaves made him wince. Explosions roared around the cottage, shaking its walls. He'd planted the charges at strategic spots of cover where someone creeping up would be likely to hide. He'd made sure the bombs were good and dirty, lots of noise and shrapnel, plenty of smoke and flames. Arranging them had been a force of habit, an obedience to Eliot's rule—no matter how safe you think you are, there's always something more you can do to protect yourself.

He drew his Mauser. A projectile blew a hole in the door. A tear gas canister thumped on the carpet, rolling, hissing. He coughed from the thick white fumes, shooting at the door, knowing what would happen next. As soon as the gas filled the room, the door would be shattered, men would burst in.

He swung to a window, freed its lock, and raised it, pushing the shutter. The night was filled with smoke and flames. A man thrashed on the ground, screaming from the agony of his burning clothes. Another man saw the movement of the shutter. As he turned to aim, Chris shot him twice in the chest.

The front door blew apart.

Chris spun toward Landish, aiming, unable to see him in the white gas filling the room. He heard a heavy thump as if Landish had toppled his chair, seeking cover. Footsteps charged up the outside steps. Again no time. He leapt from the window, running as he struck the ground. Angry voices filled the cottage. Charging through the dark, along the cliff top, away from the flames, he imagined the hit team in gas masks searching the cottage, discovering the open window. But by then he'd be far away. In the dark, they wouldn't know which way he'd gone. They'd never find him.

He raced harder, clutching the Mauser, blinking from sweat. Away from the flames, he felt released, sprinting wildly through the night.

Landish'll tell where Saul is. Got to warn him.

Then he heard it. Behind him.

Closer, faster, louder.

Footsteps. Someone was chasing him.

19

"Untie my hands," Landish blurted. The tear gas made him cough.

A grim-lipped man in black applied a treated cloth to Landish's eyes. Another tugged at the ropes.

The windows had been opened, the shutters unlatched. A sea-breeze wafted the gas from the room.

Landish stumbled to a table, grabbing the phone. He dialed impatiently. Crucial seconds passed. He told the operator the number in Falls Church, Virginia. Trembling, he clutched the table for balance, unconsciously fingering the five-inch strip of aluminum attached to the back of his belt. The strip was magnetically coded. As soon as his guards had discovered his disappearance, they'd have activated an emergency procedure, using electronic sensors to trace the code on the metal strip. On land, the sensors worked only for a limited distance, blocked by obstacles and the curve of the earth. But from a satellite or a surveillance plane—both of which MI-6 had in readiness—they were as effective as any other high-altitude scanning device. Twelve hours after Landish had been abducted, his security force would have known where his captors held him prisoner. The rest of the time would then have been devoted to setting up the rescue.

Landish felt the room swirl, hyperventilating. The phone buzzed. It kept buzzing, making him cringe. But someone finally answered.

"Eliot," Landish demanded, fearing he might not be available. "Seventeen plus three."

The man's gruff voice became alert. "I'll put you through."

In seconds that seemed like minutes, Eliot answered.

"I've found your Black Princes," Landish said.

"Where?"

"They were at my home."

"Dear God."

"A woman's with them."

"Yes, I know. What happened?"

232

"They abducted me." Landish told him everything. "Remus escaped. We're hunting him. Romulus and the woman have gone to Paris."

"Why?"

Landish told him.

"Kochubey? But he's KGB."

"That worries you."

"The opposite. Remus killed a Russian at the Abelard house in Bangkok. They put out a contract on him. We don't have to get involved. They'll owe me a favor for telling them how to get the man who helped him."

20

Chris's opponent gained on him. The rocks along the top of the cliff made running difficult. In the dark, Chris couldn't see where he was going. He felt tempted to spin and shoot, but the night would obscure his target. Worse, his muzzle flash would make him a target, and the noise from the shot would attract the others.

His chest burned. His heart pounded. But the fierce, steady, urgent breath of his pursuer surged ever closer. He strained his legs to their maximum, muscles aching. Sweat soaked his clothes. The rapidly approaching footfalls warned of imminent contact.

Through blurry vision, he noticed a patch of white ahead. It sloped to his right toward the cliff. A darker spot in its middle became a trough. The white was chalk.

A niche.

He dove to it, rolling, absorbing the impact along his shoulders and hips. Scuttling down, he grabbed outcrops, scrambling. The trough became steeper. Instead of sloping, it veered straight down, an indentation like a three-sided airshaft, its craggy sides providing hand- and footholds.

Clambering, he heard the scrape of his hunter's shoes on the rocks above him. Shards of chalk cascaded over him, cracking his shoulders and scalp. His hands bled as he scurried lower.

If I can reach the bottom, he prayed. Wind tugged his hair. The surf on the beach roared louder as he neared it.

Slipping, he almost fell, but he wedged his shoes against a ridge. Squirming over it, he reached a slope, stumbling down to the stony beach. A five-foot slab of chalk provided cover. Fumbling in his pocket, he grabbed the silencer for the Mauser, screwing it on the barrel. Spreading his legs for balance, he aimed his right arm stiffly, raising his left hand to support it.

There. A shadow moved down the niche. He shot. The pounding surf obscured both the silencer's spit and the bullet's impact. He couldn't be sure he'd struck the shadow. In the dark, he couldn't aim properly, couldn't line up his front and rear sights. He shot above and below where he'd seen the shadow.

Move. If he stayed behind this chalk slab any longer, he'd give his hunter time to calculate his position. Hunched, he ran to another slab, then another, rushing farther along the beach away from the cottage. Behind him, the night glowed from the flames on top of the cliff. The thundering surf made it useless for him to listen for anyone racing toward him. He turned, moving backward, studying the now distant niche.

Unable to see it anymore, he assumed his hunter couldn't see him either. Swinging forward, he ran again. The beach was like a tunnel, whitecaps crashing on the right, the chalk cliff stretching on the left. But far ahead, at the tunnel's end, he saw the pinpoint lights of a village. He raced harder.

If he could steal a car . . .

The cliff angled lower, sometimes an incline more than a precipice. When the bullet singed his hair, he dove in surprise to the rocks. The shot had come from the dark ahead of him, a silencer muffling both the sound and the muzzle flash, aided by the surf and the gloom.

He silently cursed. His hunter had never climbed all the way down the niche back there. Realizing the trap Chris would prepare, the man had crawled back up to run along the cliff top. Knowing Chris would eventually hurry along the beach away from the cottage, he'd hoped to find another way down, get ahead of Chris, and intercept him.

Trapped.

I can't go back. They must be searching that end of the beach now. They'll split up, heading both ways along the top and bottom of the cliff. Eventually they'll get this far.

Outflanked.

The sea and the cliff on either side. Ahead and behind him . . .

Something moved. In front of him to the left against the cliff, its pale white Chris's only advantage, providing a screenlike background against which a shadow scurried.

Flat on the rocks, he swung his aim with the shadow, tracking it. The moment he shot, he rolled. A bullet struck the rocks beside him, so close even the surf couldn't obscure its brittle crack as it ricocheted toward the sea.

He rolled again, frantic to keep his gaze toward the cliff, and this time when a bullet whacked the rocks, splinters slicing his thigh—the sharp hot pain irrelevant—he saw his target clearly, a hunkered figure sprinting closer, dropping to one knee, aiming.

Chris fired sooner, excited as the shadow lurched off balance. Despite the surf, he thought he heard a wail. He couldn't stay down here, stalking and dodging till the others found him. Now, in the few seconds given to him, he had to take his chance, charging to his feet, sprinting across the stones. He saw the man—in black, his left arm wounded, fumbling for something among the rocks.

Chris stopped and aimed. He pulled the trigger.

Nothing happened. The Mauser held eight rounds.

He'd shot them all.

His stomach scalding, he rushed ahead, dropping the Mauser, drawing his knife from the sheath up the left sleeve of his jacket.

The man saw him coming, gave up groping for his handgun, rose, and drew his own knife.

21

Amateurs hold a knife with the blade pointed down from the bottom of the fist, the thumb curled around the top of the handle. In that position, the knife must be raised to shoulder level, the blow delivered downward. That takes time. It's awkward.

Street gangs hold a knife with the blade protruding from the top of the fist, above the thumb. This position permits a variety of blows delivered from waist level, angled up or down or to each side. The

235

common stance is similar to a fencer's—one arm held sideways for balance while the other arm slashes and parries. The tactic is graceful, dancelike, dependent on rapid lunges, quick retreats, and speedy footwork. It's effective against an amateur or a member of another street gang. Against a world-class killer, though, it's laughable.

Professionals hold a knife as street gangs do—the blade at the top of the fist—but there the similarity ends. Instead of dancing, they stand flatfooted, legs spread apart for balance, knees bent slightly, body crouched. They raise their free arm, bending it at the elbow, extending it across the chest, as if holding an invisible shield. The arm itself is the shield, however, the wrist turned inward to protect its major arteries. The other arm, holding the knife, doesn't slash straight ahead or sideways. It jabs up on an angle, ignoring the opponent's stomach and chest —a stomach wound might not be lethal; ribs protect the heart—aiming toward the eyes and the throat.

Chris braced himself in this position, startled when his enemy did the same. He'd learned to fight this way at Andre Rothberg's killer-instinct school in Israel. The method was unique. The only way his opponent could have learned it was by going to that school.

The implication filled him with dismay. Had Landish too sent private warriors to Rothberg? Why? How else were Landish and Eliot connected? What else were they involved in?

He jabbed with his knife. His enemy blocked the blow with his arm, sustaining a wound, ignoring it, jabbing toward Chris, who felt the blow pierce the back of his wrist. The sharp blade stung, blood spurting. If there'd been time, Chris would have wrapped his jacket around his defensive arm, but since he hadn't been able to, he was fully prepared to accept extensive damage. A mangled arm meant nothing compared to survival.

Again he jabbed. Again his opponent used his arm to block the thrust, taking another cut. The arm was crimson, its sliced tissue parting. In turn, Chris blocked a jab, the blade so keen he hardly felt the shredding impact on his arm.

A stand-off, each man's reflexes equal to the other's. Flatfooted, crouched, Chris began to circle his enemy, cautious, slow, searching for weakness. His enemy pivoted to continue facing him. Chris hoped to force the man to stay in the middle of the circle. On the perimeter's wide loop, Chris wouldn't get dizzy as fast as the man who turned constantly at the center.

But the man understood what Chris intended. Matching Chris's

236

tactic, he began his own wide circle, their orbits intersecting, almost a figure eight.

Another stalemate, both men equally matched. When Chris had received his martial arts training, Ishiguro had said, "The way of the samurai is death. In a fifty-fifty life-or-death crisis, simply approach the crisis, prepared to die if necessary. There is nothing complicated about it. Merely brace yourself and proceed."

Chris did so now. Rejecting self-concern, he concentrated solely on the ritual. Jab and block, continue to circle. Once more. Then again. His arm throbbed, bloody, shredded.

But his perceptions were undistracted, heightened, totally pure, his nervous system tingling. Jab, block, and circle. Years ago Lee, his karate instructor, had said, "There is nothing more exhilirating than to fight in the dark, facing death." At killer-instinct school, Rothberg had said, "If both opponents have equal knowledge and skill, the younger man with the greater stamina shall be the victor." Chris, who was thirty-six, judged his opponent to be twenty-nine.

The cardinal rule in a knife fight is don't allow your opponent to back you into a corner.

Slowly, relentlessly, Chris's hunter forced him against the cliff. Chris found himself wedged between ridges of chalk. He jabbed in a frenzy. His hunter ducked, then lunged beneath Chris's arm.

The blade plunged in to its hilt.

Chris gagged. His larynx snapped. An artery burst. His mind went blank as he choked on his blood.

22

"You're sure?" Eliot sounded hoarse as he clutched the phone in his greenhouse. "There's no mistake? No chance of error?"

"None. The kill was verified. I examined the body myself," Landish said on the scrambler-protected long distance line. "The man who helped destroy my roses—Remus—is dead."

Eliot's chest felt cold. In desperation, he distracted himself by thinking of business. "You cleaned the area?"

"Of course. We burned the cottage to destroy their fingerprints. We left before the authorities arrived. They'll never know who was there."

"And the body?" Eliot had trouble swallowing.

"It's been taken to my private plane. The pilot will truss it with weights and drop it at sea, too far out for the tide to bring it in."

"I see." He frowned. "You seem to have thought of everything."

"What's wrong? Your voice sounds strange."

"I didn't realize I— Nothing."

"What?"

"It's not important."

"We've still got to deal with Romulus and the woman."

He struggled to pay attention. "I've already made arrangements. The moment I have word, I'll call you."

Eliot's arm felt numb as he set down the phone. He didn't understand what was happening in him. For the past three weeks, since the Paradigm hit, his single purpose had been to find Saul and eliminate him before he could reveal who'd ordered the job. The president could never be allowed to learn why his friend had been killed. In the process, Chris had become a danger too, but now that problem was solved. With one of them dead and the other located, he'd almost achieved his goal, had almost protected himself. Then why, as he'd tried to tell Landish, did he feel remorse?

He remembered the first time he'd taken Chris and Saul camping —Labor Day, 1952. The boys had been seven then, two years under his influence. He vividly recalled their innocent excited faces, their desperate need for affection, their eagerness to please him. More than any of his foster children, they'd been his favorites. Strangely, his throat aching, he felt gratified that Chris, though doomed to fail, had postponed his death so well. Yes, he admitted he had no right, but after all he'd taught the boy, and he couldn't help feeling proud of him. Godspeed, he thought.

Thirty years? Could so long a time have gone so fast? Did he mourn for Chris, he wondered . . . or for himself?

Soon Saul would be dead as well. The KGB had been warned. If they acted quickly, they'd spring their trap. The crisis at last would be over, the secret safe. Only two more foster children would remain, Castor and Pollux, now guarding the house. The others had died in faithful service.

I might outlive all my sons, he thought, sadly wishing Saul could be reprieved.

But that was impossible.

He suddenly felt uneasy. What if Saul escaped? *Unthinkable.*

But what if he did? He'd learn Chris was dead.

And come for me.

He'd never give up.

I truly think nothing could stop him.

BOOK FOUR
RETRIBUTION

FURIES

1

Saul stared through the windshield toward a misty streetlight, his rented Citroën parked in the middle of a line of cars along a residential block. He sat close to Erika, his arm around her, apparently just another couple in the City of Lovers. But he didn't allow himself to enjoy being near her. He couldn't become distracted. Too much depended on this mission.

"If Landish told the truth, we'll soon have some answers," Erika said.

Her Mossad informants had learned that Victor Petrovich Kochubey would be at the Soviet embassy tonight, performing Tchaikovsky's Violin Concerto at a reception in honor of the new Franco-Soviet alliance. "But you can't grab him there," the informants had said. "Various intelligence networks have set up surveillance cameras around the clock to watch all the entrances. If anyone looks suspicious, the police'll arrest them. No one's supposed to embarrass relations with the Soviets. France and Russia are getting along too well these days. Your best bet's to grab him later when he returns to his apartment on the Rue de la Paix."

"But won't he be guarded?" Saul had asked.

"A violinist? Why would he need protection?"

At eight minutes after one, Kochubey drove past in his Peugeot, its headlights flashing. Erika got out and walked along the street. Kochubey—in his fifties, tall, with sensitive but heavy features—locked his car, carefully holding his violin case. He wore a tuxedo. Erika approached him as he reached the stoop to his apartment house. The street was deserted.

He spoke first. "This late at night, a lady shouldn't be out alone. Unless, of course, you have a proposition—"

"Victor, shut up. In my purse, I've a very large pistol aimed at your crotch. Please go to the curb and wait for a car to pull up."

He stared but did so. Saul stopped the car, climbing from the driver's seat into the back where he searched Kochubey and took the violin case.

"Gently! It's a Stradivari!"

"It'll be safe."

"As long as you cooperate." Erika drove.

"Cooperate?" Kochubey's mouth opened and shut nervously. *"How? I don't even know what you want!"*

"The messages."

"What?"

"The ones you gave to Landish."

"You remember," Erika said. "To pass to Eliot."

"Are the two of you insane? What are you talking about?"

Saul shook his head, rolled down his window, and balanced the violin case on the rim.

"I said be careful!"

"The messages. What was in them?" Saul tilted the case out the window.

"A Stradivari can't be repaired!"

"Then buy another one."

"Are you crazy? Where would I find—?"

Saul took his hands from the case. It started falling.

Kochubey wailed and grabbed for it.

Saul pushed him away and snatched back the case. "The messages."

"I never knew what was in them! I was a courier, nothing more! You think I'd risk execution by breaking the seal?"

"Who gave them to you?" Saul held the case out the window.

"A KGB bureau chief!"

"Who?"

"Alexei Golitsin! Please!" Kochubey's hands trembled to grab the case.

"I don't believe you. Golitsin was shot for treason in '73."

"That's when he gave me the messages!"

"In '73?"

Saul frowned. Hardy had said Eliot disappeared in '54, then again in '73. What did a KGB officer shot for treason have to do with Eliot's disappearance? What had happened in '73?

244

"It's the truth!" Kochubey said.

"Perhaps."

"The Stradivari! Please!"

Saul balanced it out the window. Headlights flashed by. He thought about it, shrugging. "This is pointless. If I dropped the case, what reason would you have to change your story? With Amytal, we'll soon learn what you really know." He set the case on the floor.

"Thank God."

"Thank me."

2

They drove from Paris.

"Who do you work for?"

"No one."

"Where are you taking me?"

"Vonnas."

"Ah."

Kochubey's sudden mood shift bothered Saul. "You know it?"

The musician nodded, strangely pleased by the thought of visiting the small town fifty kilometers north of Lyon. "Perhaps you'll allow me the pleasure of eating at Le Cheval Blanc."

"It's not on the expense account."

Kochubey abruptly scowled. "You Americans are skinflints. Truth serum leaves such a bad aftertaste—like liver without butter or bacon. Very well." He squinted angrily. "We've a good three hours of driving ahead of us. Since you won't discuss your credentials, I'll talk about mine."

Saul groaned, sensing what was coming, and wished he could sedate him, but that would interfere with the Amytal.

Kochubey leaned back, smiling perversely, his large head framed by long, prematurely white hair in the style of composers and musicians from the previous century. He loosened his tie and rested his hands on the cummerbund of his tuxedo. "I don't suppose you attended my performance."

"We weren't on the guest list, I'm afraid."

"A pity. You'd have been given a lesson in Soviet idealism. You see, Tchaikovsky was like Lenin, and the similarity shows itself in the violin concerto, for the great composer had a theme in mind, as did Lenin. To arrive at his goal, he wove in transitional phrases, just as we in the Soviet Union have an ideal, and we move toward it, not in constant revolution, but in transitional phrases due to adjustments we've had to make because of the war and our economy. I won't say we've reached our finale, but we've come a long way in sixty-five years, have we not?"

"I'll admit you're well organized."

"An understatement. But I was talking about the great composer. The concerto opens simply, and you think the obvious strains contain the message. But underneath, other strains lie hidden, half-heard, half-guessed, as if the master were saying, 'I've a secret to tell you—but not a word to others.' It's like a whispered code to a member of our espionage network, or a sign of brotherhood among the people."

Saul grew tired quickly, fighting off sleep as Kochubey went on and Erika raced along the Autoroute du Sud toward Lyon. Forty minutes before reaching the city, she turned on the gravel access road that would in the next year become the Geneva-Macon spur of the expressway. Along the route, heavy road equipment had been parked for the night. The sharp crack of gravel pelting the underside of the car made Saul apprehensive.

He peered past the Citroën's headlights toward a heavy tanker trunk that rumbled in his direction. Frowning, he watched it suddenly veer.

It blocked the road.

Vans streaked from behind the heavy equipment, flanking the Citroën. Arc lights blazed from the dark.

"My eyes!" Hand up to shield them, Erika swerved to miss the truck, stamping the brakes. The Citroën skidded, jolting against a bulldozer, throwing her forward. Her head whacked the steering wheel, spewing blood.

The impact knocked Saul down. Scrambling up from the floor, he stared at her, moaning, unconscious. He couldn't carry her and get away, he realized. His frantic hope was to force the occupants of the vans to chase him, lose them, and double back for her. He grabbed at Kochubey's lapel as he opened the door, but the fabric tore away.

On his own, he leapt out, dodged the bulldozer, and raced to avoid

246

the spotlights. Doors banged open on the vans. He heard a car skidding to a stop on the road. Men shouted. Footsteps crunched on the gravel. The spotlights tracked him, throwing his urgent shadow across the muddy field. He stumbled in a rut, flailing his arms for balance, charging forward, desperate to reach the murky trees beyond the spotlights. Metal scraped. He tensed his shoulders, anticipating the wallop of a high-powered bullet, feeling a sting instead. In his neck: a dart. A second dart stung his hip. He flinched from an excruciating jolt. His vision failed. He fell to the mud, his knees jerking up to his chest, his arms twisting inward, convulsing. And that was all.

3

When he wakened, he knew enough to keep his eyes shut and listen. Groggy, he lay on a wooden floor. The pain in his left forearm must have been a puncture wound from a hypodermic. With enough Brevital in him, he could have been out for hours, only to be wakened by Kochubey's urgent shouts to someone else in the room. The handcuffs at his wrists behind his back were cold, not yet warmed by his body. Whoever was in the room must have recently brought him here and cuffed him.

Kochubey kept shouting. "What are they after? Why haven't you protected me better? You obviously knew I was in danger!"

Saul heard a different voice, deep and smooth. "Comrade, if you play a scale with your left hand and a contradictory scale with your right . . ."

"It's impossible to tell if the mode is major or minor! Any school boy—but what's that got to do with—?"

"The left and right hands had to be incompatible. If you'd known my intention, you wouldn't have been convincing to Romulus, whose faulty interpretation was essential to the trap. Now please stop shouting, or perhaps you'd enjoy practicing your music in the port of Hodéida in Yemen."

Saul peered through barely open lids in time to see Kochubey's face go pale.

"Relax, Victor," the voice said. "I'll supply you with a nice warm overcoat and send you on the high-speed train back to Paris."

While the man addressed Kochubey, Saul was able to recognize the ferretlike face between a black leather Tyrol hat and the high collar of a green loden coat. Boris Zlatogor Orlik, GRU colonel and Paris section chief for the KGB. Orlik prided himself on never having directly killed or stolen secrets or passed disinformation. Instead he was a theorist, a methodical planner whose exploits rivaled those of Richard Sorge, the master Soviet operative against Japan in the Second World War. It was Orlik who'd proven that GRU Lieutenant Colonel Yuri Popov was a spy for the CIA from '52 to '58, and that GRU Colonel Oleg Penkovsky was a spy for MI-6 in '62.

As Kochubey left, Saul didn't close his eyes fast enough.

"Ah, Romulus, I see you're awake. Forgive me for raising my voice, but sometimes with men like Kochubey it's necessary."

Saul didn't bother pretending he was still asleep. Squirming to sit up, he studied the room—a den with paneled walls, rustic paintings, a fireplace. "Where am I?"

"Near Lyon. A modest château I sometimes use for interrogation."

"Where's Erika?"

"Down the hall. But you needn't worry. A doctor's with her. She's fine, though she's got a nasty headache."

So did Saul. He slumped against a chair. His thoughts spun. "How did you find us?"

"The international language."

"I don't—"

"Music. Besides the Stradivari, the violin case contained a microphone and a homing device."

Saul groaned in disgust. "Kochubey was so convincing I didn't think to check it."

"But you almost dropped it out a window. I'll admit you had me nervous for a moment."

"That still doesn't answer my question. How'd you know we'd grab Kochubey?"

"Your agency told us."

"That's impossible."

"The information was specific. Since it was our man Remus killed in Bangkok, your people offered us the courtesy of letting us eliminate you."

248

"Eliot." Saul sounded as if he cursed.

"So it seemed to me as well."

"But how did—?"

"We'll get to that. First let me set the stage." Orlik gestured toward a window. "Dawn is breaking. If you think of escape, that's natural. But listen to what you're up against. You're on the edge of the Pilat Regional Park. There's a town to the south called Véranne, another to the north called Péllusin. No doubt you anticipate we have dogs, so you'd take to the wooded high ground—toward Véranne. But there you'd have to avoid the village. By night, you'd be stuck in the soft earth of the graveyard or the open fields. Wherever, we'd catch up with you. Our darts would give you another headache, and we'd have to start all over. Granted, a confrontation in a graveyard would be romantic. But the reality is it's dawn and we need to talk. I'm sorry I can't offer you a Baby Ruth."

Saul narrowed his eyes.

"You're well informed."

"Depend on it. Would you like some breakfast? Please don't think I've laced the croissants or coffee with anything. It never works properly."

Despite himself, Saul laughed.

"Good, let's be friendly." Orlik removed the handcuffs.

Puzzled, Saul rubbed his wrists, waiting till Orlik poured and drank the coffee. At last he had to ask. "Then you know about Eliot's orphans?"

"I'm sure it's occurred to you the Latin word for patriotism comes from the same root as father. *Pater. Patriae amor.* You saw your father as an extension of your country. Trained to defend it, you did everything he told you, unaware you were loyal to him—but not your government. His scheme was so brilliant the others adopted it."

Saul stopped drinking. "Others?"

Orlik studied him. "You must have known. Why else would you pick up Landish?"

"Others?"

Orlik frowned. "You really don't—? I assumed you'd reached the same conclusion I had. 1938."

"Make sense. Eliot wasn't even in government then. '54 is when he disappeared."

"And again in '73."

"But that time one of your men, Golitsin—"

"Not mine, but he did work for the KGB."

"—was involved, except your people shot him for treason."

"Then you have made progress."

"For Christ's sake!"

"Please, you'll have to be patient. I thought you could tell me some things. I never guessed I'd be telling *you.*"

"Then tell me, dammit! What's going on?"

"1938. What does that mean to you?"

"It could mean Hitler and Munich . . . or the Abelard sanction."

"Good. Then that's where we'll begin."

4

When Hitler met with Chamberlain and Daladier in Munich, a different meeting took place that same day in Berlin. Hitler—with Mussolini next to him—demanded that England and France renege on agreements they'd made with Czechoslovakia, Austria, and Poland to protect those countries against invasion. Hitler's intentions were obvious, but England and France did nothing to stop him, hoping he'd be satisfied if he expanded Germany's territory into those adjacent countries. The men at the other meeting, the one in Berlin, knew better, however. After all, they directed espionage for Germany, England, France, the Soviet Union, and the United States, and they understood that Hitler's invasion of those other countries wouldn't be the end of his need for power but only the start. A war was coming, so vast and destructive it would dwarf all others before it. Though heads of state chose to ignore the implications, the directors of intelligence could not, for they realized the role they would play in the coming war, and they had to make preparations. Since the First World War, their community had dwindled. Conditions had changed. Traditions had been forgotten. With a new conflict about to begin, it was time to reorganize, to agree on principles and establish rules, one of which was the Abelard sanction.

"I've always admired the imagination of the men who created it," Orlik said. "Such a brilliant refinement, so clever a variation. But there were other consequences of that meeting in Berlin, the most important of which was the recognition of the bond shared by those men. Because of their profession, they realized they formed a group larger than politics, transcending differences between their nations. One year countries might be friends, the next year enemies, the year after friends again. Such instability was senseless, based on the whim of politicians. It allowed the intelligence community to practice its skills, to enjoy the risks, but the men in Berlin understood that at heart they were closer to each other than to their governments. As well, they suspected the risks were becoming too huge. While they realized the need for rules, the leaders of their governments seemed to recognize no rules at all. How could the world survive if politicians refused to agree on limits? Someone had to act responsibly. Of course, before the war, they couldn't have predicted how serious this question would become. But even before atomic weapons, the issue of responsibility aggravated the intelligence community. Hitler's excesses became intolerable. We know some German intelligence officers collaborated with the English. These same German operatives attempted to assassinate Hitler. The bomb failed to kill him, and of course they were executed."

"You're suggesting a pattern?"

"What I've told you is fact. What follow are my suppositions. The men at the Abelard meeting agreed unofficially to act as—what shall we call them?—watchdogs on their governments, to see that international rivalry remained within acceptable bounds. A certain amount of conflict was necessary, of course, for the intelligence community to justify itself, but beyond a certain point, every nation stood an equal chance of losing, so the plan was set in motion. Stalin, remember, had begun his purges. My countryman, Vladimir Lazensokov, was executed a few months after he came back from the Abelard meeting. Did Stalin learn about that meeting and what Lazensokov had agreed to? Who can say? But his execution, in tandem with Hitler's reprisals for his attempted assassination, made the watchdogs in the intelligence community much more circumspect. They delegated their responsibility to carefully chosen protégés. Tex Auton, America's representative at that meeting, chose his adopted son Eliot, for example. Percival Landish chose his own son. The French and German representatives did the same. Lazensokov, I believe, foresaw his execution and made arrangements beforehand."

"You're talking about Golitsin?"

"Then you follow my logic. Golitsin, who was executed for treason in '73, had secret business with Landish and Eliot, and two other men in French and German intelligence. No doubt you'd soon have learned about them. The parallels are remarkable. The five men at the Abelard meeting trained surrogates who refused—despite their ambition—to achieve the highest positions in their networks. Instead they secured jobs just below the upper echelon where they wouldn't be threatened by the whim of politicians. To keep those jobs secure, they each compiled a secret collection of documented scandals, which they used as leverage against anyone foolish enough to try to remove them from power. These men have retained their positions since after the war and thus have been consistent influences on their governments. They've sabotaged operations. Your U-2 incident and Bay of Pigs, for example. To moderate the less enlightened members of their agencies, they've insisted an enemy spy had infiltrated them. As a consequence, each network has been so busy investigating itself only a moderate level of espionage has been maintained, and thus a form of control has been established. Acting responsibly—or so they imagine—these men ensure an international status quo."

"Eliot's disappearances in '54 and '73?"

"Meetings. To cement their relationship, to reaffirm their intentions. They needed to coordinate their efforts. They met as seldom as they could but as often as they had to."

"One problem with your theory."

"Oh?"

"Each man couldn't do all that on his own. They'd have needed personnel and financing."

"True. But in your own case the CIA has an unlimited unrecorded budget. No one knows exactly how much money it receives or where that money goes. If accounts were kept, secrecy would be impaired. Appropriating funds for a private operation wouldn't be difficult. The same rule applies to the other networks."

"Eliot and the others would still have needed help. They'd have had to delegate authority. Eventually someone would have talked."

"Not necessarily. Think about it."

Saul felt his stomach sink.

"You and Remus didn't talk. Or Eliot's other orphans. I suspect the idea came from Auton; it functioned brilliantly. For years, you and the others have been working for Eliot in his attempt to comply with the implications of the Abelard meeting, to obey his foster father's directive."

"The Paradigm job he asked me to do."

"Apparently he thought it was necessary. We were blamed for it. So was Israel. Neither of us wants the Arabs to align themselves with the United States. The question is what did he hope to achieve."

"That's wrong. The question is why did he ask me to do it and then try to kill me afterward."

"You'll have to ask him."

"If I don't kill the bastard first." His bowels contracted. "They all had orphans."

"The final parallel. Landish, Golitsin, and the others—each recruited foster sons in orphanages, guaranteeing loyalty without question, sacrificing their children when they had to."

"It keeps getting sicker." Saul raised his hands. "If I could—"

"That's why you're still alive."

Saul squinted, raging. "Get to the point."

"Like Lazensokov before him, Golitsin too foresaw his execution and chose a surrogate. I've discovered who, but I fear my efforts have been discovered. My opponent is clever and powerful. If I become too dangerous to him, he'd easily destroy me. As a consequence, I've concentrated on the men in the other networks who inherited the legacy."

"But why? If they sabotage their networks, they're helping you."

"Not if they act in accord, Golitsin's replacement along with the others. They're interfering with the natural order. I'm a Marxist, my friend. I believe in Soviet domination. There are evils in our system, but they're insignificant compared to—"

"What?"

"The utter obscenity of your own. I want to destroy these men. I want to let the dialectic take its course, upset the status quo, and complete the Revolution." Orlik smiled. "When I received the directive to intercept and kill you, I couldn't believe my fortune."

"And that's it? You want me to go after these men? So you can protect yourself?"

Orlik nodded.

"My fight's with Eliot. To get out of here, I'll have to compromise. I see that. But to help, I'll need a lot more compromise from you."

"No, I've got Erika. You wouldn't let her die. But there's something else."

Saul frowned.

"You claim your fight's with Eliot? You're wrong. It's at least with another."

"Who?"

"You wondered how Eliot knew you'd come to Paris?"

"Say it!"

"Chris is dead. Landish killed him."

5

Erika choked.

The bedroom had no windows. Saul wanted to scream, to smash the walls. Rage overwhelmed him, so intense he thought he'd burst. Grief wracked his muscles, shaking him till he ached. "It should have been me."

She moaned.

"He wanted to take my place—to go to Paris with you and grab Kochubey while I watched Landish." Saul fought to breathe. "Because he had a feeling I'd be killed. But I wouldn't do it!"

"Don't."

"I wouldn't listen!"

"No, it wasn't your fault. The lowest card stayed. If you'd taken his place—"

"I'd have died instead of him! To bring him back, I'd gladly die!"

"That isn't what he wanted!" Erika stood, unsteadily raising a hand to the bandage around her head. "He didn't ask to change places with you so he could save his life. He thought he'd be saving *yours*. It wasn't your fault. For God's sake, accept what he gave you." She shook, starting to weep. "Poor Chris. So fucked up. He never knew any . . ."

"Peace?" Saul nodded, understanding. He and Chris had been trained to cancel all emotion except dependence on each other and love for Eliot. In Saul's case, it had worked. He'd never been bothered by the things Eliot asked him to do—because he couldn't bear to disappoint his father.

But Chris . . .

Saul's throat ached. . . . Chris had been different. His conditioning had failed. The killing at last had tormented him. He must have gone through hell trying to satisfy Eliot and deny his conscience. Even the monastery couldn't save him.

Tears streamed down Saul's face, their unaccustomed warmth shocking. His eyes stung, swollen. He hadn't cried since he'd been a five-year-old at Franklin. He clung to Erika, weeping.

At last his own conditioning failed. Anger aggravated sorrow, grief fed rage till something broke in him, a lifetime's restraint letting loose so grim a resolve its power frightened him. He'd never experienced anything like it, a surging need that for all its pain promised utter satisfaction.

"You bastard." He gritted his teeth. "For those candy bars, you'll pay." The hate in his voice astonished him.

"That's right." Erika's voice shook. "Put the blame where it belongs. Not on you. On Eliot. He caused it. He and Landish and those other sonsofbitches."

Nodding, Saul raged. In fury, he understood. He had to get revenge for Chris.

The sharp knock startled him. A key scraped in the lock. He swung to the opening door as Orlik's ferret face appeared with a guard. "Our agreement was fifteen minutes."

"I'm ready." Saul seethed, impatient. "Set it up."

"I already have. You leave right now, though Erika remains, of course. As my insurance."

"If she's harmed."

"Please." Orlik looked offended. "I'm a gentleman as much as a professional."

"Insurance?" Erika frowned.

"If you prefer, an added incentive."

"What you don't understand," Saul said, "is I've got all the incentive I need."

"To do it your way," Orlik said. "But I want you to do it mine. When my enemy looks for someone to blame, it has to be you, not me." His eyes gleamed. "I hope you've recovered from the sedative."

"Why?"

"You're about to accomplish an amazing escape."

6

Saul scrambled to the top of the ridge, catching his breath as he scanned the twilit landscape. Behind him, mist filled the valley. Ahead, thick fir trees beckoned. Smelling their resin, he charged among them, hearing the bay of dogs on his trail. They'd been louder since he'd crossed the meadow back there. He'd tried to find a stream and race along it, hiding his scent, but luck had failed. Sweat stuck his shirt to his chest.

The dogs sounded louder.

Orlik had predicted correctly. Against the dogs, Saul's best choice was north toward the wooded high ground. He hoped to find a cliff the dogs couldn't climb, a chasm they couldn't jump across. But again his luck had failed him.

Evening made the forest damp. His sweat felt slick as he scrambled through the undergrowth. The dogs barked closer. Passing an open swath to his right, he saw the dots of lights in a town, but he couldn't risk heading there. Orders would have been received, sentinels posted. His best route was farther north, through the territory he liked best— the high hills and the forest. He loved the smell of the loam he raced across.

Thick brambles tore his clothes. Dense branches raked his skin. Despite the swelling stings, he felt exhilarated. Adrenaline spurred his senses. As if he'd struggled through a maze, he rejoiced in release. He triumphed.

Except for the dogs. They crashed through the bushes, relentless, closer. Leaping a deadfall, he charged up a shadowy slope, hearing forest animals skitter away as if they sensed an imminent kill. He chose a game trail to his left, rounding a boulder, scrambling toward a plain.

And found himself in the graveyard Orlik had predicted. Headstones jutted before him, silhouetted against the gloaming. Marble angels spread their wings. Cherubs mourned. Against the dying sunset, mist created halos. Everything seemed preordained. He darted among the graves. A wreath and then a single blossom caught his attention.

He heard the scratch of claws behind him. He turned to face the undergrowth and reached in his pocket. Orlik had told him not to use it till necessary.

Now it was. He screwed off the cap and poured the pungent cloying chemical on a newly filled-in mound. At once he darted past a hedge and disappeared in the gathering night. The flowers smelled of funerals.

But not for him, he thought. And not for the guards he'd slammed with the heel of his palm at Orlik's chateau, holding back. Though his enemies, they'd live. And Orlik would get what he wanted, a convincing escape without the sacrifice of his men.

Behind, he heard the anguished howl of the dogs, their nostrils tortured, useless. They'd scrape at their faces till the smell of blood obscured the chemical. But they wouldn't chase him any longer.

There'd be a funeral all right. Not his, but soon, he thought, anticipating. He was too much in love with hate to squander it.

7

The car was hidden where Orlik had said it would be—in the shadows behind a boarded-up service station on a secondary road outside Lyon. A three-year-old Renault, its gray inconspicuous, blending with the night. Saul approached it warily, checking the road and the trees around the station before he crept from bushes toward the side away from the road. He'd taken a French MAB 9-mm pistol from one of the guards at Orlik's château. Aiming it, he peered through the window toward the back floor. Seeing no one, he opened the car and found—as Orlik had promised—keys beneath the front mat. He checked to make sure the car had not been booby-trapped, using matches he found on the dash, scanning the engine, then crawling underneath to inspect the suspension. He opened the trunk, where he found the clothes and equipment Orlik had guaranteed he'd supply. Though Saul had other sources, money and identification he'd hidden years before in various countries, he was reassured by Orlik's adherence to their bargain. For certain he intended to made good on his own.

Even so, he was bothered that Orlik hadn't released Erika, though he understood the logic. Orlik had put himself under suspicion by allowing Saul to escape. It would be more believable if Erika hadn't escaped as well. She'd be a way of forcing Saul to do things as Orlik wanted. But he couldn't subdue the suspicion Orlik had another motive. What if when this was over Orlik planned to use her to lure Saul back, then kill them both and present them as trophies, absolving himself from responsibility for what Saul had done?

The complexities were quicksand, sucking him deep. But this he knew—Orlik wouldn't betray them till his purpose was achieved. In the meantime, Saul's direction was clear before him, extremely simple.

Chris was dead. There would be hell to pay.

He started the Renault. It idled easily, sounding recently tuned, its gas tank full.

He drove to the road, his headlights gleaming through the dark. He chose a lane, then another, watching for pursuit lights in his mirror. Seeing none, he turned onto the next main road and, obeying the limit, headed west.

Orlik had chosen his targets, five, the descendants of the original Abelard group. But Orlik hadn't stipulated who came first.

He planned to abandon this car as quickly as he could. Despite his search, he might have missed a transmitter beeping his location to a surveillance team staying far enough back to hide their lights. They didn't matter.

Nothing did.

Except revenge. It gave him pleasure to think the skills his father had taught him would be the weapons he'd use to destroy him.

Hey, old man, I'm coming.

He clenched the steering wheel so hard his knuckles ached.

And sometime in the night, Chris sat beside him, face gaunt, eyes dead, grinning as if they were kids again, about to start another adventure.

The best kind. Getting even.

8

"What? Excuse me? I didn't hear what you said." Eliot slowly roused himself. He sat at the desk in his study, peering up as if he'd been concentrating on important papers, though there were none and the lamps were off and the drapes were closed. He squinted at the open door, at a husky man outlined by the light from the hall.

The man had his legs spread, his arms slightly away from his sides. He was tall, his face square.

Eliot frowned. For an instant he didn't recognize the man—or rather he feared he did. It looked like Chris.

Had Chris survived and come for him? Impossible. Landish had guaranteed Chris was . . .

Dark against the light, the shape looked . . .

Dead? Impossible. Then was it Saul who, having slipped past the guards around the house, was now confronting him?

Not yet. Too soon. But the explanation disturbed him, for he realized the figure reminded him not only of Chris and Saul, but all the others, nine pairs, eighteen orphans, all his foster sons. He told himself he'd loved them. Didn't his throat ache when he thought of them? Wasn't his grief a proof he hadn't acted callously? His pain in sacrificing them had made his mission more heroic.

Fifteen now were dead, though—maybe another if Saul became too eager. Saul wasn't likely to, however. The pattern seemed predetermined. I've never believed in luck, he thought. Or fate. I put my faith in skill. But as he studied the figure in the doorway, he experienced a momentary hallucination, all his dead children superimposed on one another. He shivered. He'd chosen their cryptonyms from Greek and Roman mythology, indulging his love of complexity, but now he recalled something else from that mythology—the Furies. The avenging Shades.

He cleared his throat, repeating, "I didn't hear what you said."

"Are you all right?" Pollux stepped forward.

"What makes you think I wouldn't be?"

259

"I heard you talking in here."

Troubled, Eliot didn't remember having done so.

Pollux continued, "I couldn't figure who you'd be talking to. For sure, nobody got past me. Then I thought of the phone, but where I stood in the hall I could see it was still on the hook."

"I'm fine. I must be . . . thinking out loud, I suppose. No need to worry."

"Can I bring you anything?"

"No, I guess not."

"I could heat up some cocoa."

Nostalgic, Eliot smiled. "When you and Castor were young and you came to visit, I used to bring cocoa to you. Remember? Just before you went to sleep."

"How could I forget?"

"Our positions have been reversed it seems. And do you plan to take care of your father in his old age?"

"For you? You know I'd do anything."

Eliot nodded, in pain from emotion. Fifteen others had given everything. "I know. I'm fine. I just need time to myself. I love you. Have you eaten?"

"Soon."

"Make sure you do. And your brother?"

"He's down the hall, watching the back."

"I'll join you shortly. We'll talk about the old days."

Pollux departed. Leaning back exhausted, Eliot fondly remembered the summer of '54 when he had taken Castor and Pollux to . . . was it Yellowstone Park? Too many years had passed too quickly. His recollection sometimes failed him. Perhaps it had been the Grand Canyon. No. That had been in '56. Castor had—

With a shudder, he realized how horribly wrong he was. His mind recoiled with dismay. Not Castor and Pollux. No, dear God, it had been another pair, and he almost wept because he couldn't remember who. Chris and Saul perhaps. His Furies crowded closer. His mouth filled with bile.

He'd left the office in midafternoon as soon as his assistant had brought the news.

"Romulus escaped? But everything was arranged, the trap confirmed! The KGB claimed they had him!"

"And the woman. Yes." The assistant spoke reluctantly. "But he got away."

260

"How?"

"They caught him near Lyon. He broke from a château where he'd been taken to be executed."

"They were supposed to kill him on the spot!"

"It seems they wanted to interrogate him first."

"That wasn't the agreement! How much damage did he do? How many guards did he kill?"

"None. The escape was clean."

It troubled him. "But they killed the woman?"

"No, they're questioning her to find out where he went."

He shook his head. "It's wrong."

"But they claim—"

"It's wrong. They lie. It's a trick."

"But why?"

"Someone let him go."

"I don't see what the motive would be."

"Isn't it obvious? To come for me."

The assistant narrowed his eyes.

And that was when Eliot, realizing his assistant thought he was paranoid, had left the building, taking Castor and Pollux with him. Since then, he'd been sitting in his shadowy den, protected for now by guards around the house and his two remaining faithful sons in here.

But he couldn't continue like this forever. He couldn't merely wait. Despite the Shades that haunted him, he didn't believe in fate. I've always depended on skill, he thought. And wile.

I taught him. I can outguess him. What would I do if I were Saul?

The moment he knew what question to ask, the answer came all at once. Thrilling, it gave him another chance. But only if he acted quickly.

He had to get through to Landish.

Saul would savor revenge, making stops along the way, increasing the terror.

Landish'll be his first target. We can set up a trap.

9

Again he felt he'd been here before, seeming to see not only Franklin but the walls of Andrew Sage's estate as well. Everything was coming together. Eliot had used the school to pervert him. One of the consequences was the Paradigm job. Understanding, he grimly delighted in his sense of heading back to where it all began. When he'd blown up Sage's estate, he'd felt nothing. There'd been a job to do. He'd done it for Eliot. But everything was different now. For the first time, he looked forward to a kill. Comparing the walls of Sage's estate with Landish's estate, he realized the change in himself. He *wanted* to kill, and it pleased him that the method he'd chosen was the method he'd used to kill Sage. He savored the irony, using Eliot's tactics against him. I told you, Landish, how I'd punish you if you lied. Dammit, my brother's dead. Imagining the walls of Franklin School, he felt his eyes burn, swollen with tears.

He turned to his weapon. He could have chosen a rifle and simply have shot Landish from a distance. But that wouldn't have satisfied him, wouldn't have been complete enough, a fulfillment of his threat. Landish had to die in a certain way.

But his determination created a problem. Landish either was more cautious or else had learned of Saul's escape, for security on the estate had tripled. Guards patrolled in abundance. Visitors were asked for credentials and then were searched. The walls had now been equipped with closed-circuit cameras. It wasn't possible to infiltrate the grounds as he had before. Then how could he plant the explosives? How could he blow up not just Landish but—I told you what I'd do; they represent everything I hate—those fucking roses?

It was the largest remote-controlled model plane he could buy. He'd gone to half a dozen of the largest hobby shops in London before he found it. A miniature Spitfire with a three-foot wingspan and a half-mile range. His own guided missile. He wiped his misted eyes while he made adjustments, smiling. A toy. If Chris had been here, he'd have laughed. The corrupted child had chosen a plaything to get back at his father.

The model was fueled. He'd tested it earlier at another location. He had no trouble making it work. It responded to radio signals, maneuvered through the sky by a stick on a transmitter. It climbed and banked and dove precisely as he wished. But the plane had cargo: five pounds of stolen explosive, evenly distributed along the fuselage and taped in place. The added weight affected the model's performance, retarding its takeoff, making it sluggish in the air. But not enough to matter. The weapon would do its job. He'd gone to an electronics store and bought the parts he needed for a detonator, anchoring it to the undercarriage, controlled by its own transmitter. He'd taken care that the plane and the detonator were linked to different frequencies. Otherwise the explosive would have gone off when he activated the transmitter for the plane.

He waited. Dawn came slowly, bringing no warmth. Though he shivered, hate burned his soul.

He knew his target wouldn't have hidden somewhere else. The roses were too important. Landish would fear for them and be unable to stay away.

He thought of Chris, enjoying the wait, imagining the satisfaction he soon would know. At seven, he tensed as a white-haired figure, flanked by guards, left a rear door of the mansion, approaching the greenhouse. He feared it was someone else disguised as Landish, but through binoculars, he recognized the old man. No mistake. His gardening coat looked somewhat bulky. He was wearing a bulletproof vest.

It won't do you any good, you bastard.

As soon as Landish and the guards went into the greenhouse, Saul crept back through the trees. He carried the plane, along with the transmitters in a knapsack on his shoulder, crossing a meadow, its grass too wet with dew to be a takeoff strip. A country road worked perfectly. Seeing no cars, he started the plane and guided it faster till it left the ground and struggled for altitude. Its engine droned. When it was high enough to clear the trees, he returned through the meadow, keeping the plane in sight above him as he shifted through the woods to reach the bluff overlooking Landish's estate. Because of the dew, his pants clung cold to his legs, but even that felt pleasant. Birds sang. The early morning air smelled fresh. He pretended to be the child he never was. Had never been allowed to be.

His toy. His drying tears made his cheeks feel stiff as he smiled. He worked the controls, raising the plane to its limit—a speck against the pale blue sky—aiming it toward the estate. The guards turned, puzzled by its drone. A few cocked their heads. A man with a dog pointed up. Though they couldn't see him from this distance, he crouched behind bushes, manipulating the controls. His pulse thumped louder as the plane veered over the grounds.

The guards seemed paralyzed, then abruptly snapped into motion, urgent, nervous, appearing to sense a threat but not knowing what it was. He urged the plane to its maximum height, then forced it into a dive. As the plane streaked toward the greenhouse, its shape enlarging, its drone increasing, a few men ran toward the greenhouse. Others shouted. Several raised rifles. He heard the crack of shots, seeing the guards jerk from the recoil. Twisting the control stick, he began evasive maneuvers, tilting the plane to the right, then the left, veering, spinning, diving. Other guards began shooting. He studied the greenhouse. Through its glass, he saw a small white-coated figure turn to face the commotion. Only Landish had worn white. He stood among roses, a third of the way along a row. Saul aimed the plane directly at him. So many shots cracked they became a rattle. The plane responded sluggishly. For a terrible instant, he feared it had been hit, but then he realized the weight of the bomb affected the dive. He compensated, moving the plane less abruptly. When it struck the glass, he imagined Landish gasping. He pressed the second transmitter. The greenhouse disintegrated. Shards of glass arced, glinting. Guards dove for cover, obscured by smoke and flames. As a rumble drifted across the valley, he fled, imagining specks of rose petals drifting on, soaking up Landish's blood.

10

The phone rang, making Eliot flinch. He stared, forcing himself to wait while it shrilled again before he had control enough to pick it up.

"Hello?" He sounded cautious, expecting to hear Saul curse in triumph, threatening. He had to convince Saul to meet with him, to lure Saul into a trap.

What he heard was his assistant. "Sir, I'm afraid we've got bad news. An emergency cable from MI-6."

"Landish? Something's happened to him?"

"Yes, sir, how did you know?"

"Just tell me."

"Somebody blew him up. In his greenhouse. He was heavily guarded. But—"

"Dear God." When Eliot learned how the bomb was delivered, his heart felt numb. Landish hadn't stopped him.

It was Saul all right. He wants to let me know how clever he is. He's telling me he can get at me no matter where I am or how well I protect myself. Eliot shook his head in dismay.

Why should I be surprised? I taught him.

Murmuring "Thanks," he hung up. In the dark, he fought to calm himself, to clear his mind, to analyze his options.

Feverish, he shivered, struck by the thought that he hadn't been in danger since he'd worked undercover in France in the war. Since then, he'd risen so high his only risk had been political. No ranking intelligence officer had ever been executed for treason. Only operatives in the field ever faced death. At the worst, he'd have received a prison sentence, probably not even that—to avoid publicity, high-level traitors were often merely dismissed, their capacity to do damage ended. With his collection of scandals to use as blackmail, he might even have claimed his pension.

No, his only fear had been discovery. Because of pride and his determination not to fail.

But the fear he now suffered was fierce. Not intellectual. Instinctive. Reflexive terror. He hadn't felt this way since a night in a drainage ditch in France when a German sentry had thrust at him with—

His heart almost burst from the strain. His paper-thin lungs, brittle from years of cigarettes, heaved heroically.

I won't give up. I've always been a winner. After nearly forty years, he faced again the ultimate. And didn't intend to fail.

A father against his son? A teacher against his student?

All right, then, come for me. I'm sorry Chris is dead, but I won't let you beat me. I'm still better than you.

He nodded. The rules. Don't go to your enemy. Make him come to you. Force him to fight on your own territory. Make him face you on your own terms.

He knew a way. Saul was wrong if he thought he could get at him no matter where he was or how well guarded. There was a place. It offered absolute protection. And the best part was it followed the rules.

Standing quickly, he walked to the hall. Pollux straightened, attentive. Eliot smiled.

"Bring your brother. We need to pack." He paused at the stairs. "It's been too long since we went on a trip."

11

In London, Saul ignored the rain at the window. He'd closed the draperies. Even so, he turned on the lights only long enough to see the numbers he dialed on the phone. Again in darkness, he lay on the bed, waiting for an answer. In a while, he'd shower and change his clothes, then eat the fish and chips he'd brought here with him. After that, he'd pay for this room, having used it for just an hour, and head for his next destination. He could sleep en route. There was much to do.

The phone stopped buzzing. "Yes?"

It sounded like Orlik, but he had to be sure. "Baby Ruth."

"And roses."

Orlik. The Russian had given him numbers—pay phones where he could be reached on certain days at certain times for information and instructions.

"I assume you've heard the terrible news about our English friend," Saul said.

"Indeed. Sudden, but not unexpected. And not without consequences," Orlik said. "There's been considerable activity among his associates. It seems they fear additional sudden news about themselves."

"Have they taken precautions?"

"Why? Would that disturb you?"

"Not as long as I knew where to find them."

"Travel's good for the soul, I understand."

"Can you recommend some places?"

"Several. I know of a winery in France's Bordeaux district, for example. And a mountain retreat in Germany's Black Forest. If the

Soviet Union's to your liking, I suggest a dacha near the mouth of the Volga on the Caspian."

"Only three? I expected four."

"If you went directly to the fourth, you might lose interest in the others," Orlik said.

"On the other hand, I'm so looking forward to seeing the fourth I might not be able to concentrate on the others."

"I've a friend of yours who's anxious for you to finish your travels so you can get back to her. We agreed you'd follow directions. If you don't do what I want, what point is there in my helping you? I had in mind you'd pay your next visit to my disruptive colleague in the Soviet Union."

"And take the pressure off you? Think again. You're helping me only so I'll take care of him. Then you'll blame me and be in the clear."

"I've never pretended otherwise," Orlik said.

"But once you're safe, you might decide you can deal with the others by yourself. You'll arrange for me to be killed and come out a winner all the way around."

"Your suspicion hurts my feelings."

"I'm in this for one reason only—Eliot. I'll deal with the others later. There's no guarantee I can do them all. Maybe I'll make a mistake and die before I get to the others. If I take them in the order you want, maybe I'll never reach Eliot."

"All the more reason to be cautious."

"No. Listen carefully. I have a question. If I hear the wrong answer, I'm hanging up. I'll get to Eliot on my own. If Erika's harmed, I'll come for you the way I did for Eliot."

"You call this being cooperative?"

"The question. I assume he knows I've escaped and what happened to Landish. He'll have to figure I'm coming. He'll make arrangements. In his place, I wouldn't stay at home. I'd want the best protection I could find, the safest location. *Where do I find him?*"

Rain rattled against the window. In the dark, he clutched the phone, braced for Orlik's response.

"I don't like being threatened."

"Wrong answer."

"Wait! What's the matter with—? Give me a chance! Eliot now? Then the others in exchange for Erika?"

"Unless I feel you're using her as a trap."

"You have my word."

"The answer."

Orlik sighed, then told him. Saul hung up.

His heart raced. The location Orlik had told him was brilliant. What did you expect? he thought. Despite his hate, he admitted Eliot's genius.

The best, the most controlled of arenas. Chris would have understood.

12

A large black van stood outside the farmhouse. Approaching it, Orlik frowned. His tires crunched on the gravel lane as he parked his Citroën well away from the unfamiliar vehicle, making sure he was pointed back down the lane. He shut off his lights and motor but left the key in the switch. Cautious, he got out, scanning the night.

If he'd seen the van from a distance, he'd have stopped and circled the farmhouse, investigating. But the van had been placed so he wouldn't notice it till he reached the end of the lane. He couldn't have retreated without alerting his visitors. Assuming the night hid guards in addition to his own, he had no choice except to go inside apparently unconcerned.

Lamps glowed from several windows. There. As he neared the house, he noticed a shadow to the right at the corner. Positioned just beyond the spill of light, the figure evidently intended Orlik to glimpse him.

To the left, the screech of crickets abruptly stopped. So that side had someone too. But again the warning could so easily have been prevented by avoiding movement that Orlik had to guess the hidden sentries were letting Orlik know they were there.

To watch my reaction. If I've done nothing wrong, I shouldn't look nervous. If I did what they suspect, though, maybe I'd prove it by trying to run.

He had no doubt who they were. After Saul's "escape" from the château outside Lyon, Orlik had taken Erika south to this farm near Avignon, wanting to hide her—in case Saul attempted to rescue her

268

instead of completing his bargain. Saul could never have found this place. The French authorities didn't know what was going on. So who did that leave? Who else was involved and had ways of tracking him here?

Two conclusions. A member of his staff, suspicious about Saul's escape, had informed against him. The second: Orlik's superiors were here to interrogate him.

"You," Orlik said in Russian. "To the right. Be careful stepping back. There's a cistern behind you. Its cover won't hold your weight."

He heard no response. Smiling, he continued forward—but not to the main door, instead to an entrance near the right side.

He went in, smelling veal and mushrooms from supper. A narrow hall went left past the kitchen toward the lights in the living room. A muscular guard stood outside a padlocked door.

"Open it," Orlik said. "I have to question her."

The guard looked sullen. "They won't like that."

Orlik raised his eyebrows.

"You're expected." The guard pointed down the hall.

I know who informed against me, Orlik thought. He's in the right place. He'll get what he deserves. "They'll have to wait. I told you to open it."

The guard frowned. "But—"

"Are you deaf?"

Squinting with anger, the guard pulled out a key and freed the lock.

Orlik stepped in.

The room had been stripped of furniture Erika could have used as a weapon. She'd been allowed jeans and a flannel shirt, but her shoes had been taken in case she broke free and tried to run. Her belt, a potential weapon, had been taken as well. She glared up from where she sat on the floor in a corner.

"Good. You're awake," Orlik said.

"How can I sleep with these lights?"

"I need information." Turning, Orlik nodded to the guard and closed the door.

He crossed the room. Grim, he pulled a Soviet Makarov 9-mm pistol from behind his suitcoat.

She didn't flinch.

He studied her, brooding, deciding.

"So it's time then?" Her eyes were as dark as coal.

He rehearsed the scene he anticipated in the living room and nodded. "Yes, it's time." He handed her the pistol.

Her pupils widened.

Leaning close, he smelled the fragrance of her hair.

He whispered. Finished, he straightened. "My one consolation is that though you don't want to, you'll be helping me."

Needing the friendly contact of flesh, he stooped and kissed her. On the cheek. As he would a sister. Considering what awaited him.

He turned and left the room. The guard seemed impatient.

"I know," Orlik said. "They want me."

He walked along the hall. The living room grew brighter as he neared it. Plain, sparse, drab. A sooted fireplace. A threadbare sofa. A creaky rocking chair.

On which a gaunt joyless man surveyed him.

Orlik concealed his surprise. He'd expected his immediate superior or at worst the European director. But the man confronting him, more thin-cheeked and ferretlike than even himself, was the quarry he'd hunted, the Russian descendant of the Abelard group, the Soviet equivalent of Eliot.

A man named Kovshuk. Wearing black. He halted in the rocker, voice clipped, speaking Russian. Stern guards flanked him.

"I'll be plain. You had instructions to kill the American. You disobeyed. You arranged his escape. I assume you intend him to kill me."

Orlik shook his head. "I don't know what . . ." He sputtered. "Naturally I'm honored to see you. But I don't understand. I can't be held responsible for inferior assistants. If they're so clumsy—"

"No. I don't have time for theatrics." Kovshuk turned to a guard. "Bring the woman. Use whatever method you like. Make her admit what she knows. Document their crimes. Then kill them together."

"Listen."

"Interfere, I'll kill you right now. I want to know where the American is." Kovshuk turned to the guard again. "I told you, bring her."

Orlik watched the guard disappear. "You're mistaken. I want the American as much as—"

"Don't insult me."

Orlik's senses quickened. He carried a second gun. With no other choice, he drew it. If he killed the remaining guard before—

But Kovshuk had anticipated, already drawing his own gun, shooting.

Orlik took the bullet in his chest.

The impact jolted him. He lurched back, eyes wide, toppling. Despite the blood spewing from his mouth, he managed a grin.

He'd lost.

But won. Because from the hall he heard sharp pistol cracks, recognizing the Makarov's sound, confident both his disloyal assistant and Kovshuk's bodyguard were dead. The woman was as skilled as she was erotic.

A door banged open.

His senses faded. Nonetheless he heard the Makarov bark again. He'd warned her about the guards outside and where they were positioned.

He imagined her running through the night.

He grinned at Kovshuk. Heard the Citroën roar. The Makarov barked again.

And he died.

13

Erika's bare feet were slick with blood. She'd gashed them on the gravel lane as she raced from the house toward Orlik's Citroën. The key had been in the ignition as Orlik had promised. Her bloody feet slipped off the clutch and accelerator. Angry, she applied more pressure, switching gears, roaring faster down the lane, the rear wheels fishtailing, the night like a wall before her. She didn't dare flick on her headlights. Though she might skid off an unseen curve, she had to avoid the risk of making the lights a target.

As it was, the roar of the engine made a sufficient target. The rear window imploded. She heard repeated staccato bursts from automatic weapons, a sequence of wallops jolting the car. In the mirror, she saw strobelike muzzle flashes, recognizing the distinctive crack of the submachine guns.

Uzis. She'd had too much experience with them to be wrong. Suddenly understanding what Saul had felt like in Atlantic City, she skidded around a bend in the road she barely spotted in time.

Her thoughts intruded on her instincts. Why would Russians prefer Israeli weapons?

No time. Bleeding on the clutch, she jerked the gearshift higher. The dark was thicker away from the house. The Citroën scraped against a tree. She couldn't postpone it any longer, turned on her lights, and stared at a massive shadow crashing from the underbrush.

A van. She jerked the steering wheel to the left and floored the blood-slick accelerator. The Citroën veered past the front of the van, sliding sideways, its rear end whacking against a stump. The taillight shattered, but the wheels churned gravel, gaining traction, rocketing forward. She surged past the roadblock, seeing a tunnel of trees and bushes—at the end of which a country road beckoned.

Other Uzis rattled. The second taillight shattered. Good, it distracted their aim. She geared down, skidding from gravel to tar, aiming left on the country road. On a straightaway, she switched to high gear and watched the speedometer climb past 120 kilometers, urging it to the top.

She knew she'd be chased. The Citroën shuddered as if from structural damage. She had to run with it till it fell apart. Or she found a better car.

But the open road was before her, and her purpose was vivid. Orlik's whispered warning had been explicit, the interrogation before him, the threat they both faced, the reprieve he was granting her. Prepared, she'd shot the man who came for her—and the guard in the hall. She'd killed the sentries who flanked the house. Though her bare feet stung from gravel, specks of which were imbedded in her soles, she felt exhilarated, free and with a goal.

Saul needed her. Orlik had told her where he was.

But racing through the night, seeing headlights in her rearview mirror, resting her hand on the pistol beside her, she couldn't avoid the thought that earlier had occurred to her. The Uzis. Why would Russians prefer Israeli weapons?

The answer troubled her. Because the man who waited for Orlik at the house had been the Russian equivalent of Eliot. His guards, like Eliot's, had received killer-instinct training as their final preparation. They'd been taught to act like Israelis, and the consequences would be blamed on . . .

Erika clenched her teeth. On Israel.

She raged past farms and orchards. If the headlights gained on her, she'd stop and take her chances, blocking the road, blowing her pursuers to hell.

But despite the Citroën's shudders, she kept her distance, roaring through the dark.

Orlik's final whisper repeated itself in her mind. "Saul's headed for Eliot. The old man chose the perfect sanctuary. It's a trap."

But for whom? For Saul or Eliot?

She knew this much. Orlik had told her. A province. A city. A mountain valley.

Canada.

And she would get there.

REST HOMES/
GOING TO GROUND

1

The highway became so steep Saul switched from second gear to first, hearing the strain on the Eagle's engine, forcing the station wagon higher. He'd chosen this model because, while it looked conventional, it had four-wheel-drive capability. On the one hand, he didn't want to seem conspicuous. On the other, he didn't know how rugged the terrain would get before he reached his destination.

The terrain looked imposing enough already. An overpacked car with out-of-province license plates was stalled on the shoulder, its hood up, its radiator steaming. The driver—a harried man with his hands spread attempting to reassure his frightened wife and children—had evidently not been familiar with techniques of driving in the mountains. Probably he'd used too high a gear or worse, an automatic transmission, either of which would put too great a stress on the motor. Going back down, the driver would likely use his brakes instead of his gears to control his speed and end up burning the shoes and drums out.

Driving was complicated by more than just the steepness of the road. That slowed a car, but so did the long procession of laboring traffic above, retarded by an exhaust-belching semitruck at the head of the line. In frustration, Saul felt he crawled at a rate of millimeters instead of kilometers. The sharp switchbacks made driving worse. Angled left, Saul would suddenly reach a hairpin turn and try to keep the Eagle from stalling as he swung the steering wheel hard to the right, squeezing past downward traffic.

Above, beyond 10,000 feet, swollen mountains obscured the sky, snowcaps glinting. Granite ridges, studded with fir trees, zoomed down, furrowed as if a giant's fingers had gouged at them. The Canadian

274

Rockies, though strictly speaking this section was known as the Coast Mountains, but Saul thought of them as an extension of the Rockies farther inland. Together, these British Columbia ranges were so huge and rugged they dwarfed the Colorado mountains he was familiar with, overwhelming him.

Below, the plain he'd left had a different splendor. Wooded slopes dipped to grassland, then to the sprawling expanse of Vancouver, its expensive highrises contrasting with underground shopping centers, sleek subdivisions, and landscaped homes. The impressive Lions Gate suspension bridge stretched across Burrard Inlet, linking districts.

Paradise in the sun. A sea breeze dispelled the heat. To the west, sails gleamed in the sound. Beyond, Vancouver Island's mighty hills protected the city from ocean storms while the sheltered strait of Juan de Fuca admitted the warm Pacific current.

A perfect combination of climate and scenery. Saul squinted with hate. A perfect locale for a "rest home." Eliot—God damn him—had chosen his battlefield well.

He bristled, aggravated by the slow-moving traffic, anxious to reach the easier road at the top. To get there.

And pay back his father.

Mercifully, the road leveled off. Between slopes of pine, the belching semitruck squeezed toward the crushed rock shoulder, allowing traffic to go around. Saul put the Eagle in second gear, increasing speed, watching the heat gauge dangerously near the top creep lower as the motor worked less hard. He felt a breeze through his open window.

A speed limit sign said 80 kilometers. He stayed below the limit, noticing another sign—in French as well as in English—that warned about sharp curves. The slopes formed a V through which he focused on a towering peak as if he aimed through the notches on a rifle sight. Determined, he steered through corkscrews, mustering patience.

Soon now. Take your time. Eliot's counting on you to be so anxious you make mistakes.

He veered down a winding road to a wooded valley. To the left, he saw a glacial lake as blue as a diamond. To the right, a campground crammed with mobile homes advertised horseback riding and nature walks. The air was dry and warm.

These mountains were pocked with similar valleys. He quickly glanced at his terrain map as he drove. Orlik's instructions had been precise till now, bringing him thirty miles northeast of Vancouver. But from here, he had to rely on half-remembered rumors. After all, when he'd been younger, why would he have guessed he'd ever need a rest home? A safe house maybe, but . . .

There. He saw it on his map. Two ridges over. Cloister Valley. "Remember that," Eliot had said. "If you're ever desperate enough to need a rest home, think of being cloistered. Go to that valley. Look for a sign. The Hermitage."

Saul fought the urge to speed. He passed a fisherman on a bridge who paused in his angling to sip a bottle of beer. Labatt's. If this had been Cloister Valley, Saul would have taken for granted the fisherman was a sentry. But for now, the scenery was innocent. The sun glared directly overhead, its reflection making him put on Polaroids. With the claustrophobic peaks, though, sunset would come much sooner than he was used to. Though he couldn't rush, he couldn't dawdle. Timing was everything. He had to get there before dusk.

The map was precise. He reached a T intersection, turned right, and passed a log cabin motel. The road flanked a tumbling stream. He heard its splash. As he angled up a ridge, pines blotted the sun. He cursed.

His brother would never again feel cooling shadows.

2

Safe houses, rest homes. The designers of the Abelard sanction had been wise, understanding short-term as opposed to long-term goals. An operative, threatened, on the run, needed hope. Without it, what was the point of belonging to the craft? A neutral zone, a respite—even at Franklin, "home free" had been the goal of games—was paramount. An operative required the chance to scuff the ground and say, "All right, you beat me, but dammit all, I'm still alive. And dammit worse, you've got to let me back in play. I got here, see. I'm neutralized." A guaranteed sanctuary, inviolable, where any attempt to kill meant instant reprisal.

But a safe house was temporary, designed for operatives and hired hands. What if you'd risen so high and made so many enemies you could never dare leave the safe house? What if your hunters hated you so much they'd never stop waiting for you to come out? It wouldn't matter how many guards you had to protect you as you left—you'd still be killed.

Clearly something better was needed than just the protection of what amounted to a motel. How many paces of your room could you tolerate—how many records could you listen to, how much television could you watch—before the walls squeezed in on you? The constantly repeated daily pattern eventually made a safe house a prison. Boredom became unbearable. You started to think about sneaking away, risking your hunters. Or maybe you saved them the trouble, sticking a gun in your mouth. A week of safety? Wonderful. Maybe a month. But what about a year? Or ten years? In a place like the Church of the Moon, even safety became damnation.

Something better, more ultimate, was needed, and the Abelard designers in their wisdom had imagined further. *Rest homes.* Permanent sanctuaries. Complete environments. Absolute satisfaction.

For a price. Faced with death, an outcast would gladly pay the limit for guaranteed immunity and every comfort. Not a safe house. A rest home. Always and forever. Desperation rewarded.

There were seven Abelard safe houses.

Rest homes, though, were complicated. Sweeping, huge, complete. Only three of them. And because their clients tended to be elderly, climate was a factor. Not too hot and not too cold. Not moist but not obscenely dry. A paradise in paradise. Because of the need for long-term security, the rest homes had been situated in traditional neutral countries, their politics stable—Hong Kong, Switzerland, and Canada.

The Cloister Valley. British Columbia. Canada.

The Hermitage.

Eliot had sought retirement, hoping to lure Saul into a trap.

But as Saul urged the Eagle higher, reaching the treeline, passing snow, about to descend to another valley, thinking of Chris, he murmured through his teeth, "What's good for the goose is good for the fucking gander."

Traps could be turned around.

3

He reached a crossroads, pausing to study his map. If he headed right again, he'd veer up a slope, go through a narrow pass, and, angling down, reach Cloister Valley. He assumed he'd find a weatherbeaten sign —nothing blatant certainly—for the Hermitage. An unaware traveler wouldn't know if it meant a lodge or someone's cottage. Trees would hide the property. No doubt a padlocked gate and a potholed lane would discourage curiosity.

He also assumed there'd be sentries down the lane to turn back unwelcome visitors. Every entrance to the valley would be watched. A country store would be a surveillance post, a gas station would be staffed with guards, a fisherman sipping Labatt's would this time have a walkie-talkie in his knapsack. From the moment Saul reached the pass, his every movement would be reported.

In themselves, these precautions didn't bother him. After all, a rest home needed security. Its administration would be professional, using first-rate tradecraft. What did bother him was that some of the sentries along the road would belong to Eliot, not the rest home.

That's the way he'd do it, Saul thought. Distribute a hit team through the valley, wait till I was spotted, and kill me before I ever got on the grounds. The rules forbid interference once I'm on neutral territory, but nothing says he can't kill me on the way. The entire valley isn't protected, only the land owned by the rest home. I'd be foolish to drive through the valley.

But he knew another way. Instead of turning right and heading up the pass, he went straight ahead. Three elk grazed in a meadow beyond a stream. A pheasant flew across the road. He studied a line of aspen to his right, glanced at his map, then back at the trees. What he looked for shouldn't be far. Wind fluttered the leaves, their silver undersides turning up, glinting in the sun. That made him conscious of the sun's lower angle. Three o'clock. At the latest, to take advantage of the remaining light, he had to be ready by five.

A half-kilometer farther on, he saw it. There, to the right through the trees, a lane so obscured by undergrowth he wouldn't have noticed if he hadn't been warned by the map. No cars ahead. None in his rearview mirror. Stopping, he flicked a switch on the left side of the steering column and converted the Eagle into four-wheel drive. He entered, snapping bushes.

The lane was narrow, bumpy, arched with trees. A hundred yards along, he braked. Getting out, swatting mosquitos in the forest's stillness, he walked back to the road. The bushes had been broken too severely to spring up and hide where he'd entered the lane. All the same, in theory no one in this valley ought to care.

In theory.

He dragged a fallen limb across the mouth of the lane, using it to prop the branches so they stood as if they hadn't been broken. Someone looking closely would see the cracks along their stems, but a passing motorist wouldn't notice. Several days from now, the bushes would lose their leaves, but by then it wouldn't matter if anyone guessed this lane had been used. His concern was for tonight and tomorrow. He propped up a second row of bushes, studied his work, and decided they looked as natural as he could expect.

He continued driving up the lane. Branches scratched the Eagle. Bushes scraped its bottom. Furrows jostled him. He reached a fallen limb too large for him to drive across. Getting out, he shifted it, then drove ahead and for precaution walked back, placing it across the lane again. Farther up, he bumped across a stream, hoping the water wouldn't soften his brakes, frowning as a boulder whacked his muffler.

But the Eagle had a high suspension, and the four-wheel drive worked perfectly, surviving its torture, gaining traction on a brutal hill. The map didn't show any buildings ahead. That puzzled him. He wondered who'd built the lane and why. Loggers? Hydro crews needing access to pylons through the mountains? Someone who owned this section and used it for hunting?

He hoped he wouldn't find out.

4

Disappointingly, the lane disappeared in the knee-high grass of an upper meadow.

End of the line. He couldn't risk driving through the grass. His tracks would be obvious from the air. He had to assume the Hermitage used surveillance choppers. Strictly speaking, the rest home's guards wouldn't have much reason to check this bordering valley, but Eliot's people would. Since they knew Saul was coming, they'd be extra cautious.

He glanced at his watch—four-thirty—then at the sun behind him, dipping toward the mountains. Dusk soon.

Move. He parked the Eagle off the lane, hidden by bushes from the ground and by trees from the air. Raising the hatch, he took out his equipment.

He'd arranged it skillfully in a Kelty pack: beef jerky, peanuts, dried fruit (protein and carbohydrates he wouldn't have to cook), extra clothes, all wool (in case of a storm, the hollow fibers of wool dried fast without needing a fire), a sleeping bag filled with Dacron (like the wool, it dried fast), fifty yards of nylon rope, a knife, first-aid kit, and canteen, already filled, though when he got higher he'd trust the streams. He wore thick-soled mountain boots, designed to help his feet support the weight of the pack.

Hefting its metal frame to his shoulders, he tightened the straps and cinched the waist belt. In a moment, he'd adjusted his balance to the extra bulk. He eased his pistol along his side where the pack wouldn't pinch it against his skin, then locked the car and started up.

Around the meadow, not across it. He still couldn't leave a trail. Skirting mountain flowers, he reached the other edge, hiking steadily through the foothills, climbing steeper, harder. Sweat soaked his shirt, forming rivulets between his shoulder blades beneath his pack. At first, he judged his direction by sight alone, knowing the ridge he wanted, but as deadfalls blocked his way, as trees hid his view and draws meandered, he checked his map repeatedly, comparing its contour lines to features around him, aligning it with his compass. Sometimes he found a sparsely wooded slope that seemed an easy climb in the direction he needed to go, but the map warned otherwise. Or else he chose a gully so thick with boulders he wouldn't have considered it if the map hadn't shown it soon became a gentle rise. Forewarned of a cliff beyond the next hill, he veered a quarter-mile out of his way to reach a stream he followed up a steep but climbable gorge.

He stopped to swallow rock salt, drinking. At high altitude, the body worked harder than normal, sweating abundantly. But the dry air evaporated sweat so quickly a climber might not realize the risk of dehydration. Lethargy could lead to coma. Water alone wouldn't help, though. Salt was needed for the body to retain the water. But Saul didn't taste the salt, a sure sign he needed it. Shoving his canteen back in his knapsack, he studied the gorge he'd climbed, hearing the roar of the falling stream, then turned to the bluffs above.

Their shadows lengthened. The forest became deep green, like a jungle or clouds before a tornado. Emotions stormed inside him. His steps were relentless, fierce. The thought of jungle had reminded him of missions with Chris in Nam, of a war they'd fought because Eliot wanted them to experience combat. He remembered escaping with Chris from the choppers in the mountains of Colorado because their father had betrayed them.

Chris, he wanted to scream. Remember the summer Eliot took us camping in Maine? The best week of my life. Why couldn't things have turned out differently?

The spongy loam of the forest led higher. Through a break in the trees, he saw the pass he aimed for, a saddlelike ridge between two peaks. He climbed past slabs of granite, the last rays of sunset glinting through the pass, a beacon through the dusk. He reached the entrance, more determined now. Too excited to feel the weight of his pack, he hurried to a sheltered bluff from which he gazed at the valley below.

It wasn't much different from the valley behind him. The peaks, the forest, were similar. A river, the Pitt, ran through it. The map said the next valley over was Golden Ears Provincial Park. But as he stared at alpenglow from the dying sunset, he saw all the difference that mattered.

The valley was bisected by a road, roughly east to west. Another road cut across it, heading toward the park beyond. But the northwest sector . . . there. . . . A sizable area was clear of trees. He guessed its lawn filled a hundred acres. Through binoculars, he identified stables, a swimming pool, a jogging track, a golf course.

In the midst of it all, a massive lodge reminded him of a place at Yellowstone where Eliot once had taken him and Chris.

Rest home. Haven.

Death trap.

5

In the night, it rained. Among his equipment, he had a sheet of waterproof nylon. Stretching it across two boulders, anchoring the sides, he made a shelter. Hunched beneath it, wearing his thick wool clothes, his sleeping bag around him, he ate, barely tasting the peanuts and jerky, peering at the dark. Rain pelted the nylon, dripping off the front. His cheeks felt damp. He shivered, unable to sleep, thinking of Chris.

At dawn, the drizzle changed to mist. He crawled from his sleeping bag and relieved his bladder among some rocks. He washed in a nearby stream, shaved, and scrubbed his hair. Hygiene was mandatory up here—he couldn't risk getting sick. Equally crucial, he had to preserve his self-respect. If he fouled his body with dirt and odor, his mind would soon be affected. Feeling sloppy, he'd start to think that way, and Eliot would catch him making mistakes. With yesterday's sweat rinsed off, his bare skin tingling, scoured to a glow, he regained energy, welcoming the goosebumps raised by the chill. Resolve became sharper. Rage surged through him. He was ready.

His clothes felt damp only a moment. His body warmed their hollow wool fiber, causing vapor to rise like steam. Assembling his equipment, he hefted the backpack to his shoulders and started grimly down the mountain.

This far from the Hermitage, he didn't worry about sentries. The terrain was too wild. With several passes leading into the valley, it would take too many men to watch every approach. The main thing was he'd avoided surveillance—and probably snipers—on the road. As he got closer, though, he expected guards, especially near the rest home's site in the valley's northwest corner. Despite his eagerness, he descended carefully, knowing how easy it was to injure an ankle under the stress of going down.

The sun came out at noon, adding to the heat of exertion. A cliff stretched so far in both directions he had to loop his rope around his pack, lower it, pull up one end of the rope to free it, then rappel. At last, by midafternoon, he reached the basin.

Calculating.

If snipers watched the road, they'd want a clear wide line of fire. That suggested they wouldn't hide in the trees, where all they'd have was a brief glimpse of a car. More likely, they'd prefer an elevated position, a bluff above the trees with a view for miles.

Concealed by a boulder, he peered from a ridge toward lower ridges, slowly shifting his gaze from left to right, inspecting details.

It took an hour. He finally saw them, two, a half-mile apart, watching both ends of the road. Each lay in tall grass on a bluff, wearing brown and green to match the terrain, a telescopic-sighted rifle in position. He wouldn't have noticed them if each hadn't moved slightly, one to reach for a walkie-talkie, the other a minute later to drink from his canteen. Across the road, a gate in a fence was equidistant between them, no doubt the entrance to the rest home.

The protocol was important. Outside the rest home, the valley was fair to use as a killing ground—there'd be no punishment to the snipers; they wouldn't have broken a rule.

But what about directly in front of the gate? What if someone demanding sanctuary was shot as he reached the fence? A rest home was meaningless if no one could get inside. Logic suggested a buffer zone around the place, a small ambiguous strip—no more than a hundred yards perhaps—that wasn't protected but wasn't unprotected either. A gray area, requiring prudence. An assassin might not risk execution by killing outside a rest home, but he'd face inquiries. There'd be an investigation before he was absolved.

The ambiguity could work to Saul's advantage. I have to show myself to reach the fence, he thought. A mile down the road, I'd be dead the instant they spotted me. But what about directly outside the gate? Would they hesitate, pondering the rule?

In their place, I'd shoot.

But I'm not them.

He crept back from the boulder, entering bushes, working lower.

His map protected him. In the crowded trees, he couldn't see the bluffs the snipers lay on. Without a chart and a compass, he could easily wander into their sights. But having marked their positions on the map, he studied contour lines, carefully choosing a middle course through rugged terrain toward the gate. His progress was slow. This close, he had to scan the undergrowth ahead of him in case another sniper watched the gate.

He stopped, not needing to see the gate—his map showed he was in a trough fifty yards from the road, separated by thick shrubs and trees. All he had to do was . . .

Nothing.

Yet. The sun was still too high. It would make him too vivid a target. The best time to move was at dusk, when there'd be just enough light for him to see up close but not enough for them to aim at a distance.

He took off his backpack, eased it to the ground, and rubbed his shoulders. His stomach cramped. Till now, he'd controlled impatience. His goal had been distant. There'd been much to do. But with the rest home fifty yards away, with Eliot almost in his grasp, he ached from tension.

Waiting was agony. To keep his mind alert, he studied his surroundings.

A squirrel run along a branch.

A woodpecker tapped a tree.

The woodpecker stopped.

The squirrel threw up its tail, barked once, and froze.

6

His skin crawled.

Drawing his pistol, Saul crouched and swung to stare around him, quickly attaching a silencer. Alone, the woodpecker's sudden quiet meant nothing. In tandem with the squirrel's behavior, it became significant. Something—someone else?—was out here.

His position was risky. Three hundred and sixty degrees of space to defend, and no suspicion of where the threat would come from.

If there was a threat.

He had to assume it. Think. If there's a sniper, he isn't behind you. Otherwise you'd have passed him. He'd have made his move by now.

Then he's ahead or on your flank. Trusting his instinct, Saul ignored his back and concentrated on the trees above this trough along the road. He heard me coming and waited for a target. When I stopped, he started to wonder if he was wrong. Maybe he isn't used to the forest and he thinks the noise was an animal.

But he can't take the chance. He'll have to find out.

Or maybe I'm the one who's wrong. Maybe it's me who spooked the squirrel. He shook his head. No, the squirrel kept running after it saw me. Something else made it freeze.

Sweat trickled past his eyes. *Where?*

A patch of green shifted slowly to his left.

His backpack stood upright beside him. Saul toppled it to the left —as a distraction, to make it seem he was diving to the ground. At the same time he pivoted to the right, coming up behind a bush, aiming at the patch of green.

A man in camouflage sighted a rifle where the backpack had fallen. Shooting, Saul heard three spits from his silencer as his bullets struck the man in the face and throat.

But he hadn't been quick enough. The man squeezed off a shot just before he lurched, unable to scream because of blood gushing from his throat. The crack of the rifle echoed through the forest, the bullet walloping the backpack.

Saul didn't bother getting his gear. He didn't pause to see if the man was dead. He didn't have time. He charged up the rim of the trough, scrambling through the undergrowth, not checking to see if someone else was ahead of him. It didn't matter. The shot would have warned them all. They'd turn, glaring at the forest, aiming their weapons. When they couldn't raise their partner on his walkie-talkie . . .

They'll know I'm here. They'll radio for help and . . .

Now or never. Branches lashed his face. He scraped past a stump. But he kept sprinting, bursting from the trees, abruptly facing the road.

The fence was tall.

Barbed wire.

Shit. Not breaking stride, he veered toward the gate. At least, it was lower.

Something cracked on the asphalt behind him, a shot rumbling from a bluff. He zigzagged, a second bullet whacking the pavement ahead of him. He hit the fence, barbs tearing his clothes, ripping his hands. A third bullet snapped the strand of wire he reached for, whipping it forward, then back at his face. His cheek stung, bleeding. Clambering, he grabbed the top, swung over, and jumped.

Bending his knees as he hit the ground, he rolled.

But something stopped him.

Boots and bluejeans. An angry man pointed a magnum revolver at his chest.

Another man flanked him, wearing a brown checked hunting shirt, aiming a rifle toward the hills.

At once, the shooting quit. Of course. He'd reached the rest home. They didn't dare kill him now.

"You'd better have a damn good reason—"

Saul dropped the Mauser, raising his hands. "It's my only weapon. Search me. I won't need it now."

"—for coming here."

"The best." Blood dripped from his upheld palms, but he almost laughed. "Abelard."

It was all he had to say to gain asylum here.

7

They forced him back to the cover of trees and did indeed search him, totally, making him strip.

His scrotum shrank. "I told you the Mauser's all I have."

They checked his clothes.

"What's this packet taped to the inside of your shirt?" Instead of waiting for an answer, one guard tore the seal, opening the plastic, scowling. "Papers." He threw the pouch dismissively on the pile of Saul's clothes. "Get dressed."

"Who shot at you?" the other guard said.

"I thought they were sentries."

"Cute. We don't shoot at guests. We protect—"

286

"But I wasn't a guest yet. Maybe some of your people thought I meant to attack."

"Sure. One man. Attack. Quit being cute. Who was it?"

"I wouldn't have come here if everybody liked me."

Engines roared, approaching.

"We'll find out."

At once two vans appeared through the trees, swerving around a curve in the lane. They skidded, brakes squealing. Before they stopped, men jumped from the sides, dressed in outdoor clothes the same as these guards, burly, square-faced, cold-eyed, some holding rifles, others handguns, walkie-talkies dangling from their shoulders.

"The shots came from over there." The first guard pointed up at bluffs to the right and left across the road.

The men scrambled forward as the second guard freed the gate.

"They've got five minutes on you," the first guard said.

"The roads are blocked." A man with a brushcut hurried through, his walkie-talkie slapping his side.

Two others with anxious silent Dobermans rushed by.

"One man's across the road," Saul said. "Fifty yards through the trees."

"By now, he'll be gone," a heavy man snapped.

"I doubt it. He's dead."

They turned as they ran and squinted at him.

In twenty seconds, they'd disappeared.

The guard in the hunting shirt locked the gate. The other glared at Saul. "You come with us."

Saul gestured toward the fence. "Who'll watch the store?"

The drivers of the vans came over, drawing pistols.

"Good," Saul said and meant it. If the rest home's security was first rate, the guards who'd found him ought to be his escorts. They knew little about him. Even so, it was more than the others did.

They took him down the lane. He expected a Jeep or another van. Instead he saw a Pontiac with high suspension and oversized wheels, capable of crashing through the forest and ramming out of mud.

He nodded in approval, getting in back. A stout metal grill separated him from the front.

The driver pulled a lever near the emergency brake, locking Saul's doors. As the car surged from the trees, the second guard studied him through the grill, his handgun propped on the seat.

"If I wanted a concentration camp . . ."

"You'll get your retirement. First you have to qualify."

"With what? A blood test?"

"If we let you in like this was a tourist trap, how safe would you feel? Relax. When you're registered, I'll even buy you a drink."

"Did you say 'buy'? You mean they're not free?"

"This isn't welfare, you know."

"It's sure not paradise either."

"Buddy, that's where you're wrong."

The Pontiac lurched down the lane. Saul gripped the seat, glancing out, seeing metal boxes attached to trees. "Electric eyes?"

"And sound detectors."

"Quiet," the driver told his partner. "You want to give him a fucking guided tour?"

The second guard's eyes narrowed, dark at Saul.

They burst from the forest.

Seeing the estate, he understood. Lawn stretched forever. To the left of what was now a paved road, golfers avoided a sandtrap, heading toward a pond. To the right, guests strolled along a white stone path near flower gardens, benches, and fountains.

A country club. A park.

The road led up to the lodge, the peaks in the background reminding him again of Yellowstone. A helicopter took off.

But he didn't allow distraction. Concentrating on the resort, he prepared himself for . . .

What? He didn't know.

The Pontiac braked in front. Unlocking Saul's door, the driver got out, then the other guard, then Saul.

They flanked him, climbing concrete stairs to a porch that stretched the width of the building. It was made from sweet-smelling cedar, solid beneath his boots. Along one side, he glimpsed the edge of a tennis court, hearing the pock of balls. An unseen player laughed in triumph. With dusk approaching, they'd soon have to quit, he thought.

Then he noticed the arc lights rimming the court.

Sentries? He studied a gardener on a riding mower, a man in a white coat running with towels to the tennis court, a repairman caulking the edge of a window. But they seemed less interested in their duties than in Saul.

Okay then.

The guards took him in through large double doors. A tobacco and magazine counter to the left, a sports shop to the right. He passed a clothing store, a record shop, a druggist, reaching a lobby, spacious and high with wagon-wheel chandeliers and a gleaming hardwood floor. A counter with mail and key slots in the wall behind it reminded him of a hotel.

A clerk spoke urgently from behind a desk. "He's waiting for you. Go right in." He pointed quickly at a door marked Private.

The guards made Saul walk ahead—through the door, down a narrow hall, to a second door, this one unmarked. Before the guard in the hunting shirt had a chance to knock, a buzzer unlocked the door. Saul glanced behind him, seeing a closed-circuit camera above the first door he'd come through.

Shrugging, he went inside. The office was larger than he'd anticipated, richly decorated, faddish, leather, chrome, and glass. The wall across from him was a floor-to-ceiling window with a view of a swimming pool—people splashing—and a café. But directly ahead of him, beyond plush carpet, a man sat at a desk, scribbling to the side of a densely typed sheet of paper.

"Come," the man said, too busy writing to look up.

Saul stepped across. The guards walked in behind him.

"No." The man glanced up. "Just him. Wait outside, though. I might need you."

They eased back, closing the door.

Saul studied him. The man was in his early forties, his round face somewhat heavy, his hair cut modishly so it covered the tops of his ears. He had a bulky chest which, when he stood, became an equally bulky stomach. He wore a red blazer and navy pants, both polyester. When he came around the desk, Saul noticed his white shoes. When he held out his hand, Saul noticed his multibuttoned digital watch. But if the man looked like a high-pressure salesman or a Chamber of Commerce booster, his eyes were sharply alert.

He's dressing a part, Saul thought. Not a salesman. A recreation director. So garish he won't seem threatening to the guests.

"We weren't expecting a new arrival." The man's smile dissolved as he glanced at blood on his palm from where he'd shaken hands with Saul.

"I had a little trouble"—Saul shrugged—"getting in."

"But no one said you'd been hurt." The director's voice was

alarmed. "And your cheek. I'll have a doctor take a look. Believe me, I'm sorry. It shouldn't have happened."

"It wasn't your fault."

"But I'm accountable for what happens here. Don't you see? You're my responsibility. Sit down and relax. Would you like a drink?"

"No alcohol."

"How about some Perrier?"

Saul nodded.

The man seemed delighted, as if his every wish was to serve. He opened a bookcase, then the door to a small refrigerator, twisting the cap off a bottle, filling a glass with ice, and pouring it full. He gave it to Saul, along with a napkin.

Drinking, Saul hadn't realized how thirsty he was.

The man looked pleased. Rubbing his hands, he sat behind his desk again. "Food?"

"Not now."

"Whenever you're ready." He tilted back in his chair, scratching his eyebrow. "I understand you came in the hard way, over the mountains."

He's starting, Saul thought. It's slick, but it's still an interrogation. "I like the woods."

"Apparently someone else did. There was shooting."

"Hunters."

"Yes. But what were they hunting?"

Saul shrugged like a youngster caught in a lie.

"But why were they hunting you?"

"I'd rather not say."

"Because you think we wouldn't accept you? That's not true. No matter what you've done, we're obligated to protect you."

"I prefer to keep my secrets."

"Understandable. But look at it our way. If we knew who wanted to kill you, we could protect you better."

"And if word got around, maybe I wouldn't be welcomed."

"By the other guests, you mean?"

Saul nodded.

"I grant your point. But I'm like a priest. I never repeat what I hear."

"What about whoever's listening?"

"There's no bug."

Saul simply stared.

290

"I admit there's interoffice communication. In case I have trouble." He reached inside a drawer and flicked a switch. "It's off."

"Maybe I made a mistake." Saul rose from the chair.

The man leaned forward. "No. I don't mean to pressure you. All I want to do is help."

Saul understood. If someone rejected the protection of a rest home, the director would have to explain to his superiors why the rest home had not been acceptable.

He sat back down and finished the Perrier.

"There's protocol to be obeyed, though," the man said.

"Naturally."

"I forgot to introduce myself. I'm Don."

You're also good, Saul thought. Now it's supposed to be my turn. "Saul."

"You gave the guards the password?"

"Naturally."

"What is it?"

"Abelard."

"Mind you, even a common gangster could have found that out. The password hasn't changed since 1938. Information gets around. You understand only operatives are allowed protection here."

"I wouldn't have it any other way." Saul reached beneath his shirt and peeled off the waterproof pouch. Sorting through several documents, he handed Don his passport. "My legal name. I assume you'll check."

"Of course." Don opened the passport, frowning. "And your cryptonym?"

"Romulus."

Don slammed down the passport. "What the fuck do you think you're—?"

Saul clicked his tongue. "At least you're real. For a minute there, I wondered if you'd try to sell me a life insurance policy."

"That's exactly what you need. You figure you can trick your way in here and—"

"Trick? Hey, somebody shot at me."

"Hired help."

"Not mine. I nearly got killed. You think I'd trust even an expert to shoot at me long distance and make it close enough to be convincing? Look at my hands. Ask your men outside how close the bullets came. I'm qualified. I gave the password. I want asylum."

"*Why?*"

"You keep . . . because the president put out a contract on me. The Paradigm hit. I killed his closest friend."

Don held his breath and shook. "Your father?"

"What?"

"Or your foster father or whatever you want to call him. I suppose you don't know he's here."

"What difference does it make? If my father's here . . ."

"He told me you want to kill him!"

"Then whoever he is, he can't be my father. Kill him? Insane. Where is this man? I want to—"

Don slammed his desk. "That's bullshit!"

The door banged open. The guards came in.

"Get out of here!" Don said.

"But we thought there was—"

"Shut the goddamn door!"

They did.

Dusk thickened through the window. Arc lights suddenly gleamed, reflecting off the pool.

Don pressed his hands on the desk. "Don't kid a kidder. He told me enough to convince me you want to kill him."

"That's not the point."

"What is?"

"The contract on me. It's legitimate. If I leave, I'm dead. Imagine how your reputation would suffer. The only director of a rest home to deny protection to a qualified candidate. The inquiry—and your execution—would entertain me. Except I'd be dead."

"You've forgotten."

"What?"

"You didn't win a contest. This place costs."

"I figured."

"Did you? It's a private club."

"Initiation fee?"

"You guessed it. Two hundred thousand."

"Steep."

"Our clientele's exclusive. They pay to keep out the riffraff."

"I prefer it that way. I've got standards too." Glancing in his packet again, Saul drew out three papers, handing them across.

"What the—?"

"Gold certificates. Actually, it's more than two hundred thousand. Naturally you'll give me credit."

"How the hell—?"

"The same way the others did."

Saul didn't need to explain.

By skimming. The CIA had unlimited funds. For security reasons, no records were kept. It was common practice for an administrator to hide ten percent of an operation's cost as an unacknowledged fee, a bonus for deposit in Swiss accounts, the best insurance policy. If mistakes were made or politics became too risky, the administrator used the account for his protection. If his life was at stake, he entered a rest home.

Saul had learned the trick from Eliot, saving a portion of every mission's budget. Again, he'd used his father's tactics against him.

"Bastard. There's more. That's just the initiation fee. Those shops you passed. The tennis courts. The swimming pool. The golf course."

"Never tried it."

"The movies. You've got to eat. Quick chicken and burgers, or gourmet. It costs. You like television? We've got satellite reception. Bullfights. Pamplona. You can watch. It isn't free. We offer anything you want—from books to records to sex. If we don't have it, we'll send for it. Paradise. But friend, does it cost. And if you can't pay your way, that's the only time I can kick you out."

"Sounds like I ought to buy stock."

"Quit jerking—"

Saul pulled out two further slips of paper. "Here's fifty thousand. Even a burger can't be that expensive. Rumor has it I can live six months here on that—and even go to the movies."

Don shook worse. "You—"

"Temper. Live with it. I qualify."

Don seethed. "Make one wrong move."

"I know. I'm dead. Just tell that to my father. The same should apply to him."

"Then you admit—?"

"I don't know what you mean. But I expect the same protection my father gets."

"Shit."

Saul shrugged. "It's a problem for you. I sympathize."

"You'll be watched."

"Paradise. I hope those burgers are worth a quarter million dollars." Standing, he walked to the door. "And now that I think about it . . ."

"What?"

"I'm Jewish. Maybe I'll get religious again. I hope those burgers are kosher."

8

Passing the guards, he heard Don call them angrily into the office. He grinned—but only till they disappeared.

His eyes smoldered. Leaving the hall, he approached the desk. "I'm checking in." His voice cracked with emotion.

He filled out a registration form. The two guards came back and stood in a corner, watching. Guests in tennis outfits walked by, glancing at him. Others in evening dress came out of a restaurant across the lobby, frowning back as they climbed a polished staircase.

Saul imagined what they thought. What was his background? His bloody ragged clothes contrasted with their wardrobes. Friends, the riffraff's here.

He saw few women—the upper echelon of the profession had traditionally formed an aristocratic men's club, the old boy network. Many indeed looked old enough for retirement. Some he recognized: an American section chief who'd been stationed in Iran when the Shah was overthrown; a Soviet who'd attracted Brezhnev's disfavor by underestimating guerrilla resistance during the Afghanistan invasion; an Argentine military intelligence director who'd been blamed for his country's loss of the Falklands war.

One pattern struck him. With few exceptions, no members of the same service associated with each other.

The clerk seemed surprised he'd been admitted. "Here's your key." He sounded puzzled. "You'll find a list of services on the table by your bed. The hospital's downstairs in—"

"I'll treat the cuts myself."

He went to the clothing store and the druggist. The two guards lingered in the background. As he went upstairs, they followed. They reached a muffled corridor, waiting outside his third-floor room.

He locked his door, impressed. The rest home's clients got the protection they paid for. His unit was equally impressive, twice the size of a normal room, a bookshelf separating the sleeping area from the living quarters. He found a tape deck and stereo, a large-screen television, a personal computer, and a modem that allowed, instructions said, a link by telephone with an information service called The Source. Everything from *The New York Times* to the Dow Jones averages could be summoned instantly on the computer's screen. Saul imagined the Wall Street news was paramount. The prices here no doubt forced a lot of clients to check their investments often. If their bills came due and they couldn't pay . . .

The furnishings were too luxurious for anyone's taste to be offended. In the oversized bathroom, he found a television, whirlpool, telephone, and sunlamp in addition to a separate tub and shower. Everything a fugitive could want.

With one exception. Freedom.

He stripped and soaked his cuts in the whirlpool, feeling the surge of water knead his muscles. Sensual, the massage reminded him of Erika, making him more determined to survive. He couldn't allow distraction. Chris. He had to concentrate on his mission. He had to avenge his brother's death. Eliot. Amid the powerful swirl of water, he shut out all enjoyment. Seething, he stepped from the tub.

His shots were up to date, so he wasn't afraid of tetanus. All the same, his barbed wire gashes needed disinfecting. The peroxide he'd bought from the druggist stung them. Bandaging the worst of them, he put on the new underwear, slacks, and turtleneck he'd bought. Their luxury embittered him.

With the lights turned off, he opened the draperies and stared down at the tennis courts. Though illuminated, they weren't in use. A solitary jogger skirted them. Saul glanced beyond toward darkness hiding the mountains.

Paradise. The word kept coming back.

He'd been successful.

Getting here wasn't the point, though. Eliot was, and despite his cavalier act with Don, he knew he'd accomplished little.

So you're in. So what? Don wasn't joking. Those guards outside will watch you. Did you figure all you had to do was simply break into the old man's room and kill him? The odds are you'd be shot before you got that far. Even if you succeeded, you'd never make it out of here alive.

That isn't good enough, he thought. I've got to kill the bastard and live.

9

"He's *what?*" Alarmed, Eliot sat up rigid in bed. "You're telling me he's here? He's actually in the building?"

"More than that. He applied for asylum," Castor said. "He registered and went to his room."

"Applied for—?" Eliot blinked, astonished. "That's impossible. The manager knows I came here because of Saul. He should have killed him. Why in God's name did he let Saul in?"

"Because of the contract against him."

"What?"

"The president's after him. The manager can't refuse admission to an operative in danger."

Eliot fumed. It wasn't supposed to be like this. The snipers outside should have killed Saul when he reached the valley. If Saul got around them, the rules of the rest home were supposed to take effect. Anyone threatening a guest faced execution. That was the law.

I wouldn't have chosen this place if I thought he could get inside.

The irony dismayed him. The Paradigm job, which had started everything, had resulted in his seeking protection here. Saul, the reason he needed protection, had used the aftermath of that job to force the manager to let him in as well.

I counted on the sanction to be my weapon. I never dreamed he'd use it against me.

"Pollux is out in the hall," Castor said. "He's guarding the door."

"But Saul won't be that obvious. He'll attack in a way we don't expect."

"Unless he never gets the chance."

"I'm not sure what—"

"If I kill him first," Castor said.

"And be killed yourself for breaking the rule?"

"I'd have an escape prepared."

"They'd hunt you forever. What would it solve? They know you're my escort. They'd assume I ordered you to kill him. I'd be blamed. And killed as well."

"Then what do we do?"

Eliot shook his head, distraught. The problem seemed insoluble. Under the circumstances, given the rules, neither side could attack, yet both sides had to defend themselves. For a moment, he reluctantly admired Saul for being more clever than he'd expected. They were here as equals, caught in a stalemate, the pressure increasing.

Who'd act first? Who'd make the first mistake?

Despite his fear, Eliot surprised himself. He was fascinated. "Do? Why, nothing, of course."

Castor frowned.

"We let the system do it for us."

10

Don knocked twice, then twice again. A guard, having studied him through the peephole, opened the door. Don glanced both ways along the hall—it remained deserted, he hadn't been noticed—and stepped into the crowded room. He faced two guards, three nurses, a doctor, and a maid. Squinting past them, he didn't see what he'd come for.

"In the bathroom," the guard at the door said.

Nodding with detachment, Don subdued an unprofessional groan, thinking, Jesus, another bleeder. As he walked to the bathroom, he heard the guard lock the door.

But the body wasn't in the tub. Instead it lay on turquoise tile, face up, grotesque, wearing pajamas, a bathrobe, both of which had been opened. A slipper had fallen off.

Thank God I was wrong, Don thought. No blood.

The top of the skull was angled in his direction, so he saw the face upside down and didn't recognize it till he stepped into the bathroom and turned. Even so, he knew from the number outside the door, cross-checked with his files, which guest had been assigned this room.

An Egyptian. The intelligence officer in charge of President Sadat's security the day he was assassinated.

But the face was so distorted that without the benefit of knowing who was supposed to be here Don wasn't sure he could have identified the man the instant he saw him directly.

The cheeks were twisted in an awful grimace. The skin, though swarthy, was also blue.

"His color," Don said to the doctor. "Cyanide?"

Lean and pasty, the doctor shrugged. "Likely. It stops the cells from getting oxygen. That would account for his skin being blue. Hard to know for sure till the autopsy's finished."

Don scowled in dismay. "But the pain on his face. Isn't cyanide supposed to be—?"

"Peaceful?"

"Yeah." Don sounded confused. "Like going to sleep."

"Maybe he had a nightmare," a guard said at the door.

Don turned, almost angry, uncertain if the guard was making a joke. But the guard seemed genuinely fascinated by the effects of poison.

"Actually," the doctor said, "it made him sick. He managed to reach the bowl, threw up, and fell on his face. We turned him over. He's been dead for several hours. The pressure of his cheek against the floor accounts for the way it's twisted. Maybe he didn't die from the poison so much as cracking his head. Or maybe he choked on his vomit. Either way, you're right—it wasn't peaceful."

"Several hours ago?"

"More or less. We obeyed the protocol and tried to revive him. Adrenaline. Electroshocks to his heart. You can see the circular marks the pads left on his chest."

"You pumped out his stomach?"

"We went through the motions, but there wasn't much point." The doctor gestured toward the people in the living room. "You'll have plenty of witnesses for the inquest. The only debatable issue is why didn't I rush him downstairs to the clinic. My professional response is he was so far gone I couldn't waste time moving him. Off the record, we couldn't rush him down and still maintain secrecy. You know the effect this sort of thing has on the other guests. Believe me, it wouldn't have mattered. He was dead."

"Who found him?"

298

"I did." The maid was trim, attractive, wearing an aproned uniform.

Don checked his watch. "At eleven at night? Since when do rooms get cleaned—?"

"We had no arrangement if that's what you mean."

"It wouldn't have mattered. There's no rule against it. But they'll ask at the inquest."

Nervous, she tried to order her thoughts. "The last few days he seemed depressed. I don't know—something about a letter from his wife." She frowned. "This morning he had the Do Not Disturb sign on his door. He wants to sleep late, I thought, so I came back after lunch, but the sign was still there. Then things got busy, and I forgot about him till a while ago. On impulse, I decided to check his door again, and when I still saw the sign, I got worried. I knocked several times. No answer. So I let myself in with the passkey."

"Found him and called security."

She nodded.

"You could have called security before you went in."

"And embarrassed him if I was wrong."

Don thought about it. "You did fine. Tell the investigators just the way you told me. You won't have any trouble." He glanced at the others. "Any weak parts we ought to be clear on?"

No one spoke.

"Okay then. Wait. There is one thing. Where'd he get the poison?"

The doctor sounded exasperated. "Where do any of them get it? These people are walking pharmacopeias. Never mind the drugs we supply. Most of them bring in their own. They know a thousand ways to kill themselves. If they don't use one way, it's another."

"You took photographs?"

"Every angle."

"Swell." Don shook his head. "A wonderful assignment, huh?"

"Eleven months since I came. Thank God, my tour's almost finished."

"Lucky." Don pursed his lips. "Wait till after midnight to move him. The halls are usually quiet then. You two," he told the guards. "Make sure the elevator's empty before—" He glanced at the body. "You know how it's done. I'll handle the arrangements. Since you're working late, you don't need to report till noon. But I'll want signed statements from you by then. Also"— he suddenly needed to get out of the bathroom—"this kind of job, you'll get the bonus we agreed on.

Use the customary explanation. He made an urgent choice to leave the rest home tonight. No one knows where he's gone." Speaking quickly, he passed the doctor. "I want the autopsy done tonight."

"The tests take longer."

"Noon tomorrow. The investigators'll be here soon. We have to prove the sanction wasn't violated. We have to be sure it was suicide."

11

In his office, Don leaned against the door. His forehead broke out in sweat. He'd managed to stay in control all the way down here. He'd even been able to endure a conversation with several guests in the lobby, acting believably, as if nothing was wrong. Now, at last in private, his nerves collapsed.

He poured two fingers of bourbon, drinking them in one swallow. Soaking a towel in the sink of his wet bar, he pressed it cold against his face.

Eleven months? Is that what the doctor had said? Just one more month and the man'd be out of here? Don envied him. His own assignment had begun only six months ago. Another half-year, and sometimes he wondered if he'd make it.

When he'd first drawn this duty, he'd been delighted. A year in paradise, his only regret it'd be only a year. Anything he wanted, free —in addition to his hundred-thousand-dollar salary. Sure, he'd suspected you don't get benefits like that unless the job's a bitch. But he'd worked in intelligence for twenty years, organizing some of the biggest operations. System, that's what he was good at. So a rest home was complicated, fine. It required delicacy, no problem. He was a specialist in public relations.

But no one had told him about the mood here. No one had warned him there'd be so much death.

Of course not. Only a handful of people knew what really happened here—former managers and the investigating board—and they were forbidden to talk. Because if word got out, who'd be crazy enough to want to come? Without the concept of a rest home, who'd want to dedicate his life to the profession? Everyone eventually made mistakes. Everyone needed a heaven.

But this was hell.

He wasn't a field operative. He'd never belonged to the covert section, the dark side, the wet crew, whatever slang applied. He was front office, white collar. Before he'd come here, he'd seen only three bodies ever, and they'd been a friend and two relatives, dead from natural causes, lying in state at a mortuary. They'd given him the creeps.

Before. But now? He shuddered.

He should have guessed. A rest home was designed for ambitious people who were losers. Anything a person wanted. For a price. With guaranteed safety. That was the promise. A hundred acres of paradise. But no one guaranteed happiness. Don, who had to stay only a year, already coveted a trip to a burger joint where he'd stopped on his drive here from Vancouver. Late at night, he dreamed of walking through a crowded mall. A hundred acres. And sometimes he felt he knew every inch. The others—those who'd been here for years and had to stay forever—felt the claustrophobia even worse. To compensate, they indulged themselves. Drugs, alcohol, and sex. Gourmet meals. But how much could you shoot up or drink or screw or eat before it didn't satisfy? A hundred acres, getting smaller every second. Every day like the one before. With subtle variations.

When you used up all the variations, though?

He wasn't contemplative. Nonetheless, he'd noticed that only the losers who disdained the physical became satisfied here. Checking the library, he'd discovered their preference for spiritual topics. Saint Augustine. The teachings of Buddha. Boethius and the wheel of fortune. It intrigued him that the survivors of a life of action became meditative and monastic.

And the rest, who couldn't adjust? They poisoned themselves, O.D.'d, slit their wrists, or blew their brains out. Maybe they offered suggestions to each other, for lately several had sat in the sauna till they fainted and died from dehydration, or else they drank wine in their hot tubs till their skin was smothered and they died from oxygen starvation. But often when they lost consciousness, they sank and drowned.

12

Saul ignored his guards as he stepped from his room. There were two of them—the same as when he'd arrived last night. A different two, however. Don hadn't been kidding. "You'll be watched." No doubt another two would take over shortly. Around the clock in shifts. Two hundred thousand bought a hell of a lot of protection.

Followed, he went downstairs. It wouldn't be difficult, he assumed, to learn the number of Eliot's room. But what would be the point? He couldn't go near it without alarming his guards. He could try to lose them, but that would cause a greater alarm. Besides, he still hadn't solved the problem of how to escape. The more he thought about it, the more he wondered if his goal was even possible. To avenge his brother, he had to kill his father, and yet—to keep himself alive—he couldn't kill him. The contradiction squeezed his brain.

There had to be a way. Deciding he didn't know enough, he began the hunt, studying the rest home, wandering through the lobby, its stores and restaurants, the medical clinic, then outside, inspecting the exercise areas, the gardens, the grounds. The guards stayed close to him. But the guests, sensing trouble, kept their distance. Their wary glances made him wonder how he could use their nervousness to his advantage.

He checked the swimming pool and the golf course. Eliot must have been told by now I'm here, he thought. So what'll he do? The logical choice would be to stay in his room—he knows I'd never risk going there. How long could he bear confinement, though? He knows I'm not about to leave. He'll refuse to hide forever. Instead of reacting to me, he'll want to force me to react to him.

But how?

Whatever, it would happen soon. Since he was to show himself eventually, he won't bother waiting. He'll accept the inevitable and break the stalemate right away.

But where? The old man's too brittle for bowling and tennis. All the same, he still needs recreation. What would he—?

It couldn't be anything else. Nodding with satisfaction, Saul came to the greenhouse under construction near the jogging track at the rear of the lodge.

He enjoyed imagining ways to use it.

But where would the old man go till it was finished?

13

"I didn't know you liked fishing."

Hearing the voice behind him, Eliot turned from the river, wide and swift, with trees and bushes crowding the banks, though here a grassy slope led down to an inlet, still and clear. The water smelled sweet, but now and then the wind brought the hint of rancid vegetation —death and decay.

The man on top of the bank had the sun behind him. The glare stabbed Eliot's eyes. He raised a hand to shield them, nodding in recognition. "You don't remember our fishing trips? I like it. But I seldom had time to indulge myself. Now that I've retired, though . . ." He smiled, reeled in his line, and set the pole on the bank.

"Oh, I remember those fishing trips, all right." Saul's voice was hoarse with rage. The sinews in his throat tightened, choking him. "Just you and me." He stalked down the bank. "And Chris." He glared at Eliot's straw hat, red checked shirt, stiff new jeans, and rubber boots. He growled, "No black suit and vest?"

"To go fishing?" Eliot laughed. "I don't wear business clothes all the time. You've forgotten how I dressed when you and Chris and I took those camping trips."

"We keep coming back to Chris." Livid, Saul clenched his fists, stepping closer.

Bending, Eliot ignored him, reaching into his tackle box.

Saul pointed as if he had a gun. "That better not be a fucking candy bar."

"No Baby Ruths, I'm afraid. Sorry. Though I wish I'd thought of one. For old time's sake. I'm only changing bait."

A foot-long trout rose. Snatching a bug off the surface, it left a widening circle.

"See what I missed. I've been using a lure when it ought to be a fly."

"Bait." Saul's nostrils flared. "I asked around. You've got two bodyguards."

"Companions. That's right. Castor and Pollux."

"McElroy and Conlin, you mean."

"Very good." Eliot nodded. "I'd have been disappointed if you hadn't done your homework."

"Other orphans you lied to." Furious, Saul glanced around. "So where the hell are they?"

"Playing tennis, I believe." Eliot picked up a second pole. "They don't go everywhere with me."

"That doesn't make you nervous—being out here alone?"

"In a rest home? Why should I feel nervous? I'm protected."

Saul stepped even closer. "Wrong."

"No, *you* are." Eliot angrily threw down the pole. "You've lost. Admit it. If you kill me here, you die as well. After all these years, I know how you think. You wouldn't be satisfied unless you got away with it. You can't, though."

"Maybe."

"That's not good enough. You'd want to be certain." Eliot's chest heaved. "That's why I'm out here alone today. I could have hidden in my room, but I'm too old to waste my time. This place is bad enough as it is. You must have sensed the mood. The guests are dead already. They just don't know enough to lie down."

"You made your grave."

"Not me." Eliot raised his chin, proud. "I'll soon have my roses again. I've got this." He gestured fiercely at the pole. "So here I am, the best chance you'll get. Kill me now, and escape across the river. Who knows? You might even get away. Otherwise, either make peace with me, or dammit, leave me alone." He stared at the river, swallowing, his outburst having weakened him. "I'd rather, though, we got along."

"It won't be that easy." Saul tasted something bitter. "One thing you owe me."

"What?"

"An explanation."

"Why? Would it make a difference? If you know about Castor and Pollux, you must have learned about—"

"There were five of you." Saul spoke rapidly, spitting his words. "The descendants of the original Abelard group. Each of you had orphans, sons, fanatically loyal. Just like Chris and me. You used us to sabotage operations you thought were wrong." He gestured, impatient. *"Get on with it."*

"You learned all that?" Eliot blinked, astonished.

"You taught me."

Studying Saul with new awareness, Eliot slowly sat on the bank. His wrinkles deepened. His skin turned a darker gray. "An explanation?" He struggled with his thoughts. For a moment, he didn't move or even seem to breathe.

He sighed. "All right, I guess you deserve . . ." He squinted at Saul. "When I was young"—he shook his head as if he couldn't remember ever being young—"just getting started in the profession . . . I used to wonder why so many foolish decisions were made. Not merely foolish —disastrous. Cruel. At a cost of so many lives. I asked my foster father."

"Auton."

"You know that too?"

Saul only glared.

"He said in his day he'd wondered the same. He'd been told the decisions only *seemed* disastrous. Underlings like himself didn't have the big picture. There was a room with maps and strategy boards. High-level politicians went there to get the big picture, and sometimes they had to make decisions that might look stupid from a narrow point of view but actually were smart if every factor was considered. He said he believed this for many years till he rose so high he was one of the men in that room, and what he discovered was that the decisions were exactly as stupid as they appeared. Those men had no big picture. They were as confused, as petty as anyone else. Eventually my promotions allowed me in that room, and I discovered what he meant. I've seen the secretary of state refuse to talk to the secretary of defense—I mean he literally turned his back on the group and sat in his chair facing a corner. I've seen men arguing about who was allowed to sit next to whom—like school kids—all the while they committed billions of dollars to interfere with foreign governments in the name of our national security, but actually because big business felt threatened by socialist factions in those countries. They endorsed dictatorships or fascist coups or—" Eliot jerked in disgust. "What we did in Ecuador, Brazil, Zaire, Indonesia, and Somalia alone makes me sick. All told, millions of people have been killed because of our interference. And the rank deception. Skilled operatives dismissed when they send in accurate reports that aren't in line with current political thinking. Then someone in the front office rewrites those reports to make them what the administration wants to read. We don't gather truth. We disseminate lies. When Auton asked me to take over for him as a descendant of the Abelard group, I grabbed the chance. Someone had to act responsibly, to try for balance and sanity."

"The Paradigm job," Saul said.

"All right, let's get to it. We've got an energy problem. So what do we do? We make an agreement with the Arabs to buy cheaper oil, provided we stop our commitments to Israel. All unofficial, of course, the negotiations conducted by American billionaires—but with the tacit agreement of our government. The ultimate result? We get to drive big cars while Israel disappears. I'm not denying the claims of Arab factions. The Mideast situation's complicated. But dammit, Israel exists. We're talking about destroying a nation."

"So you had me kill the negotiators."

"A few men as opposed to a nation. The message was clear—don't try it again."

"But after, you tried to kill *me.*"

"The president wanted to get even for his best friend's death. With that kind of power behind the investigation, you'd have been found."

"You know how I felt about you. I wouldn't have talked."

"Not willingly. But under chemicals, you'd have sent them to me. And under chemicals, I'd have sent them to the rest of the group. It had to be protected."

"That isn't logical."

"Why?"

"Because the nation you wanted to protect—Israel—was the nation blamed."

"Temporarily. Once you were killed, I planned to show you worked on your own initiative. A Jew, determined to protect your spiritual country. I'd already insured the failure of your last few jobs —to prove you were unstable. Israel would be exonerated."

"Sure. And I'd be dead. Is that what you call love?"

"You think I did it easily?" Eliot's voice cracked. "The nightmares. The guilt. Isn't my grief the proof I didn't want to do it?"

Saul shook with contempt. "Words. Castor and Pollux and me. What the hell happened to the rest? Not counting Chris, fourteen other orphans."

"Dead."

"On similar missions?"

Eliot's throat heaved. "I didn't order it. They were casualties."

"That's supposed to make it all right?"

"You'd prefer they died for the men in that room? They were soldiers."

"Robots."

"But working for someone whose values are more substantial than their government's."

"Values? You want to talk about . . . ?" Saul's chest constricted. "Here's one you never heard of. You don't betray someone you love!" He trembled, burning. "We trusted you. What else made the shit you put us through bearable? We wanted your high opinion. Love? You're so damned arrogant you think it's your right. You want to save the world? When we're all dead, there'll still be assholes in that room. And none of us will have mattered. Except for the comfort we gave each other."

"You've missed the point. Because of sons like you and operations I had you sabotage, I've saved who knows how many thousands of innocent lives."

"But Chris is dead. As far as I'm concerned, it's a damn poor trade. Hey, I don't know those other people. I'm not even sure I'd like them." Glaring, barely able to restrain himself, Saul shook his head with disgust and walked up the bank.

"Wait! Don't turn your back on me! I haven't finished yet!"

Saul didn't stop.

"Come back! Where do you think you're going? I didn't say you could leave!"

Saul swung at the top. "I'm through obeying. A son ought to comfort his aging father. Me? I'll make your last days hell."

"Not here! If you kill me, you die and lose!"

"A son gets big enough—"

"What?"

"And smart enough to crush his father. What you didn't count on was I loved Chris more than you." With a final glare, of utter contempt, Saul pivoted sharply. Stalking away, he disappeared beyond the bank.

14

The river hissed. Eliot tried to stand, but his strength gave out. Legs buckling, he slumped on the bank. Throughout the argument, he'd made sure not to glance at the wooded bluff across the river.

But now he did. In confusion.

Castor and Pollux were over there. Along with the rest home's manager, an investigator who'd come with a team to conduct an inquest on a suicide, and most important, a sniper.

He'd calculated every detail. Saul had two options. To listen to reason. Wasn't the argument—thousands of lives—persuasive? Wasn't one man's life, even Chris's, worth the sacrifice?

Or else to try to kill me.

If Saul had chosen the first, I could've lived my last days in peace, perhaps returned to my mission, and saved more lives.

If Saul had chosen the second? Trying to kill me, he would have been shot. With witnesses, I'd have been absolved. The end would have been the same.

But—Eliot frowned—something was wrong. Saul had done the unexpected, choosing neither. He hadn't been convinced, but he didn't try to kill me. Nothing was changed.

Except.

He seemed too sure. He balanced his actions carefully, never coming too close.

Had he guessed? Is it possible I taught him better than I knew? Can he read my thoughts?

It couldn't be.

15

"You were with them." Squinting, Saul sat at the top of the lodge steps, waiting.

"What?" Don stopped in surprise, putting a muddy white shoe on the bottom tier.

"You ought to do something about your wardrobe."

Don peered down at the knee ripped out of his red polyester slacks. Reflexively he picked burrs from his navy blazer. "I went for a walk."

"In the woods. I know. With them." Saul pointed past the tennis courts toward Castor and Pollux, an investigator who'd arrived by helicopter this morning, and a narrow-eyed man who carried a long slim case that might have contained a billiard cue. Or a sniper's rifle.

Approaching from the river, Eliot clutched his fishpoles and tackle box.

"My, my, he didn't catch a fish."

"What do you mean I went with them?" Don said.

"When I came here, the first thing you did was accuse me of planning to kill a guest. You slapped two guards on me. Then all of a sudden the guards disappeared, so I followed the old man to the river where he offered me the chance to kill him. Since I never intended to kill him to begin with, I didn't know what he was talking about. He's my father, after all. Naturally I felt like seeing him. But he started talking crazy, so I walked away, and you'll never guess what happened next. All of a sudden my guards came back." Saul pointed at two men on lawn chairs near him. "What would *you* think?"

"I—"

"It looks to me like that old man set me up. If I laid a hand on him, I'd be dead, and there'd be witnesses to make it legal. Don, tsk, tsk. You're not exactly watching over my interests."

The manager puffed his chest as if to argue. It deflated like an inner tube. He gave up the effort. "I had to go along. The old man insisted you'd kill him."

"And without proof, you believed him."

"Hey, he went to the investigating team. If I argued, they'd think I wasn't doing my job. A test. That's all it was. If you meant no harm, you wouldn't be hurt. If you tried to kill him—"

"But I didn't. I paid a lot for protection, and what I'm getting for it is threats. Everything's reversed. The old man just proved he wants to kill *me*. I deserve—hell, demand—equal treatment."

"What are you talking about? You're already guarded."

"House arrest. They're not protecting me. They're watching me. In the meantime, Eliot can do whatever he wants. It isn't right. He ought to be guarded as well. And not by those clones he brought with him. Your own men. He's paranoid enough to try something foolish."

"Absurd."

"If it happens, you'll wish to God you'd listened. The investigators'll ream you out. I'm telling you he's crazy. I also want those thugs of his under surveillance."

"I don't have the staff!"

"Just six more guards?"

"In shifts of three? In addition to the men I've got on you? That's twenty-four!" Don sputtered. "I need those men other places. And that's just for now! What happens when the other guests catch on? They'll want protection too! A lot of them were enemies before they retired! The only reason they're able to sleep at night is their confidence in a rest home! If they thought its neutrality could be violated . . . guests being followed everywhere? Bodyguards scrambling all over each other? A rest home's supposed to be quiet and peaceful!"

"You think the others haven't noticed you've got men watching me? When I went for breakfast this morning, everybody in the restaurant took a look at my guards and couldn't wait to get out of there."

"You've been here only two days and—"

"What?"

"Threatened forty years of tradition."

"Not me. Eliot. And you. I didn't ask for those watchdogs. What goes for me should go for him. If I'm being tailed, then dammit, so should he."

Don gestured. "I won't put guards on him. This madness can't be allowed to escalate."

"Logically you've got only one other choice."

"What is it?" Don looked hopeful.

"Do it the other way around. De-escalate. Call off your watchdogs."

310

16

Flanked by Castor and Pollux, Eliot tensed as he entered the greenhouse.

He'd been anxiously waiting for its completion. Eager as a lover, he came to his roses.

But someone else was in here. At the other end, a man straightened from under a table and ducked out the back.

Eliot frowned. "Wait a minute! What were you—?" Rushing to the door, Eliot threw it open, watching Saul cross the jogging track toward the lodge. "Come back here!"

Saul broke into a run.

"What was he—?" Eliot swung to Castor and Pollux. "Check under that table."

Puzzled, Castor knelt. He groped and murmured, "Wires."

"What?" Startled, Eliot crouched, peering under. Two wires, red and black, dangled from a hole in the table leading up to a rose bed. "Jesus."

"Not a bomb. Not here," Pollux said.

"The way he killed Landish." Eliot's eyes gleamed. "What are you waiting for? Call security. Have him stopped if he tries to leave the grounds." Eliot lurched to his feet and almost cheered. "Now I've got him. I can prove he wants to kill me."

Castor rushed to the phone.

"He figures he's a match for—wasn't even fast enough to finish before I got here." Eliot laughed. "I've beaten him." Turning, he shouted to Castor on the phone. "Tell that manager to get out here!"

"Where would he get explosives?" Pollux asked.

"The same place you would! Look around! Fertilizer! Peat moss! He could go to the druggist and mix a cocktail! All he'd need was batteries and—!" Eliot shoved his hands in the rose bed. "Help me find it!"

Pollux watched, dismayed.

17

When Don arrived, he opened his mouth. No sound came out. The greenhouse had been built to Eliot's specifications. State-of-the-art equipment. Rare varieties. All of it was ruined. Eliot had started with the bed beneath which wires dangled. Tracing the wires through soil and roses, he'd yanked and dug, tearing, throwing, lunging from one bed to the next till he was covered with dirt, and roses lay around him.

"Where? Dammit, I know it's here! He planted a bomb! I've got to find it!"

Flinging earth, he staggered against a glass wall, almost crashing through it.

Castor and Pollux rushed to help.

"Where'd he put it?"

Pushing his sons away, Eliot heaved on the wires, lurching back as they pulled free. He stared at two bare-stripped ends. "Oh, Jesus, no. The bastard . . . ! There wasn't any . . . !" Sobbing, the old man sank to the floor.

18

I've had it, Don thought. A stunt like that. He's made as much trouble as he's going to.

It had taken an hour for him to deal with the disturbing aftermath of what had happened at the greenhouse—medical attendants examining Eliot before they escorted him back to the lodge; bomb specialists verifying the absence of explosives. But at last he'd been able to get away. Raging into the gym at the lodge, he faced the attendant. "Grisman's supposed to be here."

"He left a minute ago."

Don slammed back through the door. Too furious to wait for the elevator, he pounded up the stairs. Grisman'll want to change his clothes.

Sweating, telling himself he had to get back in shape, he reached the third floor, pivoting in time to see Grisman go in his room. "Hey, stop right there! I want to talk with you!"

But Grisman didn't hear. Already in his room, he shut the door.

Don stormed down the hall. "You bastard."

Two rooms away, the blast jerked him off his feet. Concussed, his ears rang as the door blew off Grisman's room.

"No!" Stunned, Don crawled to the door. Guests jerked open other doors. He didn't pay attention.

"Grisman!" Smelling sulphur, Don squirmed in.

The room was destroyed, the stereo, television, and computer shattered, the walls charred. Embers smoldered on the bed. The smoke alarm shrieked.

"Grisman!"

Coughing, he lurched to the bathroom.

There! On the floor! Thank God, he was breathing!

19

"You can't be serious! You think I—!"

"Either you or them." Don pointed at Castor and Pollux.

"He made the bomb himself!" Eliot said.

"And set it off? Ridiculous. It almost killed him."

"Almost? You think this is fucking horseshoes! Isn't it obvious? He took cover in the bathroom before he set it off!"

"But why would he—?"

"To blame it on me, for Christ's sake! He pulled that stunt with the wires to make it seem I was angry enough to pay him back!"

"Or maybe you rigged the wires yourself. To blame it on him. To make it seem he was playing with bombs and one went off."

"You dumb . . . You think if I rigged a bomb it wouldn't have killed him?"

"I think the bylaws say if a guest keeps causing trouble I can give him a refund. I'm requesting a hearing. What I'd dearly like—I don't know who's at fault, so I'll pick both of you—is for you and your son to settle your problems somewhere else."

20

Saul lingered in the lobby, glancing toward the elevator and the stairs. His flashburns hurt, but he felt too excited to care. Pretending interest in a window display of jogging shoes, he studied the reflection of the entrance to the restaurant.

At seven, his patience rewarded, Eliot—flanked by Castor and Pollux—came down the stairs. They went in the restaurant. Waiting a minute, Saul followed.

The guests reacted at once, setting down forks, swallowing thickly, glancing from Saul to Eliot, then back again. Feeling the tension, several demanded checks. Others, coming in, took one quick look and retreated to the lobby. The room became nervously quiet.

Though Eliot faced the entrance, he studied the menu, spoke to Castor and Pollux, and deliberately avoided noticing Saul.

"I'd like that table over there," Saul told the maître d'.

"May I suggest the one over here, sir—in the corner?"

"No, the one across from the old man suits me fine."

He didn't give the maître d' a chance to argue. Walking across, he sat so he stared directly at Eliot six feet away.

Eliot tried to ignore him. Other guests got up and left. Surrounded by empty tables, Saul kept staring.

Eliot sipped water.

Saul did, too.

Eliot broke off a piece of garlic bread.

Saul did the same.

314

They chewed in unison.

Eliot wiped his mouth with a napkin.

Saul reciprocated, keeping his eyes on Eliot's. It gave him pleasure to know he was using one of Chris's tricks against their father. Chris had told him about the monastery. "Some of us were desperate to stay. A few, though, wanted to leave. They didn't have the courage to say so. What they did was make a nuisance of themselves. The best way? To mock a companion at dinner. Sit across from him and mimic every action. There's no defense. Your opponent gets trapped in your repetition. You follow him, but he follows you. He can't break the pattern. It drives him crazy. Eventually he complains. The irony is the monastery's director can't tell if you're making trouble or the other guy's just imagining things."

Saul mimicked Eliot's every movement.

A hand to the chin.

A scratch on the eyebrow.

An exasperated sigh.

It took ten minutes. Eliot suddenly threw down his napkin, stalking toward the lobby, followed by Castor and Pollux.

"Was it something he ate?" Saul asked the empty room.

21

He came down to the lobby, puzzled, having been informed that he had a visitor. The rest home permitted them, provided credentials were in order and a search revealed no weapons. But he couldn't imagine who would want to see him. Eliot, he suspected, was retaliating.

When he saw who it was, however, he felt his stomach shrink. He stopped, amazed. "Erika? How did—?"

Wearing a tan skirt and yellow tanktop, she crossed the lobby, smiling, hugging him. "Thank God, you're alive."

Her arms around him, he had trouble breathing. Time stopped. "I can't believe you're here," he said. Trembling, confused, he leaned back. "Orlik . . . How . . . ?"

"He's dead." She looked disturbed. "Before he was killed, he let me escape. He told me where you'd gone. I'll explain it later." She frowned at his face, her voice concerned. "What's happened to you?"

"These flashburns?" He gingerly touched his cheeks, then glanced around the lobby, echoing her words. "I'll explain it later." He smiled in anticipation of describing what he'd done.

But she shook her head, frowning harder. "Not just the burns."

"Then what?"

"Your eyes. I don't know how to describe . . . They're . . ."

"Go on. Say it."

"Old."

He flinched, feeling as if he'd touched an electric current. Disturbed, he had a sudden need to change the topic. "Let's go." He tried to sound casual. "I'll show you the grounds."

The sun was powerful. His head throbbed as they walked on a white stone path beside a fountain, the mountains encircling them.

But he couldn't forget what she'd said. "I haven't been sleeping well."

She faced him abruptly, worried. "Your cheeks. They're—"

"What about them?"

"Haggard. Look at you. You've lost weight. You're pale. Are you feeling all right?"

"I've—"

"What?"

"Almost beaten him. I've nearly won." His eyes flashed, and yet were black.

She stared at him, appalled.

"There's a hearing tomorrow," he said. "To decide if we should be told to leave. As soon as he's off the grounds—"

She interrupted emphatically. "It isn't worth what it's doing to you. You've changed. For God's sake, leave. I've got a car. We could—"

"Not when it's almost over."

"It'll never be over. Listen to me. I know I told you to get revenge. But I was wrong."

"You couldn't be if it feels this good."

"But you'll lose."

"Not if I stay alive."

"No matter what. This isn't professional anymore. It's personal.

316

You're not emotionally equipped for that. You'll suffer the rest of your life."

"For avenging my brother?"

"For killing your father. Your conditioning's too strong."

"That's what he's counting on. But I'm beating him." His voice had the sharp edge of hate.

And Erika suddenly knew she had to get out of here. The place felt like death. It was wrong. She'd never felt such revulsion.

Her only hope was to tempt him to go with her. She'd planned to stay the night, but she sensed she had only the afternoon.

They told each other what had happened since they'd been together last. They returned to the lodge, went up to Saul's room, and slowly undressed each other. She didn't care about the sex. She wanted to lure him, to save his soul.

But even as they embraced, covering each other with nakedness, Saul shuddered in alarm. He knew it wasn't possible, but it seemed Chris lay beside him, dead eyes reproving him.

Guilt wracked his mind. I shouldn't be here. I have to be hunting Eliot.

But loneliness insisted. Joining with Erika, he suddenly realized not two but three of them thrashed on the bed. Not only he and Erika, but Chris as well.

"Love you!" he exclaimed. "Oh, God!"

And Erika, knowing something terrible had happened, also knew she'd lost him.

22

"You won't even stay for dinner?"

She glanced at the lodge, revolted. "I have to go."

"I hoped you could—"

"Help you? No, it's wrong. This place is—Come with me."

He shook his head. "I haven't finished."

"It doesn't matter if you kill him. Don't you see? He's already won.

He's destroyed you." Tears rolled down her cheeks. She kissed him. "I lost you ten years ago. Now I've lost you again." She shook her head sadly. "I'll miss you."

"In a week, I'll have what I want. I can join you."

"No."

"You're telling me not to come?"

"I want you to. But you won't."

"I don't understand."

"I know." She kissed him again. "That's the trouble." Getting in her car, she rubbed her tear-swollen eyes. "In case I'm wrong, the embassy can tell you where to find me."

"There's a place I know in Greece," he said. "The sea's so blue—"

Her throat made an anguished noise. "I bet. And the waves roll in, and the swimming's—Don't I wish. Guess what?" She raised her chin; it trembled. "I've been thinking about resigning. See you, love. Take care." She started the car and drove down the lane.

23

Unsettled, he watched till her car disappeared in the trees, heading toward the valley road. Something felt empty in him. His brain reeled, disoriented, as if an outside influence had intruded on a perfect closed system. What's happening to me?

Confused, he turned to walk up the steps to the lodge, suddenly understanding what she'd tried to tell him. I stayed. Till the old man's punished, I'll never join her.

But by then it'll be too late. She offered herself, and instead I chose my father.

How can she accept me after that?

Remembering his uneasy feeling about the rest home, he suddenly wondered if he'd damned himself. He almost leapt from the steps to run to a car and . . .

What? Chase after her? Tell her I'm going with her?

Thoughts of Eliot intruded. Paralyzed on the steps, he peered again toward the road between the trees. Pressure built in him. Anguish tore his soul. His will tilted one way, then the other. What to do? Whom to choose? Chris seemed to stand before him, his sad eyes narrowed in accusation.

Paralysis changed to resolve.

24

Don paced, gesturing angrily toward the swimming pool beyond the wall-sized window in his office. Though the day was hot and bright, the pool was empty. "All the stunts you've been pulling, you've made the guests so nervous they don't want to leave their rooms. The restaurant's deserted. The grounds—hell, I could send out naked dancing girls, and nobody'd be there to notice. Rumors of your . . . disagreement, shall we say? have got around. The smart money outside says stay away from here, pick the rest home in Hong Kong or Switzerland. Talk about trouble. The bunch of you are it."

The trouble he referred to was composed of Eliot, Castor, Pollux, and Saul. They sat—Eliot and his escorts separated from Saul, watched by guards—as Don continued. "So here's the situation. The rules of the sanction force a rest home to accept an operative in need, provided he pays the necessary fees. But the rules don't force a director to put up with disruptive guests. I've contacted my superior and explained the problems here. I've been in touch with the supervising board. I've requested a hearing and received a judgment. The Abelard rules say if a director has sufficient cause—and Christ, do I have sufficient cause! —he can instruct a guest to pack his bags." Don pointed at the door. "And leave."

Eliot straightened angrily. "And have this man try to kill me the instant I leave the grounds?"

"Did I say I'd let him try to kill you? We're not animals. The board's prepared to compromise. You paid for services you didn't receive, so here's a check refunding the balance of your fees. It's only fair. You devoted your life to the profession. You deserve a chance. So what we're giving you is twenty-four hours. That's plenty of time for a man of your experience. You could disappear forever, given your contacts. Take all night. Relax. Tomorrow morning, though, at eight o'clock—that's checkout time. I want you out of here. And one day later, Grisman has to leave as well. Maybe then the other guests can enjoy themselves again."

Twisting in his chair, Eliot fumed at Saul.

Who merely grinned and shrugged.

25

The sun dipped relentlessly toward the mountains, casting a ruddy glow through the window of Eliot's room.

"It doesn't make a difference," Eliot blurted hoarsely into his phone. "I don't care how many men it takes or what it costs. I want this valley bottled up tomorrow. I want him killed as soon as he leaves the rest home. No, you're not listening. Not the team who tried to stop him from getting in here. What's the matter with you? I'm sick of losers. I said I want the best." His knuckles ached from his tight grip on the phone. He scowled. "What do you mean there's nobody better than Grisman? I am. Do what you're told."

Eliot slammed down the phone and turned to Castor. Pollux was out in the hall, where guards sent by Don kept Eliot and his escorts under house arrest. "You confirmed the reservations?"

Castor nodded. "Air Canada out of Vancouver bound for Australia. Seven o'clock tomorrow evening."

"That ought to give us plenty of time."

Castor raised his shoulders. "Maybe not. Romulus knows he'll never be able to find you if he's twenty-four hours behind. The chances are he'll try to break out of here before then."

"Certainly he will. I'm counting on it. He'll want to chase me as soon as possible . . . and that's my advantage."

Castor frowned. "I don't see how."

"What I told that idiot on the phone is true. Nobody's better than Romulus. Except myself. And the two of you. I supervised his training.

320

I can outguess him. The mistake I made from the start was delegating other men to do my work."

"But you ordered a team to seal off the valley."

Eliot nodded. "Romulus expects me to do that. If I didn't provide a distraction, he'd sense the greater trap. Of course, the team might get lucky and kill him." He pursed his wrinkled lips, musing. "I doubt it, though. The wilderness is his home. If he leaves the way he came in, even a thousand men couldn't watch every outlet through the mountains."

Castor brightened. "In that case, though, we'd be protected. Going through the mountains takes time. He'd still be far behind us. He couldn't catch up."

"And that's why he'll choose another way."

Castor's bright look darkened, his frown returning. "But what way is that? And how can we stop him?"

"Pretend you're him. It's not too hard to predict what he'll do. Logically he's got only one choice."

"It might be logical to you, but—"

Eliot explained, and Castor nodded, confident again, impressed.

26

The sun was three-quarters down. Shadows lengthened across the valley, at first almost purple, then gray, soon black tinged with mist.

Saul didn't notice. He kept his room dark, sitting cross-legged on the floor, clearing his mind, preparing himself. He knew the door to his room was being watched by guards outside to prevent him from making a move against Eliot while the old man was still inside the rest home. He assumed that Eliot and his escorts were under surveillance as well.

It didn't matter. Despite his need, he couldn't risk killing Eliot here. Since arriving, his primary intention had been to achieve revenge and yet survive to enjoy the satisfaction of knowing he'd repaid his debt of honor to Chris.

His brother. Anger flashed inside him. He concentrated to subdue it. Now that his goal was close, he had to purge himself of distraction, to reach the purity of a samurai, to prove himself the professional Eliot had taught him to be.

As he meditated, arriving at a core of perfect resolution and stillness, consolidating his thoughts, instincts and skills, he silently repeated a mantra, over and over.

Again and again. He sensed his brother's spirit merging with him. Chris. Chris.
Chris. Chris.
Chris.

27

The morning was bleak. Clouds hung low, the air damp and chilly with the threat of rain. A dark blue Chevy station wagon—no chrome, no whitewalls, nothing to draw attention to it—waited on the gravel driveway before the lodge.

Two servants filled the back with suitcases and garment bags, then shut the hatch and waited at a distance.

Precisely at eight, the door to the lodge came open. Eliot, Castor, and Pollux, flanked by guards, stepped out on the porch. Don walked directly behind them.

Eliot wore his uniform—his black suit and vest, his homburg. He paused when he saw the car, then turned to the right, squinting sullenly at Saul, who stood at the end of the porch, flanked by other guards.

A gloomy mist began to fall. Eliot's nostrils widened with contempt. The tense moment lengthened.

Turning abruptly, the old man gripped the rail and eased himself down the steps. Castor opened a back door for him, closed it as soon as his father was settled, then got in the front with Pollux and turned the ignition key. The motor engaged at once, sounding like a large V-8.

The station wagon pulled away, its tires crunching on the gravel. Saul narrowed his vision till all he saw was the window of the Chevy's hatch. Intense, he focused on the back of Eliot's head, on the silhouette of the homburg.

But the old man never looked back at him.

The Chevy moved faster, shrinking, its roar diminishing. Soon its dark blue merged with the green of the forest.

Watching it disappear, Saul bristled, his heartbeat thunderous.

Haughty, Don came over. "Long time to wait, huh? Twenty-four hours. Bet you're tempted to run to the motor pool and steal a car to chase after him."

Saul stared at the road between the trees.

"Or the chopper in back," Don said. "Bet you can barely hold back from making a try for it, huh? It sure is tempting, isn't it?"

Saul's eyes were black as he turned to Don.

"Go on and try," Don said. "That's why I let you out of your room this morning. So you could watch the old man drive away and maybe lose your cool. Do it. Fall apart. Make a break and try to chase him. You've been a pain in my ass since you got here. I'd love to see you shot to pieces for disobeying the board's directive."

Still Saul didn't answer but instead slipped past him, calmly heading toward the door to the lodge.

"No?" Don asked behind him. "Don't feel like making trouble today? My, my. Well, that's a change."

The guards flanked Saul as he opened the door.

"In that case, pal, go back to your room and stay there." Don's voice snapped. "Twenty-four hours. That's the agreement. Tomorrow morning, you can chase him all you want." He rose to his fullest height. "Provided you can find him."

Saul glanced indifferently at him and walked inside.

He'd thought it through with care last night, analyzing various plans . . .

When everything was considered, there'd really been only one choice.

28

Don rubbed his eyes. It had to be he was seeing things. This couldn't be happening. With eyeblink speed, Grisman did something with his elbows as he walked inside. At once the guards behind him tumbled back, collapsing against each other, toppling. As they did, the door to the lodge slammed shut. The lock shot home.

"What the—? Jesus!" Pushing away from each other, scrambling to their feet, the guards cursed, rushing to the door, jerking at it, pounding angrily.

Don in turn felt frozen, disbelieving, dismayed. It wasn't possible. He'd felt so confident when he taunted Grisman he'd have bet his bonus that the goddamn troublemaker had finally been put in his place.

Oh, fuck, no. It couldn't be. Grisman was actually doing it, making a break.

"The motor pool!" Don shouted. "The chopper pad! Stop pounding at that goddamn door, you assholes! Head him off!"

Already Don was racing down the steps. He twisted hysterically to the left and lunged toward the side of the lodge.

29

It hadn't been complicated. Once Saul had decided on the only logical tactic, he'd simply imagined various scenarios, looked ahead, and predicted when he'd have the best opportunity to implement his plan. At the first likely moment, he acted. On the porch, in the open, in the presence of Don and many guards, with Eliot barely off the grounds, who'd have expected Saul to make trouble that soon? Cer-

324

tainly not Don and the guards. Their confidence had been his advantage.

By the time the guards had recovered enough to lunge at the bolted door, Saul was sprinting through the lobby. No guests were in view, but several staff members froze openmouthed in surprise. To the left, at the fuzzy corner of his vision, Saul detected a hurried gesture as the desk clerk lunged for a phone. Behind him, Saul heard muffled pounding as the guards tried to break through the door. He raced toward a hallway beside the staircase, sensing motion to his right: a guard coming out of the restaurant, seeing Saul, hearing the shouts, understanding, and drawing a pistol.

The roar of shots was amplified by the polished walls of the lobby. Bullets walloped against the banister on the staircase, flinging splinters. But already Saul had reached the protection of the corridor. Charging harder, he veered toward a door at the end, in an alcove behind the staircase, yanking it open just as a guard on the other side reached for the knob. The man must have heard the shots and hurried to investigate. But he wasn't prepared for the heel of Saul's palm slamming against his rib cage. As the man groaned, falling, Saul tugged an Uzi from his grasp and swung to spray the hallway behind him. The guard out there dove frantically for cover.

Saul didn't wait. No time. He leapt across the man he'd dropped, then raced down a short set of stairs, yanking at a ceiling-high metal case with towels, soap, and toilet paper on shelves. The unit crashed behind him, objects cascading, forming a barricade in the narrow corridor.

A puzzled maid appeared at an open door to the right, understood quickly what was happening, and ducked back, frightened. Again Saul spun with the Uzi, fired a warning volley at the guard in pursuit, and charged out a door in back.

When he'd first arrived at the rest home, he'd automatically obeyed one of Eliot's rules and scouted his hunting ground, familiarizing himself with the layout. Now as he burst outside, he faced the short flight of concrete steps he'd expected. He took them three at a time and rushed ahead.

The clouds hung lower, gray and dismal. The bleak grounds stretched before him, the mist-enshrouded motor pool to his right, the chopper pad to his left.

As drizzle dampened his cheeks, chilly in contrast with his burning sweat, he knew exactly where to go and what to do.

30

Out of breath, stumbling frantically along the side toward the back of the lodge, Don yelled to the guards before him, "Dammit"—he puffed—"split up! Head him off!" He stopped and panted, wiping drizzle off his face. "The chopper pad! The motor pool!" The guards obeyed.

Straining to breathe, mustering strength, Don lurched into motion once again, swerving around to the back of the lodge as a guard crept out, his pistol trained.

"Where is he?" Don shouted.

"He came through this door." The guard kept his voice low, crouching beneath the concrete steps, warning, "Get down before he shoots you."

"He's not armed."

"He grabbed an Uzi off Ray."

"That was *Grisman* shooting in there?" A tingle ran up Don's spine and made him shiver. "I thought it was . . . Jesus!" He dove to the lawn, his shivering worse as the wet grass soaked his checkered pants and burgundy sport coat. "Where the hell is he?"

Hunkered, the guard kept switching his aim to different sections of the grounds.

Don struggled with paralyzing fear and surprised himself by rolling toward the guard, scrambling down the concrete steps, and hunching near the door. "Your walkie-talkie. Give it to me."

Not shifting his gaze from the grounds, the guard pulled the radio from its holster on his belt and handed it over.

Don pressed the send button, alarmed by the croaking sound his voice made. "This is the director. Motor pool, check in."

He released the button. Static crackled.

"No sign of him," a voice said. "We're still searching."

"Chopper pad," Don blurted into the radio.

"Negative," a voice said. "We've established a perimeter around the bird. With this many guns against him, he'd be nuts to make a try for it."

Don flinched as the door came open behind him, another guard creeping out.

"I just left Ray," the new guard said. "A doctor's with him."

Don took a moment before he realized the implication. Again his spine tingled. "You mean he's alive?"

"Grisman slammed his chest. Broke some ribs. The doctor says Ray's gonna live, though."

"I don't understand. Grisman's too good to make a mistake like that. I can't believe he slipped up."

"Unless it wasn't a mistake."

"You're telling me Grisman deliberately didn't kill him?"

"If Grisman had wanted to, he would have. All he'd have needed was a little more force behind the blow."

"Then why the hell didn't he? What's he thinking of?"

"Who knows?" The guard made a sound that might have been a chuckle. "Maybe he didn't want to piss us off."

Abruptly the walkie-talkie crackled. "There! I see him!"

"Where?" Don yelled, his voice unsteady as he held the radio near his mouth. "The motor pool? The—?"

"Not even close! The stupid bastard's way the hell past the jogging track and the greenhouse!"

"*What?*"

"He's running across the grounds! The river! He's headed toward the river!"

Don leapt up, lost his balance and nearly fell, then started running toward the drizzle-enshrouded greenhouse. The two guards sprinted past him. Other guards converged out of nowhere.

31

Saul gripped the Uzi and raced through the increasing drizzle, his legs like pistons, his chest like a bellows. He heard murky shouts behind him. At once the shouts seemed louder. He ran faster, legs pounding, adrenaline fueling him.

A shadow seemed beside him. On his left. Glancing quickly that way, he knew he had to be imagining things. Even so, he would have sworn he saw Chris. They seemed to pace each other. Then Chris gained distance on him. You never used to be faster than me, Saul thought. Excitement almost made him grin. You were smarter, but I was stronger. Think you can get there ahead of me, huh?

Well, brother, you're wrong.

As a rifle cracked, echoing behind him, Saul forced himself to the limit, stretching his legs, gaining on Chris. An Uzi rattled in the distance. Saul came abreast of Chris. He urged his legs to work harder.

The shouts became close.

Chris disappeared, and through the drizzle, Saul faced the river, pounding toward a bank near the spot where he'd argued with Eliot. He crashed through shrubs down a slope. Reached a rocky outcrop.

And dove.

The cold water numbed him instantly. The force of his dive took him down into blackness. The surge of an undercurrent swept him along. He twisted beneath the water, struggling to level off and fight to the top. His overworked lungs rebelled, demanding air, threatening to inhale. As a roar began behind his ears, he surged and kicked and strained, breaking the surface, gasping, hearing gunshots, diving back down as bullets peppered the river.

The strength of the current amazed him. Where he'd argued with Eliot, the water had seemed almost placid. But that had been a kind of cove, away from the river's flow. Here powerful hands seemed to twist and tug at him. Desperate for air, he fought to the surface once more, and as soon as he caught a breath, he ducked back down, too quick to hear further shots but not too quick for him to realize how far the current had already taken him.

He'd left the guards behind, he understood with relief. Now all he had to do was fight the river. Get to the other side, he kept thinking. Dismayed, he realized he didn't have the Uzi anymore.

But he was alive. The first step in his plan had been accomplished. Raising his head above the surface, breathing deeply, he kicked and stroked and aimed himself toward a tree dipping into the water a hundred yards down on the opposite shore.

32

Staring despondently toward the river, Don brushed rain-soaked strands of hair from his forehead, sickened by the frantic pounding of his heart. That fucking Grisman, he silently cursed. Chasing after him nearly gave me a heart attack. "Any sign of him?"

A guard shook his head. "The other team hasn't checked in yet, though."

Don nodded. As soon as he'd understood what Grisman intended to do, he'd radioed to other guards, telling them to post themselves farther down along the river. "Sooner or later he's got to come up for air. The water's too cold for him to stay in it long."

The guards continued scanning the river.

"You never know," Don said, pulling his rain-drenched slacks away from his thighs. "Maybe we'll get lucky. Maybe the bastard drowned."

Two guards turned to him, their brows furrowed skeptically.

"All right, all right," Don said. "I don't believe it either."

Static crackled on the radio. "We just missed him," a voice said.

Don jerked up from the rock on which he'd been sitting. "Say again. Repeat," he told the radio.

"We missed him. About a quarter mile down from your position. Just as we got here, he crawled up on the other side and disappeared in some bushes."

"But I didn't hear shots."

"We didn't have time. You want us to swim across and continue after him?"

Don watched as the guards around him turned to study his reaction. Pausing, he glanced at the angry gray sky. "Just a second," he told the radio. He asked his guards, "So what would *you* do?"

"He didn't kill Ray," a guard reminded him. "He could have, but he didn't."

"So you're saying let him go?"

"I'm saying he didn't kill Ray."

Don thought about it, finally nodding. He pressed the send button on the radio. "Cancel. Return to the lodge."

"Repeat," the voice said. "Request confirmation."

"He's off the grounds. Out of our jurisdiction. Go back to the lodge."

"Roger. Affirmative."

Don set down the radio. The guards continued studying him. "Besides," he said, deciding to let them feel confided in, "I've got a hunch that the old man sent for teams to watch the exits from here—in case Grisman tried this kind of stunt. He'll be running into snipers shortly. I'd just as soon none of you got caught in their fire."

"Suits me," a guard said. "I wasn't thrilled with the notion of hunting Grisman on his turf. Hit and run in the forest. That's his specialty."

"Well, it's Eliot's problem now," Don said. Though angry, he nonetheless began to feel buoyant now that the crisis was over. "We did the best we could. I suppose Grisman left a car out there somewhere when he came in, but those woods are so thick it'll take him hours to reach it. By then, Eliot'll be out of the country. The difference is the same—whether Grisman stayed here for twenty-four hours or wandered around the forest. Either way, the old man got his head start." He turned, his legs weary as he started back to the lodge. Rain trickled down his neck. Even so, he suddenly felt amused. "It's a hell of a thing," he told a guard walking beside him. "Sometimes an operative tries to break into a rest home. But breaking *out?* Especially if you haven't killed here? That's a new one."

33

There were arrangements to be made, of course. For one thing, Don had to contact his superior and explain what had happened. He considered this task so important he didn't even wait to put on dry clothes before he made the call. Back at the lodge, dripping on the carpet in his office, he spoke into the phone while he peered through the wall-sized window at the rain making dots on the swimming pool. He sneezed once. His voice shivered a couple of times from the chill of his wet clothes soaking into his bones, but by and large he managed to sound professional and calm. "I agree, sir. The board will want a detailed report. I'm preparing one now. The point I want to emphasize is this. Sure, Grisman got away. I accept the blame for that. It shouldn't have happened. No excuses. But we promised the old man time, and practically speaking he still has it. No real harm's been done."

The conversation ended with Don's superior cautiously telling him to wait for the board's decision. In the meanwhile, Don assured him, things were finally back to normal.

Hoping there wouldn't be repercussions, Don set down the phone, gulped a shot of bourbon, and went to his room, where he soaked himself for half an hour in an almost scalding tub. His emotions pulled him in different directions. On the one hand, he still felt angry. Grisman had been such a nuisance, had caused so much trouble that Don had looked forward to taunting him. And now that Grisman had escaped, the sonofabitch had caused even more trouble. *Dammit, I wish we could have caught him before he reached the river. I'd have shot the bastard myself.*

On the other hand, Grisman was finally gone. The crisis was over. The rest home, as Don had told his superior, was back to normal, if anything about this awful place could ever be described as normal.

On balance, Don felt relieved.

He put on freshly pressed green slacks, a crisp yellow shirt, a brand-new beige checkered sport coat. Tossing down another shot of bourbon—his limit for the day—he stretched his arms, at last relaxed.

He went downstairs to his office, rested his white shoes on his desk, turned on his dictation machine to begin his report, and frowned as the roar of an engine passed so close it shook the window behind him.

Now what? he thought in disgust.

His heart plummeted. A terrible premonition squeezed his stomach, making him fear he'd throw up the bourbon.

He grabbed the phone, pressing three buttons to contact—

But it wasn't necessary. A fist pounded on the door. Before Don had a chance to say "come in," the captain of guards threw open the door.

"That goddamn Grisman!"

"Say it."

"All that shit about swimming the river, escaping into the forest!"

"Tell me."

"He was jerking us around! He didn't want to go through the forest! A feint! That's all it was! To put us off balance! As soon as we relaxed surveillance on the chopper, he came back! That's him up there! He stole the goddamn bird!"

Oh, fuck, Don thought and, thinking of the board's reaction, wondered if he could come out of this alive.

34

Saul shivered in his soaked wool clothes and wanted to cheer in triumph. The two men guarding the chopper had been so relaxed after Saul's escape that they hadn't seen him crawl to the greenhouse, then across the jogging track to the fountain, finally to the flower garden, the bench, themselves.

Again, he'd made sure to disable them without killing. That was important. If he killed within the confines of a rest home, he'd be pursued by the fullest might of the profession. He'd likely never catch Eliot, and for sure he'd never survive to enjoy his revenge. Hell, if necessary, the world's intelligence community would hunt him with missiles, anything to guarantee his punishment for violating the sanctity of a rest home.

This way, however, the worst crimes he'd committed were rough-ing up personnel and stealing a chopper. Compared to violating the sanction, what he'd done was roughly analogous to getting in a fight and stealing a car. The decision makers would understand the control he'd exercised. They'd know he wasn't attacking the system but instead only getting even with Eliot. This wasn't political; it was personal. And understanding the duel in progress, perhaps they'd make allowances.

He hoped.

But his principles made sense at least, and more to the point, Saul took delight in sensing Chris would have approved. Indeed it seemed that Chris sat next to him, grinning, urging him on. Saul grinned in response. He hadn't flown a chopper in seven years, but Eliot had trained him well, and he needed only a minute to feel confident at the controls. He lifted off the pad, swooped past the rest home, and soared up over the trees along the perimeter. On the seat beside him, he had a jacket he'd taken from one of the guards and two Uzis plus several loaded magazines. His heart soared along with the chopper. Eliot logi-cally had only one choice. Oh, sure, he could pretend to leave but actually stay in the area, hoping Saul would pass him. But considering the head start Eliot had been guaranteed, it was smarter for him to drive as fast as he could, reach Vancouver, and catch a flight to the farthest corner of the world, where, Saul admitted to himself, he had no chance to find him. Naturally Eliot would have hired men to watch the rest home, killing Saul when he was allowed to leave. The chopper—and less ideally a car—had been his only practical options.

This, more than anything, was to Saul's advantage. The area was wilderness. Few roads went through the region. Saul remembered the route he'd used to reach the rest home. Nothing complicated. Calculat-ing in the reverse, he knew he couldn't go wrong if he chose whatever road headed southwest toward Vancouver. Eliot had a two-hour lead. But that was on a zigzagging road whose route was controlled by the complex topography of the mountains, while Saul could chase him as the crow flew. What was more, the chopper was faster than the station wagon. Much, much faster.

Forty minutes, Saul guessed. Everything'll be finished then.

He imagined Chris would have cheered.

35

The drizzle thickened, falling harder. When Saul had taken off, the weather hadn't been a problem. Now, however, the rain was dense enough to reduce visibility and make the chopper's controls feel unstable. Studying the meandering road below him, Saul began to worry about crashing into an unseen barrier, a tree, a cliff, a hydro pylon obscured by low-hanging clouds. He had to watch for sudden changes in the terrain.

His sole consolation was that the gloom had discouraged travelers. The traffic below him was sparse, most of it vans and motor homes. The few cars he saw were easy to identify and dismiss. A Ford LTD. A VW Sirocco. A Pontiac Firebird.

But no Chevy station wagon.

In the first minutes of the hunt, he hadn't been concerned. After all, Eliot should have passed through several valleys already. Though it never hurt to be thorough, Saul really didn't expect to see the station wagon yet.

But the minutes accumulated. Thirty. Thirty-five. Forty. As the rain fell harder and the roaring helicopter became less responsive to commands, Saul feared he'd miscalculated. Had Eliot anticipated Saul's response and headed inland instead of to the coast? Had Eliot gone to ground somewhere, hoping Saul would lose the trail by running past him to Vancouver? Check and countercheck. The possible variations were like a dizzying maze whose exit could never be found.

He forced distraction from his mind. He couldn't allow himself to doubt the course he'd chosen. He didn't dare lose patience. Committed to this plan, he had to follow through. There wasn't any other way now.

Five minutes later, his determination received its reward. Below, not far in front of him, he saw the reduced shape of a dark blue Chevy station wagon veer around a wooded curve, heading southwest.

His chest expanded.

But at once he subdued his excitement. The color and model were the same. Still, coincidence wasn't impossible.

He urged the chopper down for a closer look. No chrome, no whitewalls. Getting better, he thought. Roaring nearer, he saw the outlines of three passengers, two in the front, one in the back. It puzzled him that they didn't turn back to investigate the commotion behind them. They seemed to be men, though, and the passenger in the rear wore a hat. Even better. Then Saul was close enough to see the license plate through binoculars. The same as the one on the car at the lodge.

He raged, swooping faster, closer. Ahead, to the right, a semicircle of trees had been cleared. A rain-soaked gravel parking area was rimmed by picnic tables. The place was deserted.

In a fifty-fifty life-or-death crisis, simply approach the crisis, prepared to die if necessary. There is nothing complicated about it. Merely brace yourself and proceed. So Ishiguro, Saul's judo instructor, had taught him years before in the *dojo*. Saul braced himself and proceeded now, making an instantaneous decision, though he didn't intend to die.

He zoomed above the road, roaring closer. Breasting it on the left, he shifted his controls to the right and veered toward the station wagon.

A great deal happened at once. Saul briefly saw Castor's alarmed face behind the steering wheel. If Castor had stayed on course down the road, if the chopper's landing struts had touched the station wagon, the chopper would have lost its equilibrium and flipped against the Chevy, consuming both in a massive blast of flame. Granted, Eliot would have been destroyed, but Saul had no intention of dying with him.

Castor reacted as Saul expected, twisting sharply on the steering wheel, veering in the only unobstructed direction, toward the parking area, the picnic tables, the trees.

Saul did the same, speeding parallel to the Chevy, forcing Castor not to stop, instead compelling him to keep rushing toward the trees. At the final moment, just before the chopper would have disintegrated on impact with the forest, Saul jerked the controls and swooped up, clearing the treetops. Enclosed in the chopper's plexiglass, his hearing tortured by the roaring flap of the blades, he knew he must have imagined the sound of a crash behind him.

Imagination or not, it gave him satisfaction. Abruptly turning, he swooped back toward the parking area, seeing the Chevy's front end crushed against a boulder between two trees. Setting the chopper down hurriedly, he left the rotors on idle, grabbed the two Uzis and their full magazines, and jumped to the soggy gravel. Rain lashed his face. Even as he stooped to keep from being decapitated by the revolving blades, he began to fire, lunging at the wrecked station wagon, noticing steamy antifreeze gushing from its radiator, riddling the car with bullets.

But something was wrong. The Chevy's windows didn't break. Its doors weren't torn apart by his barrage.

He scowled. The station wagon was armored. Its glass was bulletproof. He charged through puddles toward it, firing another volley. The bullets walloped fenders and doors but still did little damage.

No one moved inside. Cautious as he hurried forward, peering through a rain-spattered window, he saw Castor slumped across the broken steering wheel, blood gushing from his forehead. Next to him, Pollux was . . .

A mannequin. A dummy dressed in the denim jacket Pollux had worn.

And Eliot? In the back seat, a second mannequin lay on its side, wearing a black suit, a homburg fallen to the floor. That was why they hadn't turned toward the roar of the chopper.

He spotted the two-way radio built under the dashboard and realized at once the terrible danger he was in. Reflexes spurred him. Racing past the station wagon toward the trees, he felt a bullet from behind him sear his arm. Another bullet tore bark from a pine tree. The bark stung his jaw.

He didn't stop to whirl behind a tree and return the fire. He didn't wonder who was shooting at him or how the mannequins had come to be in the car. He just kept charging through the trees, gaining distance, desperate for time to think.

Because the two-way radio said it all. Dammit, Saul thought, why the hell didn't I realize? How could I have been so stupid? From the moment Eliot left the rest home, he must have kept in touch with the lodge. He'd have known I stole the chopper. Jesus, he probably counted on it. The mannequins must have been hidden in the station wagon when he left. The old man outguessed me all the way.

And the sniper shooting at Saul? It had to be Pollux, who'd followed Castor in another car. If Saul hadn't seen the mannequins and the two-way radio, if he hadn't darted toward the trees the instant he sensed the trap, Pollux would have killed him. Eliot would have been the victor.

No! Saul inwardly screamed. No, I won't let him beat me! I've got to get even for Chris!

He scurried deeper through the trees and rain, shifting direction when he knew Pollux couldn't see him. The road, Saul thought. I've got to get back to the road.

Pollux, of course, would be stalking him, aiming toward the sound of rustling bushes and snapping branches, and for that reason, Saul intended to make all the noises he could. He meant to lure Pollux into here. And as soon as Pollux was far from the road, Saul planned to use silence, creeping instead of racing, confusing Pollux, gaining a chance to retreat to the road.

For Pollux didn't matter. Eliot did. And the thickening rain made Saul shiver with understanding. Would an old man expose himself to such terrible weather if he didn't have to? Eliot's plan had been to use Castor as a decoy while Pollux came in from the rear and caught Saul by surprise. But Eliot must have considered the possibility that there'd be a fight. Would Eliot wait unprotected in the second car? Would he hide in the rain in the woods? Not likely. The old man would prefer a place warm and safe.

Dear God, the old man's somewhere along the road I followed. He's holed up, probably in a cabin, a motel, a tourist lodge. He'd never wait at the airport for his plane—if he intended to take a plane at all.

But Saul had flown over several motels. With sufficient time, he could retrace his route and check them all. But that was the point. There *wasn't* time. Pollux would continue hunting him. The provincial police would soon be here to investigate the accident. *I have to get away,* he thought.

In twenty minutes, sweating despite the cold, intensifying rain, Saul reached a bend in the road a half mile away from the picnic area. Despite his silence and care, he felt a persistent prickly spot between his shoulder blades, where Pollux's bullet might strike him.

Have to find Eliot. Have to—

Hearing a motor approach around the bend, he waited to make sure it wasn't a police car. Seeing a battered van, he lurched from the trees and waved to make the driver stop. When the long-haired kid behind the steering wheel tried to veer around him, Saul aimed the Uzi. The kid blanched, slammed on screechy brakes, and got out, holding up shaky hands. "Don't shoot me." He backed up and started to run.

Saul scrambled into the van. Its gears whined as he tugged the shift into first. With a lurch, it started forward. Speeding along the road, he passed the picnic area, where the helicopter's blades continued to turn.

The driver's door on the station wagon hung open. Castor—

Wasn't dead. Holding his stomach, he stumbled from the wreck. But Castor heard the rattle of the van and glanced toward the road in time to notice Saul behind the wheel.

Blinking, Castor shook his head as if he doubted what he saw.

Abruptly he straightened with a wince. Blood streaming from his forehead, he lurched toward the trees, no doubt for Pollux.

That was all right, Saul thought, disappearing from the picnic area. In fact, it was fine. It couldn't be better.

He soon saw a dark green Ford parked along the road, probably the car Pollux had used to follow Castor. Determined to be thorough, Saul stopped and got out of the van, aiming, checking the Ford, but it was empty. The mud on the far side revealed no footsteps where an old man might have gone to take cover in the forest.

Saul nodded, more confident of his suspicion.

He whirled to peer through the rain down the road toward the picnic area. Pollux was sprinting in his direction, Castor hobbling behind him. Pollux halted when he spotted Saul, but as he raised his pistol, Saul rushed to get into the van. A bullet whacked the rear hatch. Saul felt elated, pulling away. It wouldn't be long now.

Two bends down the road, certain his pursuers couldn't see him, he turned left down a gravel lane and soon turned left again, shielding the van in a thick grove of trees. He jumped down to scramble, hunched in the rain, toward the edge of the road, and hid behind dense bushes, watching, waiting.

A minute passed. He swelled with satisfaction, seeing what he wanted. His ruse had worked.

The green car raced past. Pollux looking desperate as he drove. Next to him, Castor stared through the windshield, no doubt straining for a sight of the van.

Saul knew he could have shot them as they went by, assuming the car wasn't armored as the Chevy had been. But what would that have gained? They weren't Saul's objective. Eliot was, and Saul was hoping Castor and Pollux would rush to protect their father.

Lead me to him.

Soon now, he thought, running back to the van. The end was close.

He felt it intensely. Very soon.

36

But he couldn't let them know they were being followed; he had to stay back out of sight. In their place, he'd have periodically checked his rearview mirror, out of habit, just as he did now—to make sure he himself wasn't being followed, by a police car, for example. Such a precaution had its drawbacks, though. If he couldn't let Castor and Pollux see him, he couldn't allow himself a glimpse of *them*. As a consequence, he had to hide the van near every motel and lodge he came to, sneaking up in search of their car.

The process was tedious, frustrating. After the fourth lodge he checked, he began to fear he'd overlooked the Ford. The police must have reached the scene of the accident by now. The long-haired kid must have told them his van had been stolen. They had to be searching for him.

And what about the guards from the rest home? They'd be hunting him as well. They'd have sent for help. The only good thing was that the rest home didn't have another chopper. They'd have to pursue him in cars. But eventually they'd be coming down this road.

His need to retain his freedom fought to overcome his need to punish Eliot. Give up the hunt, a dark voice warned him. You'll never find the old man before the cops or the guards arrive. You tried, but circumstances worked against you. There'll be other chances.

No, he told himself. If I let him slip away, he'll run so far and burrow so deep I'll never find him. He won't leave a trail. It has to be now. There won't be another chance.

Thirty minutes later, at the seventh place he checked, two parallel rows of cabins with parking spaces in the middle, he found the dark green Ford.

A neon sign in front of the office said Rocky Mountain Inn. The sign was illuminated in the gloomy rain. The Ford had been parked with its back end toward a middle unit on the left, the trunk left open.

Hiding the van down the road, Saul climbed through rain-swept trees to a bushy ridge that gave him a view of the cabin behind the Ford.

He watched from cover as the cabin door cracked slowly open. Pollux glanced out, then quickly put a suitcase in the trunk and closed the lid, ducking back inside.

Saul squinted. All right, then. He gritted his teeth. I got here just in time. They're about to leave.

He quickly calculated. The Uzi wasn't accurate from this distance. If he positioned himself behind a cabin across from the Ford, he could shoot when Eliot came out to the car.

But he had to get down there fast. He found a sheltered draw that sloped to the cabins and scrambled down over deadfalls, choosing a spot behind a middle cabin in the row opposite the Ford.

The rain became thicker, darker, colder. As he waited, not showing himself, listening for the sound of the heavy engine starting over there, he began to have misgivings.

It's too easy, he thought.

It felt like a setup. Eliot wouldn't allow his escorts to park their car directly in front of his cabin. They sense I'm around. They're using the car as a decoy.

Still Saul remained convinced that Eliot was here.

Which cabin, though?

He remembered what he'd seen from the ridge above these units. Twenty of them, ten on each side. Because of the rain, the tourists had apparently decided not to go out sight-seeing today. How else explain the vehicles in front of fourteen cabins? Of the six empty slots, two flanked the cabin in front of the Ford. A third empty slot was down near the office. A fourth was on that side but at the opposite end, to the right, in back, almost into the forest. The remaining two were over here on *this* side.

Heart aching, Saul remembered a game he and Chris had liked to play when they were at the orphanage. The game had been introduced to them by Eliot. He'd called it the shell game. "Con men trick suckers with it at carnivals," he'd said. "It works like this. Three empty shells. Set them in a row. Put a pea under one. Then rearrange the order of the shells—several times—as fast as possible. Like this. Now tell me. Which shell hides the pea?" Neither Saul nor Chris chose correctly. "Which goes to prove," Eliot said, "the hand is quicker than the eye. Except I want you to practice this game till you always know which shell hides the pea. I want your eyes to be quicker than anyone's hand."

The shell game. Remembering, Saul fumed. But now instead of three shells, there were six. Which cabin held the pea?

He had to reduce his choices. Would Eliot pick a cabin near the office and the road? Not likely. He'd prefer to hide where the cover was best—in the middle. But then again maybe not. What about the cabin on the opposite end over there—the one closest to the forest?

Saul shook his head. Too far from the road if he had to get away from here fast.

Still its isolation would be an advantage in a fight; few people would hear the commotion.

Again he felt stymied.

What about the cabin on each side of the one where the Ford was parked? They were obvious possibilities. Accordingly Saul discounted them.

But what if Eliot had chosen to hide behind the obvious? The complexity continued to baffle him.

A stalemate. Eliot wouldn't show himself till he felt safe. Saul in turn refused to act till he knew he wouldn't be facing a trap. But Eliot knew, just as Saul did, that the police would investigate the accident and come looking for the stolen van. The cops'd be here soon.

And so would the rest home's guards.

Something had to happen to break the stalemate.

Someone had to move first.

He made a decision. It was arbitrary. But deep in his soul, it felt right. Where would I hide if I were Eliot? Away from Pollux in the cabin over there. I'd want to see what happened. Safely away from the Ford. I'd stay in a cabin over here.

The possibilities reduced, at least in theory, he shifted through the rain toward the supposedly empty cabins, both of them on his left.

"So you guessed."

The ancient voice was startling.

Saul twisted sharply, aiming at the space between two cabins.

And found himself staring in shock at Eliot. The old man had been standing out of sight in front of an empty cabin. Now he showed himself, drenched by the rain.

More exhausted and wizened than Saul had ever seen him, the old man shrugged. "Well, what are you waiting for? Go on and shoot."

Saul wanted to, with all his heart, amazed at himself—because no matter how much his rage compelled him, he couldn't force himself to pull the trigger.

"What's the matter?" his father said. "Isn't this what you wanted? My compliments. You've won."

Saul wanted to scream, but his throat squeezed shut till he couldn't breathe. His chest contracted till he thought his lungs would be crushed.

"You figured it out," his father said. "God damn, I taught you well. I always said, pretend you're the enemy you're hunting. And you guessed. You sensed I'd be in a cabin on this side."

The rain fell so hard Saul couldn't be sure if his cheeks were wet from raindrops or from tears. "You bastard."

"No more than yourself. Go on," his father said. "I've admitted you've beaten me. So pull the trigger."

Again Saul had trouble speaking. "Why?" he murmured hoarsely.

"Isn't it obvious? I'm old. I'm tired."

"You still had a chance."

"For what? To die? Or see another of my children die? I'm sick of it. I've got too many ghosts. Furies. On the riverbank, when you came to me while I was fishing, I tried to explain why I'd done the things you blame me for."

"I can't forgive you for killing Chris."

"I was wrong to ask you. Shoot me." Rain slicked Eliot's thin gray hair to his forehead. "Why hesitate? Your attitude's not professional." Eliot's black suit clung pathetically to him, utterly soaked. "Your father's telling you to kill him."

"No." Saul shook his head. "If you want it, then it's too damned easy."

"True. I understand. Revenge isn't satisfying if the man you hate won't resist. Very well. If that's the way it's to be, then by default you've made a choice."

Saul and Eliot stared at each other.

"I don't suggest a reconciliation," Eliot said. "But I wonder if a grudging acceptance might be possible. I'm your father. No matter how much you hate me, we still share a bond. As a favor, in memory of when you loved me, let me live my last few years in peace."

Saul almost shot him then, tempted by the thought of denying Eliot what he wanted.

But he realized he'd been talking with Eliot long enough for Castor or Pollux to have killed him where he hesitated in the open. Eliot had truly surrendered.

No, not here, not now, he thought. He couldn't shoot. Not face to face—if his father refused to fight back.

"After everything you taught me, I failed."

342

His father raised his eyebrows sadly, quizzically.

"Or you didn't teach me well enough," Saul continued. He lowered the Uzi. "And maybe that's all to the good. I'm finished. I'm resigning. Fuck the agency. Fuck you. There's a lady I know. Instead of playing games with you, I should have gone away with her."

His father brooded. "I never told you. Back in '51. Perhaps you wondered why I never married. See, I had to make a choice. The agency or . . . Well, I'm not sure my choice was the right one." Thunder rumbled. The old man peered at black rolling clouds. "I always wondered what became of her." His eyes narrowed, nostalgic. Then his mood broke, and he tugged at his suit. "You and I, we're ridiculous." He sounded amused. "Standing in the rain. A young man like you, you don't seem to mind getting wet. But these old bones . . ." He chuckled in self-derision. "Thank God, this is over." He held out his hand; it shook. "I've got some Wild Turkey in my suitcase. A farewell drink might be in order. To chase the cold away."

"You told us never to drink. You said it dulls the mind and the senses."

"I didn't expect you to share it with me. But now that you've retired, what difference does it make?"

"Old habits die hard."

"I know. Forgive me. No matter how hard you try, you'll never be normal. That's something else to haunt me."

Eliot turned wearily, stepping up on the cabin's porch, shielded from the rain by an awning. He gestured across to the cabin behind the Ford. Pollux stood nervously in the open doorway over there, but seeing the signal from Eliot, he relaxed his shoulders. In a moment, he went back in the cabin, shutting the door.

Saul approached his father.

"Inasmuch as we'll probably never see each other again," Eliot said, "I want to share a secret with you."

"What?"

"About Chris and the monastery. Something that happened to him there. It helps, I think, if you know about it." The old man went in his cabin, rummaging through a suitcase, finally raising a fifth of Wild Turkey. "There ought to be a glass around here. Good." He poured a small amount of whiskey into it. "Sure you won't join me?"

Saul neared him impatiently. "What about Chris? What happened in the monastery?"

Behind him, the slight creak of the open door was his only warning. He automatically leaned ahead, stooping to protect his renal artery. It happened swiftly, the brush of cloth, the rush of air. But not a knife, instead a glint of piano wire flashing from above him, streaking past his eyes toward his throat.

A garotte. The weapon was usually hidden under a collar. Two wooden handles, pulled from a shirt pocket, snapped into hooks on each end of the wire, prevented an assassin from cutting his fingers while he controlled the strangulation.

Saul jerked up his hands to protect his throat, the gesture instinctive, also a mistake.

Andre Rothberg: *Use only one hand to protect your throat. Keep your other hand free so you can fight. If the wire traps both hands, you're dead.*

Saul corrected his impulse, wrenching his left hand free. His right hand, shielding his larynx, was caught by the wire. Behind him, Castor, who'd been hiding behind the open door, applied more pressure.

Saul dimly heard Eliot say, "I'm sorry. But you know I can't trust you. What if you woke up tomorrow and decided you wanted to kill me anyhow?" He shut the door. "This way's better. There'll be no shooting. No frightened tourists. No calls to the police. We'll have time to get away. I regret having tricked you, though. If it makes any difference, I love you."

A garotte kills in two ways: by strangling the victim, by cutting his throat. In its simplest form, it's nothing more than a strand of piano wire. But the better type uses several strands, twisted under pressure, with industrial diamonds imbedded among them. As a consequence, if a victim manages to raise a hand to stop the garotte from touching his throat, the assailant can use the edge of the diamonds to cut through the victim's fingers.

That began to happen now.

Saul struggled, feeling the diamond-studded wires saw back and forth across the fingers he gripped protectively over his voice box. The diamonds gnawed his flesh and ground his bones. Blood streamed down his arm. Even with his hand as a buffer, he felt the pressure of the garotte squeezing off his air. He gagged.

The door came open. Pollux stepped in, briefly distracting Castor.

It gave Saul time. Though his mind swirled from lack of oxygen, he drew his free arm forward, making a fist, bending the elbow, ramming it back as hard as he could. The blow struck Castor's chest. Andre

Rothberg had taught Saul well. The elbow smashed Castor's rib cage. Bones cracked, impaling a lung.

Groaning, Castor released his grip and staggered back.

Saul didn't waste time removing the garotte. As Castor sagged, Saul swung, feeling a sharp pain in his elbow, realizing he'd fractured it, but that didn't matter. Rothberg's training was based on the theory that a few parts of the body could still function as weapons, even though injured. The elbow was one of those parts.

Saul straightened his arm, ignoring the pain, continuing to swing. The side of his rigid hand caught Castor's brother, Pollux, in the throat. The damage was lethal. Pollux dropped uncontrollably, convulsing.

Incredibly, despite the massive trauma to his chest, Castor had still not fallen. A palm thrust to his shattered ribs jerked him back. He trembled in death throes, collapsing.

Saul tore the garotte from his throat and whirled toward Eliot. "I meant it. At the last, I couldn't do it. I wouldn't have killed you."

Eliot blanched. "No. Please."

Saul picked up the Uzi he'd dropped in the scuffle. "Now," he demanded fiercely. Stepping ahead, he embraced his father. Clutching him with his injured arm, he used the other to raise the Uzi to almost point-blank range.

Eliot squirmed.

Hugging him, Saul pulled the trigger. He kept it pressed back. The Uzi rattled, ejecting empty casings, making a noise like a sewing machine.

And stitched out his father's heart.

"You never had one anyhow." Saul dripped with blood as his father's shuddering body slid from his grasp. "For Chris," Saul moaned.

And realized he'd begun to cry.

He wrapped a handkerchief around his bleeding fingers. The bones, though gnawed by the garotte, would heal. The pain was intense, but he ignored it, hurriedly taking off his bloody wet clothes, putting on Pollux's dry jeans and denim shirt.

There was much to do. The guards and the police would soon be here. He didn't dare return to the stolen van, so he'd have to take the Ford, though tourists alarmed by the shots would see him drive away in it. He'd found its keys on Pollux. To be safe, he'd soon abandon it. If he could reach Vancouver, he'd be able to disappear.

And then? The police would have no leads.

But what about the profession? Would he still be hunted? Till he knew he was free, he couldn't join Erika.

Rain gusted in as he opened the cabin's door. He glanced back at Eliot's body. For Chris, he'd said. Now his voice cracked.

"And for me."

EPILOGUE

THE SANCTION'S AFTERMATH

ABELARD AND HELOISE

France, 1138.

Peter Abelard, onetime canon of the church of Notre Dame, formerly revered as the greatest teacher of his day, had fallen from eminence for love of his beautiful student, Heloise. Castrated by her angry uncle because of her pregnancy, pursued by jealous enemies eager to take advantage of his disgrace, he founded a safe house, the Paraclete, and invited Heloise, now a nun, to be in charge of a convent there. His emasculation prevented them from joining in love, but profoundly devoted to one another as brother and sister, they composed the documents—Abelard's history of his calamities, Heloise's letters—that became the basis for the legend of their tragic passion. After repeated attempts to regain his former glory, Abelard died, dejected, weary, some say of a broken heart. Disinterred from the priory of Saint Marcel, his body was secretly delivered to Heloise at the Paraclete, where after more than twenty years of mourning she died and lay in the ground beside him. Their remains were moved several times during centuries to come but were finally put to rest in the tomb that bears their name in the cemetery of Père-Lachaise in Paris.

Where they found eternal sanctuary.

UNDER THE ROSE

FALLS CHURCH, VIRGINIA (AP)—A powerful explosion last night destroyed a greenhouse behind the home of Edward Franciscus Eliot, former Chief of Counterespionage for the Central Intelligence Agency. Eliot, a rose enthusiast, was murdered six days ago while on vacation in British Columbia, Canada. His funeral in Washington, Tuesday, showed a rare accord between Democrat and Republican legislators, who as one mourned the loss of a great American. "He served his country selflessly for more than forty years," the president said. "He'll be sorely missed."

Last night's explosion, investigators said, was caused by a massive thermite bomb. "The heat was incredible," a Fire Department official announced at a press conference. "What it didn't burn to ashes, it melted. We couldn't get near the greenhouse for several hours. I can't imagine why anybody would want to destroy it. I'm told those roses were gorgeous, some of them extremely rare, one of a kind. It's senseless."

The mystery deepened when firefighters clearing the wreckage discovered a locked steel vault beneath the greenhouse. CIA personnel, in cooperation with the FBI, sealed off the area.

"We worked all night to open it," a spokesman said. "The heat from the thermite bomb fused the locks. We finally had to cut it open. The vault had been used to store documents, that much we know. But what the documents contained is impossible to determine. The heat soaked through the walls of the vault. The documents were seared into dust."

REDEMPTION

Enjoying the heft of the shovel in his hand, Saul threw dirt along the bank of the ditch. He'd been working for several hours, enjoying the strain on his muscles, the trickle of honest sweat. For a time, Erika had dug beside him, helping to extend the ditch, but then the baby had started to cry in the house, and she'd gone inside to nurse him. Afterward, she'd braid and bake the challah dough for their Sabbath bread. Watching her walk to the house, made from concrete blocks painted white, the same as the other dwellings in this settlement, he'd smiled in admiration at her strength and dignity and grace.

The sky was turquoise, the sun molten white. He wiped his brow and got back to work. When his network of irrigation trenches was completed, he'd put in vegetable seeds and grapevines. Then he'd wait to see if God would do His own part and send the rain.

He and Erika had come to this settlement—north of Beersheba and the desert region—six months ago, just before the baby was due. They'd wanted to help extend the nation's frontier, but disillusioned with international rivalry, they'd stayed away from land contested by the Arabs, preferring to develop the nation inward rather than out. But borders were never far. An unexpected attack was always possible, so he took care to have a weapon with him everywhere. A high-powered rifle lay near the ditch.

As far as the sanction was concerned, he thought he'd protected himself. In theory, the intelligence community had still been after him, so after punishing Eliot he'd contacted his network along with representatives from MI-6 and the KGB. His revelation of the conspiracy involving descendants of the original Abelard group had gone a long way to put him back in their good graces. They'd felt bitter pleasure in knowing that their suspicions about internal sabotage of their operations had been justified. Taking steps to undo the damage Eliot and his group had caused by interfering, they let global tensions assume their natural course.

351

Saul's own network required a further gesture of good faith before they'd absolve him of blame, however. The documents, Saul had said. Eliot's collection of scandals. The blackmail that had kept him in power. "But no one knows where those documents are," the agency had said. "No, I do," Saul had said. He'd been thinking about those documents since Hardy had first explained about them. Where would Eliot have hidden them? Pretend you're him. In Eliot's place, where would I have hidden them? A man obsessed by verbal games. Whose life had been based on *sub rosa*. Under the rose? The old man couldn't have chosen any other hiding place. Refusing to hand over the documents lest someone else take advantage of them, Saul had suggested a compromise, blown up the greenhouse, and destroyed them. The president, despite his public praise of Eliot in death, had felt immensely relieved.

But the rules of the sanction were supposed to be absolute. Saul received only unofficial immunity. "What we're agreeing to do is look the other way," a senior intelligence officer told him. "If you hide well enough and don't raise your head, we promise not to come looking for you."

And that was good enough for Saul. Like Candide in his garden, he retreated from the world, enjoying the pleasant exhaustion of manual labor, digging his irrigation ditch. He reflected on the grave Chris had dug in Panama. Now life instead of death would come from turning the ground. Old habits fade hard, however, and when not engaged in establishing a home for Erika, their son, and himself, he taught the youth of the village how to defend themselves if the settlement was ever attacked. He was foremost a warrior, after all, and though he'd disowned the profession, his talents could be put to constructive use. It struck him as ironic that many of the boys he trained had been adopted by the village: orphans. This time around, the process seemed justified. But as he tossed more dirt from the ditch, he remembered that Eliot too had felt justified.

He'd expected revenge to be satisfying. Instead it filled him with misgivings, haunting him. A lifetime of love, no matter how misguided, couldn't be dismissed, any more than his love for Chris could be dismissed. Or his love for Erika. If things had somehow been different. In somber moments, Saul debated with himself. Perhaps what he'd really wanted was the tension of the rest home to last forever. Punishment prolonged. Eliot and himself eternally trapped there. Bound by hate.

And love.

But then Saul's mood would lighten. Glancing at the broad warm sky, smelling the hint of rain in the air, he'd listen to Erika talking to their baby in their house, their home. He'd swell with affection, wholesome, unlike the perverted affection Eliot had created in him, and realize that his father had been wrong. "No matter how hard you try, you'll never be normal": one of the last things his father had said to him. You bastard, you were wrong. And Saul, who in a special sense had always been an orphan, delighted in the thought of being a father to his son.

He set down his shovel, thirsty, retreating from the highest heat of the sun, picking up his rifle, walking toward his home. Entering its shadows, he sniffed the fragrance of tomorrow's challah, walked to Erika, and kissed her. She smelled wonderfully of sugar, flour, salt, and yeast. Her strong arms, capable of killing in an instant, held him tight. His throat ached.

Drinking water from a cool clay pot, he wiped his mouth and crossed the room to peer down at his son in a blanket in his cradle. Friends from the settlement had remarked at first about his name.

"What's wrong with it?" Saul had asked. "I think it's a good name."

"Christopher Eliot Bernstein-Grisman?"

"So?"

"Half Christian, half Jewish?"

"Chris was a friend of mine. In fact, you could say he was my brother."

"Sure. Chris Grisman. They'll love it when he goes to school. And what about Eliot?"

"I used to think he was my father. Now I'm not sure what he was. No matter. I'm what he made me."

The friends didn't understand. But sick in his heart, Saul didn't either.

Even more than the name for the boy, the friends from the settlement drew attention to something unique outside the Bernstein-Grisman home. It seemed a miracle, they said.

A sign from God that the settlement had been given a blessing. How else could it be explained?

A man (with a past, it was rumored in the settlement, and not without respect) who'd never grown anything in his life? And in such brittle ground?

A large black rose.